The city is chic and the
men are seductive!

ONE KISS
IN... *Paris*

ROBYN GRADY
MYRNA MACKENZIE
DANA MARTON

ONE KISS

IN... COLLECTION

April 2015   May 2015   June 2015

July 2015   August 2015   September 2015

ONE KISS
IN... *Paris*

ROBYN GRADY
MYRNA MACKENZIE
DANA MARTON

Published in Great Britain 2015
by Mills & Boon, an imprint of Harlequin (UK) Limited,
Eton House, 18-24 Paradise Road, Richmond, Surrey, TW9 1SR

ONE KISS IN... PARIS © 2015 Harlequin Books S.A.

The Billionaire's Bedside Manner © 2011 Robyn Grady
Hired: Cinderella Chef © 2009 Myrna Topol
72 Hours © 2008 Dana Marton

ISBN: 978-0-263-25391-7

025-0715

Harlequin (UK) Limited's policy is to use papers that are natural, renewable and recyclable products and made from wood grown in sustainable forests.The logging and manufacturing processes conform to the legalenvironmental regulations of the country of origin.

Printed and bound in Spain
by CPI, Barcelona

The Billionaire's Bedside Manner

ROBYN GRADY

One Christmas long ago, **Robyn Grady** received a book from her big sister and immediately fell in love with Cinderella. Sprinklings of magic, deepest wishes come true—she was hooked! Picture books with glass slippers later gave way to romance novels and, more recently, the real-life dream of writing for Mills & Boon.

After a fifteen-year career in television, Robyn met her own modern-day hero. They live on Australia's Sunshine Coast with their three little princesses, two poodles and a cat called Tinkie. She loves new shoes, worn jeans, lunches at Moffat Beach and hanging out with her friends on eHarlequin. Learn about her latest releases at robyngrady.com and don't forget to say hi! She'd love to hear from you!

For the gorgeous Jade Pocklington for her
input on all things French!
With thanks to my editor, Shana Smith, for her
unfailing support and advice and belief
in my stories.

One

"Just shout if it's a bad time to drop in."

The instant the words left her mouth, Bailey Ross watched the man she had addressed—the man she knew must be Doctor Mateo Celeca—brace his wide shoulders and spin around on his Italian, leather-clad feet. Brow furrowed, he cocked his head and studied her eyes so intently the awareness made Bailey's cheeks warm and knees go a little weak. Mama Celeca had said her obstetrician grandson was handsome, but from memory the expression "super stud" was never discussed.

When Bailey had arrived at this exclusive Sydney address moments ago, she'd hitched her battered knapsack higher as she'd studied first the luggage, set neatly by that door, then the broad back of a masculine frame standing alongside. Busy checking his high-tech security system, Mateo Celeca had no idea he'd had company. Bailey wasn't normally one to show up unannounced, but today was an exception.

Remembering manners, Mateo's bemused expression eased into a smile…genial but also guarded.

"Forgive me," he said in a deep voice that hinted at his Mediterranean ancestry. "Do we know each other?"

"Not really, no. But your grandmother should have rung. I'm Bailey Ross." She drove down a breath and thrust out her hand. But when Dr. Celeca only narrowed his gaze, as if suspecting her of some offense, Bailey's smile dropped. "Mama Celeca did phone…didn't she?"

"I received no phone call." Sterner this time, that frown returned and his informal stance squared. "Is Mama all right?"

"She's great."

"As thin as ever?"

"I wouldn't say thin. After enjoying so much of her Pandoro, I'm not so thin anymore, either."

At her grin, Mateo's cagey expression lightened. A stranger lands on your elite North Shore doorstep with a half-baked story, looking a mess after fifteen hours in the air, who wouldn't dig a little deeper? But anyone who knew Mama Celeca knew her delicious creamy layer-cake.

Looking like a sentinel guarding his palace, Mateo patiently folded his arms over the white button-down shirt shielding his impressive chest. Bailey cleared her throat and explained.

"This past year I've backpacked around Europe. I spent the last months in Italy in Mama Celeca's town. We became close."

"She's a wonderful woman."

"She's very generous," Bailey murmured, remembering Mama's final charitable act. She'd as good as saved Bailey's life. Bailey would never be able to repay her, although she was determined to try.

When a shadow dimmed the light in the doctor's intelligent dark eyes, fearing she'd said too much, Bailey hurried on.

"She made me promise that when I arrived back in Australia, first thing, I'd drop by and say hello." She stole another glance at his luggage. "Like I said…not a good time."

No use delaying her own day, either. Now that she was home, she needed to decide what her next step in life would be. An hour ago she'd suffered a setback. Vicky Jackson, the friend she'd hoped to stay with for a couple of days, was out of town. Now she couldn't go forward without first finding a place to sleep—and finding a way to pay for it.

Mateo Celeca was still studying her. A pulse in his strong jaw began to beat before his focus lowered to his luggage.

Bailey straightened. *Time to go.*

Before she could take her leave, however, the doctor interjected. "I'm going overseas myself."

"To Italy?"

"Among other places."

Bailey frowned. "Mama didn't mention it."

"This time it'll be a surprise."

When he absently rotated the platinum band of his wristwatch, Bailey took her cue and slid one foot back.

"Well, give her my love," she said. "Hope you have a great trip."

But, turning to leave, a hand on her arm pulled her up, and in more ways than one. His grip wasn't overly firm, but it was certainly hot and naturally strong. The skin on skin contact was so intense, it didn't tingle so much as shoot a bright blue flame through her blood. The sensation left her fizzing and curiously warm all over. How potent might Mateo Celeca's touch be if they kissed?

"I've been rude," he said as his hand dropped away.

"Please. Come in. I don't expect my cab for a few minutes yet."

"I really shouldn't—"

"Of course you should."

Stepping aside, he nodded at the twelve-foot-high door at the same time she caught the scent of his aftershave...subtle, woodsy. Wonderfully male. Every one of her pheromones sat up and took note. But that was only one more reason to decline his invitation. After all she'd been through—given how narrowly she'd escaped—she'd vowed to stay clear of persuasive, good-looking men.

She shook her head. "I really can't."

"Mama would have my head if she knew I turned a friend away." He pretended to frown. "You wouldn't want her to be upset with me, would you?"

Pressing her lips together, she shifted her feet and, thinking of Mama, reluctantly surrendered. "I guess not."

"Then it's settled."

But then, suddenly doubtful again, he glanced around.

"You just flew in?" He asked and she nodded. He eyed her knapsack. "And this is all your luggage?"

Giving a lame smile, she eased past. "I travel light."

His questioning look said, *very*.

Mateo watched his unexpected guest enter his spacious foyer. *Sweet,* he noted, his gaze sweeping over her long untreated fair hair. Modestly spoken. Even more modestly dressed.

Arching a brow, Mateo closed the door.

He wasn't convinced.

The seemingly unrehearsed sway of hips in low-waisted jeans, no makeup, few possessions...Bailey Ross had described his grandmother as "very generous," and it was true. In her later years Mama had become an easy touch. He didn't doubt she might have fallen for this woman's lost-kitten look and his gut—as well as past experience—said Miss Ross had taken full advantage of that.

But Mama was also huge on matchmaking. Perhaps Bailey Ross was here simply because his grandmother had thought she and her grandson might hit it off. Given how she tried to set him up with a "nice Italian girl" whenever he visited, it was more than possible.

His first instinct had been to send this woman on her way... but he was curious, and had some time to spare. His cab wasn't due for ten minutes.

Taking in her surroundings, his visitor was turning a slow three-sixty beneath the authentic French chandelier that hung from the ornately molded second-story ceiling. The crystal beads cast moving prisms of light over her face as she admired the antiques and custom-made furnishings.

"Dr. Celeca, your home is amazing." She indicated the staircase. "I can imagine Cinderella in her big gown and glass slippers floating down those stairs."

Built in multicolored marble, the extravagant flight split midway into separate channels, which led to opposite wings of the house. The design mimicked the Paris Opera House, and while the French might lay claim to the Cinderella fable, he smiled and pointed out, "No glass-slippered maidens hiding upstairs, I'm afraid."

She didn't seem surprised. "Mama mentioned you were single."

"Mentioned or repeated often?" He said with a crooked, leading grin.

"Guess it's no secret she's proud of you," Bailey admitted. "And that she'd like a great-grandchild or two."

Be that as it may, he wouldn't be tying any matrimonial knots in the foreseeable future. He'd brought enough children into the world. His profession—and France—were enough for him.

She moved to join him. Her smile sunny enough to melt an iceberg, her eyes incredibly blue, Bailey and Mateo descended a half dozen marble steps and entered the main reception room. Standing among the French chateau classic decor, pausing before the twenty-foot-high Jacobean fireplace, his guest looked sorely out of place. But, he had to admit, not in a bad way. She radiated *fresh*—even as she suppressed a traveler's weary yawn.

Was there reason to doubt her character? Had she fleeced his grandmother or was he being overly suspicious? Mama could be "very generous" in other ways, after all.

"So, what's first on the itinerary?" She asked, lowering into a settee.

"West coast of Canada." Mateo took the single saloon seat. "A group of friends who've been skiing at the same resort for years put on an annual reunion." The numbers had slowly dwindled, however. Most of the guys were married now. Some divorced. The gathering didn't have the same feel as the old days, sadly. This year he wasn't looking forward to it. "Then on to New York to catch up with some professional acquaintances," he went on. "Next it's France."

"You have friends in Paris? My parents honeymooned there. It's supposed to be a gorgeous city."

"I sponsor a charitable institution in the north."

Her eyebrows lifted as she sat back. "What kind of charity?"

"Children without homes. Without parents." To lead into what he really wanted to know—to see if she'd rise to any bait—he added, "I like to give where I can." When she bowed her head to hide a smile, a ball of unease coiled low in his stomach. With some difficulty, he kept his manner merely interested. "Have I said something funny?"

"Just that Mama always said you were a good man." Those glittering blue eyes lifted and met his again. "Not that I doubted her."

Mateo's chest tightened and he fought the urge to tug an ear or clear his throat. This woman was either a master of flattery or as nice as Mama obviously believed her to be. So which was it? Cute or on the take?

"Mama is my biggest fan as I am hers," he said easily. "Seems she's always doing someone a good turn. Helping out where she can."

"She also plays a mean game of Briscola."

He blinked. *Cards?* "Did you play for money?" He manufactured a chuckle. "She probably let you win."

A line pinched between Bailey Ross's brows. "We played because she enjoyed it."

She'd threaded her fingers around the worn denim knees of her jeans. Her bracelet was expensive, however—yellow-gold and heavy with charms. Had Mama's money helped purchase that piece duty free? If he asked Bailey straight out, what reply would she give?

As if she'd read his mind and wasn't comfortable, his guest eased to her feet. "I've held you up long enough. You don't want to miss your flight."

He stood too. She was right. She wasn't going to admit to anything and his cab would be here any minute. Seemed his curiosity with regard to Miss Ross's true nature would go unsatisfied.

"Do you have family in Sydney?" He asked as they crossed the parquet floor together and she covered another yawn.

"I was raised here."

"You'll be catching up with your parents then."

"My mother died a few years back."

"My condolences." He'd never known his mother but the

man he'd come to know as Father had passed away recently. "I'm sure your father's missed you."

But she only looked away.

Walking alongside, Mateo rolled back his shoulders. No mother. Estranged from her father. Few possessions. Hell, now *he* wanted to write her a check.

He changed the subject. "So, what are your broader plans, Miss Ross? Do you have a job here in town to return to?"

"I don't have any real concrete plans just yet."

"Perhaps more travel then?"

"There's more I'd like to see, but for now, I'm hanging around."

They stopped at the entrance. He fanned open the door, searched her flawless face and smiled. "Well, good luck."

"Same to you. Say hello to Paris for me."

As she turned to walk away, hitching that ratty knapsack higher on one slim shoulder, something thrust beneath Mateo's ribs and he took a halting step toward her. Of course, he should let it alone—should let her be on her way—but a stubborn niggling kept at him and he simply had to ask.

"Miss Ross," he called out. Looking surprised, she rotated back. He cut the distance separating them and, having danced around the question long enough, asked outright. "Did my grandmother give you money?"

Her slim nostrils flared and her eyebrows drew in. "She didn't give me money."

Relief fell through him in a warm welcomed rush. As she'd grown older, Mama had admitted many times that she wasn't overly wealthy by design; she had little use for money and therefore liked to help others where she could. There was nothing he could do to stop Mama's generosity—or gullibility as the case more often than not proved to be. But at least he could leave for his vacation knowing this particular young woman hadn't left his grandmother's house stuffing bills in her pocket.

But Bailey wasn't finished.

"Mama *loaned* me money."

As the stone swelled in his chest, Mateo could only stare. He'd been right about her from the start? She'd taken advantage of Mama like those before her. He took in her innocent looks and cringed. He wished he'd never asked.

"A…loan," he said, unconcerned that his tone was graveled. Mocking.

Her cheeks pinked up. "Don't say it like that."

"You say it's a loan," he shrugged, "it's a loan."

"I intend to pay back every cent."

"Really?" Intrigued, he crossed his arms. "And how do you intend to do that with no job, no plans?" From her reaction to his question about her father, there wouldn't be help coming from that source, either.

Her eyes hardened. "We can't all have charmed lives, Doctor."

"Don't presume to know anything about me," he said, his voice deep.

"I only know that I had no choice."

"We all have choices." *At least when we're adults.*

Her cheeks flushed more. "Then I chose escape."

He coughed out a laugh. This got better and better. "Now my grandmother was keeping you *prisoner?*"

"Not your grandmother."

His arms unraveled. Her voice held the slightest quiver. Her pupils had dilated until the blue was all but consumed by black. But she'd told him what he'd stupidly wanted to know. She'd accepted Mama's money. He didn't need or want excuses.

"Goodbye, Miss Ross." He headed inside.

"And thank you, Doctor," she called after him. "You've

killed whatever faith I had left in the male species." A pulse thudding at his temple, he angled back. Her expression was dry. Sad. *Infuriating.* "I honestly thought you were a gentleman," she finished.

"Only when in the presence of a lady."

Self-disgust hit his gut with a jolt.

"I apologize," he murmured. "That wasn't called for."

"Do you even want to know what I needed to escape?" She ground out. "Why I needed that money?"

He exhaled heavily. Fine. After that insult, he owed her one. "Why did you need the money?"

"Because of a man who wouldn't listen," she said pointedly, her gaze hot and moist. "He said we were getting married and, given the situation I was in, I *didn't* have a choice."

Two

"You're engaged?" Mateo shook himself.

"No." In a tight voice, she added, "Not really."

"Call me old-fashioned, but I thought being betrothed was like being pregnant. You either are or you aren't."

"I...*was* engaged."

Slanting his head, he took another look. Her nose was more a button with a sprinkling of freckles but her unusual crystalline eyes were large and, as she stood her ground, her pupils dilated more, making her gaze appear even more pronounced. Or was that scared?

I didn't have a choice.

An image of the degrees decorating his office walls swam up in Mateo's mind. Time to take a more educated guess as to why Mama might have sent this woman. He set his voice at a different tone, the one he used for patients feeling uncertain.

"Bailey, are you having a baby?"

Her eyes flared, bright with indignation. *"No."*

"Are you sure? We can do tests—"

"Of *course* I'm sure."

Backing off, he held up his hands. "Okay. Fine. Given your circumstances, it seemed like a possibility."

"It really wasn't." Her voice dropped. "We didn't sleep together. Not even once."

She spun to leave, but, hurrying down the steps, she tripped on the toe of her sandal. The next second she was stumbling, keeling forward. Leaping, Mateo caught her before she went down all the way. Gripping her upper arms, he felt her shaking—from shock at almost breaking her neck? Or pique at him? Or was the trembling due to dredging up memories of this engagement business in Italy?

She was so taken aback, she didn't object when he helped her sit on a step. Lifting her chin, he set out to check that the dilation in her eyes was even, but with his palm cradling her cheek and his face so close to hers, the pad of his thumb instinctively moved to trace the sweep of her lower lip. Heat, dangerous and swift, flared low in his belly and his head angled a whisper closer.

But then she blinked. So did he. Spell broken, he cleared his throat and got to his feet while she caught her breath and gathered herself.

He might be uncertain about some things regarding Bailey Ross, but of one he was sure. The constant yawning, tripping over herself…

"You need sleep," he told her.

"I'll survive."

"No doubt you will."

But, dammit, he was having a hard time thinking of her walking off alone down that drive and Mama phoning to ask if he'd looked after her little friend who'd apparently had such a hard time in Casa Buona. Given her stumble, her jet lag, Mama would expect him to at least give Bailey time to recuperate before he truly sent her on her way. And that was the only reason he persisted. Why he asked now.

"So…who's this fiancé?"

Closing her eyes, she exhaled as if she was too tired to be defensive anymore.

"I was backpacking around Europe," she began. "By the time I got to Casa Buona, I'd run out of money. That's where I met Emilio. I picked up work at the taverna his parents own."

Mateo's muscles locked. "Emilio Conti is your fiancé?"

"*Was.*" She quizzed his eyes. "Do you know him?"

"Casa Buona's a small town." Emilio's kind only made it feel smaller. Mateo nodded. "Go on."

Elbows finding her knees, she cupped her cheeks. "Over the weeks, Emilio and I became close. We spent a lot of time with his family. Time by ourselves. When he said he loved me, I was taken off guard. I didn't know about loving Emilio, but I'd certainly fallen in love with his parents. His sisters. They made me feel like one of the family." Her hands lowered and she brought up her legs to hug her knees. "One Saturday, in front of everyone, he proposed at the taverna. Seemed like the whole town was there, all smiling, holding their breath, waiting for my answer. I was stunned. Any words stuck like bricks in my throat. When I bowed my head, trying to figure out something tactful to do or say, someone cried out that I'd accepted. A huge cheer went up. Before I knew what had happened, Emilio slid a ring on my finger and…well…that was that."

Bailey ended by failing to smother a yawn at the same time the sound of an engine drew their attention. His ride—a yellow cab—was cruising up the drive.

"Wait here," he said, and when she opened her mouth to argue, he interrupted firmly. "One minute. Please." He crossed to the forecourt and spoke to the driver, who kept his motor idling while Mateo walked back and took a seat on the step alongside of her.

"Where do you plan to go now? Do you have anywhere to stay?"

"I'd hoped to stay with a friend for a few days but her neighbor said she's out of town. I'll get a room."

"Do you really want to waste Mama's money on a motel?"

"It's only temporary."

He studied the cab, thought of the dwindling group of guys doing their annual bachelor bash in Canada and, as Bailey pushed to her feet, made a decision.

"Come back inside."

Her look said, *you're crazy.* "You're ready to leave. The meter's running."

He eyed the driver. Best fix that.

He strode to the vehicle, left the cabbie smiling at the notes he passed over and heard the engine rev off behind him as he joined Bailey again.

Her jaw was hanging. "What did you do?"

"I'd thought about cancelling the first leg of my trip anyway. Now, inside." He tilted his head toward his still open front door.

"Flattering invitation." Her smile was thin. "But I don't do *fetch* or *roll over,* either."

Mateo's chin tucked in. She thought he was being bossy? Perhaps he was. He was used to people listening and accepting his advice. And there was a method to his madness. "You say the money Mama gave you is a loan. But you admit you have no income. No place to stay."

"I'll find something. I'm not afraid of work."

Another yawn gripped her, so consuming, she shuddered and her eyes watered.

"First you need a good rest," he told her. "I'll show you to a guest room."

Another *you're crazy* look. "I'm not staying."

"I'm not suggesting a lease, Bailey. Merely that you recharge here before you tackle a plan for tomorrow."

"No." But this time she sounded less certain.

"Mama would want you to." When she hesitated, he persisted. "A few hours rest. I won't pound on the door and get on your case."

She glared at him. "Promise?"

"On my life."

All the energy seemed to fall from her shoulders. He thought she might disarm him with a hint of that ice-melting smile, but she only nodded and grudgingly allowed him to escort her back inside.

After ascending that storybook staircase, Mateo Celeca showed her down the length of a wide paneled hallway to the entrance of a lavish room.

"The suite has an attached bath," he said as she edged in and looked around. "Make yourself at home. I'll be downstairs if you need anything."

Bailey watched the broad ledge of his shoulders roll away down the hall before she closed the heavy door and, feeling more displaced than she had in her life, gravitated toward the center of the vast room. Her own background was well to do. With a tennis court and five bedrooms, her lawyer father's house in Newport was considered grand to most. Her parents had driven fashionable cars. They'd gone on noteworthy vacations each year.

But, glancing around this lake of snowy carpet with so many matching white and gold draperies, Bailey could admit she'd never known *this* kind of opulence. Then again, who on earth needed this much? She wasn't one to covet riches.

Surely it was more important to know a sense of belonging... of truly being where and with whom you needed to be. Despite Emilio, irrespective of her father, one day she hoped to know and keep that feeling.

After a long warm shower, she lay down and sleep descended in a swift black cloud.

When she woke some hours later in the dark, her heart was pounding with an impending sense of doom. In her dream, she'd been back in Casa Buona, draped in a modest wedding gown with Emilio beckoning her to join him at the end of a long dark corridor. She shot a glance around the shadowy unfamiliar surrounds and eased out a relieved breath. She was in Sydney. Broke, starting over. In an obstinate near-stranger's house.

She clapped a palm over her brow and groaned.

Mateo Celeca.

With refined movie-star looks and dark hypnotic eyes, he did all kinds of unnerving things to her equilibrium. One minute she was believing Mama, thinking her grandson was some kind of prince. The next he was being a jerk, accusing her of theft. Then, to really send her reeling, he'd offered her a bed to shake off some of the jet lag. If she'd had anywhere else to go—if she hadn't felt so suddenly drained—she would never have stayed. She wasn't about to forgive or forget his comment about her not being a lady.

She swung her legs over the edge of the bed at the same time her stomach growled. She cast her thoughts away from the judgmental doctor to a new priority. Food.

After slipping on her jeans, she tiptoed down that stunning staircase and set off to find a kitchen. Inching through someone else's broad shadow-filled halls in the middle of the night hardly felt right but the alternative was finding a takeout close by or dialing in. Mateo had said to make herself at home. Surely that offer extended to a sandwich.

Soon she'd tracked down a massive room, gleaming with stainless steel and dark granite surfaces. Opening the fridge she found the interior near empty; that made sense given Mateo was meant to be on vacation. But there was a leftover roast, perhaps from his dinner earlier. A slab went between two slices of bread and, after enjoying her first mouthful, Bailey turned and discovered a series of floor-to-ceiling glass panes lining the eastern side of the attached room.

Outside, ghostly garden lights illuminated a divine courtyard where geometrically manicured hedges sectioned off individual classical statues. Beyond those panes, a scene from two thousand years ago beckoned…a passionate time when Rome dominated and emperors ruled half the world. Chewing, she hooked a glance around. No one about. Nothing to stop her. A little fresh air would be nice.

She eased back a door and moved out into the cool night, the soles of her bare feet padding over smooth sandstone paths as she wandered between hedges and those exquisite stone figures that seemed so lifelike. She was on her third bite of sandwich when a sound came from behind—a muted click that vibrated through the night and made the fine hairs on her nape stand up and quiver. Heart lodged in her throat, she angled carefully around. One of those figures was gliding toward her. Masculine. Tall. Naked from the waist up.

From behind a cloud, the full moon edged out and the definition of that outline sharpened…the captivating width of his chest, the subtle ruts of toned abs. Bailey's gaze inched higher and connected with inquiring onyx eyes as a low familiar voice rumbled out.

"You're up."

Bailey let out the breath she'd been holding.

Not a statue come to life, but Mateo Celeca standing before her, wearing nothing but a pair of long white drawstring pants. She'd been so absorbed she'd forgotten where she was, as well as the events that had brought her here. Now, in a hot rush, it all came back. Particularly how annoyingly attractive her host was, tonight, with the moonbeams playing over that hard human physique, dramatically so.

When a kernel of warmth ignited in the lowest point of her belly, Bailey swallowed and clasped her sandwich at her chest.

Mateo Celeca might be beyond hot, but, at this point in her life, she didn't care to even *think* about the opposite sex, particularly a critical one. Her only concern lay in getting back on her feet and repaying Mama as soon as possible, whether the doctor believed that or not.

"I didn't mean to wake you," she said in a surprisingly even voice that belied how churned up she felt.

"You tripped a silent alarm when you opened that door. The security company called to make sure there'd been no breach. I thought it'd be you, but I came down to check, just in case."

Bailey kicked herself. She'd seen him fiddling with a security pad when she'd arrived. Heaven knew what this place and its contents were insured for. Of course he'd have a state-of-the-art system switched on and jump when an alert went off.

"I was hungry," she explained then held up dinner. "I made a sandwich."

She wasn't sure, but in the shadows she thought he might have grinned—which was way better than a scowl. If he started on her again now, in the middle of the night, she'd simply grab her bag and find the door. But he seemed far more relaxed than this morning when he'd overreacted about the money Mama had loaned her.

"You usually enjoy a starry stroll with your midnight snack?" He asked as he sauntered nearer.

"It looked so nice out."

"It is pleasant."

He studied the topiaries and pristine hedges, and this time she was certain of the smile curving one corner of his mouth as he stretched his arms, one higher than the other, over his head. She wanted to fan herself. And she'd thought the *statues* were works of art.

"Are you a gardener?" She asked, telling herself to look away but not managing it. Bronzed muscles rippled in the moonlight whenever he moved.

"Not at all. But I appreciate the effort others put in."

"This kind of effort must be twenty-four seven."

"What about you?" He asked, meandering toward a trickling water feature displaying a god-like figure ready to sling a lightning bolt.

"No green thumbs here." Moving to join him, she tipped her head at the fountain. "Is that Zeus?" She remembered a recent movie about the Titans. "The god of war, right?"

"Zeus is the god of justice. The supreme protector. Perhaps because he could have lost his life at the very moment he entered the world."

"Really? How?" Moving to sit on the cool fountain ledge, she took another bite. She loved to hear about ancient legends.

"His father, Cronus, believed in a prophecy. He would be overthrown by his son as he had once overthrown his own father. To save her newborn, Rhea, Zeus's mother, gave him up at birth then tricked her husband into thinking a rock wrapped in swaddling clothes was the child, which Cronus promptly disposed of. He didn't know that his son, Zeus, was being reared by a nymph in Crete. When he was grown, Zeus joined forces with his other siblings to defeat the Titans, including his father."

She couldn't help but be drawn by Mateo's story, as well as the emotion simmering beneath his words. Had she imagined the shadow that had crossed his gaze when he spoke of that mother needing to give up her child?

"What happened to Zeus after the clash?" She asked.

"He ruled over Olympus as well as the mortals, and fathered many children."

"Sounds noble."

"The great majority of his offspring were conceived through adulterous affairs, I'm afraid."

Oh. "Not so good for the demigod kids."

"Not so good for any child."

Bailey studied his classic profile as he peered off into the night...the high forehead and proud, hawkish nose. She wanted to ask more. Not only about this adulterous yet protective Roman god but also about the narrator of his tale. Not that Mateo's life was any of her business. Although...

For the moment he seemed to have put aside his more paranoid feelings toward her, and this was an informal chat. In the morning she'd be well rested and on her way, so where was the harm in asking more?

Making a pretense of examining the gardens, she crossed her ankles and swung her feet out and back.

"Mama mentioned that you left Casa Buona when you were twelve."

His hesitation—a single beat—was barely enough to notice.

"My father was moving to Australia. He explained about the opportunities here. Ernesto was an accountant and wanted to look after my higher education."

"Have you lived in Sydney since?"

He nodded. "But I travel when I can."

"You must have built a lot of memories here after so long."

Who were his friends? All professionals like him? Did he have any other family Down Under?

But Mateo didn't respond. He merely looked over the gardens with those dark thoughtful eyes. From the firm set of his jaw, her host had divulged all he would tonight. Understandable. They were little more than strangers. And, despite this intimate atmosphere, they were destined to remain that way.

A statue caught Bailey's eye. After slipping off her perch, she crossed over and ran a hand across the cool stone.

"I like this one."

It was a mother, her head bowed over the baby she held. The tone conjured up memories of Bailey's own mother…how loving and devoted she'd been. Like Rhea. Both mothers had needed to leave their child, though neither woman had wanted to. If she lived to one hundred, Bailey would miss her till the day she died.

"Is this supposed to be Zeus as an infant?" She asked, her gaze on the baby now.

Mateo's deep voice came from behind. "No. More a signature to my profession, I suppose."

His profession. An obstetrician. One of the best in Australia, Mama had said, and more than once.

"How many babies have you brought into the world?" She asked, studying the soft loving smile adorning the statue's face.

When he didn't reply, she edged around and almost lost her breath. Mateo was standing close…close enough for her to inhale that undeniable masculine scent. Near enough to be drawn by its natural heady lure. As his intense gaze glittered down and searched hers, a lock of dark hair dropped over his brow and jumped in the breeze.

"…to count."

Coming to, Bailey gathered herself. He'd been speaking, but she'd only caught his last words.

"I'm sorry," she said. "To count what?"

His brows swooped together. "How many babies I've delivered. Too many to count."

Bailey withered as her cheeks heated up. How had she lost track of their conversation so completely?

But she knew how. Whether he was being polite or fiery and passionate, Mateo exuded an energy that drew her in.

Indisputable.

Unwelcome.

Heartbeat throbbing in her throat, she lowered her gaze and turned a little away. "Guess they all blur after a time."

"Not at all. Each safe delivery is an accomplishment I never take for granted."

The obvious remained unsaid. Even in this day and age, some deliveries wouldn't go as planned. No matter how skilled, every doctor suffered defeats. Just like criminal lawyers.

She remembered her parents speaking about one client her father had failed to see acquitted. The man's family had lost nearly all their possessions in a fire, and her father donated a sizable amount to get them sturdily on their feet again. She'd felt so very proud of him. But he seemed to lose those deeper feelings for compassion after her mother passed away.

As Mateo's gaze ran over the mother and child, Bailey wondered again about *his* direct family. He'd lived with his grandmother in Italy. Had come to Australia with his father. Where was his mother?

"I'm turning in," he said, rolling back one big bare shoulder. "There's a television and small library in your room if you can't get back to sleep." That dark gaze skimmed her face a final time and tingling warmth filtered over her before he rotated away. "*Sogni d'oro,* Bailey."

"*Sogni d'oro,*" she replied and then smiled.

Sweet dreams.

Mateo sauntered back inside, his gait relaxed yet purposeful.

He was a difficult one to work out. So professional and together most of the time, but there was a volatile side too, one she wondered if many people saw. More was going on beneath the sophisticated exterior…deep and private things Mateo Celeca wouldn't want to divulge. And certainly not divulge to a troublesome passerby like herself. Even if they had the time to get acquainted, he'd been clear. She wasn't the kind of woman the doctor wanted to get too close to.

Bailey thought of those shoulders—those eyes—and, holding the flutter in her tummy, concurred.

She didn't need to get that close either.

Three

Early the next morning, Mateo strode out his back door and threw an annoyed glance around the hedges and their statues. Not a sign of her anywhere. Seemed Bailey Ross had flown the coop.

After knocking on her bedroom door—politely at first—thinking she must be hungry and might join him for breakfast, he'd found the room empty. The shabby knapsack vanished. No matter her consequences, she shouldn't have taken money from an elderly, obviously soft-hearted woman. Equally, she ought to have had the decency to at least stay long enough to say "thanks for the bed," and "so long."

He'd practically laughed in her face when she'd vowed to pay that "loan" back. After this disappearing act, he'd bet all he owned neither he nor Mama would hear from Miss Ross again. She was a woman without scruples. And yet, he couldn't deny it—he was attracted to her.

After her stumble yesterday, when he'd cupped, then

searched, her face, the urge to lean closer and slant his mouth over hers had been overwhelming. Last night while they'd spoken among the shadows of these gardens, he'd fought to keep a lid on that same impulse. Something deep and strong reacted whenever she was near. Something primordial and potentially dangerous.

He'd felt this kind of intense chemistry once before, Mateo recalled, looking over the statue of mother and child Bailey had found so interesting last night. Unfortunately, at twenty-three he'd been too wet behind the ears to see that particular woman for what she was: a beautiful, seductive leech. He'd fallen hard and had given Linda Webb everything she'd wanted. Or, rather, he'd *tried*. Expensive perfume, jewelry, even a car. She was an unquenchable well. Took twelve months and a ransacked savings account before he'd faced facts—unemployed Linda hadn't wanted a fiancé as much as a financier.

Unlike Mama, he had no problem with being wealthy. He'd worked hard to achieve this level of security and he wouldn't apologize for doing well. He also liked to be generous— but only where and when his gifts were put to good use and appreciated. That cancelled out the likes of Linda Webb and Bailey Ross.

Giving up the search, Mateo rotated away from a view of bordering pines at the same time he saw her.

Beyond the glass-paneled pool fence, a lithe figure lay on a sun lounge, floppy straw hat covering the back of her head and the teeniest of micro bikinis covering not much of the rest. An invisible band around Mateo's chest tightened while his clamoring heartbeat ratcheted up another notch. Last night in the moonlight she'd looked beyond tempting, but in an almost innocent way. There was nothing innocent about the way Miss Ross looked this morning.

Those bikini bottoms weren't technically a thong, but

far more was revealed by that sliver of bright pink fabric than was covered. Minus the jeans, her legs appeared even longer, naturally tanned. Smooth. His fingertips, and other extremities, tingled and grew warm. He couldn't deny that every male cell in his body wanted to reach out and touch her.

One of Bailey's tanned arms braced as she shifted on the lounge. The disturbed floppy hat fell to the ground. When she blindly felt around but couldn't find it, she shifted again, pushing up on both palms. A frown pinched her brow and, as if she'd sensed him standing nearby, her gaze tipped higher then wandered across the lawn.

When their eyes connected, hers popped and she sprang up to a sit while Mateo fought every impulse known to man to check out the twin pink triangles almost covering her perfect breasts. With difficulty, he forced his face into an unaffected mask.

Get a grip. You're a medical doctor. An obstetrician who has tended hundreds of clients.

But there was a distinction between "work" and this vastly different environment. Irrespective of profession, he was still a man, complete with a man's urges and desires. Under normal circumstances, being physically attracted to a member of the opposite sex was nothing immoral. Trouble was…he didn't *want* to be attracted to Bailey Ross. Whether she was a victim or a schemer, she was a drifter who seemed to court trouble.

As Bailey swiped her T-shirt off the back of the lounge, Mateo set his hands in his trouser pockets and cast an aimless glance around. When he was certain her top half was covered, he crossed over.

"I took an early morning dip," she said as he entered the pool area.

"When I couldn't find you inside, I thought you'd run off."

She frowned. "I wouldn't leave without saying goodbye."

"Unless I was your fiancé?"

"I'm grateful for the bed," she said, standing, "but not appreciative enough to listen to any more of your put-downs."

He moved to the rock waterfall, wedged his hands in his pockets again and, after debating with himself several moments, said calmly, "So tell me more about your situation."

"So you can scoff?"

"So I can understand."

Dammit, one minute he was wanting to help, offering her a bed, the next he was lumping her in the same class as Linda. Was Bailey genuine about paying that money back, or were her dealings with Mama merely a side issue for him? Was his interest more about that long fair hair, those blazing blue eyes?

That, after his last comment, seemed to have lost a little of their fire.

Folding back down again, she set that straw hat on her lap and explained.

"After that night...the night Emilio proposed," she said, "his sisters jumped into organizing the wedding. Emilio set the date two months from the day he shoved that ring on my finger. He wouldn't listen when I told him it was a mistake. He only smiled and tried to hug me when I said this had all happened too fast. Everyone kept saying what a great catch he was."

"Not in your opinion."

"Sure, we had fun," she admitted. "Up to that point. But after that night, whenever I got vocal and tried to return his ring, Emilio got upset. His face would turn red and beads of sweat would break on his brow. He'd proposed, he'd say, and I'd accepted. I'd taken his family's charity by working at the taverna and sleeping under their roof. We were getting married and he knew once I got over my nerves I'd be happy. I didn't have nearly enough money for a ticket home. I was trapped." Looking at her feet, she exhaled. "One day at Mama's place, I broke down. We were alone and when she asked what was wrong I told her I couldn't go through with the wedding. Everyone else might have been in love with Emilio but I wasn't."

"Why not call your father?"

Regardless of disagreements, family was family. His own father had been there through thick and thin. Or rather the man he knew as a father was.

"If I introduced you to Dad," she plopped her hat back on her head, "you'd understand why. I went overseas against his advice. The last thing he said to me was that if I was old enough not to listen, I was old enough to figure out my own problems." Her voice dropped. "Believe me, he wouldn't want to know."

"You've made a few mistakes in the past?" An insensitive question, perhaps, but he was determined to get to the bottom of this maze.

"Nothing monumental."

"Until this."

Screwing her eyes shut, she groaned. "I knew I could've said no to Emilio on the day of the wedding, but I couldn't bear to think of everyone's meltdown, particularly his. Or I could simply have packed up and stolen off in the middle of the night and moved on to the next town. But Emilio proved to me he wasn't the kind to let go what he believed was his. He'd come after me and do all he could to bring me back."

From what Mateo remembered of Emilio, he had to agree. Beneath the superficial charm lived a Neanderthal.

Moving to a garden crowded with spiky Pandanus palms, Mateo swept his foot to move stray white pebbles back into their proper bed.

"What makes you so sure he won't come here?"

"I'm *not* sure. I mailed him a package from the airport. The letter explained how I wished he'd listened and I wasn't coming back. I put his ring in, as well. Hopefully that will be enough."

Mateo grunted. "He's thick but not entirely stupid." When she glanced over, curious, he explained. "The summer before I left Italy, a twelve-year-old Emilio tried to call me out. Can't recall the reason now but certainly nothing to warrant a fistfight. When Emilio and a couple of friends cut me off in an alley, I defended myself. Emilio didn't bother me after that."

Surrounded by memories, Mateo absently brushed more pebbles into the garden bed. How different his life would have been if he'd stayed in Casa Buona. What if no one had come for him all those years ago in France? What would have become of him then? If Mama hadn't offered her help to this woman—if what she said was true—what would have happened to Bailey?

"I'm going to pay her back," Bailey insisted. "If it takes five years—"

"Mama may not *have* five years."

Her head went back as if she hadn't considered Mama's advanced age. But then one slender shoulder hitched up and she amended. "I'll get a loan."

A loan to pay a loan. "With no job?"

Sitting straighter, she crossed those long tanned legs. "I'm fixing that."

"Looks like it," he muttered, eyeing the pool sparkling with golden east coast sunshine. Linda was always on the verge of getting a job too.

Bailey's jaw tightened. "Accepting Mama's money wasn't any moral highlight—"

"And yet you did accept."

The frustration in her eyes hardened before the irritation evaporated into resignation. She slowly shook her head. "Someone like you...you could never understand what it's like to feel powerless."

Oh, but he *did* know. And he'd spent his entire adult life making certain he never felt powerless again. He'd done it through hard work, not lying around a pool. Although part of her plan had merit.

"Getting a loan is a good idea," he said, "but not from an institution. There's interest. If you get behind, there are fees."

"Maybe I should throw some cash at a roulette wheel," she groaned.

"I have a better idea. I'll pay Mama the money you owe—"

"What?" She shook her head. "Absolutely not!"

"—and you can pay me back."

"I don't want to owe *you* anything."

"So you're not serious about paying her back as soon as possible?"

She eyed him as Little Red Riding Hood might eye the big bad wolf.

"What are the terms?" She finally asked.

"A signed agreement. Regular repayments."

"Why would you do that for me?"

"Not for you. For my grandmother." The amount Bailey owed wouldn't make a dent in any of his accounts but he liked to think that, for once, Mama wouldn't be left out of pocket by virtue of her soft heart.

Bailey pushed to her feet, paced around the back of the sun lounge, studied him and then, defiant, crossed her arms. A few more seconds wound out before she announced, "Well, then, I'd better get cracking."

That floppy hat stuck on her head, she fished her jeans out of her knapsack and drove her legs through the denim pipes. When he realized he'd been staring while she wiggled and scooped her bottom into the seat of her jeans, he jerked his gaze away and heard her zip up. He'd already faced the fact Miss Ross wasn't the kind of woman with whom he wished to become more involved than he already was.

In time, he looked back to see her heading for the pool gate, that knapsack swinging over a shoulder. "Where are you going?"

"To get a job. I'll be back by five to sign that contract. And about those repayments..." She stopped at the gate and her glittering blue eyes meshed with his. "I want them as steep as possible."

His eyebrows jumped. "To get the debt paid off in record time?"

"To get you out of my life ASAP."

As she strode away, Mateo gave himself permission to drink in the sway of those slim hips and long hair. High on each thigh, his muscles hardened as his thoughts gave over to how those curves and silk might feel beneath his fingers, his lips....

Regardless of whether she took Mama's money or not, she was attractive and fiery and...something more. Something he would dearly love to sample.

Whether it was good for him or not.

Four

Bailey visited every employment agency she could find, unfortunately with little success. Although initially there seemed to be some prospects, they turned out to be either charity work or commission-based jobs, like knocking on doors.

Time and again she'd been asked about qualifications. No high school diploma. One year of an apprenticeship at a hair salon. She'd been a school crossing guard, helping kids cross streets for a while. Mainly she'd performed waitress work.

She'd been directed to a hospitality recruitment agency. Placements were available at exclusive establishments but she didn't have the experience necessary to be put forward as a candidate. Many courses to enhance her skills, however, were available. But they cost money and Bailey didn't have the time to spare. She needed to start earning. Needed to start paying back and showing Mateo Celeca she wasn't a con artist but merely someone who'd needed a hand up.

As weary as she felt after a full day trekking around the city, she tried to keep her spirits high. Her mother had always said there was good in every situation. Bailey didn't quite believe that; what was so good about having a stroke take a parent out at age thirty-five? But Bailey did believe in never giving up. Her mother would have wanted her to stay strong and believe in herself, even now when she'd never felt more alone.

In the busy city center, with traffic and pedestrians grinding by, she'd pulled out her bus timetable and had found a suitable link when a familiar voice drew her ear. Masculine. Tense. The tone sent simultaneous chills and familiar warmth racing over her skin. She hadn't heard that voice in over a year. Back then it had told her not to come home begging.

Her heart beating high in her throat, Bailey looked carefully over her shoulder. Her father stood on the curb, phone pressed to his ear, announcing his displeasure over a jury verdict gone wrong.

In an instant, Bailey couldn't draw enough breath. She had the bizarre urge to run—both toward her father and away from him. Never would she have simply waltzed up to his door and thrown out her arms, and yet now—with him available such a short distance away—she couldn't help but relive those much earlier days…times when her dad had taken her horseback riding, or suffered answering inane questions from an eight-year-old while he worked on depositions. When she'd come down with tonsillitis he'd rushed her to the doctor. He'd even taken time off to nurse her back, complete with spoon-fed antibiotics.

And that was a full year after her mother had died.

Bailey's throat convulsed at the same time her eyes misted over.

He was right there.

A now-or-never feeling fell through her middle as she

moved one foot forward, and another. Maybe he hadn't meant to sound so harsh. So final. Maybe he *wouldn't* turn her away. She was his only child, after all. Perhaps he'd cry out in surprise and wrap his arms around her. Tell her that he'd missed her and ask that she come home with him now. Straight away.

An uncertain smile quivering on her lips, she'd cut the distance separating them by half when a cab swung into the curb. Before Bailey could think to call out, Damon Ross had flung open the door and, phone still at his ear, slid into the backseat. Her hand was in the air, a single word on her tongue, when the cab cut into a break in traffic and shot away.

Her hand lowered and stomach dropped. Blinking furiously, she fought back the bite of rising tears and disappointment. But, no matter how much it hurt, that bad timing was probably best. The cab swerving in at that exact moment had saved her from herself. Her father had said she'd regret dropping out of school and while that was one thing he'd been right about, there was a whole lot more that had never needed to be said. But it was too late for those kind of regrets. Nothing could be done about the past.

Determined, Bailey walked a straight line to the bus stop.

Now the future was all that mattered.

She'd told him five, but Bailey didn't get back to Mateo's mansion until six. Answering the bell, he threw open the door, took in her appearance and frowned. Bailey drew herself up, entered the foyer and fought the impulse to ease the sandals off her feet, grimy with city dirt. God, she must look like an urchin in need of a warm meal and a bath.

He closed the door. "No luck on the job front?"

"There are a few possibilities." She firmed the line of her mouth and almost succeeded in squaring her shoulders. "I'll be out again tomorrow. I just wanted to let you know I haven't skipped town. I have every intention of going through with my end of the deal." Taking up his offer of a loan and signing a contract that would legally commit her to paying every penny back, the sooner the better. She wanted this episode of her life over as much as Mateo must, too.

But then she stopped to take in his attire—custom-made trousers and a black jersey knit shirt that covered his shoulders and chest like a dream. His scent was hot and mouth-wateringly fresh. His shoes were mirror polished.

"Are you on your way out?"

Seemed she was destined to show up on his doorstep whenever he was about to head off.

"I spoke with a friend today," he said. "We went to university together. I delivered his baby boy."

"Having an obstetrician friend must come in handy."

He conceded a smile. "Alex's wife worked in real estate," he went on in that rich deep voice that resonated like symphony base chords through the foyer. "Rental properties. Natalie still works a couple of days a week to keep her hand in."

"Smart lady."

And you're telling me all this...why?

As if reading her thoughts, he explained. "Since my trip's been delayed, I suggested we catch up for dinner. Alex thought you might like to come."

At the same time a muscle in his jaw flexed, a wave of anticipation, and apprehension, rippled between them and Bailey fought the urge to clear her ears.

"Your friend doesn't know me. You barely know me and, call me paranoid, but I have the impression you don't like me much."

His closest shoulder hitched and dropped. "We have to eat." She narrowed her eyes at him. Since when had "he" and "she" become "we"? "Unless you have other plans," he finished.

Her only other plans entailed checking into an affordable hotel. The more interesting question was, "How did you explain me to your friend?"

"I told him the truth."

"That I took money from your grandmother and you don't mean to let me out of your sight until I've paid back every cent?"

"I said you were a friend of Mama's returned to Australia."

Bailey held that breath. His expression was open. Given she'd kept her word and come back today, were his suspicions about her character being unfavorable starting to wane? Not that his opinion of her should matter…only, if she were completely honest, for some reason they did.

He thrust his hands in his trouser pockets. "Of course, if you're not hungry—"

"*No*. I mean, I *am*." In fact, now that food had been mentioned, her empty stomach was reminding her she hadn't eaten since a muffin several hours earlier. But…wincing, she looked down and felt the day's dust on her skin. "I'll need a shower."

"Table's not booked till seven-thirty."

Bailey nibbled her lower lip. There was something else. Something any female would be reluctant to admit. "I, um, don't have another dress." From the look of Mateo's crisp attire, jeans and a T-shirt wouldn't cut it.

When his gaze skimmed her frame, her eyes widened. She'd felt that visual stroke like a warm slow touch.

He gave a sexy slanted grin. "What you're wearing," he said, "will be fine."

Twenty minutes later, showered and somewhat refreshed, Bailey followed Mateo to the garage. She was determined not to drink in the way the impression of his shoulder blades rolled beneath that black shirt or recall how delectable that back had looked so bronzed and bare in the moonlight last night.

As much as she'd like to, she couldn't deny she was physically attracted to the man. That didn't mean she should dwell on bone-melting images of him as she had done while standing beneath the showerhead mere moments ago. She hadn't been able to pry her thoughts from memories of Mateo strolling among those lifelike statues. Worse, she couldn't help but speculate on how those strong toned arms might feel surrounding and gathering her in, or how the bow of his full lower lip might taste grazing languidly back and forth over hers....

Now another image faded up in her mind—Mateo Celeca, gloriously naked and poised above her in that beautiful big upstairs bed. Her throat immediately thickened and beneath her bodice, nipples peaked and hardened. Slowing her step, Bailey pushed out a breath. She might have been engaged to Emilio but he'd never affected her this way. No man had. Why should that be so when, not only had she and Mateo locked horns, they'd only known each other a day?

In the garage, he showed her to the passenger side door of an expensive low-slung vehicle. A Maserati, if she wasn't mistaken. Odd there wasn't at least one or two other sports cars housed in the overly spacious garage. Or, perhaps, something classier to more aptly suit his station, like a Bentley or Rolls.

The garage door whirred up and soon they were cruising down the tree-lined drive and out on to a quiet street bordered by wide immaculate sidewalks where women in designer tracksuits walked poodles showing off diamanté collars. These people couldn't have the foggiest idea how the other half lived.

"I phoned someone else today," Mateo said, changing gears.

"Mama?" She guessed, and he nodded. "I wanted to be half settled before I called or wrote her."

"She figured that."

"Did you tell her that you invited me to stay last night?" She asked, feeling a little awkward over it. Not that Mama would mind in the least.

"I told her you rested at my house overnight and you were out looking for a job." Large sure hands on the steering wheel navigated a corner. "She said you should stay until you were earning and set up some place."

Closing her eyes, Bailey groaned as her cheeks grew hot. Mama was a lovely lady. She was only showing that she cared. But, "I'm sure you told her I'd be fine."

"I said I'd offer."

"You *what?*"

"I said you could stay for a couple of days until things were sorted out."

Bailey thought that statement through. "You mean things like our loan agreement?"

He gave an affirmative grunt. "And it's not as if the house isn't big enough to accommodate one more." He skated over a defining look. "For a few days."

Before she could argue, he turned the conversation toward the couple they'd be dining with that night—Natalie and Alex Ramirez. But Bailey's thoughts were stuck on Mateo's offer to stay in his home. She didn't want to sponge. But a few days grace to set herself up would be heaven-sent. She was willing to work at anything to get her life back on track, and quickly. Surely a job would turn up in the next day or two.

When they pulled up at a well-to-do address, Bailey's stomach flipped. She shouldn't be surprised that the Ramirez abode almost rivaled Mateo's in size and grandeur. Of course his friends would be wealthy. But beyond that, despite her nerves, she was curious to meet people the doctor liked to spend time with and perhaps learn a little more about the enigma that was Mateo Celeca. She only wished she was dressed more appropriately, and that she had a better pair of shoes to wear out. Dinner with this type meant more than pulling up a chair in a pizza joint.

Mateo slid out of the car. When he opened her door, she accepted his hand and a flurry of sparks shot like a line of lit gunpowder up her arm. Easing out into the forecourt, although her heart was thumping, Bailey managed to keep her expression unaffected. She'd felt this buzz before, when he'd caught her yesterday and, holding her chin, had looked into her eyes. Tonight the effect was even more pronounced. If an everyday act like hands touching caused this kind of physical reaction, she couldn't fathom how something of consequence might affect her...like a no-holds-barred penetrating kiss.

Did Mateo feel it too?

A stunning brunette holding a young child dressed in a blue jumpsuit, and a tall, dark-haired man answered the door. At the same time the man—Alex Ramirez—stepped aside to show his guests through, his wife put out her free hand. Her nails were French tipped. The princess-cut diamond solitaire was enormous. "You must be Bailey. I'm Natalie and this little fellow is Reece." She bounced the baby and he smiled and squealed again. "Come in, and bring that handsome devil with you."

Mateo leaned in to brush a light kiss on Natalie's cheek before shaking his friend's hand heartily then returning close to her side again, as if he could sense her anxiety. As if they might be a genuine couple.

As they all moved into a sumptuous living room, furnished with contemporary leathers and teak, Bailey took in Natalie's exquisite dress. Cut just below the knee, the lilac fabric shimmered beneath strategically placed downlights. The effect was dazzling, bringing out her complexion and intensity of her long dark hair. Her shoes matched the dress, lilac, delicate heels. Her toenails were painted red. Had she enjoyed a professional pedicure earlier that day?

Glancing down, Bailey cringed.

Her own toes hadn't seen a lick of polish in too long to remember.

Everything in Casa Buona had been so relaxed. She hadn't needed much, although, in order to travel light—to leave quickly when she had—she'd left a number of pretty skirts and tops behind, casual bright wear that suited work at the taverna. Despite the way it had all ended, she'd enjoyed being part of the staff there, serving tables, joining in on the songs and chatter afterward when the kitchen had closed for the night.

How would *this* evening end? With brandy and cigars in the study for the men, most likely. Perhaps flutes filled with Cristal offered to the ladies. And when Mateo drove her home…

Standing beside the liquor cabinet, Alex rubbed his hands together. "What can I offer you to drink?"

"I'm fine," Bailey replied, "thank you." Given her inquisitive thoughts regarding Mateo, better she stayed well clear of beverages that would only weaken inhibitions.

"Ice water for me, Alex," Mateo said, moving to stand alongside her, close enough to soak in the natural heat emanating from his body. "You and Natalie can indulge a little tonight."

"It's true." Natalie rubbed her nose with her baby's. "It isn't often we get a night off."

The little boy giggled and held his mother's cheeks. When his fingers caught in her perfectly coiffed hair, Natalie only laughed, but then worried over a strand wrapped around one tiny finger. Alex walked over, unwound the hair from around his boy's finger then kissed the baby's palm with a loud raspberry that sent the child into peals of laughter.

Bailey's chest squeezed. This trio was the picture of the perfect family. The happiness they so obviously shared lit all their faces. What they had couldn't be bought.

That's what *she* wanted one day. The kind of marriage that took a person's breath away. The kind of love her parents had once shared. They'd been so happy. When she was young, she'd never stopped to think it might not last.

When she refocused, a feathery feeling brushed over her. She looked across. Mateo was looking at her, a curious light shining in those dark eyes, a sexy grin curving one side of his mouth. A pulse in Bailey's throat began to beat fast. She blinked then, uncertain of where to look, concentrated on Alex who sent her an ambiguous smile before returning to the bar to see to the drinks.

Natalie spoke to her husband as he poured a water then what looked like scotch for himself.

"Honey, I might change his diaper for Tammy before we go." Natalie explained to Bailey, "Tammy's the wonderful lady who looks after Reece when I go into the office a couple of times a week. She's catching up on her knitting in the family room until we leave."

"Mateo mentioned that you work outside of the home."

"It's a great balance. Only four hours each day—" Natalie rubbed noses with her baby again "—and then I'm dying to get back to him." She met Bailey's gaze. "Want to help me change him?"

Bailey's knees locked. She'd done some babysitting but never one so young. "I'm not sure I'd be any help."

Natalie only smiled. "You look like a quick study."

They left the men, who were busy discussing football, and moved into a nearby room—a downstairs nursery. Bouncing the baby, Natalie crossed to a white lacquered changing table where she gently lay her bundle down then set about unbuttoning his suit.

"Mateo mentioned you know Mama Celeca?"

"I lived in her town for a few months."

"I've heard so much about her. Alex says she's the biggest darling ever. He went with Mateo to Italy one summer a long time ago. Apparently Mama tried her best to get both of them married off."

She seemed so genuine, Bailey couldn't help but like her. Couldn't help but feel relaxed and at home, even in a dress that looked more like a rag next to Natalie's exquisite creation.

Bailey brushed a palm over the baby's soft crown and carried on the thread of their conversation.

"Lucky for you Mama's matchmaking didn't succeed."

"Lucky isn't the word." Natalie peeled back the diaper and let out a pleased sigh. "I love when there's no messy surprises. Could you hand me a fresh diaper, please?" Natalie cast a glance to her right. "They're in that lower drawer."

Bailey dug one out while Natalie cleaned up, shook on powder then slid the fresh diaper under the baby's bottom.

"Mateo mentioned that you're in between jobs," Natalie said, pressing down the diaper tabs.

"I was out looking today." *All* day.

"Find anything?"

"Not yet."

Natalie took both the baby's feet and clapped the soles together, but the baby's smile was a little slow to bloom this time. Must be past his bedtime, Bailey thought.

"What are you interested in?" Natalie asked, scooping her baby up. "Do you have office skills?"

"Afraid not. I've been waitressing, serving and general cleanup."

"In Italy?" Bailey nodded and Natalie beamed. "What an adventure."

Bailey arched a brow. "It certainly was that."

"I don't know of any waitressing positions, but we're always after good cleaners for rentals at the agency."

Bailey's heart leapt. "Really?"

With the baby's head resting against her shoulder, Natalie headed for the door. "You're probably not interested—"

"No," Bailey jumped in. "I mean, *yes*. I *am* interested. When do you think I could start?"

"I'm going in Monday. I'll give you the address."

"I'd appreciate that." A *lot*. "Thank you."

Natalie's pace had slowed. The baby's eyelids were drooping now. He was about to drift off. "Would you like a cuddle before we leave?"

Bailey gave a nervous laugh. She would. He was so adorable and full of smiles. But what if she took him and he cried? She'd feel terrible. But, as if to reassure her, little Reece stretched his arms out to her and found a drowsy smile.

"Seems at least one of you wants a cuddle," Natalie joked. But then she saw Bailey's hesitation. "He's a darling, honest. The worst he'll do is pull your nose."

Bailey blew out a shaky breath. "Well, I've never had my nose pulled before." She put out her arms.

The baby weighed more than she thought. Close up, his heavy-lidded eyes looked even bluer. And he smelled divine— all fresh and new. No wonder Natalie and Alex were so happy. They had it all.

"He likes your bracelet." Natalie touched the dangling charms that Reece was fingering too. "So do I. Did you get it overseas?"

"It was a gift." And then Bailey admitted what she hadn't in a very long while. "A gift from my mother."

"Then it's doubly precious. Do your parents live in Sydney?"

"My father does. My mother passed away."

Natalie's beautiful face fell. "Oh…I'm so sorry, Bailey."

"It was a long time ago."

The sudden lump in Bailey's throat made speaking a little difficult. Over a decade had passed since her mother's death. Not everyone would understand why her grief hadn't faded. But something about Natalie made Bailey feel as if she would. As if the two of them could be more than acquaintances. That, maybe, they could be friends.

Still, she didn't want to mire down the conversation, not when Reece was mumbling adorable things she couldn't quite understand and hiccuping in such a cute way.

But Natalie's expression had grown alarmed. Slanting her head, she held out her arms.

"I think you'd better give him back."

Bailey's heart sank. "Did I do something wrong?"

"No, no. It's just I think he's about to—"

Natalie didn't move quickly enough. Reece gave another hiccup. Heaved a little. Then a lot. Next his dinner came up.

All over the front of Bailey's dress.

Five

When Natalie barged into the room, Mateo and Alex had been discussing the state's current public hospital concerns. Mateo immediately dropped the conversation and peered past Natalie's shoulder. Bailey wasn't in tow and Natalie's hands were clasped tight before her. Seemed unlikely—Natalie was one of the sweetest people he knew. But Bailey was a relatively unknown quantity. Had the women had a disagreement?

Natalie pulled up in front of her husband. "Can you ring and let the restaurant know we'll be late?"

Standing, Alex caught her arm. "Is the baby all right?"

"Too much milk after dinner, I'm afraid."

Alex lowered his hand. "Another accident?"

"All over poor Bailey."

Mateo was no stranger to babies' assortment of surprises. He not only cared for pregnant women before and during delivery, he looked after their concerns postpartum. Many days, his practice was filled with the sights, sounds and smells of children of all ages. He'd been chucked up on more often than some people brushed their teeth. Part of the job. He wasn't sure Bailey would be quite so cool with it, particularly given the trying day she'd had.

Setting down his glass, Mateo rose too. "I'll take her home."

"No need. Bailey's fine," Natalie said. "Other than needing a quick shower and a fresh change of clothes, and I have a stack of outfits in my pre-baby wardrobe she can wear." She ran her hand down her husband's sleeve. "Tammy's settling the baby now. I'll go see how Bailey's doing."

As she sailed away, Alex fell back into his chair. The grin on his face said it all. "She's an amazing woman, isn't she?"

"You're a lucky man."

Alex leaned closer and lowered his voice. "So, now we know they'll be occupied for a while yet, tell me about it."

"Tell you what?"

"About your date."

"She's not a *date*."

"She's an attractive female accompanying you to dinner. If she's not a date, what is she?"

"Difficult to work out," Mateo admitted. "Like I said on the phone, she appeared on my doorstep yesterday morning." He went into more about the engagement and her dramatic flight from Italy, the loan and Bailey's search for a job to pay it back. "When I phoned Mama today, she confirmed that she'd told Bailey to drop in." Mateo dropped his gaze to the glass he rotated between his fingers. "Mama also asked me to watch out for her until she can make amends with her father."

"Trouble there too?"

"I'm sure whatever's gone on before could be sorted out with one or two calm conversations."

"Family rifts aren't usually that easy to solve." Alex took a long sip of scotch.

"Either way, it's none of my business."

"So where's Bailey staying?"

"I said she could stay with me—just for a few days." Alex coughed as if his drink had gone down the wrong way. Mateo frowned. "What?"

Alex tried to contain his amused look. "Nothing. I mean, Bailey seems very nice."

"But?"

"But nothing, Mateo. I'm only surprised that you've opened your home to her. You haven't done that in a while."

"You mean since Linda." Mateo slid his glass onto the side table. "This isn't the same."

Alex studied his friend's face and, inhaling, nodded and changed the subject.

"What's happening with the vacation?"

"I haven't made any firm decisions yet."

"But you're still going to France, right?"

It was more a statement than a question. His annual pilgrimage to Ville Laube was a duty he never shirked. But, of course, it was more than simply an obligation. He enjoyed catching up with the people who ran the orphanage. Although seeing the children conjured up as many haunted feelings as good. Each year he saw so many new faces as well as those who had lived there for years.

One little boy was a favorite. Remy had turned five last visit. Dark hair and eyes, solemn until you pitched him a ball—any kind. Then his face would light up. He reminded Mateo of himself at that age. Leaving Remy last year had been difficult.

When he returned this year, Mateo hoped that little boy was gone. He hoped he'd found a good family who would love and support him. He wondered what kind of man Remy would grow into. If he would learn from the right influences. Whether he'd always have plenty to eat.

Mateo confirmed, "I'll go to France."

"Maybe Bailey would like to go too."

Mateo all but lost his breath. Then he swore. "You're not trying to step into Mama Celeca's matchmaking shoes, I hope."

"Just an idea. You seem…interested."

"You saw us together for less than a minute."

"It was all the time I needed to see that you think she's different."

"Hold on." Mateo got to his feet. "Just because you've found the one, doesn't mean I need to be pushed down any aisle."

"Maybe it'd make a difference if you didn't fight it quite so hard?"

"Fight what?"

Both men's attention flew in the direction of that third voice. Natalie stood in the living room doorway. While Mateo withered—*was Bailey a step behind, within earshot?*—Alex pushed to his feet and crossed to his wife.

"Nothing, honey," he said, stealing a quick kiss. "Is the baby okay? How's Bailey?"

"Judge for yourselves."

When a stylish woman, wearing an exquisite pink cocktail number and glittering diamond drop earrings, slid into the room, Mateo did a double take then all but fell back into his seat.

Bailey?

While the bikini-girl turned glamour-queen crossed the room, looking as if she'd worn Chanel all her life, Natalie clasped her hands under her chin and exclaimed, "Isn't she gorgeous?"

Mateo knew he was smiling. He wanted to agree. Unfortunately he was too stunned—too delighted—to find his voice.

"The first time Mateo and I came to this place, we were twenty-two," Alex explained as a uniformed Maxim's waiter showed the foursome to a table next to the dance floor.

"Twenty-three," Mateo amended, his hand a touch away from Bailey's elbow as they navigated tables of patrons enjoying their meals and tasteful atmosphere, including tinkling background music. "You'd just had a cast off your arm after a spill on your skateboard."

"You rode a skateboard at twenty-three?" Natalie laughed as she lowered into a chair the waiter had pulled out for her.

Alex ran a finger and thumb down his tie. "And very well, might I add."

While the waiter draped linen napkins over laps, Bailey tried to contain the nerves jitterbugging in her belly. She'd dined at similar establishments, although not since her mother had died. In the old days her family had enjoyed dinner out at least once a week, but never to this particular restaurant. Wearing this glamorous dress and these dazzling earrings, not to mention the fabulous silver heels, she felt as if a magic wand had been waved and she'd emerged from her baby throw-up moment as a returned modern-day princess. For a day that had started out horrendously, she was feeling pretty fine now. Not even tired. Although catch-up jet lag would probably hit when she least expected it.

Until then she'd lap up what promised to be a wonderful night.

Some people you couldn't help but like. Natalie and Alex were that kind of folk. And Mateo…she'd wondered what he'd be like in friends' company. His smile was broader. His laugh, deeper. And when his gaze caught hers, the interested approval in his heavy-lidded eyes left her feeling surreal and believing that tonight they might have met for the first time.

"I must confess," Natalie said, casting an eye over the menu. "I love not having to think about the dishes."

"I help with that," Alex pointed out, teasing.

"And I love you for it." Natalie snatched a kiss from her husband's cheek then found Bailey's gaze. "Do you like to cook?"

"I'm no expert. But I would like to learn how to prepare meals the way they do in Italy." The dishes she'd enjoyed there had been so incredibly tasty and wholesome.

Natalie tipped her head toward Mateo. "You know your date's a bit of a chef?"

Her *date?*

Hoping no one noticed her blush, Bailey merely replied, "Really?"

"We go over for dinner at least every month," Natalie added.

Mateo qualified, "Nothing fancy. Just a way of remembering home."

"His crepes are mouth-watering," Natalie confided.

Bailey thought for a moment. "Aren't crepes French?"

"Mateo spent his first years there." As soon as the words were out, Natalie's expression dropped. "That probably wasn't my place to say."

While Mateo waved it off, Bailey puzzled over what the drama with France could be. He must have seen her curiosity.

"I lived in an orphanage the first six years of my life."

All the air left Bailey's lungs as images of dank, dark corridors and rickety cots with children who lacked love's warm touch swam up in her mind. She couldn't imagine it, particularly not for Mateo Celeca. Her lips moved a few times before she got out a single, "Oh."

"It wasn't so bad," Mateo said, obviously reading her expression. "The people who ran it were kind. We had what we needed."

"Mateo sponsors the orphanage now," Alex chipped in as, wine menu in hand, he beckoned a waiter.

Bailey sat back. Of course. Yesterday Mateo had mentioned he was a benefactor. She hadn't thought beyond the notion that any donations would be the act of someone who had the means to make a difference to others' lives. She hadn't stopped to think his work in France might be more personal. That he was paying homage to a darker past and wanted to help those who were in the same underprivileged position he'd once been.

"It's difficult for them to find funds," Mateo was saying, pouring more water. "A small bit goes a long way."

"You're too modest," Alex said.

Natalie added, "Wouldn't surprise me if one day you come back with someone who needs a good home."

"I'm hardly in a position."

Mateo's reply sounded unaffected. But Bailey detected a certain faraway gleam in his eye. Would Mateo consider adopting if he *were* in the position? If he were married?

She tried to focus on Natalie's words…something about looking forward to dessert. But, as much as she tried, Bailey couldn't shake the vision of Mateo playing with a child of his own with a faceless Mrs. Celeca smiling and gazing on. Not her, of course. She wasn't after a husband—or certainly not this soon after her recent hairy experience. One day she wanted to be part of a loving couple—like Natalie and Alex—but right now she was more than happy to be free.

Did Mateo feel the same way? Natalie wondered, stealing a glance at the doctor from beneath her lashes. Or could Mama's perennial bachelor be on the lookout for a suitable wife slash mother for an adopted child?

* * *

Finishing dessert, a moist, scrumptious red velvet cake, Bailey gave a soft cry when some chocolate sauce slipped from her spoon and caught the bodice of her dress. She slid a fingertip over the spot to scoop up the drop, which only smeared the sauce. Bailey didn't wear these kinds of labels, but she knew something about the price tags. Often they cost more than her airfare home.

With dread filling her stomach, Bailey turned to Natalie. "I'll pay to have it dry-cleaned."

But Natalie wasn't troubled.

"Keep the dress, if you want. It's too snug on me after the baby anyway. In fact, there's a heap of things you could take off my hands, if you'd like."

Eyes down, Bailey dabbed the spot with her napkin. She was grateful for the offer but also embarrassed. Over dinner, they'd discussed her travels and lightly touched on the Emilio affair. Mention had been made of Mateo's suggestion she stay a couple of days as well as Natalie's proposal of work. Now the offer of a designer wardrobe…

She was beginning to feel as if she constantly had her hand out.

Bailey set aside the napkin. "That's very kind, Natalie. But you don't need to do that."

"Chances are I won't wear them again. Some mothers are eager to get back their pre-baby bodies but I quite like the fuller me."

"Hear, hear," her husband cooed close to her ear. "Now if you've finished dessert, what say we dance? Just you and me."

Natalie laughed. "Oh, you love when the three of us dance together in the living room."

"Of course." Alex kissed her hand and found his feet. "But this moment I'm happy to have only you in my arms."

As they headed for the dance floor, Bailey sighed.

"You're right. They're a magic couple. Have they been together long? The way they look at each other, anyone would guess they'd fallen in love yesterday."

"They've been together a couple of years."

"I thought they might have been school sweethearts," she said, watching them slow dance to the soft strains of a love song drifting through the room while misty beams played over their heads.

"Natalie grew up in far different circumstances than she enjoys now. Very humble beginnings."

Bailey was taken aback. "She looks as if she might've been born into royalty."

"Tonight, so do you."

Bailey's breath caught high in her chest. Was he merely being polite or was the compliment meant to have the reaction it did? Suddenly she didn't know where to look. What to say. But her mother had said to always take a compliment graciously. So, gathering herself, she lifted her eyes to his and smiled. "Thank you."

Her heart was thumping too loudly to maintain that eye contact, however, so she found Alex and Natalie on the dance floor. Natalie was laughing at something her husband had said while Alex gazed down at his wife adoringly. They radiated wedded bliss.

"It was a good day," Mateo said.

"Which day?"

"The day I helped bring their son into the world."

Elbow on the table, Bailey rested her chin in the cup of her hand. "I bet you had everything prepared and everyone on their toes."

"Quite the opposite. When she went into labor, we were at Alex's beachside holiday house. It happened quickly." He peered over toward the couple. Natalie's cheek was resting on Alex's shoulder now. "She'd miscarried years before. Alex was concerned for mother and child both."

"But nothing went wrong?"

Mateo smiled across. "You saw Reece tonight."

Bailey relaxed. "Perfect."

"Alex had always longed for a son."

"I suppose most men do," she said, wondering if she'd get a reaction.

"Most men…yes." Then, as if to put an end to that conversation, he stood and held out his hand. "Would you care to dance?"

Bailey's throat closed. Perhaps she should have seen that coming but she was at a loss for words. Mateo looked so tall and heart-stoppingly handsome, gazing down at her with those dark, penetrating eyes. Eyes that constantly intrigued her. She wanted to accept his offer. Wanted the opportunity to know the answer to her earlier question—how it would feel to have his arms surround her. Here, in this largely neutral, populated setting, she could find out.

She placed her hand in his. That telling warmth rose again, tingling over her flesh, heating her cheeks and her neck. His eyes seemed to smile into hers as she found her feet and together they moved to the dance floor, occupied by other couples, some absorbed more in the song than their partner, others locked in each other's arms and ardent gazes.

Bailey couldn't stop her heart from hammering as Mateo turned and rested a hot palm low on her back while bringing their still-clasped hands to his lapel. Concentrating to level her breathing, she slid and rested her left hand over the broad slope of his shoulder at the same time the tune segued into an even slower, more romantic song and the lights dimmed a fraction more.

They began to move and instantly Bailey was gripped by the heat radiating from his body, burrowing into and warming hers. Her senses seemed heightened. She was infinitely aware of his thumb circling over the dip in her back. Her lungs celebrated being filled with his mesmerizing scent. Strangely, all the happenings around them faded into a suddenly bland background. When a corner of his mouth slanted—the corner with that small scar—her pulse rate spiked and her blood began to sizzle. She'd wanted to know. Now she did. Having Mateo's arms around her—soothing and at the same time exciting her—was like being held by some kind of god.

"So you'll be working for Natalie's agency?"

"While I was dressing—make that *re*dressing—Natalie explained they'd lost three cleaners in the past couple of weeks."

"You don't mind the work?"

"I'm grateful for it. And it won't be forever."

He grinned. "Sounds as if you're making plans."

Seeing her father today cemented what she'd already come to realize. Education was the key to independence. "I'm going to apply to college."

"Do you know what you'll study? Teaching? Nursing?"

"Maybe I should become a doctor," she joked. "Dr. Bailey Ross. Neurosurgeon." She laughed and so did he, but not in a condescending way. "I want to do something that makes people happy," she went on. "That makes them feel good about themselves."

"Whatever you choose I'm sure you'll do well."

"Because you know I'm an A student, right?"

"Because I think you have guts. Persistence will get you most places in life."

Unless you were talking about her father. The more she'd tried, the more he'd turned his back. Cut her off. There came a time when a person needed to accept they should look forward rather than back.

But then she retraced her thoughts back to Mateo's

words—*I think you have guts.* She gave him a dubious look. "Was that another compliment?"

A line cut between his brows. "Tell you what. We'll make a deal. I promise not to mention the money you owe Mama in a derogatory way if you promise something in return. It has to do with my vacation."

She couldn't think what. Except maybe, "You want me to house sit?"

"I want you to come with me to France."

Bailey's legs buckled. When she fell against him, bands of steel stopped her from slipping farther. But the way her front grazed against his, his help only made her sudden case of weakness worse.

Siphoning down a breath, she scooped back some hair fallen over her face. "Sorry. Did you just say you want me to go to France with you?"

"I got the impression you hadn't seen Paris."

"I was saving it for last. I never got there."

His smile flashed white beneath the purple lights. "Now's your chance."

She took a step back but more deep breaths didn't help. She cupped her forehead.

"Mateo, I'm confused."

He brought her near again and flicked a glance over his shoulder at the couple dancing nearby. "Blame Alex. He suggested it."

She tried to ignore the delicious press of his body, the masculine scent of his skin, the way his hard thigh nudged between hers as he rotated them around in a tight circle. "You know I don't have money for a ticket to Europe." Her jaw hardened. "And I won't take any more charity."

"Even if you'd be doing me a favor, keeping me company?" His dark gaze, so close, roamed her face. "One good turn deserves another."

"That's not fair."

His mouth turned into a solemn line. "There wouldn't be any conditions."

Bailey blinked. Maybe because he was Mama's grandson, she hadn't considered he might be trying to buy more than her company.

With the lights slowly spinning and couples floating by, oxygen burned in her lungs while she tried to come up with an appropriate reply to a question that had knocked her for a loop. After an agonizingly long moment, she felt the groan rumble in his chest and his grip on her hand loosen.

"You're right," he said. "Crazy idea."

"It's not that I wouldn't *like* to go." She'd always wanted to see Paris. It was her biggest disappointment that she'd planned to save France for last rather than enjoying that country first. "But I've just got back," she explained. "I'm starting that job Monday." She finished with the obvious excuse. "We don't know each other."

He dismissed it with a self-deprecating smile. "Like I said. Forget I spoke."

But as his palm skimmed up her back and he tucked her crown under his chin while they continued to dance, although she knew she really should, Bailey couldn't forget.

At the end of the evening, she and Mateo dropped Natalie and Alex off then drove back to his place in a loaded silence.

Her breathing was heavier than it ought to be. Was his heartbeat hammering as fast as hers, or was she the only one who couldn't get that enthralling dance and tempting offer out of her mind? Mateo had asked her to jet away to France with him. What had he been thinking? What was she thinking still considering it after having already told him no?

Bailey pressed on her stomach as her insides looped.

Admittedly, she was uniquely attracted to Mateo Celeca; he had a presence, a confidence that was difficult to ignore. But how did she feel about him beyond the physical? Yesterday, after he'd tried to degrade her over the money she'd loaned, she'd thought him little more than a self-serving snob. And yet, tonight, when she'd met his friends...had been his *date*...

Her stomach looped again.

After that episode with Emilio, the last thing she wanted was to get caught up in a man. Any man. Even when he gave generously to the orphanage where he'd spent his earliest years. Even when she felt as if she'd found a slice of heaven in his arms.

Since that dance, the air between them had crackled with a double dose of anticipation and electricity. If, when they got home, they started talking, got to touching, she didn't know if she'd want to stop.

After they pulled into the garage, Mateo opened her door and helped her out. Their hands lingered, the contact simmered, before his fingers slipped from hers and he moved to unlock the internal door and flick on the lights. Gathering herself—straightening her dress and patting down her burning cheeks—Bailey followed into the kitchen.

"Care for a nightcap?" he asked, poised near the fridge.

Bailey clasped the pocketbook Natalie had loaned her under her chin and, resolute, made a believable excuse.

"I'm beat. Practically dead on my feet. Think I'll go straight up and turn in."

As she headed out, Bailey laughed at herself. He might not even *want* to kiss her. She could be blowing this awareness factor all out of proportion. But prevention was always better than cure. She'd accepted his invitation to stay a couple more nights. She didn't want to do something they both might regret in the morning. And if they got involved that way, there *would* be regrets. Neither was looking for a relationship. She certainly didn't want to get caught up in a man who, only yesterday, had as good as called her thief. A man who might set her pulse racing but who could never get serious about a woman in her situation.

And yet, he had asked her to France….

When Mateo reached the foot of the staircase, he stopped and turned to face her. Standing there, simply gazing at one another in the semi-darkness, she had this silly urge to play down the scene, stick out a hand and offer to shake. But, given past experience, probably best they didn't touch.

"Thank you for the lovely evening," she said.

"You're welcome."

Still, he didn't move.

"Well…" Clutching her pocketbook tighter, she set a foot onto the lowest stair. "Good night."

"Good night, Bailey."

When she began to climb, he started up too. They ascended together until they hit a point where the stairs divided into separate branches. A fork in the road.

Her stomach twisting with nerves, she chanced a look across. He was looking at her too, a masculine silhouette a mere arm's length away.

Swirling desire pooled low in her belly and she frowned. "You're not moving."

"Neither are you."

Rolling back her shoulders, she issued a firm and final, "Good night."

She hiked the rest of the stairs, right to the top. But before she could head off down to her suite, curiosity won out again. She edged a gaze over her right shoulder, to where she'd left Mateo standing seconds ago. What she saw sent her heart dropping in her chest.

He was gone. And wasn't that what she'd wanted? What she knew was best for both their sakes?

Still, she stared at that vacant spot a moment more, feeling strangely empty and no longer so pretty in her pink designer dress. Shifting her weight, she finally rotated back…and ran right into Mateo's solid chest.

Her heels balanced on the edge of the stairs, Bailey toppled back. But before she could fall, his arm hooked around her waist, pulling her effortlessly against him. *Déjà vu.* With the bodice of her dress pinned to his chest—with every one of her reflexes in a tailspin—she worked to catch her breath before croaking out, "I thought you were tired."

"*You* said you were tired." His dark eyes gleamed. "I'm wide awake."

When she felt his hardness pressed against her belly, she gulped down another breath only to feel him grow harder still. Any doubts she may have had were blown away. The way her own blood was throbbing, taking this steadily growing attraction further seemed frighteningly inevitable.

"Maybe…" She wet her suddenly dry lips. "Maybe we should have that nightcap after all."

His gaze dropped to her lips. "What kind of nightcap?"

"What would you like?"

His mouth came to within a whisper of hers.

"I'd like you."

Six

He didn't waste time waiting for her reply. Bailey supposed he saw all he needed to know in her eyes. He angled and, before she could think beyond *I need you to kiss me,* she was in his arms and he was moving down the hall, away from her suite, headed for his.

The tall double doors of his suite were open. He didn't bother to kick them shut after he'd carried her through. Nor did he switch on any lamps. What she could make out in the shadows was courtesy of the light filtering in from the hall as well as the moonbeams slanting through a bank of soaring arched windows that looked out over that garden and its statues below.

He stopped at the foot of his bed and his voice dropped to a low rasp.

"This is what you want?"

Instinctively, her palm wove around the sandpaper of his

jaw. She filled her lungs with his scent then skimmed the pad of her thumb over the dent in his chin.

"Yes," she murmured.

His chest expanded, his grip tightened then he lifted her higher in his arms as his head came purposefully down. When his mouth claimed hers, Bailey couldn't contain the moan of deepest desire the sensation dragged from her throat. She didn't want to contain *anything*. And as his mouth worked magic against hers and his stubble grazed and teased her skin, she pressed herself up and in, needing to feel even closer. Needing him as close as it got.

Her fingers wound through his hair while his throat rumbled with satisfaction and the kiss deepened. Even as her mind and body raged with desire, she was lucid enough to recognize the simple truth. Whatever it was that had sparked when they'd met, it had grown to a point where now they were downright hungry for each other. *Starving* for each other's touch in a primal nothing-held-back, nothing-taboo, kind of way. She could never get enough of this burn…of the flames that already leapt and blazed nearly out of control.

When his lips gradually left hers, she felt dizzy. Her eyes remained closed but she heard and felt his breathing. At the edges of her mind, she wondered…why was this coming together so intense? So combustible?

He dipped to sit her on the edge of the mattress. With moonlight spilling in, she dragged the dress up over her head then, in her lingerie, watched as he wound the shirt off his shoulders, the sleeves from his arms. When he was naked, he bent near, slid an arm around her waist and drew her up to stand again. Holding her chin, he ran the wet tip of his tongue along the open seam of her mouth while, at her back, he unsnapped the strapless bra with one deft flick. His palm pressed down the dent of her spine and slipped into the back of her panties. She whimpered as her womb contracted and quivered…a tantalizing prelude to the climax she couldn't wait to enjoy.

His fingertips pressed and seared into her flesh while his mouth covered hers completely again, and all the time her insides clenched and pulsed while her limbs and mind went to mush. She wanted this heaven to go on forever. But even more, she wanted him bearing down on top of her. Inside of her. Filling and fulfilling her *now*.

Her hands ironed down his sides. When she reached his lean hips, she urged him forward, toward her and the bed. With their mouths still joined, she felt his smile before he broke the kiss long enough to wrench back the sheets. With a determined gleam in his eyes, he crowded until the back of her legs met the cool edge of the mattress. His big hands ringed her waist and her feet left the ground long enough for him to lay her gently down. He followed a heartbeat behind.

Looming above her, everything seemed to still as he searched her eyes in a world of midnight shadows. His deep low voice seemed to fill the room.

"I didn't ask you to stay here for this."

She drew an aimless pattern through the hair at the base of his throat.

"I know."

"Although I'm not sorry you agreed."

She matched his grin. "I'm not sorry you asked."

He dropped a tender kiss at the side of her mouth, a barely there touch that shot a fountain of star-tipped sparks through her every fiber.

"Come with me to France," he murmured against her lips.

She groaned. The temptation was huge. She'd said no and had meant it. She was starting a job Monday. She didn't want to take more charity. But those considerations didn't seem quite so solid since he'd carried her to his bed.

Closing her eyes, she sighed. He was kissing the sensitive spot beneath her left lobe.

"What if I say please?"

She bit her lip. He was *killing* her.

"I'll tell you what." She filed her fingers up over his burning ears, through his hair. "I promise not to say no again if you promise not to ask."

He moved lower to nuzzle the arc of her neck. "I don't like when you say no."

"To everything but that, Mateo…" She hooked her leg around his hip and drew him close. *"Yes, yes, yes."*

Mateo couldn't stop to think about how his unexpected encounter with Bailey Ross had come to this. How they'd gone from strangers to opponents to lovers in less than two days. As he tasted a leisurely line along the perfumed sweep of her shoulder, he only knew these sensations were too intense to analyze. More intense—more vital—than he'd ever had before.

When her heel dug into the back of his thigh, letting him know again she was on the same page, he ground up against her but then grit his teeth and blocked that insistent heady push. Tonight would be sweet torture. He'd need every ounce of willpower to keep this encounter—his pleasure—from peaking too soon.

Working to steady his breathing, his pace, he sculpted a palm over the outside of one full breast as he shifted lower. His mouth covered that nipple before his teeth grazed up all the way, tugging the tip of the bead. Her hands had been winding through his hair but now she dug in and held on as she shuddered and moaned beneath him. He heard her desperate swallow and listened, pleased that her breathing sounded more labored than his own. Savoring the way her breasts rose and fell on each lungful of air, he twirled his tongue around that tip and tried to ignore the fact his every inch was ready to explode.

With her leg twined over the back of his, her pelvis began to move in time with the adoring sweep of his tongue. She murmured something he didn't catch. But he wouldn't ask and stop the bone-melting rhythm their bodies had fallen into. He didn't want to interrupt for a moment the feel of her body stirring beneath his. He could lie here all night, doing precisely this.

If only his erection wasn't begging for more.

He repositioned again, higher to savor the honey of her lips at the same time his touch wove down: over her ribs, the curve of her waist, the subtle flare of a hip, then up over the same terrain. He was performing a repeat descent, stroking and playing—anticipating the added treasures he'd discover this time around—when she grunted, shifted and pushed against his chest.

He froze. Then, eyes snapping open, he rolled away. What was wrong? Had he hurt her?

When she slid over too—on *top* of him—he held his brow and almost laughed with relief.

"What are you doing?"

Crouched on his lap, she slid her hips one way and the other then tossed back the hair fallen over her face. "What do you think?"

She slid *up* a little this time then down over his throbbing shaft. That sent him reeling way too close to the edge. He was thrilled she was so completely in the zone that she wanted to take the reins, but any more of that kind of maneuvering and he'd reach the finish line way too soon.

He flipped her over so she lay on her back again, him firmly on top. While she peered up at him, a saucy glint in her eyes, his hand burrowed between them, down the front of her panties, and his erection grew heavier still. She was warm and moist. When his touch curled up between her folds and pressed against a woman's most sensitive spot, she let out a time honored sound that told him she was ready.

Leaning over, he opened his bedside drawer, found the pack then tore a single foiled wrap with his teeth. As he rolled on protection, her fingers sluiced up and down his sides. Oh, he wanted to take this slower. Make it last. But this time, with this lady, that wasn't going to happen.

Sheathed, he positioned himself, took a long slow kiss from her welcoming mouth then eased inside. Her walls clamped around him at the same time her hips lifted and she opened her mouth wider, inviting him deeper.

With one arm curled around her head, he drove in and clenched every muscle as a mind-tingling burn hardened him more. He felt as if he was drowning in a lake of fire. All exposed nerve endings and profound sizzling need.

Bailey trailed her fingers down his neck, felt the cords bulging and pulsing, and melted more. The way he moved with her left her breathless while his mouth on hers raised her up. She wanted this moment to go on forever. Never wanted the steep waves of pleasure to wane or fade. And yet they both needed to go that bit further. Needed to be thrown up to the stars and explode on their way back down.

He was snatching slow kisses from her brow, from her cheek, holding her hip securely as his strokes grew ever stronger and longer. The friction was scolding, the pleasure beyond what she could take.

And then his kisses stopped and his body grew still and hard. She sensed his every tendon stretched trip wire tight, could feel his heart thumping and pounding in his ears. The mind-altering fire at her core intensified, somehow changing in dimension and in shape. Then, in one finite moment, in less time than it took to suck down a breath, all the universe contracted into a single high-voltage speck. Beyond that nothing existed. Nothing but black.

When he thrust again—when he hit that secret wanting spot—she threw back her head, spread her wings and flew.

Seven

"Tell me more about France."

At the sound of Bailey's voice filtering though the predawn mist, Mateo lifted his head off the pillow and dropped a kiss on her silky crown.

They'd made love well into the night. The first time had been incredible. Incomparable. But over far too quickly. The second time they'd slowed down enough to thoroughly explore each other's bodies and share their most intimate needs. The third time they'd come apart in each other's arms might have been the best…the time when he'd truly begun to see that this joining meant more than simply great sex. The connection they shared, the amazing way they fit, was special.

That didn't mean he'd changed his mind about getting serious. About settling down. Invariably marriage meant children. Children of his own. But his practice was his life. He'd put all he had into doing his best and building a home that was his. He had everything he needed. Everything and more. He felt secure, and that was life's most valuable gift.

If he were to become a husband...a father...well, he couldn't think of a more vulnerable place to be. There were concerns over the complications in the womb, worry about childhood disease, not to mention the fact that in this world he had no living family now, other than Mama. If fate stepped in and left his child without parents...

Mateo swallowed against the pit formed in his throat.

This is why he never let himself analyze relationships too deeply, particularly following the "after all she could get" Linda incident. He was a man of influence and means who could choose what course his life should take. Tonight he'd chosen to act on the undeniable chemistry he shared with Bailey. Given she'd asked about France a moment ago, he hoped they could continue to enjoy the attraction a while longer. For however long it might last.

Nestled in the crook of his arm, she twined to rest her chin on her thatched hands, which lay on one side of his chest.

"What's it like?" She asked, looking beautifully rumpled and sleep deprived but content. "Everyone seems to love Paris. Did you ever get into the city when you were young?"

"As a child?"

"Uh-huh."

"I didn't know Paris existed."

She sat up a little, bracing her weight on an elbow as she searched his eyes in the misty light. Outside, the morning sun peeked over the distant rise, painting a translucent halo around her head.

Her voice softened when she asked, "Were you very lonely there? At the orphanage, I mean."

Mateo's jaw tensed. His first instinct was to push her question aside. If anyone, including Alex or Natalie, brought up his childhood, he rarely gave away too much. The past was past…even if it was never forgotten.

But lying here with Bailey after the extraordinary night they'd shared, he felt closer to her this minute than anyone he'd known. That shouldn't be. He'd loved and respected Ernesto. He adored Mama. He had friends he would do anything for and, he was certain, vice versa.

And yet, he couldn't deny it. Whatever drew him to Bailey Ross was a force unto itself. He wanted to share more than his bed with her tonight. He wanted to open up…at least this once.

"I wasn't lonely," he began. "I had many friends and adults I knew that cared for us all." He thought more deeply and frowned. "I did feel *alone,* which is different, but I was too young to understand why. I never knew my parents. No one explained about the 'who' or the 'when.' I didn't realize a life outside the orphanage existed until my fifth birthday."

Sitting up, she wrapped the sheet around her breasts, under her arms. "What happened on your birthday? I don't suppose you had a party."

"From what I can recall, the day was pleasant enough. Everyone sang to me after lunch. I got a special dessert along with two friends I picked out." He searched his memory and blinked then smiled. "I received a gift. People from town donated them. I tore open the paper and found a wooden train. Green chimney," he recalled. "Red wheels. I thought I was made." But his smile slipped. "Then my best friend said he was going away. That a mother and father were taking him home."

Bailey tucked her knees up and hugged her sheet-clad legs. "It mustn't have made sense."

He flinched at a familiar pang in his chest and for a moment he wanted to end that conversation and talk about the France people found in travel books. The "gay Paree" with which Bailey would identify. But she wasn't listening to this story to snatch some voyeuristic thrill. He saw from her unguarded expression that she wanted to learn more about the man she'd made love with tonight. He wanted to learn more about her too. So, to be fair, he took a breath and went on.

"I knew some children were there with us, then, suddenly, they weren't. No one spoke about it, or if they did, I didn't have the maturity to latch on and work the steps out. But this time, with Henri, I began to see."

"You realized something was missing."

He nodded.

Yes, missing. Exactly.

"From a second-story window," he said, "where the boys slept, I watched Henri slide into a shiny white car and drive away with two people, a man and woman. I shouted out and waved, but he didn't look up. Not until the last minute. Then he saw me. I think he called out my name, too."

With her blue eyes glittering in the early dawn light, she tipped nearer and held his arm.

"Oh, Mateo…that must have been awful."

Not *awful.* "Eye-opening. Unsettling. From then on I was more aware of others leaving. More aware that I was left behind. I tried to find him a few years back. It would be great to see him again. Hear if his memories match mine."

Henri had been his first friend.

Mateo touched the scar on his upper lip—the one he'd received when Henri had thrown a ball too hard and he'd missed catching it—then, dismissing the pang in his chest, he swung his legs over the side of the bed and reached for the water decanter. After pouring two glasses, he offered her one.

She drank, watching him over the rim of her glass.

"How did Mama Celeca find you?" she asked, handing the empty glass back.

"Not Mama. Ernesto." He took another mouthful and set both glasses down. "Years before, he'd been in love with a woman who'd carried his child. A friend, returning from France, let Ernesto know he'd heard that Antoinette had given birth in a town called Ville Laube and had offered her baby boy up for adoption there. Ernesto flew straight over. He found the orphanage his friend had described but not his boy."

Clutching the sheet under her chin, Bailey sagged.

"I thought you'd say that *you* were Ernesto's child."

"Not through blood. But apparently my parents were Italian, too. I was left there when I was three, but I don't remember any life before the orphanage."

She shifted and he waited until she'd settled alongside of him.

"One day after Henri had gone," he went on, "I saw this sad looking man sitting alone in the courtyard under a huge oak. His hands were clasped between his thighs. His eyes were downcast. When I edged closer, I saw they were bloodshot. He'd been crying. I knew because some times in the mornings I had bloodshot eyes too."

His throat closed as the memory grew stronger and flooded his mind with a mix of emotions, sounds and smells from the past. The scent of lavender. The noise of children playing. The deepest feeling that, if only he knew this sad man, he would like him.

But, "I didn't know why the man was unhappy. I had no idea what to say. I only knew I felt for him. So I sat down and put my hand over his."

Mateo looked across. In the growing light, he thought he saw a single tear speed down Bailey's cheek. Ironic, because after that day he couldn't remember ever crying again.

"And he took you home," she said.

"Home to Italy, yes. And later here to Australia."

"So Mama Celeca isn't your real grandmother?"

"She's always treated me as though she is. She accepted me from the moment Ernesto brought me back to Casa Buona. I helped Ernesto in his office during the day and hung out with Mama in the kitchen in the evenings."

"Where she taught you to cook."

Remembering the aromas and Mama's careful instructions, he smiled and nodded. "The old-fashioned way."

"The *best* way." She turned more toward him. "Did Ernesto find his boy?"

"No." And that was the tragedy. "Although he never gave up hope."

"Did he ever marry?"

"Never. He died two years ago."

"I remember. Mama told me."

"He wanted to be buried back home. Mama was heartbroken at her son's death, but that, at least, gave her a measure of comfort." He voiced the words that were never far from his heart. "He was a good son. A good father. Last year I had a call from a woman, Ernesto's biological son's widow. After he'd been killed in a hit-and-run, she'd found papers from the orphanage that helped her track Ernesto down. She'd wanted him to know."

She lowered her head and murmured, so softly, he barely heard. "Is all this why Natalie thinks you might bring home a child from France one day?"

"Adoption rules were more flexible in the country back then."

"You'd have no trouble proving you could care for a child. I haven't known you long but I know you'd make a good father...like Ernesto."

A knot twisted in his chest. Sharp. Uncomfortable. He'd already explained.

"I'm too busy for a child." He looked inside and, flinching, admitted, "Too selfish."

When his temple throbbed, he turned to plump up his pillow. They ought to get some sleep, Bailey especially.

They lay down again, front to front, curled up tight. Mateo was drifting when she murmured against his chest.

"When are you expected in France?"

"Next week."

"I told Natalie I'd start work for her in two days' time." She lifted her head to glance out the window at the ever-rising sun. "Make that tomorrow."

Mateo was suddenly wide awake. If Bailey was thinking about changing her mind and coming with him...

"Natalie won't hold anything against you for taking a week off."

In fact, he was sure she'd be happy at the news. Natalie made no secret of the fact that she would love to see her husband's best friend settled with someone nice. Not that that was in the cards.

She snuggled into him more. "I'd feel as if I were copping out."

"Visiting the Eiffel Tower, the Louvre, perhaps. But the orphanage?" He skimmed a hand down her smooth warm arm. "It's not a cop-out."

After several minutes, her breathing grew deeper and he thought she was finally asleep. He was letting oblivion overtake him too when she spoke again.

"Mama's right."

He forced his heavy lids open. "About what?"

She rubbed her cheek against his chest and murmured in a groggy voice, "You are a good man."

Eight

As Mateo predicted, Natalie wasn't the least bit upset when the following day, Bailey rang to explain.

"I know I'm only starting," she began, sitting behind Mateo's desk in his home office. "I'm so grateful for the chance, but I was wondering if I could possibly ask for the week after next off?"

"Are you all right?"

"I feel great." In fact, better than great. "Mateo asked whether I might like to fly with him to France."

Bailey jerked the receiver from her ear as Natalie squealed down the line.

"Sorry," Natalie said. "I'm just excited for you. For you both. And I'll need to go through my wardrobe with a fine-tooth comb. In late October, you're going to need some warm clothes over there."

The following day Bailey dived into the first of her cleaning jobs. The work was constant and anything but glamorous, but she rolled up her sleeves and took pride in making sure the floors were spotless and that the kitchens and bathrooms sparkled. She was being constructive, pushing forward, earning her way and feeling rewarded because of it.

When Friday came, Bailey was exhausted by the time she got to Mateo's place. But she was also elated. When he opened the door for her, she threw out her hand.

Mateo took the slip of paper she held. "What's this?"

"A printout of the receipt from my transfer."

Mateo had set up an account solely for the purpose of her loan repayments.

When he smiled, he truly looked pleased.

"We should celebrate."

"What do you suggest?"

"Dinner at this little Italian taverna five minutes from here. Unless you're too tired…"

"No." Suddenly she was feeling pepped up. She *should* celebrate. This was a noteworthy step toward reaching her goals. "But on one condition. I pay my way."

One brow hiked up. "You're supposed to be saving, not spending."

"We go dutch or we don't go."

They went and enjoyed a carafe of Chianti, twirled and slurped spaghetti, paid half each and, when they arrived home, made love as they'd done every night since their first.

Afterward, as they lay tangled in each other's arms and Mateo stroked her hair, Bailey thought back on the week, feeling happier than she had in a long while. She'd had fun backpacking around Europe and she'd enjoyed herself in Italy—before Emilio had cornered her the way he had. But now, here with Mateo, she'd stepped up to a different level of understanding.

Funnily enough, she felt settled. Living in this grand palace with a strong-minded millionaire doctor…unbelievable, but she felt as if she belonged.

But this hyper exhilaration was only temporary. It wasn't real. Wouldn't last. Staying in this extraordinary house with this extraordinary man was a fairy tale she happened to fall into. Clearly, Mateo had been with other women but he'd never committed, as Mama had told her more than once. There was no reason to believe that what they'd shared this week would last either.

She was a big girl. She was fine with that.

Smoothing a palm over his chest, she smiled softly. This time with Mateo might be temporary, but she planned to enjoy each minute and, when it was over, cherish every memory. It was a temporary happy ending to an unpleasant episode in her life. And Paris was yet to come!

Two days later they flew halfway around the world on the sumptuous private jet Mateo hired. Nibbling on mouth-watering cheese and fruit platters, feeling as if she were lounging at a luxury retreat rather than an aircraft, Bailey was certain she would never view air travel the same again.

It was early evening when they landed at Charles de Gaulle. The weather was cool in the City of Light, but the darkening sky held no threat of rain or sleet. Bailey tugged Natalie's silk-lined designer jacket higher around her ears and, loving the chilly nip on her nose—so different from the warm weather in Australia this time of year—slid into the back of the chauffeur driven limousine, with Mateo entering behind her. She guessed her mother would have felt just as excited when she'd arrived in this famous city years before.

As the driver performed a pared down city tour, she lapped up the scenery while Mateo pointed out noteworthy spots. The iconic spire of the Eiffel Tower, the history effused Arc de Triomphe. Then they passed the Louvre and the Pyramid.

Bailey sighed. "I wonder if there's a person in the world who doesn't want to see the *Mona Lisa*."

His hand found hers and squeezed. "We'll spend an entire day there."

"Before or after we've spent a morning strolling along the Seine? And I want to sip coffee at a gorgeous sidewalk café and gaze up at the obelisk at the Place de la Concorde."

Mateo nuzzled her hair. "We'll do it all. I promise."

They checked into one of the best hotels in the city, only steps from the Champs-Elysees. Bailey held her pounding heart as she took in magnificent glittering chandeliers, mirror polished floors, classic marble statuettes and fountains of fresh scented flowers. She wasn't interested in being wealthy. Money did *not* buy happiness—ask her father. But this kind of experience was different. It was about appreciating another culture. About absorbing history. Enriching one's life by seeing how others communicated and lived. This hotel was a prime example of crème de la crème. Tomorrow they would move among the less fortunate…children without family or homes of their own. Children who lived as Mateo had once done.

As Mateo checked in at the reception desk, Bailey absorbed his effortless sophisticated air. Calling into that orphanage each year must be a bittersweet experience. Were his memories of that place still sharp or were those long ago days more like a dream…as these days would no doubt be to her in a few years' time?

When they reached their suite, Bailey drifted toward a twinkling view, visible past a soaring window, while Mateo wasted no time coming up behind and enfolding her in his arms.

"It's said that Paris in daytime is only resting," he murmured against her hair. "That the city only comes to life at night. So," his breath felt warm on the sweep of her neck, "are you ready to take on the town?"

"I'd love to say yes, but I need sleep." And she didn't want to be dead on her feet tomorrow when they reached their first and most important destination—the orphanage.

"Hungry then?" He twined her arms around his and pressed her extra close. "Or perhaps we ought to check out that fine piece of furniture."

Eyes drifting closed, she hummed out a grin. He meant that canopied bed.

Turning her back on the view—on the glittering spectacle of Paris at night—she rotated until they were facing one another then gifted his stubbly jaw with a lingering kiss.

"I like that idea," she murmured. "Let's freshen up first."

"Only if we do it together."

He led her through to a marble finished room, featuring a classic clawfoot tub, big enough for two. After kissing her thoroughly, a toe-curling taste of what was to come, he left to order up refreshments.

Floating, Bailey ran the gold gooseneck faucet, added salts and bubble liquid into the rising water then, humming, twirled her hair up and set it with a single pin. After stripping off her shoes and Natalie-sponsored clothes, she threaded her arms through an oversized courtesy robe but stopped when she caught her reflection in the window.

Holding her fluttering stomach, she wanted to imprint this precise moment…this dreamlike feeling…into her memory forever. Beyond that pane, Paris was buzzing with music and laughter and life. Even more amazing, beyond that door, Mateo Celeca was looking forward to sharing this bath with her.

Tying the robe's sash, she lowered onto the edge of the bath's porcelain rim and took stock.

Two weeks ago she'd been near desperate to get home,

for the chance to start again. Two weeks ago she'd thought constantly about her father…reliving those earlier happier years…regretting that their relationship had come unstuck. When she'd seen Damon Ross in the city during that exhausting second day back in Australia, her heart had screamed out for her to walk over. To give them another chance. The cab's timely arrival had put a stop to that idea, thank heaven, because there was nothing she could say that she hadn't said before. Nothing she could do that would mend those flattened fences. She'd tried in the past, over and again. The more she'd persisted, the more her father had only wanted to push her away.

One day, perhaps, they'd talk again, Bailey decided, swirling a hand through the deepening warm bubble-filled pool. But that couldn't happen until she'd proven herself to herself. She was young. With the right attitude she could accomplish anything. Go anywhere.

Right now, however, she wanted to help Mateo accomplish his goals here in France. Of course, she also wanted to enjoy this time they had here as lovers. Still, she was mindful of keeping this whirlwind romance in perspective. It would be ridiculously easy to fall in love with an amazing man like Mateo Celeca only to be left behind.

After this time together, that he was so successful and she was so definitely not didn't worry her so much. His state of mind, as far as commitment was concerned, did. She'd briefly wondered whether he might want to find a wife and adopt that little boy he'd spoken about. But Mateo was married to his career and wanted to keep it that way. He'd confessed he was too busy for a family of his own. Too selfish.

Despite his mansion back home and all his lavish possessions, she couldn't believe he was self-centered. Although Mateo kept him well hidden, the orphaned boy he'd once been was still there deep inside. The boy who'd had no one and nothing. She felt the bracelet heavy on her wrist and smiled softly. People had different ways of dealing with the past.

The adjoining door fanned open and Bailey, brought back, pushed herself to her feet. Mateo entered the room carrying a silver service tray holding two champagne flutes and a dish of sliced pear. At the sight of him, the tips of her breasts tingled and her blood instantly heated. But for the white serving cloth draped over his forearm, he was naked.

Her gaze drank him in…tall, toned and completely comfortable in his own gorgeous bronzed skin.

"I hope you didn't answer the door to room service dressed like that," she said, holding off tightening her robe's sash.

"I doubt they'd bat an eye."

With his gaze lidded and hot, he sauntered closer. After placing the tray on a ledge next to the bath, he poured the champagne then handed over a flute. The glasses pinged as they touched.

"To Paris," he said.

"To Paris," she agreed and sipped.

As the bubbles fizzed on her tongue then slid down her throat, Mateo selected the largest piece of pear, bit in and watched juice sluice down his thumb.

"Delicious," he said and licked his lips.

He offered her a taste. But when she moved to take a bite, he lowered the fruit and touched the piece to the hollow of her throat, drawing a calculated circle before sliding the pear farther down.

Pulse rate climbing, Bailey closed her eyes and waited for the cool to glide between the dip of her cleavage, under the folds of her robe. Instead Mateo lowered his head and sucked at the juice slipping a single line down her throat.

Soaking up each and every thrilling sensation, Bailey sighed and let her neck rock back.

As his mouth slid lower, the sash at her waist was released. A moment later, cool air feathered over her exposed breasts, her thighs, at the same time a big palm trailed the plane of her quivering belly then higher, over her ribs and tender swell of each breast.

He nipped her lower lip and spoke of the near overflowing tub. "That bath needs attention."

Winding her arms around his neck, she whispered in his ear, "Me first."

Nine

Although the morning was far too fresh to leave the top down, Mateo arranged a late model French convertible for the road trip.

From Bailey's wide-eyed expression as they cruised beyond the city limits, she was in thrall of the unfolding country scenes...roads lined with trees whose leaves had been kissed with the russets and reds of autumn and far-reaching vineyards busy with the business of harvest. She marveled at the *colombage* houses with their geometric half-timber patterns. Mateo had obliged when she'd begged to stop at a rustic farmhouse with a leaded-glass feature that highlighted a coat-of-arms on the lintel above.

And there was so much more ahead of them.

He didn't dwell on the niggling doubts that had surfaced since she'd accepted his invitation to join him on this trip, although at times he had found himself wondering if he'd acted too quickly—whether he was a fool believing Bailey was cut from a different cloth than Linda. But they were here now, and he intended for them both to make the most of it.

"After we visit the children," Mateo said, stepping on the gas, "we'll go back to Paris and spend a couple of days. Longer if you want."

"Two days will be wonderful," Bailey said, focused on a tractor trundling over a patchwork of fields. "I told Natalie I'd be back on deck by next Monday."

"She won't mind—"

"I know she wouldn't," Bailey said, looking over at him, "but I've taken up enough slack. Natalie was good enough to offer me a job. I need to step up to the plate."

Changing down gears to take a bend, Mateo was deep in thought. That Natalie had offered Bailey a job didn't bother him in the least. What did rankle was the fact that she scrubbed floors to pay back money he would never miss. After the time they'd spent together, the intimate moments they'd shared, if he didn't know that she'd argue, he'd tell her to forget the debt. He'd much rather set her up in an apartment and, if she followed through with the idea, finance her way through university, like Ernesto had done for him.

Of course he'd be clear that any arrangement would not include a marriage proposal. From what she'd told him of her experience with Emilio Conti, she'd be glad of the clarification. She'd had one close call. She wouldn't be looking forward to the sound of wedding bells.

That made two of them. He liked children but he did not want the responsibility of bringing his own into this world. Life was too uncertain. No one could convince him otherwise.

They reached the town by eleven. Five minutes later, the convertible made its way up the long dirt ruts that led to the Ville Laube Chapelle, a fine example of early French architecture which had been restored over time and transformed into a children's home last century. Bailey sighed, taking in the hundred-foot steeple and angels carrying the instruments of Passion adorning the ornamental gables. Unpolished strong buttresses contrasted with the intricate foliage friezes and elevated stained-glass windows that captured then speared back the sun's late morning light.

Mateo's throat thickened enough he had to clear it. So many years on and still, whenever this scene greeted him, he was six again…feeling uncertain again.

As they parked and slid out from the car, a girl with short-cropped, blond hair, standing beneath the enormous oak Mateo remembered, gawped, dropped her skipping rope and raced inside. A moment later, children poured out through opened double doors that near reached the sky. Eager women, alternatively clapping hands to order the scattered children and patting down their dresses, followed. One lady, with chestnut hair that bounced on the shoulders of her yellow blouse, hurried to line the children up in the yard. Madame Nichole Garnier, Mateo's contact and current director of the orphanage.

Many girls held bouquets, flowers plucked from the home's gardens or nearby meadow. Every boy had their shoulders pinned back. When the assembly was reasonably quiet, beaming, Madame Garnier swept up to greet her guests.

"Monsieur Celeca, it is wonderful to see you again," she said in French. Light green eyes sparkled as she came forward and kissed him, first on one cheek then the other. She turned to Bailey. "And you've brought a friend."

"Madame Nichole Garnier." Mateo spoke in English, knowing Madame would follow suit. "This is Bailey Ross."

"Mademoiselle Ross."

"Call me Bailey."

Madame held one of Bailey's hands between the palms of her own. "And you must call me Nichole. I'm very happy you are here." Smiling, Madame held Bailey's gaze a moment longer before releasing her hand and speaking again with Mateo. "The children have been eager for your arrival." She pivoted around and beckoned a boy standing at the middle front of the group: six or seven years of age, dark hair and chocolate brown eyes fringed with thick lashes.

Mateo's chest swelled as he smiled.

Remy.

After Remy strode forward then pulled up before them, Nichole placed her hand on the boy's crown. "You remember Remy, Monsieur."

Mateo hunkered down. He'd hoped that, since last time, someone might have seen the same special qualities and warmth *he* saw in this child. He'd hoped that Remy would have found two people who would love and adopt him. Still, in another sense, he'd looked forward to seeing him again. From the boy's ear to ear grin, Remy hadn't forgotten him either.

"*Bonjour,* Remy," Mateo said.

The boy's mop of hair flopped over his eyes as he smiled and nodded several times. Then, without invitation, Remy reached and took Mateo's hand and Mateo's heart melted more as he was dragged off. He hated whenever he left, but he really ought to come more often.

Bailey looked on, feeling the connection, subtle yet at the same time unerringly strong. These two—Mateo and Remy— had a history. An ongoing solid relationship. When Natalie had suggested Mateo might bring home a child, was she speaking of anyone in particular? Did the Ramirezes know about this boy?

His little hand folded in a much larger one, Remy drew Mateo nearer the other children, still lined up and standing straight as pins. Bailey fogged up watching the girls hand over their flowers and the boys beam as they shook their benefactor's hand.

Exhaling happily, Nichole folded her arms.

"We so look forward to his visits."

"How long has Mateo been coming back?"

"This will make eight years. Two years ago he helped with dormitory renovations. Last year he sponsored the installation of a computer network and fifty stations. This year I'd hoped to discuss excursions. Perhaps, even an extended stay in Paris for the older ones."

Bailey was certain he'd like that idea.

Her gaze ran over the remarkable building that looked something like a smaller version of Notre Dame, without the gargoyles. How many stories those walls must hold.

"Has this place changed much since Mateo's time?" Bailey asked.

"The structure has been renovated many times over the centuries. Some of the furniture and facilities will have been upgraded since Mateo's time, much of it via his own pocket."

Bailey studied the children again, well dressed, obviously well fed, not a one looking discontent. The word orphanage brought up such Dickensian images…never enough food, never enough care or love. But Bailey didn't feel that here. She only felt hope and commitment.

When Mateo had greeted each child, Remy still stood beside him, a mini-me shadow.

"Remy seems quite attached to Mateo," Bailey pointed out.

"I think Mateo is quite attached to *him*." But then Nichole rubbed her arms as if she were suddenly cold. "Remy lost his mother when he was three," she confided in a lowered voice. "His father dropped him here saying he would return when he could. Four years on…" She shrugged.

No sign of him.

Bailey's chest tightened. At least she'd had her mother until she was fourteen. Had a father too, although he'd been emotionally absent these later years. But looking at that little boy…

Bailey angled her head. "Remy seems happy enough. Lively."

Was it because he was too young to fully understand there was another way to live…with a family, a mother and father?

"He's a joy." Then Nichole hesitated. "Although he doesn't speak often. There's nothing wrong with his hearing. Seems he simply doesn't care to talk most of the time." Her expression softened. "But he and Mateo have a relationship that extends beyond words."

A thought struck and Bailey's smile wavered. "Do you think Remy's father will ever come back for him?"

"I can only say Remy will always have a home here if he doesn't."

Nichole Garnier meant it as a comfort but Bailey heard a dirge rather than a choir. From the little she'd seen, this establishment was well run, with genuine carers who were dedicated to their work. Still, any comprehending child would rather be with his parents in a real home if there were any way, even if that father had once abandoned him…wouldn't he?

Hand cupped to his mouth, Mateo called out.

"Bailey, the girls want to meet you. The boys too."

Laughing, Mateo ruffled Remy's hair and Bailey and Nichole moved forward.

"Have you known Mateo long?" Nichole asked as they walked together and bands of birds warbled nearby.

"Not very."

"He's a good man."

Bailey grinned. "I keep hearing that." She'd even said it herself.

"He gives others so much joy. He deserves every happiness."

Bailey heard the tone in Nichole's voice…the suggestion theirs might be a relationship that could bloom into love and marriage. Perhaps she ought to set the older woman straight. She and Mateo might be lovers, but that didn't translate into anything permanent. He didn't *want* anything permanent.

As they met again and Mateo took her hand and introduced her, Bailey reaffirmed to herself—right now, she didn't want permanent either.

After the children dispersed, Nichole Garnier showed them around the buildings and grounds.

Although the kitchen facilities, plumbing and sleeping quarters were all twenty-first century, the exterior was undoubtedly restored medieval; and the interior, including the lower chapel, retained much of its original decoration, including intricate paintings. Having grown up in a young country like Australia, Bailey was in awe of the sense of history these children were surrounded by every day. The hallowed atmosphere made her feel insignificant, humbled, and at the same time part of the very heart of this sacred place, as if she, herself, might have strolled these soaring halls in a former time.

They enjoyed a lunch of soupe a l'oignon and quiche aux legumes after which the children sang for their adult audience. Although she understood little, Bailey couldn't remember a performance she'd enjoyed more. At the concert's close, she and Mateo provided a standing ovation while the children all bowed and grinned.

Mateo had a meeting with Nichole in the afternoon, so Bailey spent time with the children playing escargot—a French version of hopscotch—and le loup and cache-cache, or hide and seek. One little girl, Clairdy, stole her heart. Only five, Clairdy had white blond hair and the prettiest violet colored eyes. She never stopped chatting and singing and pirouetting. By the end of the afternoon, Bailey's stomach ached from laughing and her palms were pink from applauding.

For dinner they gathered in the dining hall. When Nichole said a prayer before the meal, Bailey's awareness of her surroundings swelled again and, from beneath lowered lashes, she studied her company, particularly the man seated beside her. How amazing if she could see all the world with Mateo. Even more incredible if, in between, they could stay here together in France.

Bailey bowed her head and laughed at herself.

If fairy tales came true...

After the meal, she and Mateo said good-night to the children, Madame Garnier and the others, saying they would be back the next day, then slipped outside and back into the convertible. As they drove down those same dirt ruts, Bailey searched her brain. At no time had Mateo discussed where they would be staying.

"Have you booked a room in town?" She asked, rubbing her gloved hands, relishing the car's heat.

"I own a property nearby."

"Well, it can't be the Palace of Versailles," she joked, thinking of his three story mansion in Sydney. But he didn't comment, merely smiled ahead at the country road, shrouded in shadows, stretching out ahead.

Within minutes, Mateo pulled up in front of a farmhouse, similar to the one they'd stopped to study earlier that day. With the car's headlights illuminating the modest stone facade, Bailey did a double take. No immaculate grounds. No ornate trimmings. This dwelling was a complete turnaround from Mateo's regular taste.

As Mateo opened her car door and, offering a hand, assisted her out, Bailey slowly shook her head, knocked off balance.

"We're staying here?"

"You don't like it?" he asked, as he collected their bags.

"It's not that. In fact…" Entranced, she moved closer. "I think it's wonderful." She had only one question. "Does it have electricity?"

"And if it didn't?"

"Then it must have a fireplace."

"It does, indeed." His smile glowed beneath a night filled with stars as they walked to the door.

"In the bedroom?" she asked, imagining the romantic scene.

"Uh-huh."

She studied his profile, so regal and strong. "You never stop surprising me."

At the door, he snatched a kiss. "Then we're even."

A light flicked on as they moved inside and unwound from their coats. The room smelled of lavender and was clean—he must have had someone come in to tidy up—with a three seater settee, a plain, square wooden table and two rattan backed chairs. Bailey's sweeping gaze hooked on the far wall and she let out a laugh.

"There's a fireplace in here too."

He'd disappeared into a connected room, reemerging now minus their bags. Crossing over, he stopped long enough to brush his lips over hers before continuing on and finding matches on the mantel.

"Let's get you warmed up."

Feeling warmer already, she unraveled the scarf from around her neck while taking in the faded tapestries on the walls as well as the flagstone floor, hard and solid beneath her feet. Feeling as if she'd stepped into another dimension—another time—she fell back into the settee and heeled off her shoes.

"How long have you owned this place?"

"I stayed here the first year," he said, hunkering down before the fireplace. "I came back and bought it soon after."

She hesitated unbuttoning her outer shirt. "Eight years ago?"

He'd struck a match. His perplexed expression danced in the flickering shadow and light as he swung his gaze her way.

"Why so surprised?"

"Why haven't you pulled it down and built something more your style?"

When his brows pinched more than before he turned and set the flame to the tinder, Bailey's stomach muscles clenched. She wasn't certain why, but clearly she'd insulted him. He was all about working hard to surround himself with fine things. Possessions that in some way made up for being cast off with nothing as a child. She'd have thought that here, next door to the heart of those memories, his need for material reassurance would be greatest. It was obvious from Madame's testimony and the well-equipped state of the orphanage that Mateo wanted those children to benefit from pleasant surroundings.

Still, whatever she'd said, she didn't want it to overshadow the previous mood.

"I'm sorry," she said, curling her chilled feet up beneath her legs.

"No need to be," he replied, throwing the spent match on the pyre. "You're right."

Finding a poker, he prodded until the flames were established and the heat had grown.

"I had planned to build something larger," he said, strolling back toward her. "But after I spent a few nights under this roof, I found I didn't want to change a thing. In some ways I feel more at home here than I do in Sydney."

Not so odd, Bailey thought as he settled down beside her. Roots and their memories run deep.

His gaze lowered to her hands. Holding up her wrist, he smiled. "Do you know you play with this bracelet whenever you're uncertain?"

Studying the gold links and charms—a teddy bear, a heart, a rainbow—she shrugged. "I didn't know, but I guess it makes sense."

He rotated her wrist so that the flames caught on the gold and sent uneven beams bouncing all over the room. Bailey moved closer. The heat of his hand on her skin was enough to send some of her own sparks flying.

"I've never seen you with it off your arm," he said.

"My mother put it together for me. A charm for each birthday."

Lowering her wrist, he searched her eyes.

"Until you were fourteen?" he said. *Until the year your mother died.*

"I knew about the bracelet all those years before. It was supposed to be my sweet-sixteen gift. But then Dad refused to give it to me, so..."

"You took it anyway?"

"*No.* This bracelet belonged to me but I would never have taken it without my father's consent. When my sixteenth birthday came and went, I begged for him to give it to me. It was a connection...a link to my mother that I'd waited for all that time. He said he wasn't certain I could look after it, but he didn't have the right to keep it from me."

"He gave it to you in the end."

"He never really spoke to me again after that."

"Sounds as if you both miss her very much. You'd have a lot of memories you could share."

She huffed. "You tell him that."

"Why don't you?"

"He wouldn't listen."

"You've tried?"

"Too many times."

He sat back, absorbed in the crackling fire. After a time, he said, "I'd give anything to speak with my biological father."

"What would you say?"

He thought for a long moment and then his eyes narrowed.

"I'd ask him *why*. But I'll never have the opportunity." He found her gaze again. "What would you say to your father if you could?"

She pondered the question as she never had before.

"I guess I'd ask why too."

"One day you'll have your answer."

When she shivered he wrapped his arms around her, bringing her close to the comfort of his natural warmth. His breath stirred her hair.

"Is that better?"

Looking up into his eyes, she spoke from her heart. "Everything's always better when you hold me."

When his brow furrowed, Bailey shrank into herself. Despite the atmosphere, she'd said too much. Not that her words were a lie. She'd never meant anything more in her life. She felt safe, protected, in his arms. But the way that admission had come out...

Too heavy. She'd bet that kind of "I can't live without you" talk had got a number of his previous love interests gently bumped away. But it wasn't too late to reshape her confession, to season it with the tone they were both more than comfortable with.

Pressing closer, she skimmed her lips across his sandpaper jaw, then hummed over the full soft sweep of his mouth. "On second thought, I think I need to have you hold me a little closer."

She felt his smile, heard the rumble of approval vibrate through his chest.

"But there's something stopping that," he murmured as his palm cupped her nape and she nuzzled down to find a hot pulse throbbing in his neck.

"What's that?"

"Clothes."

Delicious heat flushed through her. They'd made love so many times these past weeks, she'd lost count. But something about his voice, his touch, tonight went beyond anything that had come before. Every cell in her body quivered and let her know…whatever they shared would never get any better than this.

But this time she wanted to be the one to lead…to tease and control and drive the other insane with want.

She lifted her face to his and let his lips touch hers before she slid away from his hold and stood in the firelight before him.

"You build a good fire," she said.

He sat straighter. "You're warm now?"

"Beyond warm."

She caught the hem of her lighter shirt and drew it up over her head. The heat of the flames kissed her bare back while Mateo's intent gaze scorched her front. Her heartbeat thudding, she reached around and released her bra and let the cups fall from her breasts to the soft-pile rug at her feet. When he tipped forward, her flesh tingled and nipples hardened beneath his gaze.

She could see in his eyes that he wanted to drag her to him…wanted to kiss and taste her as much as she wanted to devour him too. But she didn't go to him. Instead she recalled how he'd entered the hotel suite bathroom the night before, without a stitch on, ready to stroke and tease.

She first released the clasp above the zip of her dress pants then eased the fabric past her hips, down her thighs. As the pants came down, she leaned over, nearer to where he sat and waited. Close enough for him to reach out and touch. When she straightened, only one item of clothing separated her from her birthday suit.

His breathing was elevated now, his chest beneath that black shirt rising and falling in the firelight. She recognized the fiery intent in his gaze. How long would he go before hauling her in?

She edged a step closer and a muscle in his jaw began to jump. When she reached for his hand and set his hot palm low on her belly, he came forward and traced his warm mouth over her ribs. Trembling inside, she drew his hand down over the triangle of silk at the apex of her thighs then slowly, purposefully, back up again. His kisses ran higher, brushing the burning tip of one breast as his touch trailed and fingers twined around the elastic of her panties sitting high on her hips.

Groaning, he nipped her nipple at the same time he dragged the scrap of silk down.

Time melted away when his head lowered and his mouth grazed what a second before her panties had concealed… tenderly and then deeply as he cupped her behind and urged her ever closer. She didn't resist when he lifted her left leg and curled her calf over his broad shoulder. She only knotted her fingers in his hair as he continued to explore, his tongue flicking and twirling at the same time the heat at her core kindled, sparked and caught light.

A heartbeat from flashpoint, she recalled she hadn't wanted to surrender to these burning sensations this soon. Now it was too late. This felt—*he* felt—too good to stop.

As she was sucked into that void, all her muscles locked, the fire raged and, dropping back her head, she gave herself over to the tide and murmured his name.

She was barely aware of being lowered down upon that soft pile rug or Mateo's hard frame lowering on top of her. As the waves began to ease and, sighing, she opened her eyes, she found the wherewithal to smile. He hadn't taken the time to take off even his shirt before he thrust in and entered her, filling her in every sense while whispering French and Italian endearments in her ear.

Her legs twined around the back of his thighs as her palms grazed up the hot, hard plate of his chest. He began to move, long measured strokes that built on that fire again. Each thrust seemed to nudge precisely the right spot as his lips sipped lightly from her brow, her cheek. When he drove in suddenly hard and fast, she gripped his head and pulled his mouth to hers. His tongue probed as his body tensed and burned above her. Then she felt the warm touch of his palm sculpting over her breast, the pad of his thumb circling the nipple before he rolled the bead and she gasped as a bright-tipped thrill ripped through her.

His mouth left hers as he levered up. Amid the flickering shadows she could see his muscles glistening and working as his hips ground against hers. She trailed her fingertips down the ruts of his abdomen. Then, scooping them lower, she fanned his damp belly before she gripped his hips, closed her eyes and moved with him, feeling the inferno growing, wishing this sensation would never end.

When he groaned and stiffened above her—when he thrust another time and never more deeply—she reached, held on to his neck and joined him, leaping off that glorious ledge again.

Ten

Later they moved into the bedroom. While Bailey slipped under the covers, Mateo built a fire before joining her. Wrapped in each other's arms, they didn't wake until after eight. He couldn't let her leave the bed until they made love again.

An hour later, Mateo met Nichole at the orphanage. They plotted a workable scheme for regular excursions to the city and surrounds, the first planned in the spring to visit the Louvre with a weekend stay over at a boardinghouse. Nichole was beyond excited for the children, many of whom had never set foot much beyond this district. With a deep sense of satisfaction, Mateo signed his name to the draft document. Opening the world could be an invaluable experience for any child, with regard to education as well as a sense of self. He should know.

They ended their meeting on another high note. A child—Nichole wasn't obliged to say who at this time—would leave the orphanage today for a new home and bright new future. Mateo left the room wondering…

Could this child be Remy? He would only be happy for him if it was.

Mateo had promised Bailey a trip to the neighboring village where she could soak up more of the rustic atmosphere she enjoyed so much. But when he found her in the large undercover area, she and her company looked so enthralled he didn't have the heart to disturb them. Bailey was playing house with a few of the younger girls, one of them Clairdy, a blond angel who Remy was fond of.

As the girls' conversation and laughter filtered through the cool late-morning air, Mateo rested back against that enormous oak-tree trunk and crossed his arms. This was the place he'd wanted to escape as a child. These were the grounds he still recalled in disturbing abstract dreams at least once a year. And yet, whenever he visited, the longer he stayed, the more difficult it was to walk away. Today— this minute, watching Bailey play with the girls—he felt that contradiction more strongly than ever. He couldn't seem to settle the opposing forces playing tug-of-war in his mind. Memories reminded him how much he'd once wanted to leave this place and yet something else whispered for him now to stay.

This, of course, was absurd. He had a practice, friends, a life back home. Here, at times, he felt almost like a ghost.

Bailey saw him and arced an arm through the air. "Mateo, come over! Clairdy and Eleanor are baking cookies. You could help."

Clairdy and an equally small Eleanor chattered on in French as they rolled and cut play dough then put the tray into their playhouse oven. Mateo smiled. Reminded him of when he'd helped Mama in the kitchen all those years ago.

"What cookies are you baking?" Mateo asked, sauntering over.

"*C'est notre recette spéciale,*" Clairdy said. *It is our special recipe.*

"Remember not to have the oven too hot or the bottoms will burn," he pointed out.

Eleanor immediately pretended to alter a temperature dial.

Clairdy patted her friend on the back and exclaimed, "*Bon travail!*" *Good job!*

"These two are inseparable," Bailey said. "I've never seen two children get along so well."

Clairdy was tugging Mateo's sleeve. "Would you like to try one, Monsieur?" she said in French.

Mateo leaned down, hands on knees. "Will they need to cool first?"

Clairdy put her hands on her hips and nodded solemnly at the oven before she told Eleanor two minutes longer and then the cookies needed to cool.

Mateo ran a palm down Bailey's back and whispered, "After the cookies, I'll take you into town."

"Perhaps the girls would like to come."

His brows lifted. *No doubt.* But, "If we take these two, they'll all want to go."

Bailey nodded earnestly, as Clairdy had done a moment ago, then said, "We could hire a bus."

He laughed. "Perhaps we could."

"How did things go with Nichole this morning?" she asked turning more toward him. Her blue eyes had never looked more vibrant.

"We worked out an excursion schedule for next year. The older children will go first."

Bailey's chin came down. "But no one will miss out."

"Everyone will get a trip," he assured her.

Happy with that, she maneuvered in front of him then wrapped his arms around her middle. Her head dropped back against his shoulder as she sighed and took in the industrious scene playing out before them. Eleanor was stepping into a fairy costume; Clairdy was handing her glittering silver wings.

Bailey snuggled back more. "I like it here."

"The climate suits you." He grazed his lips near her temple. "Brings out the pink in your cheeks."

"What about my lips?"

Mateo's physical responses climbed to red alert. With the children engrossed in their game, he pulled her around a cozy corner, gathered her snug against him and purposefully slanted his head over hers. She immediately melted against him, making him feel invincible...taller and stronger than that five-hundred-year-old oak. When their lips softly parted, he wanted to forget where they were and kiss her again.

"It's only early," he murmured against her cheek. "Perhaps we should visit home before trekking off for lunch."

She dropped a lingering kiss on the side of his mouth. "Maybe we could stay here and eat with the kids."

Frowning, he pulled back. "Am I losing my charm?"

A teasing glint lit her eyes. "Would that bother you?"

"Only as far as you were concerned."

He cupped those pink cheeks and kissed her slowly, deeply, until all the world was only them and this embrace. She might have thought he was only flattering her but his last remark was sincere. Today, that other world—with its busy office and appointments and investments and antiques—wasn't important. He wanted to think, and feel, only her.

When his lips drew away a second time, her eyes remained closed. Leaning against the stone wall at her back, she hummed over a dreamy smile.

"Perhaps we should stay here forever."

His stomach slowly twisted. Not because he disagreed but because as outlandish and flippant as her suggestion may be, he was attracted to the idea. As far as he and Bailey were concerned, this trip was supposed to be about nothing more than short-term companionship. Was meant to be about acting on physical attraction. This minute physical attraction was dangerously high...but he was feeling something more. Something new. And he wasn't entirely sure what to do with it.

A woman's voice, emanating from around the corner, brought him back. It was one of the caregivers, the auburn-haired Madame Prideux. Bailey obviously heard too. Her dreamy look evaporated a second before she straightened her blouse and patted away the long bangs from her blushing face.

"Is she looking for you?" Bailey whispered.

"No. Eleanor. She wants her to wash up and come to the office."

"Is something wrong?"

Mateo remembered Nichole's comment about a child leaving.

"My guess is," he said, "that this is little Eleanor's lucky day."

They came out from behind the corner. Eleanor was holding Madame Prideux's hand as they walked together toward the main building. Clairdy sat by herself on a miniature kitchen chair. Mateo felt this little girl's jumbled feelings as if they were his own.

"Don't worry, Clairdy," Bailey said. "Monsieur says Eleanor isn't in trouble."

Not understanding, Clairdy gave Bailey a blank look, let out a sigh then spoke in French. Bailey's eyes widened at the words Mama and Papa. Clairdy knew Eleanor wasn't in trouble. To Clairdy's mind her friend was being rewarded for being the best little girl at the orphanage.

Bailey lowered into the second tiny chair and spoke to Mateo. "Is she saying what I think she's saying?"

He nodded. "Nichole explained this morning that a couple, who've been waiting years, have jumped through the final hoop and obtained consent to adopt."

"Eleanor?"

"It would appear so."

They both studied Clairdy watching her friend walk away toward a different tomorrow. And as Mateo's gut buckled and throat grew thick, he was reminded again of all the reasons he loved coming back. And why he hated it too.

Bailey gazed down at the little girl who a moment ago had been bubbling with life. Now Clairdy's tiny jaw was slack and her shoulders were stooped. When she held her tummy and spoke to Mateo, Bailey guessed the ailment. The innocent she was, Clairdy would be happy for Eleanor finding a mother and a father—a mama and a papa—but how could she not also miss her friend? Likely envy her.

"Does Eleanor get to say goodbye to her friends?" Bailey asked as they escorted a pale Clairdy back to the dorms.

"I have no doubt."

"That's something at least. Not that I'm unhappy for Eleanor," Bailey hastened to add. "It just must be so hard on the ones left behind." She examined Mateo's intense expression as they walked. "But you know that better than me."

"There'll be someone for Clairdy too one day."

She read his thoughts—*for them all, I hope*—and had to stop herself before she blurted out, *I wish it could be me.*

But she'd known this child a couple of days. Even more obvious, she was in no position to think about children in that context and hadn't before this moment. But the brave way Clairdy held her head as they strolled up the main path brought a stinging mist to Bailey's eyes. She might have lost her mother but she'd known and loved her for fourteen beautiful years, and, as difficult to understand as he was, her father had never considered putting her up for adoption. Damon Ross cared about his daughter. These past years, he simply hadn't been able to show it.

They were all three entering the nurse's office as Remy showed up, a scuffed football clamped under his arm. When they came out a few minutes later, Remy was still there, waiting to see how Clairdy was. Something older than his years shadowed that little boy's eyes; he knew she needed a friend more than medicine. Remy said a few words to Mateo—something in French, of course. Mateo nodded and Remy took Clairdy's hand and led her upstairs to the girls' dorm to rest.

They both watched until the pair disappeared around the top balustrade. Bailey let out a pent-up breath. She couldn't stop thinking about what her mother would've done in this situation.

"We could stay and read her a story," she suggested and stepped toward the stairs, but Mateo's hand on her arm held her gently back.

"She might like to be alone with Remy now."

Bailey wanted to argue, but it was as much herself as Clairdy she wanted to console. This was a small taste of what Mateo must see each time he visited. There was the fabulous welcome and smiling familiar faces, time set aside to make plans for improvements he knew would be appreciated. But those same faces who were overjoyed to see him couldn't help but be sad when he drove away. He must want to take each and every one of these children home with him, and realizing he couldn't...

Bailey hung her head.

A lesser man might simply send a check.

As they moved away from the building toward that big sprawling tree out front, Mateo circled his arm around her waist. "Let's take a drive."

She hesitated but then nodded. If they went out, talked, her mind, and his, would be taken off a situation over which they had no power. And she had to be happy for Eleanor and pray that Mateo was right. A perfect family was around the corner for Clairdy. Remy too.

Mateo drove over that ancient stone-bridge and into the village with a towering gothic church, two restaurants, one bakery...and right on through.

Bailey shot over a glance. "Where are we going?"

"Thought you might like to see something a little different. A fortress. A ruin now. Word is it's haunted."

Determined not to be sullen, she set her mittened hands in her lap. "I'm in."

After a few more minutes traveling along the country road, they reached the foot of a rocky cliff that jutted over the river. Ascending a series of rock slabs that served as steps, Bailey, with Mateo, reached near the summit a little out of breath. But given their incredible surroundings, she soon forgot her tired legs.

"Nine-hundred-years ago this began as a motte—a large mound—and wooden keep," Mateo told her. "An earlier word for keep is *donjon*."

It clicked. "As in dungeon?"

He winked, took her hand and led her toward the ruins. "By the fifteenth century, the fortress consisted of three enclosures surrounding an updated keep. Only the château of the second enclosure still stands."

Bailey soaked up the sense of history effused in the assorted moss-covered arches, sagging stone steps, the remnants of sculptures hanging to cold gray walls. Above what once must have been an imposing door rested a worn coat of arms. Shading her eyes, she peered up. A giant might have taken a ragged chomp out of the second story wall.

"Who are the ghosts?" she asked. "Why do they haunt?"

"It's said that a lord once kept his daughter locked in this tower. Apparently no man was good enough, but everyone knew the true reason. The lord didn't want to lose his only child." Holding her elbow, he helped her over rubble through to a cool interior that smelled of mold and earth. "Then, one day, a knight rode through and was invited to stay for the evening meal. The knight heard the maiden singing and crying. He asked if he could speak with her. But the lord wouldn't allow it."

Bailey had been picking her way up the stairs. Now she swung around to face him. "Don't tell me they both died while the knight was trying to rescue her?"

"The knight succeeded in freeing his lady and they rode away that night to be wed. The father was furious and set out on horseback to bring his only child back. Taking a jump, his horse faltered and the lord broke his leg. Infection set in. He took six weeks to die, but he moaned and howled for his daughter's return until his last breath. He wanted her forgiveness," he added.

Bailey studied the lonely crumpling walls and coughed out a humorless laugh. "Funny thing is that lord never enjoyed his daughter's company while he had it."

Reading between the lines, Mateo crossed the dirt floor and joined her midway up the steps.

"If you'd like to see your father when we get back," he said, "I'd be happy to go with you."

She cupped his bristled cheek. "Thanks, but I can't see any happy ending there either."

"I'm sure if you gave him a chance—"

"Maybe he should give me one for a change." Gathering herself, she blew out a breath. She didn't want to discuss it. There was no point. "I wish it were different, but it's not."

A muscle in his cheek pulsed as he considered her response.

"I suppose it's not easy."

Bailey frowned. Did he mean for her or her father? How would he handle the situation if he ever became estranged from his child? How would he handle any situation as a father? She wanted to ask. And now seemed the time.

"Natalie mentioned at dinner that night she wouldn't be surprised if one year you came home with a child from France."

His face hardened. "Natalie's sweet but she doesn't have all the facts."

"What are the facts?"

"For a start, nowadays the adoption process in France is a longwinded one."

"So you've looked into it?"

"Madame and I have conversed for many years."

Be that as it may, he hadn't answered the question. "Then you've never considered adopting?"

His voice and brow lowered. "Remy will find a perfect home."

"Maybe it could be with you."

The muscle pulsed again before he headed back down the steps. "It's hard, Bailey, I know, to think about leaving those kids behind. But they're well looked after. I do what I can."

Bailey let out a breath. Of course he did, and far more than most people would. Resigned, she admitted, "It's probably best we're leaving tomorrow or I might never want to go. Those kids have a way of wrapping themselves around your heart."

From the foot of the stairs, he found her gaze. "That's the

way it is. When you have to stay, you don't want to. When you're free to leave…" His gaze dropped away.

That's the way it was for her with Mateo, Bailey realized walking with him back out into the open. When she'd had nowhere to go and Mateo had convinced her to stay to rest up, she'd been intent on leaving. She'd ended up sharing his bed for two weeks then flying with him here. And in these few days she'd become frighteningly used to the sight of him sitting before a flickering fire in their cottage. Used to his earnest evaluating walks around the orphanage, as well as his warm smile when any one of the children brought him a drawing or sang him a song. She felt so *close* to him. As if they'd known each other before.

What would happen when they returned to Australia? She'd be earning her own money…would be free to live her own life. She had no real reason to stay at the Celeca mansion any longer.

Only now she wasn't so keen to go.

Eleven

Mateo looked over the children playing in the late October sunshine and ran damp palms down his trouser legs. He and Bailey had spent three days at the Chapelle. At the end of each day they returned to his stone cottage to talk and make love into the night. The French countryside this time of year, the children's laughter mixed with memories…he didn't want to leave.

Bailey didn't want to go either. If she hadn't seemed so determined to start work again next week, he'd tell her they would stay a few more days. She seemed to fit here among the trees and the quiet.

He wanted to see more of her when they returned to Australia. But he also wanted to be clear on his position. He was not after marriage. Children of his own. If she accepted that, he'd be more than happy to continue what they shared for however long it lasted.

Bailey was strolling along the paved path with Madame

Garnier. Clairdy walked a step behind, looking a little recovered from her news yesterday about her friend leaving. Shoving his hands in his pockets, Mateo headed toward them. All those years ago, he'd been overjoyed when Ernesto had taken him away from here, like his friend Henri had left before him. The friend he'd so love to know again. It hurt to see that little girl's malaise but that's all he could wish for each of these children. That one day soon they would find a family of their own.

A stiff breeze tugged at his coat. He examined the sky. Rain on the way. He should call Bailey now, say their goodbyes and, if they were going, head off.

Bailey and Madame strolled over.

"Are you ready to leave, Monsieur?" Madame asked.

Mateo folded Bailey's gloved hand in his. "We'd best go now or the mademoiselle will miss out on seeing Paris."

Nichole clapped twice, loudly, and children, coming from everywhere, promptly lined up.

"Monsieur Celeca must leave now," Nichole said in French. "Would you all thank him and the mademoiselle for visiting?"

In unison, the children said in French, "Thank you. We will miss you."

But even as Mateo's chest swelled at the sight of so many adoring little faces and their heartfelt words, his gaze skated up and down the line and soon he frowned. One was missing.

"Where's Remy?" he asked.

"Remy is a little under the weather today." Madame reached into a pocket. "He asked that I give you this."

She fished out a handmade card. When Mateo opened the paper, his heart torqued in his chest then sank to his knees.

Don't forget me, Monsieur.

There was a drawing of a smiling boy holding a football.

Mateo groaned, then, setting his jaw, started off. "I'll go see him."

But Madame's firm hand on his arm pulled him up. Her green eyes glistened with sympathy and understanding.

"I think, Monsieur, it is best that you don't. I'll keep an eye on Remy. He'll be fine, I promise."

Mateo held Nichole's gaze for a long tortured moment as his thoughts flew and a fine sweat broke on his brow. She knew that if he went upstairs to Remy he would want to take him. And he *couldn't*. For so many reasons. He had to go and let Remy find a couple who wanted a family. That boy didn't need an overworked, set-in-his-ways bachelor.

After the women and Clairdy hugged, he and Bailey headed to the car, and the children began to sing. Emotion biting behind his eyes, Mateo fought the urge to look back. Seeing out the corner of his eye that Bailey's hands were clenched together, it was all he could do not to. But he was scared that if he did, he would see Remy, standing as *he* had once stood, at a second-story window, wondering if two friends would ever meet again.

Mateo barely spoke the whole drive to Paris. Whenever Bailey tried to make conversation, he answered and that was all.

From the first, she'd been aware of the connection he and Remy shared. Now Mateo felt terrible leaving that little boy behind. More terrible than she felt leaving Clairdy, and that was bad enough. But as Mateo had said, he did what he could. Neither of them was in a position to do any more…even if they desperately wanted to.

Still, she wished she could have the happy, talkative Mateo back again.

As the convertible hurled them ever closer to Paris and away from the Chapelle, Bailey told herself not to dwell on the possibility of Mateo being a father to Remy as Ernesto had been a father to him. Watching farmhouses and fields whiz by, she reminded herself that Mateo had a bachelor lifestyle—a busy career—that didn't correlate with having children. Remy deserved a family who were prepared to give up anything and everything to adopt him. When Mateo flew over next year, Remy might well be gone. And that was best.

Wasn't it?

They checked into the same hotel on the Champs-Elysees and, as if neither of them wanted to dwell on where they had been—how different it felt to be back in the bosom of luxury as opposed to snuggling beneath the patchwork quilt of their stone cottage—they had their bags taken to their suite and immediately set off to sightsee.

As they strolled arm in arm along the Champs-Elysees, Mateo explained, "The people of Paris refer to this avenue as *la plus belle avenue du monde*. The most beautiful avenue in the world."

Bailey had to agree. Finally soaking up the sights she'd heard so much about felt amazing. The atmosphere was effused with so much history and courage and beauty. Every shop and tree and face seemed to greet her as if they were old rather than new friends.

She cupped a hand over her brow to shield the autumn sun from her eyes. "It seems to go on forever."

"Two kilometers. It ends at the Arc de Triomphe, the monument Bonaparte built to commemorate his victories."

They strolled beside the clipped horse-chestnut trees and lamplights, passing cinemas, cafés and so many speciality shops, before stopping for lunch at a café where the dishes marked on a chalkboard menu ranged from sweet-and-sour sea bass and lobster ravioli to more casual fare such as club sandwiches. After taking a seat among the pigeons at one of the many sidewalk tables, Bailey decided on the crab and asparagus salad, while Mateo liked the sound of braised lamb with peaches.

"Is this a favorite café when you're in town?" She asked, sipping a glass of white wine.

"This is my first time eating here."

"Then I think today we've found the perfect place to simply sit and watch."

He raised his glass. "A favorite Parisian pastime. Keeping an eye out for the unique and the beautiful."

Bailey had been watching a pair of young lovers, laughing as they meandered down the avenue. Now her focus flicked back to Mateo and the intense look in his dark eyes made her blush. He wasn't looking at the beautiful view. He was looking at her.

They enjoyed their meal then headed off to the Louvre on the bank of the Seine. Bailey couldn't stop from beaming. So much to take in…over thirty-five thousand works of art dating from antiquity to modern times…Da Vinci, Rubens as well as Roman-Greco and Egyptian art collections…she felt deliciously lost as more and more worlds unfolded before her. She adored Michelangelo's *The Slave* and openly gaped at the *Venus de Milo*. But she fell completely in love with Canova's *Psyche Revived by Cupid's Kiss*.

Cupid's wings were raised behind him, his head slanted over the unconscious Psyche's as he held her close. Bailey was in awe of the depth of emotion the master had captured in marble.

"This is my favorite," she decided. "You can see how in love with her he is."

"Legend has it that Venus was jealous of Psyche's beauty," Mateo said, wrapping his arms around her from behind. "She sent her son, Cupid, to scratch Pysche with an arrow while she slept. When Psyche awoke, she would fall in love with the first man she saw: a hideous creature that Venus planned to plant in the bed. But Cupid woke Psyche and, startled, he accidentally scratched himself as well. Under the arrow's spell, they fell instantly in love."

"And lived happily ever after?"

"They had a spat and Venus put some more obstacles in the way. The last sent Psyche into a dead sleep, that only Cupid's kiss could cure."

She sighed. "Like in *Sleeping Beauty*."

"Like you in the mornings," he murmured against the shell of her ear.

She smiled and admitted, "I'm not the lightest of sleepers."

"Waking you is my favorite time of the day."

He brushed his lips down the side of her throat and the backs of her knees turned to jelly. But she was well aware of their public surroundings.

"You want to get us thrown out."

He chuckled. "We're in *France*."

While Mateo continued to nuzzle her cheek, she thought again of the sculpture and its legend. "What happened at the end of their story?"

"Our old friend Zeus blessed their union and gifted Psyche immortality. She and Cupid had a daughter, Voluptas, the goddess of sensual pleasure."

Bailey's eyes widened. "*Voluptas*. Bet she has a story or two of her own."

Laughing—his old self again—he led her away.

They cruised around the exhibits until the museum closed up at ten. But outside they found the city sparkling and very much awake. Making their way along the Seine, they drank in the river's shimmering reflections and music floating over the cold night air.

He released her hand and drew that arm around her waist. "What would you like to do tomorrow?"

"That's easy." She cuddled in as they walked. *"Everything."*

"In a single day?"

"We have a day and a half," she corrected. "And I put myself entirely in your hands."

"Entirely?"

"And exclusively."

He growled playfully, "I like the sound of that," then turned her in his arms to steal a bone-melting kiss that sparked a wanting fire low in her belly and kept it burning.

They found a warm place to enjoy coffee and share a pastry, then walked again. When dawn broke—a palette of pink and gold soaking across the horizon—cold and worn out, she yawned and couldn't stop.

Mateo raised his hand to hail a cab. "Time to turn in."

"But—"

"No buts," he growled before opening the back passenger door of the cab that had pulled up. "We have another big day coming up."

She didn't like when he was bossy. Even if he was right. Nestled in the back seat, she rested her cheek against his shoulder. Smiling drowsily, she found she couldn't keep her eyes open. As her lids closed, all the sights and sounds and smells of their day in Paris flooded her mind. She snuggled more against his warm hard chest and murmured, "I loved our night. Love it here. I love…*I love…*"

Mateo waited for Bailey to finish. But, with the sun rising—with the full day they'd had—she was asleep before her last words were out. After pressing a kiss on her brow, he too closed his eyes.

When they arrived at the hotel, he roused himself and eased away. But Bailey didn't wake, so he carefully scooped her up in his arms and, entering the lobby, asked the doorman to follow him to an elevator and help him into his suite. A few minutes later, the concierge swiped open the suite's door and, on Mateo's orders, hurried to draw back the bed's covers before bidding him a hushed very good morning.

Searching Bailey's contented face, Mateo carefully laid his sleeping beauty upon the sheets. She stirred when he removed her coat and shoes but after he stripped and lay down to join her, she curled up against him and huddled deeper as he drew the covers up around her chin. His body cried out for rest but he didn't want to give into sleep.

The view was too good.

As he stroked her hair and watched growing light play over the contours of that button nose, the curve of her lips, Mateo's chest grew warm. Despite lingering memories of the Chapelle earlier today, he'd never known this depth of peace. The feeling that he had what he needed to survive, to be happy, was right here with him now in his arms.

He'd mulled it over before. Now his mind was made up. No more wondering if Bailey was anything like his manipulative ex. When they were home again in Sydney, he'd make it official. He would make their current living arrangement more permanent. No contracts. No rings. Just an agreement to share each other's company.

And his bed.

Twelve

At nine the next morning, a soft caress at the shell of Bailey's ear stirred her from her dreams. Smiling, stretching and sighing, she rolled over and remembered where she was and with whom. In Paris with the most incredible man.

Mateo dotted a kiss on her nose, on her cheek.

"You were sleeping soundly." His voice was deliciously husky the way it always was first thing in the morning, and she found herself sighing at her body's reaction to the desire evident in his hooded eyes and slanted smile. Coiling her arms around his neck, she brought his lips to hers while his hot palm trailed up her side. Within seconds her heartbeat was racing.

She couldn't remember the last of that cab ride last night. Couldn't remember how she'd arrived back in this suite. She did know, however, that this minute she felt amazingly snug, wonderfully safe. She remembered their agreement... today she was entirely, exclusively his. How she wanted to pull the covers up over their heads and spend the next few hours in bed.

Reluctantly breaking the kiss, he murmured against her lips. "It's time to get up."

Groaning, she dragged the back of her hand over her tired eyes. *Bossy again.* "What time is it?"

"Time to see Paris."

A second passed when she could have smoothed her fingers over his muscled shoulder and drawn his mouth back to hers. But this was their only full day left in France. She couldn't pass that up, even for such a compelling reason.

With not nearly enough sleep, Bailey was slow to shower and dress. But the moment they were back on the Parisian streets, coats pulled up around their ears, she was bubbling with excitement.

They visited Notre Dame, the legendary home of the hunchback, then went on to an artist's paradise, Montmatre et Sacre Coeur, situated on a hill in the north of Paris. It boasted the famous Moulin Rouge at its base and the famed Sacre Coeur Basilica, with its inspirational equestrian statue of Joan of Arc, at its summit. She made sure Mateo took plenty of snapshots.

After changing for dinner back at their suite, they took the elevator to the top of the Eiffel Tower where they caught the last of the sunset. Gazing over the city's buildings and monuments draped in a coat of gold, Bailey tried to imprint her mind with every inch of the breathtaking panorama. Mateo circled his arm around her waist and handed his camera to a German tourist who ensured the moment was captured.

He thanked the man then asked her, "Are you hungry?"

"I'm starving." They'd had a bagel on the run, but that was hours ago. "What do you have in mind?"

"A special treat."

As they descended, Mateo revealed his biggest surprise of the day. He'd booked well in advance a table at The Jules Verne, one of Paris's most exclusive restaurants, situated on the tower's second floor.

They were shown to a table by a window facing north across the fountains and enjoyed a night of exquisite cuisine, the best of champagne, while surrounded by a glittering blanket of city lights.

When the waiter removed their dessert dishes, Mateo slid a hand across the white linen tablecloth. His fingers folded around hers.

"Did you enjoy the meal?"

"I enjoyed *everything*."

He grinned, and the smile lit his eyes. His index finger had begun to toy with her bracelet's charms...the heart, the bear.... He looked down but then frowned and took a closer look.

"You ought to have that catch checked out. It's near worn through."

Worried, she inspected the clasp then each of the charms to make certain none were missing. "Guess it should be worn. I don't take it off." Bailey's stomach looped and knotted at the thought of losing it. "After so long, I wouldn't feel whole without this around my wrist."

"We'll get a safety chain for it tomorrow."

"I'll look after it when we get home."

Mateo didn't look pleased. But it wasn't his place to insist.

He reached and took her hand again, angling her wrist to study the charms. "Have you added to it since your sixteenth?"

"It's never felt quite right. It'd have to be a really special charm." She didn't own much, but this possession was sacred. Not that her father would understand that. Even now he probably thought she was a day away from harming or losing it.

"What about you?" She asked, looking up from their twined hands; hers looked so small and pale compared to his. "Do you have any childhood mementos hidden away?"

Mateo's gaze grew distant and his brows knitted before he shook his head. "No. Nothing material."

Bailey's heart went out to him. Given all his chattels back in Sydney, that answer made sense.

"But I do have something," he said. "A memory I treasure."

She sat straighter. "Memories are good."

"The day Ernesto came back to the Chapelle for me. It was spring and everyone was playing outdoors. He called me over, beside that old oak and he said, 'Mateo, if you'd like to be my son...'" His Adam's apple bobbed before he seemed to come back from that distant spot. Then he shrugged and gave an offhanded smile. "How's that. I've forgotten the rest."

From the way his dark eyes glistened, she didn't think so. But she understood. Memories were the most valuable of all keepsakes. He was entitled to protect his. He'd certainly given her some amazing memories these past days to cherish.

Leaning closer, she confessed with all her heart, "I'll never forget our time here."

When his gaze darkened more and his jaw jutted almost imperceptibly, Bailey sat back as a shadowy feeling slid through her. They'd shared so much. Seemed to have gotten so close. But was that open admission too much? Had she sounded too much the lovesick schoolgirl?

But then a smile swam up in his eyes and the tension seemed to fall from his shoulders. He lifted her hand, dropped a light kiss on the underside of her wrist and murmured against her skin, "I won't forget either."

After dinner they strolled again, but the weather had turned even chillier and, while they'd been lucky so far, Bailey smelled rain on the way. She tried her best but when she couldn't keep her teeth from chattering, Mateo stopped to turn and envelope her in his coat-clad arms.

"I'll take you back to the suite," he said.

Her heart fell. "I don't want to go in yet."

"We can always come back."

Come back? She searched his eyes. Was she reading him right? "You mean...to France?"

"And sooner than I usually plan."

Bailey couldn't take a breath. It was a generous, wonderful offer but...should she read more into it? She supposed she ought to ask herself, *How much more did she want?* They'd been sleeping together, enjoying each other's company, but did she want a relationship, *if* that's what he was saying?

Her smile quavered at the corners as she tried to contain her whirling mix of emotions. As they headed for a cab stand, she smiled a jumpy smile and said, "I'd like that."

Thirteen

Mateo made love to Bailey that night feeling both content and never more conflicted. Caressing her silken curves as they played upon the sheets…kissing every sensual inch of her and only wishing there were more. He couldn't deny that he wanted to keep this woman in his life even if, with every passing hour, he felt himself treading farther into dangerous ground.

After the Emilio affair, it was safe to presume Bailey wasn't interested in exchanging vows and wedding bands. He'd invited her back to Paris and she'd agreed. Would she presume, too, that he would also invite her to live under his roof on a more permanent basis? In time, would she expect more? Deeper commitment?

Diamond rings?

Mateo slept on the problem and when they stepped out to bid the City of Light good morning, with Bailey looking so vibrant and fresh on his arm, he made a decision—one he hoped she would be happy with. But now wasn't the time to discuss it.

He arranged for them to spend the morning on a cruise, absorbing the sights from a different point of view. They boarded near the Pont-Neuf Bridge.

"Its name literally means the new bridge," Mateo said as they settled into window seats beneath a Perspex roof that allowed an unhindered view of the sights, including the many graceful arches of the stone bridge. "But this is the oldest bridge in Paris."

Bailey narrowed her gaze on a distant point then tipped forward. "Look there."

She pointed out a couple standing at the center of this side of the bridge in the midst of a passionate kiss. Before their lips parted, the man swept the woman up in his arms and twirled her around. They were both laughing, bursting with happiness.

Bailey melted back into her seat. "I bet he just proposed."

Mateo's chest tightened at her words, at her tone. Shifting, he got comfortable again and explained, "The *Pont-Neuf* is rumored to be one of the most romantic places in the city."

She laughed. "Is there anywhere in Paris that *isn't* romantic?"

He gave an honest reply. "Not this trip."

All expression seemed to leech from her face before she blushed…her cheeks, her neck. From the look, she'd gone hot all over. That made him smile but also made him want to pull back. He really ought to rein it in. Although she knew his mind on the subject, he didn't want to confuse the issue. Companionship was good. A marriage proposal was not.

After a leisurely time enjoying the sights from the river, he helped her off the boat. Her posture and thoughtful look told him she wasn't looking forward to leaving this behind and boarding that jet. But he had one more surprise before they left. One that would, hopefully, surpass all the others.

As they meandered along the avenue, she said, "Suppose we'd better get back to the suite and pack."

He kept a straight face. "I need to duck in somewhere first."

"Souvenir shopping?"

He twined her arm around his. "In a way."

He hailed a passing cab. When they arrived at their destination, Bailey didn't seem able to speak. Her eyes merely sparkled, edged with moisture, as she clasped her hands under her chin.

"It didn't seem right that we leave without visiting here," he said, stepping out from the cab.

"The Paris Opera," she breathed.

"I have tickets, but the matinee starts soon." He extended his hand to help her out. "Let's hurry."

He escorted her toward a magnificent facade adorned with numerous towering rose-marble columns. The highest level was bookended by two large gilded statues. The interior luxury, including mosaic covered ceiling and multiple chandeliers, had been compared to the corridors in Versailles. When Bailey spotted the 98-foot high marble grand staircase—the one his own was based on—she gasped and held her throat. As he took her arm and escorted her up the flight, she looked over and beamed.

"I don't need a ball gown or glass slippers. No one could feel more like Cinderella than I do now."

When they emerged from the theater, she was floating. She literally couldn't feel her feet descending those incredible grand stairs. The performance was a thoroughly beautiful ballet Bailey knew she would dream about for months.

As they made their way toward the exit, all those amazing

sparkling chandeliers lighting their way, Mateo checked his watch.

"We have a little time yet before we need to head off to the airport. What would you like to do?"

She remembered a mention of souvenirs earlier and piped up. "Buy a gift."

"Who for?"

"I wanted to get Natalie something to thank her for taking me on then letting me have this week off. But then I thought she'd appreciate something for Reece far more."

Chuckling, he wound her arm more securely around his. "You're right. She would."

"Maybe some kind of stuffed toy. A Gallic Rooster." Her step faltered at his unconvinced look. "It's this country's national animal, isn't it?"

"But Reece isn't a baby. He'd appreciate something more—" he thrust out his chest "—masculine."

She slanted her head. Okay. "How about a football?"

"Too young."

"Suggestion?"

"That we go to the experts."

"And that would be?"

He quickened his step and propelled her along with him. "The oldest and largest toy store in Paris."

Soon they arrived at Au Nain Bleu, the massive store that had been serving French children's play needs since the mid-nineteenth century. There were lots of stuffed floppy-eared rabbits. Bailey seemed especially taken with a pair of bunny slippers. But Mateo ushered her through to a spot where boys' toys ruled.

They looked at trucks, action figures, miniature drums. Bailey drifted toward a nearby girls' section while Mateo kept searching. After a few more minutes, satisfied, he called and gestured toward a shelf.

Bailey hurried over from a jewelry stand and picked up the pack. "A builder's kit, suitable for eighteen months to three years," she said. With a plastic hammer, automatic wrench, an "electric" drill that buzzed when you pressed a red button. "But Reece is only twelve months."

"Believe me, he'll grow into it quickly."

She quizzed Mateo's eyes and smiled.

"You would have liked this when you were young?"

"More than anything, I wanted to be a builder."

"And you ended up becoming a doctor?"

"Ernesto wanted me to make the most of my grades."

She smiled knowingly. "But there's still a part of you that wants to hammer and saw and create."

He rolled that thought over and admitted, "I suppose there is." Although he hadn't thought about it in decades. He straightened his shoulders. "Anyway, I'm sure you'll be a hit with Reece with this."

At the counter, Mateo pulled out his wallet but Bailey held up a hand. "I have money enough for this."

He wanted to argue but finally put his wallet away while she extracted some French currency. He hadn't known she'd exchanged any cash. But given her backpacker history, of course she'd be well up to speed on such things.

The lady behind the counter insisted on gift wrapping. Mateo was checking his watch again as they headed for the exit when a large well-dressed man materialized directly in front of them. With a stony expression, he studied Bailey who, looking uncertain, slid a foot back. Mateo wasn't uncertain. He was annoyed. They had a jet to catch.

Before Mateo had a chance to speak up, the man addressed Bailey in French.

"I am a security officer for the store. Please empty your pockets."

Bailey clung to his arm. "What's he saying?"

Mateo stepped in front of Bailey and demanded of the officer, "What's this about?"

"I have reason to suspect your wife has something in her pocket for which she did not pay."

Bailey's hushed voice came from behind. "Why is he upset, Mateo?"

He looked over his shoulder. "He thinks you've shoplifted."

Her eyes rounded. "That's crazy."

Yes. It was.

And yet he couldn't help but wonder why a security officer from a well reputed store should stop them if there was no basis to the accusation.

Stepping beside her again, Mateo assessed her knee-length coat. "He wants you to empty your pockets."

"What on earth does he think I stole?"

"The quickest way to end this, Bailey, is show him the contents of your pockets."

If she had nothing to hide, she would have nothing to fear and, doing his job or not, he would then demand an apology from this man. If, of course, the security guard was right…

As shoppers swirled around them and a toddler, trying a mini slide, squealed close by, Bailey reluctantly dragged something shiny from her right pocket then held out her hand, palm up. The officer preened his moustache before leaning in to take a better look. Mateo didn't need to. He knew what Bailey had hidden in her pocket.

The officer angled his head and frowned. "What is this?"

Sheepish, Bailey found Mateo's eyes. "You were right. The clasp broke when I was looking through a display. It fell in with some necklaces. I put it in my pocket and was going to have it fixed, first thing, when we got home."

Mateo let out a lungful of air. Her charm bracelet. She was lucky she hadn't lost it. He knew how much it meant to her. He should have *made* her listen.

Mateo explained the situation to the officer who accepted the story with an apology before allowing them to be on their way.

"I know what you're thinking," she said as they walked out onto the pavement. "It could have slipped off without me knowing." She cringed. "I hate to think what my father would say."

"He wouldn't be happy."

"I'm used to that. But you don't need to be upset."

He didn't reply.

As they cabbed it back to the suite, Mateo mulled over the incident. What really bothered him was that for a moment he'd been prepared to think the worst of Bailey—again. But it had been a misunderstanding, something similar to when he'd jumped to conclusions the second she'd confirmed she'd taken that money from Mama. But that hiccup was long behind them. Bailey wasn't dishonest. Wasn't manipulative.

He stole a glance at her profile as she watched the Parisian streets flash by in her borrowed designer clothes, perhaps thinking of her visit to the Champs-Elysees, and confirmed she wasn't that type. She couldn't be.

He couldn't feel this deeply about someone who was nothing better than a fraud.

Or, more correctly, he couldn't make that mistake again.

They packed, checked out and boarded the jet with time to spare. Bailey felt as if she were grieving for a friend as she gazed out the window, bid goodbye to France and the jet blasted off. She felt as if she were leaving home, leaving her family—Nichole and the children at the orphanage.

Mateo had said they would visit again, and she was over the moon about that. But now, more than before, she also needed to know what would happen to "them" when they arrived back in Australia.

As the jet climbed higher and clouds began to interfere with the view of the receding ground below, she considered hedging around the subject, trying to get an answer without sounding needy or obnoxious by asking directly. Because she hadn't the money to find her own place and wanted to pay that loan back as quickly as she could, she'd agreed to live at Mateo's home…his *mansion*.

But as close as she believed they'd become—as close as she'd come to acknowledging feelings she'd been determined to stay away from less than three weeks ago—she had to know where they were in their…well, their *relationship*. She couldn't land in Sydney and simply walk through his front door as if she owned the place. She needed to know what the next step was, and the best way was to ask straight out.

She set her magazine aside. "You know, with the wage I'll make cleaning, I should have that loan paid back in a couple of weeks."

He looked across, smiled. "That's great."

When he looked back at his obstetrician periodical, she folded her hands firmly in her lap. Since that incident at the toy store, he'd seemed distracted. A silly part of her wondered if, for just a second, he might have believed the security buffoon's accusation. But she hadn't pilfered a thing in her life. He might have set out thinking she'd shammed his grandmother but surely, after the week they'd spent together, he knew her by now. She'd even begun to think that he might be falling a little in love with her. That left her feeling dizzy and, perhaps, even a bit hopeful.

She shook herself. This mooning wasn't getting her any closer to finding out what came next. If either of them truly *wanted* a next.

She drummed four fingertips on the magazine page. "I thought I should start shopping for a place to live before then."

He froze then lowered the periodical and studied her eyes. "Do you want to find a place of your own?"

Bailey swallowed a fluttery breath. What kind of question was that? What kind of reply did she give? Honest, she supposed.

"Depends. Do you want me to?"

His gaze dropped to her hands and again she realized how naked she felt without that bracelet on her wrist. She was squirming a little when he announced, "I thought you might like to stay with me."

Her entire body lit with a blush. She coughed out a laugh, shrugged, tried to find words while attempting to sort out if she really did want to "live with a man" so soon after her pseudo engagement catastrophe, even if that man was the uber attractive, thoroughly irresistible, Mateo Celeca.

Bowing her head, she let out a shuddery breath. This was a thousand times different from Italy. She and Mateo had a connection, something she wanted to pursue…if he did.

She took a breath and looked him in the eye. "Are you sure?"

He waited two full beats where Bailey could only hear her heart pounding in her ears. Then he leaned close, stroked her cheek and murmured against her lips.

"I'm sure."

Fourteen

A week later, Bailey sat at the meals table next to Mateo's chef-standard kitchen. She'd been struggling all morning with a question. A problem. Finally now she'd made up her mind.

She pushed her coffee cup away and announced, "I'm going to do it."

Sitting alongside of her, Mateo shook out his Sunday paper, looked over and announced, "Fabulous." Then he frowned and asked, "Do what?"

Bailey let her gaze roam the hedges and statues in her favorite of Mateo's gardens—the one that reminded her so much of their time in France—then she studied the bracelet, repaired and back on her wrist. Her stomach turned and she swallowed the lump formed in her throat.

"I'm going to see my father."

The day after they'd returned, she'd gone back to work, cleaning for Natalie's firm; she'd decided to keep Reece's gift until she and Mateo saw them all together. He'd put the rest of his vacation plans on hold and seemed content to play golf and catch up with local friends. He'd said that seeing as Mama hadn't expected him, she wouldn't be disappointed and that he'd visit her and Italy sometime soon. Every night they came together but, although the words almost escaped, she didn't bring up his suggestion that they would return to France one day. There were moments when she'd caught a distant, almost haunted look darkening his eyes. At those times she guessed his mind was back at the Chapelle, wondering how little Remy was doing, as she often thought about Clairdy. She wanted to talk about it but his demeanor at these quiet times told her not to. He might not admit it but he felt guilty about leaving that boy. She understood his reasons. She wondered some times if Mateo did.

What she owed for her return airfare had been paid back and to set all the records straight she spoke to Mama on the phone, admitting that she'd taken her money under false pretenses, that she'd never planned to return to Italy. To Bailey's surprise, Mama had said she'd guessed as much and understood. She might be a dear friend of Emilio's grandmother, but she had never been a big fan of that boy... not since Emilio had tried to fight her Mateo so many years earlier.

Mama had gone on to say that when his ring had returned in the mail, Emilio had spread word that his Australian fiancée had indeed run out on him. But he hadn't pined for long. Emilio was seeing another lady, this one a visitor from Wales. Mama said she was a nice young woman and she would keep an eye out for her too.

Now that her more recent past issues were ironed out, Bailey felt a need to at least try to make some kind of amends with her father. They hadn't spoken in over a year and she'd grown a great deal since then. Perhaps it was foolish hoping but maybe he'd grown too. Whereas a couple of weeks ago, when she'd seen him on the street, she hadn't known if she were strong enough, now, this morning, in her heart she believed she could not only face her father, but if their meeting turned sour—if he still shunned and criticized her—she could do what was needed to go forward with her life.

She could forgive him and walk away.

Now the inquiring smile in Mateo's eyes dimmed and he scraped his chair to turn more toward her. "You want to go see your father now? This morning?"

When she nodded, he ran a hand through his hair, smiled and pushed his chair back. "In that case I'll get the car out."

He got to his feet but, before he could head off, she caught his arm.

"Mateo, you don't have to come."

His dark brows knitted. "Do you want me there?"

A spool of recent memories unwound...how Mateo had helped her with the money she'd owed Mama. How he'd given her a roof over her head, even when she'd insisted she didn't need one. The way he'd invited her into his life, through friends like Alex and Natalie and Nichole. The amazing time he'd shown her in France.

He'd trusted her enough to admit that he would give anything to ask his own father *why*. She'd realized that was precisely what she needed to ask too.

Decided, she pushed to her feet. "If you'd like to come, that would mean a lot."

As they pulled up outside the familiar Sydney address, Bailey dug her toes into her shoes and told herself to get a grip. She wasn't a kid anymore. She was here not because she needed her father but because she *chose* to see him. If he turned her away...well, she'd deal with it. She'd been through worse. And with Mateo standing alongside of her, she could face anything.

Mateo's strong, warm hand folded around hers.

"You'll be fine."

She tilted her head at the front yard. A good part of the greenery lay hidden behind a massive brick and iron fence.

"I grew up playing on that lawn," she said. "The summer after I got a bike for Christmas, my father built a track on the other side of that garage, complete with dirt jumps and dips. He said he'd take me to moto-X competitions, if I wanted."

"Not your thing?"

"I turned seven that year and discovered my destiny. I was going to be either a Labradoodle breeder or a Russian circus fairy."

His eyes crinkled at the corners at the same time his mouth slanted and some of the stress grabbing between her shoulder blades eased.

"I ditched after-school circus skills mid-third term," she explained. "I still love poodle crosses though. Dad said he'd set me up with my own breeder's kennel when I was older."

Mateo curled a loose strand of hair behind her ear. "Everything will be fine."

"Promise?"

"I promise you won't regret coming here today," he said, then pushed open his door.

Together they walked up the path to the front door. Mateo stood back while she flexed her hands a few times then rang the bell. Her heartbeat galloping, she waited an interminable time, but the hardwood door she knew so well failed to open.

Feeling beads of perspiration break on her brow, she glanced across. Mateo cocked his chin at the door and, with a shaky hand, she thumbed the bell again. After several more nothing-happening moments, she surrendered and threw up her hands.

"All that build-up and he's out."

She pivoted on her heel, ready to leave, but Mateo only stood firm.

"It's Sunday morning," he said, running a reassuring palm down her arm. "Give him a chance to put down the paper. Set his coffee cup on the sink."

Listening to a kookaburra laugh from a nearby treetop, Bailey gathered her failing courage and faced that closed door again. A neighbor, trimming hedges, popped his head over the fence. Smiling, Mateo nodded at the curious gray-haired man. But Bailey only blew out a done-with-it sigh.

"If my father's in there, he's not coming out."

After a few seconds, Mateo reluctantly agreed. They'd turned to leave when that heavy door cracked open. A man in a weekend checked shirt squinted at them through a shaft of steamy morning light. While Bailey's chest tightened, Damon Ross's eyes flared and his grasp on the doorjamb firmed as if his knees had given way.

"Bailey...?" His head angled as he took in more of her. "It is you, isn't it?"

She tried to swallow but her throat was suddenly desert dry. So, although it wobbled at the corners, she tried a smile instead.

"How are you, Dad?"

Stepping back, her father ran his gaze up and down again as if she might be an apparition come back to haunt him. But then his expression softened and the stern voice she'd come to know over these last years softened too. He even partway smiled when he said, "I wasn't sure I'd ever see you again."

She shrugged. "I didn't know if you wanted to see me."

Her father moved forward, hesitated, and then reached his arms out. Bringing her in, he hugged his only daughter close and for a bittersweet moment she was transported back to that day when they'd desperately needed each other. The day her mother had been laid to rest.

Bailey gave herself over to the feeling. This is how she'd dreamed this meeting would unwind. The smell of his aftershave, the warmth of his bristled cheek pressed to hers. As tears stung behind her eyes, she wanted to say how much she missed him but as he released her and edged back, she gathered herself. Hopefully, there would be plenty of time for that.

Damon Ross acknowledged the third person standing nearby. The older man drew back his shoulders and extended his hand.

"We haven't met."

Mateo, several inches taller, took her father's hand. "Mateo Celeca."

"Have you known my daughter long?"

"Only a few weeks."

Her father's calculating lawyer's gaze took Mateo in before, obviously approving, he released another smile and waved them both inside.

"Are you from Sydney, Mateo?" Her father asked, escorting them through the foyer that wasn't a quarter as large as Mateo's.

"Originally from Italy."

"The name, the complexion…" Damon Ross lobbed a knowing look over his shoulder. "I guessed Mediterranean."

The aroma of coffee brewing led them to the kitchen. While the men made small talk, Bailey discovered the cups in the same cupboard and poured three coffees before they sat down in the adjoining meals area.

The table was stacked with journals and assorted papers relating to her father's work. The rest of the room looked clean. Almost too tidy. Didn't seem so long ago that her mother's easel and paints had occupied that far corner, the one that offered the best natural light. Ann Ross had always kept a spare pair of slippers right there by the door. Of course, they were gone now. But her parents' wedding portrait still hung in the center of that feature wall. Sipping coffee, Bailey wondered whether their bedroom had changed. Whether her mother's clothes were still hanging in the wardrobe all these years later.

"You had a good time overseas?" Her father's dark-winged eyebrows arched as he lifted the cup to his pursed lips.

"Yes." Bailey fought the urge to clear her throat. "Thank you. I did."

"I'm glad." Her father held his smile. "You must have been busy."

A little nervous, she laughed. "Pretty much."

"You enjoyed it then?" Damon Ross went on.

Her fingers tightened around the cup. He was pushing the point that he had advised her not to go abroad alone. Digging to see if, true to his prediction, anything had gone wrong.

"I'm glad I went," she said, her smile verging on tight now. "I'm glad I'm back."

Her father nodded, but his buoyant expression had slipped a touch, too.

"I wasn't sure what to think," he said.

Out of the corner of her eye, Bailey saw Mateo roll back one shoulder a second before she replied. "About what?"

"About how you were doing," her father expounded as if he were telling her B followed A. "Whether you were in any kind of trouble."

"You didn't need to worry, Dad."

Damon Ross laughed with little humor. "It's not as if I've never had to worry before."

A retort, fast and hot, leapt up her throat but before she

could say a word, her father changed his tone...upbeat again.

"So," he pushed his cup aside and threaded his fingers on the table, "did you find work while you were over there?"

"I did some waitressing."

"Well, as long as it kept you out of trouble."

Bailey's face burned. There was that word again. Or was he merely being inquiring, genuinely concerned, and she was being overly sensitive? Now that she was here, shouldn't she be the better person and let any slights, intended or otherwise, sail over her head? She was mature enough to handle this.

"How did you two meet?" her father asked Mateo while Bailey took a long sip of hot coffee.

Mateo replied, "Through a mutual friend."

"Bailey's mother and I met at a church function." Damon blinked several times then dropped his faraway gaze. "But that was a long time ago."

"We recently returned from France," Mateo chipped in, sharing a covert you'll-be-fine wink with her.

Her father's wistful smiled returned. "My wife and I visited Paris on our honeymoon. Ann was taken with the country scenery. She said she felt as if she'd stepped into a Monet." His gaze wandered to his daughter and he sat back. "So, what are you doing with yourself nowadays?"

"I'm working," she announced. "For a real estate firm."

Mateo stepped in again. "Bailey and a friend of mine clicked. Natalie said Bailey had what her agency was looking for." He caught her gaze. "Didn't she, darling?"

Bailey's heart lifted to her throat. Mateo had only ever addressed her by name and yet he'd chosen this moment to call her an endearment. A well-educated, respected professional in his field, Damon Ross was challenging his daughter and Mateo was defending her without causing waves, by letting her father know she was his "darling" and insinuating she was selling properties rather than cleaning bathrooms.

She hoped the smile in her eyes told Mateo she appreciated his efforts. But honestly, she'd sooner he didn't intervene. Whatever came today, she needed to stand up for herself, not as a child standing toe to toe with a disapproving parent, but as the self-respecting adult she'd become, and without too much of her father's help.

"Bailey's going back to school," Mateo was saying.

Her father looked half impressed. "Well, well. I said one day you'd regret dropping out." While Bailey set her teeth, Damon Ross spoke again to Mateo. "My daughter didn't attain her high school diploma," he said under his breath as if she hadn't learned to spell her own name.

Bailey studied that wedding portrait and, hands on the table's edge, pushed her chair out. She'd come here hoping—she'd wanted to make their father-daughter relationship work—but she was only hurting herself. Still, she wouldn't argue. Neither would she sit here a moment longer.

As she rose, her father stopped talking and looked up at her with eyes that, for a moment, were unguarded.

"Are you pouring more coffee?" he asked.

"Actually, Dad, we have to go."

Her father got to his feet. "You only just arrived."

"We can stay awhile longer," Mateo said, standing too.

But she pinned Mateo with a firm look that said he was wrong.

"Mateo," she said, "it's time to go."

While her father muttered that he didn't know what the rush was all about, Mateo's furrowed gaze questioned hers.

She peered up at the ceiling and almost groaned. She appreciated Mateo coming—appreciated everything he'd done—but this was her business. *Her* life. She'd gone through this game with her father too many times already.

Bailey walked away and the men's footfalls followed. At the door, she leaned toward her father and pressed a quick kiss to his cheek. When she drew back, her father's gaze was lowered on her wrist. On the bracelet.

"I see you haven't lost it yet," he said.

Her gaze went from the bracelet to her father's cheated look and a suffocating surge of hurt, and guilt, bubbled up inside her.

He just couldn't let her leave without mentioning that.

On the edge, she flicked open the bracelet's new clasp. "Know what, Dad?" Slipping the chain and its jingling charms from her wrist, she handed it over. "I want you to have this."

His brow furrowed. "But I gave it to *you*."

"Not the way I needed. The way she would've wanted you to."

"Don't start on—"

"Mum didn't ask to die," she plowed on. "She didn't want to leave us. I don't need this to know she loved me. It's sad but," she slapped the bracelet in his palm, "I think you need this more than me."

She headed down the path.

Mateo remote-unlocked his car a second before she reached for the passenger side handle. Churning inside, she kept her burning, disappointed gaze dead ahead while Mateo slid into the driver's side. He belted up, ignited the engine, shifted the gear into drive. Trying to even her breathing, she felt his gaze slide over.

"Your father's waiting on the doorstep," he told her. "Don't you think you ought to at least wave?"

Her stomach kicked and she screwed her eyes shut. "Don't try to make me feel guiltier than I already do."

Not about her father's behavior but because she *had* almost lost that bracelet, and she would never have forgiven herself if she had.

Mateo wrung the steering wheel with both hands. "He was a little out of line. But, Bailey, he's your father. We were there ten minutes. Do you really want to walk away, cut him off, again?"

Eyes burning, she continued to stare ahead. Mateo might want the chance to sit down and speak with his biological father, but she knew now hers would never listen. Would never understand. He wasn't the only one who'd felt lost when Ann Ross had died.

And while they were on the subject—if she was running away, hadn't Mateo in a sense run away too, from that little boy who would love to be his son?

But she wouldn't mention that. If she did, they'd have an argument and the way she was feeling—the way she'd thatched her fingers to stop her hands from shaking—she wouldn't be the one to back down.

While she glared out the windshield, Mateo sucked in an audible breath and wrenched the car away from the curb. They drove in silence home. When she got out of the car, she tried to make her way through the house and up that staircase before any tears could fall, but Mateo had other plans. Catching up, he grabbed her arm from behind. Tamping down hot emotion, she lifted her chin and turned around.

The chiseled plains of his face were set. "We need to talk."

"Not now."

She tried to wind away but he held her firm. "Don't let this get to you."

"I'd have thought you'd approve of me walking away."

Mateo had once said he was selfish. He was wrong. He was a hypocrite. Mateo might have had a good relationship with Ernesto, but there was a little boy back in France who had silently begged for years for the monsieur to accept him. Not so different from the way she wanted to be accepted by her father.

She shook her arm free and started up the stairs. It was better they didn't discuss it.

Mateo's steps sounded behind her. "I'm not the one you're angry with."

Her throat aching, she ground out, "Please. Mateo." *Please.* She continued up the stairs. "Leave me alone."

When an arm lassoed her waist and pitched her around, she let out a gasp as she fell. But before her back met the uneven ramp of the stairs, that arm was there again, scooped under and supporting her as Mateo hovered over her, daring her to try to walk away from him again.

But he didn't speak, and the longer he stayed leaning over her as she lay on the steps, his eyes searching hers, the more her tide of anger ebbed and gradually seeped away. But the hurt remained…for herself as well as for Remy. She doubted that would ever leave.

Her words came out a hoarse whisper.

"Why does he do that?"

Mateo exhaled and stroked her hair. "I don't know."

"I won't ever go back."

"You don't have to…if that's what you want."

Frustration sparked again. "I know what I want, Mateo."

His lips brushed her brow. "I know what *I* want."

She shifted onto her elbows. "Do you?"

He hesitated a heartbeat before his mouth slanted over and took hers.

His kiss was tender and at the same time passionate. Dissolving into the emotion, needing to completely melt away and forget, she reached for his chest and struggled with his shirt buttons. As the kiss deepened, he shifted too, rolling back each shoulder in turn as she peeled the sleeves off his powerful arms.

When his mouth finally left hers, her blood felt on fire. She didn't want to think about anything but this. Not her father or France or her bracelet. Only how Mateo made her feel time and again. She couldn't deny it any longer. As much as she'd set out to keep her head and her heart, she'd fallen in love with Mateo, an emotion that consumed her more and more each day.

His eyes closed, one arm curled around her head, he murmured against her parted lips. "Perhaps we ought to take this upstairs."

She sighed against his cheek. "If you want."

His brow pinched. Before he kissed her again, he said, "I want you."

Fifteen

Finished tapping in the final answer on the last form, Bailey held her breath and hit send. If everything went according to plan, in a couple of months she'd be busy studying, sending off her first assignments, on her way to getting that degree.

Sitting back in Mateo's home office chair, she had to grin over the majors she'd chosen. What were the odds? Then again, what were the odds she'd come to feel this way, this *deeply,* about Mateo?

A week had passed since their surprise visit to her father's house…since Mateo had defended her, challenged her, then pinned her on the stairs where they'd made love in a frenzied, soul stirring way they never had before. Her skin flashed hot to even think of the avalanche of emotions he'd brought out in her that day.

Mateo cared about her. He enjoyed her company. But even more, Mateo Celeca *believed* in her. Yes, for her sake he hoped she and her father could somehow, someday, make amends, but he respected her enough not to push. The same way she wouldn't push about Remy, no matter how strongly she felt those two should be together.

More and more she was coming to believe she and Mateo should stay together too. More than common sense said he could have his choice of companions, and yet he chose to be with her. Had asked her to stay. She couldn't help but wonder….

Exhaling, Bailey pushed that thought aside and, before signing off the computer, decided to check emails. A message from her friend Vicky Jackson popped up in reply to the email Bailey had sent when she'd discovered that first day back that her friend was out of town. Vicky was dying to hear all the news. Had she seen her dad yet? Had she met anyone wonderful? As always, Vicky wanted the gossip, just like the old days, bolts and all.

Bailey glanced around Mateo's red leather and rosewood office. So many amazing collectors' items. Even the ornate silver letter opener looked as if it belonged in a museum. Would her friend since school believe what had happened over the last few months? From backpacking around Europe, to settling down in Casa Buona, to being cornered into an engagement that had sent her on a desperate flight home to Australia. Best of all she'd gone and lost her heart. A huge romantic, when Vicky found out, she would go berserk!

Fingers on keys, she jumped right in.

Vicky! You wouldn't believe how I've lucked out. So much has happened since we saw each other last. But the main thing is that I found *the* guy. A keeper!

I'm sitting here now in his home study. Make that mansion! I'm actually cleaning houses atm. Long story.

But that's only temporary. I have *so* many plans—BIG plans—and Doctor Mateo Celeca is at the center of them all—

Bailey stopped, pricked her ears and listened. Mateo's car was cruising up the drive.

She tapped out a super quick "Talk soon," hit send, then jumped up. Mateo had said she could use this laptop anytime. She didn't feel guilty about taking him at his word. In fact, she'd come to feel wonderfully at home here. But, with him being gone for four hours, she was excited to have him back. Whenever she thought of him striding toward her, that dazzling smile reaching out and warming her all over, her knees went weak. She needed his kiss. More and more she wanted so much to let him know how deeply she felt.

What would he say if she did?

Mateo entered the house aware of the weight in his shirt pocket and the broad grin on his face.

Not so long ago he'd had no intention of getting overly involved with a woman. And yet, with Bailey, he was involved up to his chin. He'd spent his whole life avoiding the ghosts and hurdles of his past. He'd only needed his friends and the possessions he surrounded himself with. To open his heart—to consider marriage and children of his own—would mean to invite in vulnerability. Take on risk.

But late last night in the shadows, after he and Bailey had made love and he'd felt so at peace, he'd questioned himself. Searched his soul.

Did he *love* Bailey Ross?

Moving down the central hall now, Mateo rolled the question over in his mind but still the answer eluded him. He did know, however, that he had never felt this attracted to a woman before. He enjoyed, without reservation, Bailey's conversations and smiles. He looked forward to seeing her, kissing her, letting her know how much he valued her. And they were certainly beyond compatible in the bedroom.

In Paris he'd made a decision. To offer her commitment—a home, his affection—without unnecessary encumbrances. This morning he'd come to a different conclusion.

He may not be certain that he loved Bailey but he was wise enough to know he would never find this connection with anyone else. Today he intended to utter words that previously had not existed in his personal vocabulary. As soon as he found her, wherever she was hiding, he intended to ask her to be his bride.

He entered the kitchen, swung a glance around. Empty. Out in "their" garden, no sign of her among the statues either. A hand cupped around his mouth, he called out, "Bailey. I'm back."

He waited but the house was quiet. Then he had a thought. Before he'd left this morning, she'd asked if she could use his computer. A bounce in his step, he headed for the office.

A few seconds later he discovered that room empty too. But from the doorway he saw the internet browser on his laptop had been left open. The world was full of hackers, scammers, looking for a window to wiggle into and defraud. A person couldn't be too careful. Needing to log off, he crossed over and saw a message hadn't been closed. He moved the curser to save the draft at the same time a few words caught his eye.

BIG plans... A keeper...

His gaze slid to the top of the screen. He skimmed the entire message, lowered into his chair and read it again. After a fourth time, Mateo's hand bunched into a tight ball on the desk. There had to be a different way to interpret it. A different light from the murky one he'd latched on to. But, for the life of him, he couldn't grasp any other implication from this message than the one hitting him square between the eyes.

You wouldn't believe how I've lucked out. I found...a keeper!

Actually cleaning houses...that's only temporary... BIG plans—and Doctor Mateo Celeca is at the center of them all—

His gut kicked then twisted into a dozen sickening knots while his hand drifted to his shirt pocket. His fingers curled over the velvet pouch inside and tightened. Was her meaning as obvious as it seemed? Had he been wrong about Bailey? Emilio then Mama...Had she wormed her way into his feelings to manipulate him too?

Had he played the fool *again?*

"Mateo!" Bailey's call came from down the hall. "Where are you?"

He snapped back to the here and now and dabbed his clammy brow with his forearm. He had to think.

"Mateo?"

The call sounded close. He looked over and saw Bailey standing at the office door, looking slightly flushed, a brilliant smile painted across her face. She rushed forward and wasted no time plopping onto his lap and snatching a quick kiss.

"Guess what I did today?" She asked, beaming.

Although his mind was steaming, he kept his tone level. "Why don't you tell me?"

"I enrolled."

He forced a smile. "You did?"

"After looking into all the faculties' courses and searching myself about what I really wanted to accomplish, you won't believe what I've decided to be."

Out the corner of his eye, that email seemed to taunt him. "What did you decide?"

"I want to study law. Not criminal, like Dad, but human rights. I want to do my best helping those who don't have the education or means or, in some cases, the status to help themselves."

"That sounds…worthy."

Absently watching the motion, she curled some hair behind his ear. Where normally he would lean in against her touch, this minute it was all he could do not to wince. She had big plans.

Who was this woman?

Did he know her at all?

"Bridging courses are the first step," she went on, "a chance to catch up on high school stuff before tackling the full on units." She let out a happy sigh. "I'm so excited." Nuzzling down into his neck, she murmured against his jaw. "I missed you today. Where have you been?"

Mateo thought of the item in his pocket, and the rock that filled the space where his heart used to beat grew harder still. He shut his eyes and groaned. God, he wished he'd never seen that note.

Her cuddling stopped. Her lashes fluttered against his neck an instant before she drew away and searched his eyes, head slanting as she reached to cup his cheek.

"Is something wrong?"

His gaze penetrated hers as his jaw clenched more. He should ask her point blank, lay it on the table, and this time he wouldn't be hoodwinked. How could he be when the truth was there on that screen in black and white?

"You left your inbox open," he ground out.

She bit her lip. "Sorry. I rushed off when I heard your car."

"You sent a message to a friend."

She blinked. "That's right."

"It didn't go through."

Her brow furrowed and her gaze shot to the screen before it slid back to him. He could sense her mind ticking over. "Did you read it?"

When he moved, she shifted and he got to his feet.

"Mateo…"

He headed for the door. His throat wouldn't stop convulsing. He needed fresh air. Needed to get out of here and be alone for a while. But she stayed on his heels.

"Mateo, tell me what's wrong."

He peered down toward the foyer, to his elaborate staircase that, as large and grand as it was, didn't really lead anywhere…except to more furniture and art and antiques. He'd accumulated so much. Right now he felt as if he'd been stripped of everything.

When she touched his arm, his stomach jumped. He tried to find his calm center as he edged around. Her beautiful pale blue eyes were clouded with uncertainty, the indigo band around each iris darker than he'd ever seen. Blood pounded and crashed in his ears. She'd been caught and she knew it.

The words—his accusation—were on the tip of his tongue when the doorbell sounded. He thought of ignoring it, but he couldn't get what he needed to off his chest with some unknown person lurking on his doorstep. Leaving a desolate Bailey, he strode over, opened the door and was caught between a groan and smile.

Alex Ramirez stood with his hands in his pockets. Natalie, looking as beautiful as ever, was at her husband's side. Reece sat perched on her hip.

"We were on our way to a picnic," Alex said, sliding his

shades back on his head. "We thought you guys might want to join us."

"It's such a gorgeous day," Natalie added breezily, but a certain shadow in her eyes let him know something was amiss. Perhaps she was just overly tired.

"A picnic?" Bailey came forward. "I'd love to get out," she said as she looked across, "but Mateo might have something planned."

Mateo stepped aside. "Come in out of the heat."

"We have plenty of food and drink." Natalie entered the foyer while Reece kicked his legs as if he was riding a horse. "There's chicken and homemade potato salad. And plenty of room in the car. When you start a family you need to trade sports cars for roomier, safer options."

Mateo didn't miss the emphasis Natalie placed on *safer* or the way Alex's lips pressed together as he looked down and crossed his arms.

Mateo folded his arms too as he shared a look between them. "Is something wrong?"

Alex said, "No," at the same time Natalie said, "Actually, we wanted to speak with you—"

Alex groaned out a cautionary, *"Nat."*

"—about France," she finished.

And something else. Something important enough for them to show up unannounced. Not that he minded friends dropping in, but beneath the cheery exterior, some kind of trouble was upsetting Nat and Alex's usual state of marital bliss. And it seemed Natalie, at least, wanted him to referee.

Unfortunately, this was far from the ideal time. But he couldn't simply turn his good friends around and on their way. Not when Natalie's eyes were pleading with him to leave with them.

Mateo unfolded his arms. "Sure," he said, smiling, "we'd love to go."

Bailey spun on her heel. "Let me just race upstairs for a moment."

Natalie headed down the hall. "Do you mind if I use a bathroom? Reece sicked up a little on his shirt. He's had a cough."

"Of course." Mateo ran an assessing eye over the baby, but he didn't look flushed or ill. A little restless perhaps. "You know where the closest one is."

Alex waited until Natalie was out of earshot before he stepped closer.

"Sorry about this."

"No need to apologize. You're welcome any time."

There were simply more convenient times than others.

"It was Nat's idea we drop in. She values your opinion." Alex shrugged. "I do too."

"What's the problem?"

"Nat wanted to pin you down to get your take on—"

"All set!"

Alex stopped mid-sentence and both men's attention swung to the stairs. Bailey was bouncing down, a big bag over her shoulder. When she reached the foyer floor, she glanced around. "Where's Nat?"

"Here we are."

Natalie emerged, baby Reece resting on her hip, his cheek on her shoulder. Carefully, she handed him over to Alex. "I'm afraid he's getting a little too heavy for Mummy to carry."

"Babies do grow up," Alex said, swinging Reece onto his own hip.

"But they still need protecting."

"In lots of ways," Alex pointed out.

Mateo opened the door. "We should go."

As they headed out the door, Bailey went to loop her arm through his but he hadn't forgotten that email. How the truth had made him feel. Grinding his back teeth, he hastened his step, caught up with Alex and helped him put Reece in his seat.

As they all buckled up and Alex pulled out down the drive, Bailey tried to keep her spirits high even though she felt completely off balance.

When Mateo had come home she'd been on cloud nine. Now, for reasons she couldn't explain, there was nothing but tension all around. Between Mateo and her. Alex and Natalie. Even Mateo and Alex! Hugging the gift bag containing that builder's kit close, she studied Reece when he coughed. Even the baby didn't seem overly happy.

As if to prove it, the little guy barked again.

Natalie swung around to check on him but Alex put his hand on her arm and spoke to those in the back, as if he wanted to divert the focus.

"So tell me, has Paris changed?"

Mateo was glaring out the window. "The Louvre's still there."

"So you said hello to the *Mona Lisa?*"

Bailey answered Alex this time. "It was amazing to see her for real."

"And the orphanage?"

Mateo again. "Going well."

"Did you see that little boy? Remy?" Natalie peered around again. "Is he still there?"

"Quite a few have found families," Mateo said, and Bailey almost shivered at his tone. A stay-away-from-that-subject-today timbre.

Still, Natalie persisted. "But not Remy? He hasn't found a home yet?"

When Mateo's hands bunched on his lap, Bailey answered for him.

"Remy's still there. Barely says a word. But his little girlfriend makes up for it. Clairdy never stops talking."

"How old is he now?" Natalie persisted. "Five? Six?"

Mateo leaned forward. "This is a good park. Plenty of shade. Great views of the harbor."

Alex pulled in and they unloaded the picnic basket from the back while Natalie and Bailey took care of the baby. They found a shady spot overlooking the blue water and spread out two large checkered blankets.

"Would you like to go again?" Natalie placed Reece down and fished for a toy to occupy him from her diaper bag. "To France, I mean?"

"Actually, we'd kind of discussed that." Bailey slid a glance over.

Mateo's chest tightened as he took in her curious look. "Depends on my schedule," he replied as he found the thermos.

Bailey could go to France again but it wouldn't be with him. She'd exchanged paying back the price of her ticket home from Italy for an all-expenses first-class trip to Europe. She'd done well. And when they were alone again, he'd tell her exactly that—a moment before he told her to pack her bag and leave.

He'd had doubts from the start. And when that security guard had delayed them in Paris, he'd suffered more than a niggle. Now he knew why. There was reason to be suspicious. Hell, even her own father didn't trust her.

"Which part did you like best?" Natalie was saying, handing Reece a clear ball with jigsaw cut-outs and corresponding shapes inside.

"There were so many amazing things." Bailey fumbled as she laid out the plastic plates and they went in all directions over the blanket. "I couldn't choose just one."

Reece threw the ball then let out another cough and another. Mateo's doctor antennae went up.

"Has he had that long?"

"A couple of days," Natalie said.

Alex added, "But the doctor explained he couldn't give him his scheduled shots until he's completely well."

"*If* we decide he should be immunized," Natalie said.

Alex ran a hand through his hair. "Nat, we've discussed this."

"No. *You* made a decision for all three of us."

Reece began to grumble. Making *shushing* sounds, Natalie folded down beside him and handed back the ball.

Alex set his hands on his hips. "Mateo, save me. Tell her children need to be immunized."

"But there are side effects," Natalie interjected. "Sometimes serious ones. There are risks, aren't there, Mateo?"

Mateo considered the two of them—Natalie so passionate about protecting her boy from possible harm, Alex in exactly the same position, just looking at possible dangers differently. No one ever said parenting was easy. This decision might be a no-brainer for a lot of folks. For others, whether or not to immunize was the beginning of a whole host of moral battles associated with the responsibilities of being a mother or father. He should thank Bailey for inadvertently showing him her true colors and saving him from all this.

"In my professional opinion," he began, "I would have to say that the benefits far outweigh any possible dangers."

Natalie's slim nostrils flared then she dropped her gaze. "It's not that easy when it's your own child, Mateo." Holding her brow, she pushed out a breath and apologized. "I'm sorry. There was just this horrible story on the news the other night about the possible effects of shots. The footage was shocking. And then Sally from work said she knew of a couple who had a similar experience with their toddler. He was never the same again." Natalie peered up with haunted eyes. "Some kids *die*. Once it's done you can't take it back."

Mateo scrubbed his jaw. Natalie did need sleep. And reassurance. This decision obviously meant a lot to her. To both of them. As it should. But it wasn't *his* decision.

When Reece began to whimper, confused at seeing his mother upset, Alex crossed over, kneeled beside his family and hugged them tight. He brushed the words over his wife's crown. "We'll work it out, darling. Don't worry."

Mateo sat down with his friends and while Bailey made chicken sandwiches, he spoke to Natalie and Alex candidly. With any vaccination there could be side effects, but most often minor ones. Immunization was a way to curb and even eliminate deadly diseases in both children and adults. Ultimately the burden of research and decision was on the parents' shoulders.

But he conceded…Natalie was right. Rationalizing must sound pat when the child concerned wasn't your own. Natalie seemed reassured somewhat.

In the dappled sunshine, they finished their sandwiches—Reece ate almost a whole one. The packing up had begun when Bailey remembered. "I left something in the car."

She returned with a gift bag and handed it to Natalie. "This is for Reece. Mateo picked it out."

Mateo averted his gaze. He'd been happy to choose the gift but memories of the day also brought back the image of that security guard and his own suspicions. Come to think of it, Bailey hadn't emptied her pockets that day. She'd merely pulled out the bracelet.

But that was all water under the bridge. As charming as she was, that email had proven her more mercenary nature beyond a doubt. Duped by her own hand. He didn't care what excuses she came up with.

Natalie helped Reece unwrap the gift. He instantly grabbed

the hammer and thumped the ground. He squealed with delight when the tool squeaked and whistled.

Alex gently ruffled his son's head. "That's my boy."

Mateo took in the scene and knew he ought to be happy for them. But, even when he wanted to deny them, the truth was that other emotions were winning out. Ugly emotions like envy and disappointment.

This morning he'd come home thinking that soon he would be a married man. He'd been prepared to do what three months ago no one could have convinced him to try. He'd wanted to risk. Was willing to try for a family of his own. After finding the truth out about Bailey, he would never consider taking that kind of risk again.

After they'd packed up, Alex and Natalie dropped them home. Mateo headed for the door without waiting. He knew Bailey would follow, and out of the earshot of neighbors, he'd tell her precisely what he thought.

Bailey stood, stunned, watching Mateo's broad shoulders roll away as he ascended the stairs to his porch then unlocked and entered the house. She held her sick stomach, unable to comprehend how he could be so angry over that email to Vicky. Yes, she'd been pretty open in suggesting she thought there was—and wanted there to be—a future for them. She knew how he felt about marriage and children. God knows she hadn't wanted to get this involved either.

But now he was acting as though she was some weirdo with an attachment disorder. After the way he'd treated her—like a princess—*dammit,* that just wasn't fair. He'd led her on, set her up to trust him and…yes, *love* him. She thought he was falling in love with her too.

Back straight, she started for the stairs.

If he thought she would cower in a corner and accept this

behavior—the way Mateo had intimated she ought to take her father's sorry treatment—he was sadly mistaken.

When she strode in the door, he was waiting for her by the stairs. Given her dark expression, he knew what to expect. She was primed to defend herself, but he wasn't prepared to let this demise ramble on. He'd get to the point. Then she could leave.

"These past years I thought I had everything I could ever want," he told her as she crossed over to where he stood. "I thought I was content. And then I met you."

A range of emotions flashed over her face. First happiness. Lastly suspicion. "I'm not sure what you're saying."

"When I came home earlier I intended to ask you to marry me."

He extracted the blue jewelry pouch from his shirt pocket, loosened the string and tipped the ring into his palm. Five carats. The jeweler said his fiancée would love it. More than ever, Mateo felt certain that she would have.

Her incredulous gaze drifted from the ring to his eyes. Then her cheeks pinked up and her throat made a muted high-pitched noise.

"When you were out this morning you bought this?"

He inspected the diamond, tipping the stone so the light caught then radiated pale geometric patterns on the walls.

"I wasn't sure of the fit," he said. "The jeweler said I could take it back." That was precisely what he intended to do now. His fingers closed over the stone and his voice lowered to a rough-edged growl. "You have no idea how betrayed I felt when I read that email."

Bailey simply stared, looking as if she were taken aback and even annoyed. "Betrayed is a pretty strong word."

He almost sneered. "I shouldn't feel manipulated when you told that friend you wouldn't be cleaning floors for long?"

"I said that because eventually I'll get my degree."

"What you said was that you had big plans. That you'd lucked out."

"Well, I did feel lucky to have—" she stopped, blinked, then coughed out a humorless laugh.

"Wait a minute. You think I'm here...that I share your bed..." Her eyes glistened at the same time her face pinched as if she'd swallowed a teaspoon of salt. "You think I'm sleeping with you for your *money?*"

He huffed. "I'm sure as hell not sleeping with you because of yours."

When her eyes filled with moisture and hurt, Mateo cursed as a blade sliced between his ribs and twisted.

He inhaled deeply. "I apologize. I shouldn't have said that."

"Mateo, if you felt you needed to say it, believe me, I needed to hear it."

She wound around him and started up the stairs.

He called after her. "So you're going."

She stopped at the same spot where they'd made love a few days before. Her face was pale. Her hands trembled, even as they gripped the banister. He imagined she felt determined... and maybe, with her plans ruined, even crushed.

Join the club.

"You truly believe I'm nothing but a gold digger?"

He should have been prepared for it. The threat of tears. The indignation. Of course she wasn't going to admit it. "Bailey, there's no other way to read it."

Through narrowed eyes, she nodded as if she were seeing him for the first time.

"I'm such a fool."

"And how does that feel?"

She ignored his sarcasm. "Could you believe I thought you

were upset because you'd found out I'd fallen in love with you?"

His head kicked back but then that certain coldness rose up again. "Don't play with me."

"This morning I thought I'd really found the perfect guy, that fate had finally smiled on me again. An intelligent, good-looking professional with a sense of humor who had a heart to boot. Hell, I thought you were way too good for me." She dropped over her shoulder as she continued up the stairs, "Turns out I'm too good for you."

Sixteen

Bailey had been packed and gone from Mateo Celeca's house in ten minutes flat. He wasn't anywhere around, and she was glad of it. Nothing he could say would change her mind about leaving, and if she'd seen his supercilious face, she would have needed to let him know again how disappointed she was. Disappointed in herself as well. For believing and hoping too much.

Now, a week later she was entering Natalie's real estate office. The receptionist buzzed through and a moment later Natalie breezed out from a back office, the smile wide on her face. She beckoned Bailey inside.

"I wasn't expecting you."

"I just finished cleaning my last house for the day. I hope this isn't an inconvenient time." Bailey took a seat while Natalie shut her office door then lowered into a chair behind her orderly desk.

"What can I do for you? Personal or private?"

"Both. You obviously don't know yet. Mateo and I broke up last week."

Her expression dropped. "I can't believe it. You said you'd had such a perfect time in France."

"We did. So perfect I fell in love with him."

Natalie nodded as if she understood. "He hasn't tried to contact you since you left?"

"No. And I don't want him to."

"He's always said he didn't want to know about vows and rings." Annoyed, Natalie flicked a pencil away. "I love Mateo but he's so stubborn on that. People come into our lives. Things change."

"Actually, Mateo bought a ring. The most beautiful ring I've ever seen."

Natalie's eyes rounded. "He proposed and you said no?"

Bailey relayed the story about the email, how Mateo had misinterpreted the message and how he wasn't prepared to view it from a different, more flattering light.

"I'm sorry," Natalie said, "but it sounds like a timely excuse to me." Bailey waited for her to explain. "For Mateo to have gone so far as to buy a diamond, he *must* be in love with you. But it doesn't sound as if he's ready to look beyond the past."

"I know he has issues with family. That he feels as if his parents abandoned him, his biological father particularly."

That was a big part of the reason he kept his emotions concerning Remy reined in so tight.

"There's something else," Natalie admitted. "Mateo was in love once before, many years ago. From what Alex tells me, she was not a nice type. She preyed on Mateo's good nature and generosity. He gave and gave but nothing was ever enough. They'd have arguments then make up. Alex said Mateo wasn't prepared to ever go through that kind of rollercoaster affair again. It scared him to think what would happen if he married a self-centered woman like that and they had a family. If he died and she abandoned the children."

Bailey tried to absorb the details as she gazed blindly at some document on the desk. "He wanted to marry her and she used him...."

"She didn't so much use him as bleed him dry."

Bailey's gaze flew up. "I wasn't with Mateo because of his money, what he could give me—"

"Oh, honey, I know."

Natalie skirted the desk and put her arms around her, but that didn't help Bailey from feeling gutted. She understood his reasoning a little better, but whatever lay in his past, Mateo was wrong to have jumped to any conclusions without giving her an opportunity to explain. She was tired of feeling as if she weren't good enough. As if she continually had to prove herself.

Moving away, Natalie leaned back on the edge of the desk. "Would you like Alex to talk to him?"

Bailey shook her head. "I'm here about my job. After the break you gave me, I wanted to give you plenty of notice. I've enrolled in classes and I'll be starting work in the university canteen closer to the time. If you don't mind, I'd like to stay on till then. I found a small place to rent and, frankly, I need the money."

The apartment wasn't much more than a room with a tiny bath attached. But it was affordable and clean and, most importantly, all hers.

"Of course you can stay on as long as you need to," Natalie said. "And I'm so pleased for you about the classes. But I do wish you'd let Alex have a word with Mateo."

Bailey found her feet. "It wouldn't work. Even if we got back together, he'd always wonder about my true feelings. Whether or not I'm a fraud." And, right or wrong, she didn't think she could ever get over the anger and disappointment that consumed her whenever she thought of his mistrust. "Still, I hope he finds someone who can make him happy."

Natalie sighed. "Alex and I thought he had."

The two women hugged and promised to keep in touch after Bailey handed in her notice. She was on her way out when she remembered to ask, "Did you and Alex come to a decision about Reece's shots?"

"We're going to take him in next week."

Bailey smiled. "I'm sure he'll be fine."

As she made her way to the bus stop, she rolled over in her mind their conversation. Given Mateo had gone so far as to buy her that ring, Natalie seemed convinced that he loved her. Bailey hadn't confessed that he'd barely batted an eye when she'd admitted that *she* loved *him*. Then again, given his doubtful nature—his ill-fated affair—he would only think she'd been playing her trump card to keep her foot in his door and her body in his bed.

Cringing, she walked faster.

She may not be a virgin but she would only ever sleep with a man if she wanted to share that most intimate part of herself with him. She hadn't been prepared to do that with Emilio, not that Mateo needed to know. The truly sad part was that she'd been burned enough by her Italian episode. Once bitten... Now, like Mateo, she couldn't imagine trusting anyone that much again. To know that he believed she would barter sex for a well-to-do lifestyle—that what they'd shared was essentially a lie—made her want to give up on relationships altogether.

As she neared the bus stop, a tall, suited figure stepped out from behind the shelter. When she recognized the height, the profile, every drop of blood froze in her veins. She was ready to turn straight around and walk away. She didn't want to see him. Didn't need to talk. But another, more resilient part propelled her on at the same time as that man came forward too.

She was shaking inside, but that didn't stop her from standing tall when she pulled up before him.

"What are you doing here? How did you know where to find me?"

"Since you left that morning after our argument," her father said, "I've kept track of your movements. I was about to take a deep breath and knock on your Mateo's front door before I saw you storm out. I contacted Mateo. He explained you two had had a falling out, and he told me which agency you worked for. The lady at the desk explained you were on their books to clean properties. I've waited around every day since, working through what I'd say when I saw you next."

Bailey swallowed against the emotion rising in her throat. "What did you come up with?"

"I don't know if she ever told you," Damon Ross said in a thick, graveled voice, "but your mother and I chose that bracelet together."

She wanted to clamp her hands over her ears. Instead she held them up. "I'm done fighting over that."

"I wanted to get you a gold pin with your name on it," he went on. "But, like always," his smile was both sad and fond, "Ann had her way. And, I'll give it to her, usually she was right. But not always." In his pristine jacket, his shoulders stooped. "Sometimes she was dead wrong."

Bailey's chest ached so badly she didn't want to take another breath. Her father had never opened up like this before. As if he genuinely wanted to help her understand. Still, that lesser part of her whispered in her ear. *Walk away. Say something that will hurt him for a change.* But she couldn't. When everything was said and done, he was her father and he was reaching out. But she needed to make him understand too.

"I know you miss her," she said, "but, Dad, I miss her, too."

He nodded slowly as his gaze trailed off.

"I thought something was wrong," he admitted. "We can all have trouble remembering where we put the keys. We've all missed appointments. But when she couldn't coordinate your activities…when she forgot to pick you up from school…" His features hardened and he thrust out his chin. "I told her I was taking her for a checkup. Yes, she was a free spirit. That's what I loved about her most. She always wanted to do it her way. But just that once—"

He paused and air leaked from his chest before he went on.

"Just that once, I wish she'd have listened." His chin firmed up again. "I should have insisted. Taken her to the doctor myself instead of buttoning my lip when she insisted it was nothing."

Her throat clogged, Bailey's thoughts raced. She couldn't get her mind around what he was saying.

"You blame yourself for her stroke?"

"Sometimes…yes, I do. Her grandmother died of an aneurysm at a young age. Her own mother died of similar complications the year before she passed." His eyes met hers and he smiled. "You're so like her. So headstrong."

"Is that why you pushed me away?"

"Makes no sense to say it aloud but I didn't want to lose you too. I made a pact the day we buried your mother that no matter how much I might want to give in to you, you'd do as you were told. I was going to protect and guide you and I didn't care if you ended up hating me because of it."

"I never hated you." Her voice cracked. "I just couldn't understand why you were so…distant. When Mom was alive, everything seemed so simple." So warm and so safe. "When she died, it felt like the biggest part of me died with her. After the funeral I felt so alone. I got mixed up with the wrong crowd and dropped out because I didn't think anyone cared."

He closed his eyes for a moment as if wishing he could take all those hurt feelings away. "Every day since you left I told myself that I shouldn't be so hard on you. I should be happy to watch you grow, make your mistakes."

She admitted, "I made a few."

"Most of them because I wasn't there the way I should have been."

He fished into his suit jacket pocket. When his hand opened, the gold chain and charms shone out like the treasure that it was. His eyes glistened with unshed tears.

"This is yours."

He took her hand and laid the bracelet in her palm. She gazed down, remembering those happy childhood days—her mother and the father she'd loved so much—and her heart rolled over. Tears ready to fall, she rested her cheek on her father's shoulder and Damon Ross at last brought his daughter close.

Mateo downed the last of his scotch, set his glass on the clubhouse counter and gestured to the bartender. He needed another drink. Make that a double.

Beside him, Alex held up a hand. "No more for me. I told Nat I'd be home by six-thirty."

Mateo argued. "We only got off the course an hour ago."

"And I'm ready to gloat to my wife about how I beat you on both the front *and* back nine." Alex's mouth shifted to one side. "Not that you've been focused on anything much lately."

Two weeks had passed since Bailey had walked out. Admittedly, he'd been preoccupied. Mateo was gesturing to the bartender again.

"I'll be back at work soon."

"And you think that'll help?"

Mateo pretended not to hear that last comment. It was high time he got back to the practice. He was going crazy hanging around that big house. Nothing to do. Only ghosts to talk to. When he'd been with Bailey he'd been happy to postpone visiting Mama. Since she'd gone, he'd considered flying to Italy to fill in the time more than anything, but he knew if he happened upon Emilio he might just punch him in the nose.

"Why don't you come back and have dinner at home with us," Alex said. "Natalie would love to see you. Reece too. I told you he had his shots earlier this week."

"A couple of times. I'm glad there weren't any serious side-effects."

Alex raised his brows. "You're not the only one. So, what about dinner?"

"Thanks. I'll have something here."

Mateo collected his fresh glass while Alex asked to settle his tab.

As Alex brought the leather booklet closer and looked over the items, he asked, "Ever heard the saying, love never comes easy?"

"I'm not in the mood for a lecture." Mateo swirled his ice.

"What about some sound words from a friend then?"

"She's gone, Alex." Mateo took a long sip. Swallowed and enjoyed the burn. "No happily ever afters here."

Alex signed and waited for the bartender to leave before he thatched his hands on the timber counter and asked, "Why do you hold on to it so fiercely?"

"Hold on to what?"

"You're not losing anything by admitting you love her."

"You know, you're right." Mateo found his feet. "Time to go."

"To that great big empty house," Alex reminded him,

following out of the crowded room filled with nineteenth hole chatter.

At the exit, Mateo stopped and rotated around. "I let Bailey know I thought she was a con."

Alex shrugged. "You were wrong."

"Yeah. I was wrong."

He'd let Bailey walk away that day two weeks ago, telling himself he had no choice. He was protecting himself. Doing the right thing. But he'd printed off that email and as the hours and then days passed, he read it over again and again. Bailey had insisted that her dialogue in that email had been that of a woman in love. In love with him. He hadn't wanted to listen. Even when his heart wanted to believe it, his brain didn't want to take the risk. Because this kind of decision was only the beginning. When you were a couple, you had to tend the garden every day, do everything you could to make certain the union survived. And if it didn't...if the marriage failed and you had kids...

Mateo headed for the cab stand.

Better that things had turned out the way they did.

Alex was on his tail. The sun was lying low, getting ready to set. The air was muggy. Stifling. Mateo was a whisker from ripping off his shirt.

"So admit it."

Mateo looked at Alex, striding beside him. "Admit what?"

"That you were wrong."

"Just did."

"To *her*."

"Sure. I suppose I could kick it off with something like... 'Hey, Bailey, I was wondering if you could ever forgive me for being the world's biggest jerk.'"

Alex tugged his ear. "That's a start."

Mateo confessed, "I found that message and—" What felt

like a sharpened pencil drove into his temple. Growling, he waved off the rest. "Ah, forget it."

But Alex wasn't letting him off. "And what?"

Mateo stopped and studied his feet. His heart.

"And suddenly…I felt as if I had nothing. Was nothing. It's weird. I have so much. Too damn much. But where it counts…" He shut his eyes. *Oh God.* "I'm empty."

"You don't have to be."

Mateo's jaw shifted as his stomach sank more. "I never knew my biological parents."

Alex rested his hand on his friend's shoulder. "You'd make a great father."

"Bailey said that to me once."

"She's a wise lady."

"And I'm a jackass."

"Not usually but in this instance…"

Mateo looked over. Alex was grinning.

He would've liked to smile back but he shrugged instead. "How do I fix this? What on earth do I say?"

"The sixty-four million dollar question." Alex flagged down a cab. "The truth is always a good place to start."

Seventeen

"Just shout if it's a bad time to drop in."

Knowing that voice, feeling her heart instantly crash against her ribs, Bailey gathered herself in record time and turned to face her attractive, uninvited guest.

"Okay," she said, devoid of emotion. "It's a bad time to drop in."

She angled back to climb her building's first flight of stairs. Mateo Celeca was right there beside her, his arms out, offering to carry her grocery bags.

"I'll help with those," he said.

Ignoring him, she kept climbing.

"Nice complex," he said when they reached the first landing.

She leveled him a glare—*Go away!*—and went on walking.

"Nat said you handed in notice at the real estate agency," he said.

She groaned and kept walking. "Whatever it is you've come to say, please, just say it."

"I thought we could catch a coffee some place."

"Thank you. No."

She tackled the last of the stairs and crossed to her apartment's front door.

"Bailey, I want to say I'm sorry."

His words hit her so hard she lost her breath. But apologies didn't make a difference in how she felt. She bolstered her resolve.

"Terrific." She placed her bags on the ground, found her key and fit it in the lock. "Goodbye."

"Also, I need to mention I was an idiot. I made assumptions and I shouldn't have."

She bent to retrieve the bags, but he'd collected them and was already moving around her and inside. Her tongue burned to let loose and tell him to get out before she called security. But why not let him see how she lived now? He might need all his "stuff" but she certainly did not. Cozy suited her just fine.

"A bit different from what you're used to," she said as he slid the bags on the modest kitchenette counter.

His brows knitted, he cast a glance around. "It's, ah, very clean."

Then, as if she'd invited him to stay, he pulled out a stool. Not happening. Since speaking with her father—making amends there—she'd progressed by leaps and bounds this last week. New place, new job and new life on the way. She wasn't prepared to take a backward step now. She would not let her past feelings for Mateo hoodwink her into thinking for a moment "this" was anything other than over.

"I understand you must feel bad about what you said and even worse about how you acted. You should. But you've said sorry. Hell, I'll even accept the apology. Now," she fanned the door open, "have a nice life."

Not quite a smile, his mouth tugged to one side. "You don't mean that."

"Actually, I don't. But *I wish you nothing but happiness* would've been even harder to believe."

A muscle leapt to life in his cheek as he pushed to his feet. By the time he'd strolled over, Bailey's pulse had climbed so high, she swore it hit a bell. But he didn't sweep her up into his arms and carry her away. He didn't even try to crowd her back against the wall and kiss her. He merely closed the door, then gestured for her to take a seat.

Holding her ground, Bailey crossed her arms.

"It's over, Mateo. I can spell it out for you if you like, but other than that, if you don't mind I have things to—"

She'd reached to turn the door handle. In an instant, his hot hand had covered hers and her gaze jumped to his, his face set and passionate. God help her, he'd never looked more handsome.

"Bailey, what we shared is a long way from over."

Wrenching back, she moved well away. She didn't need to get that close to him. Didn't need to smell his musky scent. Feel that animal heat.

"Do you think that little of me?" She asked. "*Turn on the charm and she'll forget how I suggested she could be bought.* Dr. Celeca, you could be the richest, most powerful, best looking man in the world and it wouldn't make a scrap of difference as to how I feel about you now."

"I understand."

She looked at him sideways then blinked.

"Well…*good.*"

"From the moment we met," he said, "I made assumptions. I was hard on you, suspicious. Not because of Mama and

Emilio. I'm sure I believed you on both counts near to the start."

"So you made me feel like a felon because it rains on Tuesdays?"

A smile curved his lips as he prowled two steps nearer.

"I was hard on you because you made me look at myself. Not the doctor or investor or benefactor. At the *stripped down* me with absolutely nothing to hide behind. And, *Dio buono,* that scared me like you wouldn't believe."

Breathing shallow, she rotated away. *I don't want to hear this. It won't make a difference.*

"Before I met you," he went on, "I knew what I wanted. Success. Security. If I had somewhere solid where I felt I belonged, I had everything I needed. But all the possessions in the world could never be enough because what I need can't be bought."

She shrugged. "Take a bow."

An arm wound around her waist but not firmly enough. She maneuvered out and held up both hands.

"This has gone on long enough. I'd like to say we could be friends but—"

"Dammit, Bailey, I want more than your friendship."

He hadn't raised his voice but something in the timbre set her nerves jangling and her blood racing even faster.

"I know what you want," she said. "But I'm happy the way I am. There are goals I want to accomplish and I want to achieve them my way."

"There's no room for *our* way?" he asked.

She thought of her father's admission—of how her mother hadn't wanted his help when she'd needed it most—and a sliver of doubt pierced her armor.

"I've thought long and hard about this," Mateo said, coming close again. "The way I see it, this is about trust. I needed to trust you. Now you need to trust me."

She huffed and stepped back. "Sorry. Tried that."

"And I let you down."

"Damn right you did."

"But love is about forgiveness."

"No one mentioned *love*." At least he hadn't.

"I have something for you."

She lifted her brows at his change of subject. She guessed what his something was.

"I'm not interested in your big diamond ring, Mateo."

"It's not a ring. I only hope you like it enough." He reached into his trouser pocket and retrieved something small and gold.

Bailey's heart pounded as she gazed down at the Eiffel Tower trinket nestled in the palm of his hand. She couldn't help it. Her eyes misted over and she suddenly felt so weak... so *vulnerable*.

"France was only a week out of our lives."

"The most important week," he said. "The week we fell in love. I love you, Bailey. You loved me then. I'm here because I need to know...do you love me still?"

She searched his eyes...searched her heart. The truth wasn't that simple.

"I don't know," she said.

"Because I made a mistake." Before she could answer, he went on. "An unbelievably huge mistake." Pressing her lips together, she nodded. "Your father made mistakes too. You've made mistakes."

"I don't know that I can forgive you that one."

"I understand." He stepped nearer. "I do." His palm trailed her cheek, her chin. "I'd do anything to take it back."

She closed her eyes to shut out the bitter sting and ache of emotion. "I never wanted your money."

"I always wanted you." A light kiss dropped on the side

of her mouth. "Marry me, Bailey. Be my wife. I need you in my life and you need me. Every day. Every night."

"Because you love me."

He groaned against her lips. "So much."

"And because…"

His hand covered hers and the charm. "Because…?"

Overcome with emotion, finally beaten and glad of it, she gazed into his eyes and admitted.

"Because I love you."

His eyes flashed a heartbeat before his mouth lowered and captured hers.

She was helpless to deny the pleasure, couldn't stop herself from pressing in. As one palm cradled the back of her head and his steaming hard body curled over hers, Bailey could only cling to his shoulder, grateful tears squeezing from her eyes, heart filled to overflowing.

When his lips reluctantly left hers, her head was spinning. But his smile, so close, and his hands, so warm, left her wonderfully anchored.

"Marry me," he whispered.

Another tear slid down her cheek as she took a breath and surrendered. "Yes, Mateo," she murmured. "I'll marry you. I want to be your wife."

A tingling wave of desire and contentment spiraled through her as the man she couldn't help but adore—the soul mate she couldn't help but trust in—kissed her once more. Bailey held on, smiling…belonging…believing…

All the world lay in the palm of their hands.

Epilogue

Mateo had decided this should be a surprise. Bailey argued; everyone liked to be given at least some notice before guests drop by. When he pulled up outside Ville Laube's Chapelle and Madame Garnier's face lit with amazement, then a group of children edged forward, he laughed and, leaning over, snatched a kiss from his beautiful bride's cheek.

"You see," he said. "Sometimes it's good to be caught off guard."

"I know someone who's going to be a little more than that."

But they'd already agreed. Mateo would give Remy his gift in private. There were other bombshells to drop first.

As the new Dr. and Mrs. Celeca moved forward and the crowd of kids grew larger, someone in the tower rang the bell. Nichole Garnier was one of the first to meet them. Holding her face, she looked lost for words.

Mateo kissed both Madame's cheeks.

"I don't understand," Nichole started. "We only said goodbye. How long are you staying?"

"A while." He and Bailey shared a look. *A long while.*

Mateo was about to explain when he caught sight of Remy, standing by the side, one mitten cupping his brow.

"Remy!" Mateo called out. "Come say hello."

By now children were racing around them, hugging their guests' legs and singing as if school was out for a year.

Laughing too, Madame demanded to know. "Tell me! What are you doing here?"

"Bailey and I have decided to move to France permanently. There's still a mountain of forms to fill out and sign, but—"

"Mon dieu." Madame interrupted. *"Here?"*

"Actually, over there."

When he waved toward his cottage, Nichole failed to catch her yelp of delight.

Clairdy was there dancing around, first like a ballerina then a break dancer. Laughing, Bailey crouched down beside her little friend. "Do you understand, Clairdy?"

Nichole ran a hand over the little girl's head and spoke in French. Up to speed now, Clairdy's eyes sparkled before she cartwheeled away and back again. She was telling the other children. *Monsieur and Mademoiselle are married and living here with us!*

Remy must have heard; he came running up, full speed. Mateo bent to catch his hare. The momentum swung them both halfway around. After the commotion settled enough, Mateo drew Remy away, out of others' earshot.

"I have some other news, Remy." He held the boy's hand and continued to speak in French. "Bailey and I would like you to live with us."

But Remy didn't react the way Mateo had hoped. His face filled with uncertainty and his wide eyes darted first right then left. Frowning, Mateo shifted. He hadn't explained properly.

"Remy, if you want me to be your father…" He inhaled deeply and said the words he'd held back for too long. "I'd like you to be my son."

But the boy's expression furrowed more. He looked as if he'd been given the biggest gift under the tree but for some reason couldn't open it.

With a knuckle, Mateo gently tipped up his chin. "What's wrong?"

"Monsieur, I cannot go." The boy held a hand out to where his friend stood dancing with the others. "I cannot leave Clairdy behind."

"You want Clairdy to come with us?" Mateo smiled. "To be your sister?"

"She will be good," Remy promised. "She won't talk too much. I'll tell her."

Mateo chuckled. "We've already thought about your Clairdy. If she'd like to join our little family, we'd love to have her."

Remy gave a *yip!* then raced off to tell Clairdy the good news while Mateo raveled his wonderful wife into his arms.

"I'm thinking we need a dog. How about a Labradoodle?"

Bailey wrapped her arms around his neck and stole a kiss. "You remembered?"

"Why don't we name him after your father?"

"Damon the Labradoodle?" She nodded. "I like it. He can keep you and Remy company while you work on the cottage."

"Yes. Another couple of rooms."

"A cubbyhouse out back."

Letting out a breath, he took in his surroundings…the majesty of the Chapelle surround by a pile of noisy children. "How strange that I should end up back here."

"I think it's perfect. Well, *almost* perfect." She stroked his cheek and spoke earnestly. "Mateo, now I have a surprise for you."

She tilted her chin over his shoulder.

A man was walking up and for a moment Mateo thought he knew him…the hawkish nose, those kind, light gray eyes. Something unique about the way he walked. Mateo's mind wound back, further and faster. Absently he touched the scar on one side of his lip then shook his head slowly.

It couldn't be.

The name came out a threadbare croak.

"Henri?"

Upon him now, the man hugged him tight and then Mateo knew for certain. His childhood friend who had left all those years ago. Mateo never thought they'd see each other again.

"You are the same," Henri said, laughing and clapping Mateo's shoulder.

Beaming, Mateo brushed the top of Henri's head. "You're taller!"

Henri's gaze hooked onto Bailey, her hands clasped under her chin. He exclaimed, "This is the lady we have to thank for finding and bringing us here."

Mateo pinned Bailey with a curious look.

You did this?

Looking set to burst, she nodded. Now Mateo was the one lost for words.

"I hear you're married, Mateo. And after marriage," Henri said, "comes children. I'm afraid you have some catching up to do." Henri stepped aside. A woman with three children stood behind him. "My wife, Talli. These three rascals belong to us."

The rascals, introduced as Mimi, Luc and Andre, asked if they could play then ran off to join in the other children's games while Nichole rushed inside to have more settings placed for lunch. While Talli and Bailey chatted, Mateo and Henri caught up. Henri lived many miles from the Chapelle. His adoptive father had died and his adoptive mother married again. Change of name, a few changes of address. It made sense that Mateo's search for him had come up empty.

"Until Nichole and your beautiful wife put their heads together. They left no stone unturned."

Mateo explained about Ernesto, his move to Australia and how he'd decided to give up his practice there to live and enjoy a simpler life here.

When Nichole called everyone in for lunch, Mateo held Bailey back.

"I have never been so surprised," he told her as he brought her close and searched her adoring eyes. "Thank you." And then he kissed her with all that his body and soul could give.

When their lips softly parted, he kept her near. He couldn't put into words how much he loved her. How her love had saved him.

Smiling, he shrugged. "You have given me *everything*."

Bailey's heart glistened in her eyes as she replied in French, "Then, *mon amour,* we are even."

* * * * *

Hired: Cinderella Chef

MYRNA MACKENZIE

Myrna Mackenzie is a self-proclaimed 'student of all things that concern women and their relationships'. An award-winning author of over thirty novels, Myrna was born in a small town in Dunklin County, Missouri, grew up just outside Chicago and now divides her time between two lake areas—both very different and both very beautiful. She loves coffee, hiking, cruising the internet for interesting websites and 'attempting' gardening, cooking and knitting. Readers (and other potential gardeners, cooks, knitters, writers, etc...) can visit Myrna online at www.myrnamackenzie.com, or write to her at PO Box 225, La Grange, IL 50625, USA.

CHAPTER ONE

"MR. JUDSON said that his guests want to meet the cook."

"Excuse me?" Darcy Parrish's throat nearly closed up with dread as she addressed the young serving girl who had delivered the message.

"I said that Mr. Judson's dinner guests want to meet the cook."

Such simple words. Such a simple request. Why then were Darcy's hands shaking? No question.

"That's impossible," Darcy said. "Tell him no."

She looked at the young woman's astonished and horrified face. To tell the truth she was a little horrified at her audacity, too. She had only been at Judson House a week. She'd been hired by the housekeeper while Mr. Judson was out of town and had never actually met her boss. But she knew about him. She knew a lot about him.

More than that, she knew that he *didn't* know about her. At least not some important details.

"I'm sorry, I can't do that," the young woman, Olivia, said. "It would be my job. Unlike some people, *I* need this work. I don't have charity to fall back on."

Anger burned within Darcy even as she conceded that Olivia was right. It wasn't fair to hurt another person to keep from hurting herself.

"I'm sorry, Liv," she told the girl. "Really, but…I can't go out there. You don't know how it feels to be on display, to be like a bug under a microscope…I just can't."

Olivia sighed. "I'm sorry, too, but he asked, Darcy. What can I say?"

"Say that I'm covered in flour."

"But you're not."

Darcy wanted to groan. Olivia was so young and so honest. She hadn't learned the convenient little lies that helped protect a person from life's blows. And being paraded out in front of a millionaire's guests like a pet performer would be a blow, especially once they realized her situation. Pity always followed. She wasn't going through that.

"Well then, say that I'm in the midst of making dessert." That wasn't completely true, either. The dessert only needed whipped cream on the top.

"Dar-cy," Olivia drawled.

"O-liv-i-a, please. I can't. I won't," Darcy said.

"Is there a problem of some sort?" The deep, male voice echoed through the huge kitchen, and Darcy spun in her wheelchair to face Patrick Judson, her new boss, the man who had financed the group home where she was staying.

To be honest, having been assigned this job by his house-keeper, Darcy had never actually seen her boss, but who else could it be? Entering through the door nearest the dining area, he was dressed formally for dinner in stark black and white and he looked a lot like the pictures she'd seen in the news-paper. With those broad shoulders, dark, longish hair, green eyes and a granite jaw, he might have stepped right out of a magazine or a romance novel. He was definitely the kind of man that women made fools of themselves over, even beau-tiful, women with working appendages, serious pedigrees, money and no flaws. He was Heathcliff in twenty-first century clothing, and he was also…very tall.

Darcy had always been slightly shorter than average. Tall, imposing men had always made her feel squat even when she'd been able to get around well on two legs. Now, in a wheelchair, she felt even shorter, more at a disadvantage. But she'd been a fighter all her life and she'd never been one to let her fears show.

"Mr. Judson, I appreciate the offer to meet your guests, but I'm afraid that's not possible. I have to finish the dessert." Okay, that was her story and she was sticking to it.

Patrick's gaze passed around the room, and Darcy wished she could rush over and cover the obviously finished crystal glasses of chocolate mousse. But he said nothing about that. Instead he turned to Olivia. "If the coffee is ready, why don't you serve that, Olivia?"

The young woman nodded, gathered the coffee cart and rushed out, clearly glad to be spared the storm to follow.

Now Patrick turned those dark green eyes on Darcy. "How long have you been here?" he asked. "I don't remember you."

But he was studying her so intently that Darcy knew he wouldn't ever forget her. She could no longer be totally invisible the way she liked things. She fought the urge to brush away the trace of chocolate that had dripped onto her left breast. She wished she could get up and make herself tall so that she was the one towering over someone.

As if he had read her mind, Patrick pulled up the nearest stool and sat down.

Darcy's eyes widened. The man had guests, yet he looked as if he intended to settle in for a long visit!

Now, she *did* give in to the urge to fidget, clutching the armrests of her chair. "I've been here a week," she said. "My name is Darcy Parrish."

"You're from Able House."

She raised her right eyebrow. "How could you tell?" Her tone was slightly mocking and…okay, that *was* stepping over the line…in more ways than one. Of course, he knew where she was from. Everyone in this neighborhood had fought to keep the assisted-living facility for those with spinal cord injuries out of this posh neighborhood. All except Patrick Judson, who had sponsored Able House, fought for it and made sure that it was luxuriously furnished and stocked and had every technological and administrative advantage available. Darcy was grateful—more than grateful for the chance to live in a place that catered to her needs and made her feel less dependent, but she also knew that being from Able House, being an example of Patrick Judson's largess made her a marked woman and an object of pity.

For a second Patrick looked nonplussed. Then a small amused look lifted his lips. "How did I know? It's stamped on your wheelchair," he said.

Darcy looked down. "I don't see it." Of course. He had made it up.

"It's on one of the spokes."

She bent over and read the half-upside down letters on the fat, black spoke. He was right. When she looked up, her gaze met his. Those sleepy green eyes looked right into her ordinary brown ones and she felt as if she had been sucked up into a tornado of sensation. She felt helpless.

Darcy hated feeling helpless. She had been in situations where she had no control or was at the mercy of the more powerful or advantaged too many times in her life. She had been the object of Good Samaritanism gone bad before, too, and she'd certainly been forced to deal with admiration turned to pity. The times that had happened…she didn't want to remember. Not any of them. She would have none of that in her life again. Pride mattered, and she knew enough to shield herself. But now…dammit, she *liked* this job. Moreover, she needed this job.

Ever since her accident had killed her dreams of being a police officer, she had been spiraling out of control. For the second time in her life, the first being a dark period of her childhood she didn't like to think about, she had had to rely completely on the mercy and goodwill of others, and the very thought scared her to death. But here in the kitchen, with her newfound skill? She ruled. She had discovered her talent and she totally ruled. What if she lost that just because she couldn't keep her big mouth shut?

"I'm sorry about disappointing your guests," she said, trying for a humble and deferential tone.

Now, Patrick raised his brow. "Is that so?"

Okay, she had lied enough. Besides, she never lied about things that really mattered. A person's attitude mattered. "No, not really. That is, I don't want to go out there and meet them, But, I also don't want them to be disappointed in the meal."

"They're not. That's why they wanted to meet you. To tell you how much they enjoyed it."

"I…I'm sorry, but I really don't like to be on display. I just can't do that."

He nodded curtly. "That wasn't my intent."

"You didn't know I was in a wheelchair, did you?"

"I don't know you at all."

"No reason you should. I'm just another employee." Even though she knew that was a lie. When she applied for this job, Mrs. D., the housekeeper, had noted that she was from Able House, and Darcy was almost certain that the woman had favored her because of that. Not that she didn't have the talent to do the task, because she did, but this was Chicago. Talent in the kitchen abounded, and a man with Patrick Judson's money and social standing could hire the best. He wouldn't have had to give preferential treatment to a woman just because she lived at the institution where he was the chief benefactor.

But he had. Or at least his housekeeper had.

Darcy sighed. "I'm grateful for the work."

He didn't smile. Indeed, his look was grim. "If you couldn't do the work Mrs. D. wouldn't have hired you. But I have to warn you, it's a very temporary position."

Yes, she knew that. She'd been trying not to think of that. She'd been hoping that temporary meant…not temporary.

"But for now?" she asked.

Patrick leveled a look at her and she knew this was a man who was used to getting his way. "For *today*," he stressed, "I'll make your excuses. But that's a one-time reprieve. I'm leaving Judson House soon and I'll be gone long-term. When I go, every employee here will have a new place to work. That's my promise to myself, and I can't place employees elsewhere if they are insubordinate or insist on hiding their talents. If Able House is going to succeed beyond this generation, its inhabitants have to be willing to be beacons and let their lights shine, at least in some small way. They have to be examples of success stories themselves. You and I are going to work on this, Darcy."

She stifled a groan. "On what?"

"On your fear of coming out of the kitchen and meeting people."

It wasn't exactly fear of being around people that was her problem. True, she didn't like being stared at, but she wasn't a complete hermit. She just steered clear of anything that brought her undue attention, and even then…her fear was much more than that. "I don't want to be anyone's project," she said.

"Too bad. It's just become a condition of your continued employment. You're mine now."

Darcy tried to ignore the sudden quickened beating of her heart as he stood up and started to walk away.

Darcy rolled forward. "Mr. Judson. I—"

Patrick Judson turned. "Trust me on this, Darcy. I'll make sure you have security, a good job and the means to survive without being beholden to anyone before I go."

Oh, yeah, like she hadn't heard those kinds of promises before. But in the end *she* was the only person she had ever truly been able to count on.

"I don't need security." A total lie.

He paused. "What do you need?"

Darcy didn't hesitate. "I need to finish making dessert."

"Chocolate mousse? Is it good?" he asked, a teasing tone in his voice.

"Practically orgasmic," she said. Okay, that *was* over the top. The tendency to speak her mind was a good trait for a policewoman, but it could only get her in trouble here. She opened her mouth to take back her comment, but her boss had raised one dark eyebrow.

"Well, that will be entertaining, at least," he said. "I guess I owe you, Darcy, and so do my guests. That *was* a most spectacular meal. My taste buds are still humming. Thank you." He smiled.

She couldn't help it. She smiled back. How did he do that? Most likely he did that with every woman he encountered.

"My pleasure," she said. But inside, she was trembling. Patrick Judson was everything she could never have had even before her accident. The things she knew about him and the things she knew about herself…oh, yes, he was off-limits to a woman like her. So, she really couldn't do anything that implied that she was even mildly attracted. Talk about an impossible situation!

No, it was just too irritating that her new boss was so attractive and compelling. That kind of thing was just going to end right here and now.

Except the darn man was going to turn her into some sort of hobby, a cause.

Her blood ran cold. She could barely think.

"I have to concentrate on the dessert and only on the dessert," she muttered. And this time she meant every word.

She could not even allow herself to think about letting Patrick Judson turn her into a project. But how was she going to stop him?

Patrick woke up the next morning thinking about Darcy Parrish's dark, hot rebellious eyes. There had been something magnificent and defiant about her even though he could tell that she was scared and bluffing beneath the bravado. Having raised three sisters he knew the signs.

Still, he had no business dwelling on the woman despite the fact that there was something compellingly beautiful about her. He'd found himself wondering how long her wheat-colored hair would be when freed from its ponytail and…what she was wearing beneath that red apron. He could see that she was slender, but…

"Stop it," he muttered. This was completely inappropriate. She was his employee. For now, anyway, and he had sworn to help her.

Patrick nearly let out a groan. Why had he done that? His life was too busy right now and he was halfway out the door to a trip around the world. Now that his youngest sister was going off to college he was free to pursue his own interests for the first time since his parents had died and left him a guardian at age nineteen.

This trip was all he had wanted for years. He intended to grab opportunity with both hands, and nothing was going to sidetrack him, including a pair of lovely brown eyes. At twenty-nine he was still single and he had yet to sow any wild oats. He was going to do just that. Soon enough he would marry someone like himself, from his world with his goals. He would raise his own children. Angelise would be a perfect choice for a wife, and she seemed to feel the same about him. Not that they'd actually discussed marriage, yet. That would happen in time.

But for now, the family sporting goods business offered the perfect opportunity to do all the things he'd been wanting to do. The prospect of a multi-continent trip to promote the business while engaging in adventure sports for charity loomed large. No more avoiding the reckless pursuits he craved. No more being responsible for another person's well-being. He wanted that new life, badly, and it was almost in his grasp.

Except there were just a few loose ends. Able House was one, and apparently Darcy Parrish was another.

"You're an idiot, Judson," he told himself. "She doesn't even want your help."

But she would have it. He'd taken on the responsibility of Able House not only as an example to his sisters of the value of diversity in one's life, but also as an example of the duties of the wealthy to those less fortunate. The first round of residents had all been chosen as those most likely to be able to make their own ways eventually. Potential strong role models who might offer hope to others. It was clear why Darcy had been included. She was talented, bright and bold. But he'd heard her try to get Olivia to lie for her. He'd seen her anger. Something was wrong.

Having been the one to shepherd Able House into being, he had to make sure that wrong was made right. Whether he'd known it before or not, he now knew that Darcy was in his employ and that made him responsible for her.

When he left town, he had to be sure that Able House and its residents were safe from attack. He didn't want any of his neighbors to be able to say "I told you this wouldn't work" or "I told you this would be a problem" or "We don't need any trouble bringing our property values down." These were people's lives, hopes and dreams that were at stake.

He'd been lax. He'd been concentrating on getting Lane off to college and then on his own issues. Having chosen Able House's directors with care, he'd assumed that the brand-new facility had launched cleanly.

Apparently that wasn't completely true. Darcy Parrish had more than just a smart, sexy mouth. She was willing to be in-subordinate to an employer rather than meet a group of people who had only wanted to praise and admire her. That could be problematic for future employers. Because while Darcy clearly had talent and could be a success, that wouldn't happen if she was unwilling to promote herself in the competitive Chicago culinary field. Patrick knew that Mrs. D. had hired Darcy because of her Able House connections. Her talent might never be fully recognized if she insisted on ignoring those who wanted to meet her. And that would be bad news for both her and Able House.

He wasn't going to let that happen. He was going to help her. And he was going to get some much needed coffee, he thought with a near groan. Damn, but he needed coffee if he was going to face the woman with a clear head.

Patrick just bet that Darcy Parrish made coffee that would make a man beg. Probably not a good idea to let her know that she had the power to make him beg, not with that saucy attitude of hers, he thought with a smile.

Oh, no. That wasn't how things were going to be.

"Let the games begin, Darcy," he whispered as he went in search of his pretty chef.

CHAPTER TWO

DARCY'S nerves were totally on edge. When she'd finally returned to Able House last night she'd been unable to sleep for hours knowing that today was likely to bring another meeting with Patrick Judson. The memory of the man's arresting presence had her mind spinning as she tried to think of some plausible reason she could give for not showing up. Unfortunately there was none. She was going to have to face the man.

"So what?" she whispered to herself. "He's just a man." And she had been working for him for a week. This should be no big deal.

Except it was. Patrick Judson was not only gorgeous and sexy, with a voice that made a woman think of…oh, things she had stopped thinking of a long time ago, he was also larger than life. And she was—eek!—going to be spending a little time with him.

No big deal, she repeated to herself again as she finally made it to work, bleary-eyed and tired. He'd probably give her a half-hour lecture and a few pointers and that would be it. Had she seriously worried that some rich guy was going to hang around with her and put her through her paces?

"Hey, Darce. So, I hear you're going to spend the whole day with Mr. Judson," Olivia said as Darcy came through the door.

So much for no big deal. "Who told you that?" she asked the young woman, but secretly Darcy was thinking, I am? The whole day?

"Mrs. D. told me that I would have to handle lunch alone."

Darcy hadn't run into Mrs. D. yet. She'd better go find out what was going on.

"But she said that it wouldn't be too difficult," Olivia continued. "Because Ms. Judson—Lane—is out shopping, and because Mr. Judson wouldn't be here, anyway. He has a meeting with you. I guess his guests were really impressed. Maybe he's even going to ask you to cater his wedding."

"Wedding?"

"Oh, yeah, I forgot that you haven't met Angelise Marsdon yet. She's pretty hot."

"I didn't know Mr. Judson was engaged," Darcy said. She thanked heaven that she hadn't let her crazy attraction to her boss show. Not that it ever would have even occurred to Olivia that Darcy might be attracted to anyone. Many people, maybe even most, assumed that the wheelchair stripped a person of desire.

"Oh, he isn't yet, but it's pretty clear that he and Angelise—don't you love that name?—are an item and that they're made for each other. Now that Lane is going to college in a few weeks, and all of his sisters will be out of the house, he'll be alone. That engagement's gonna happen. I just know it. You'll see. So, this meeting with Mr. J. is just about all that stuff last night, then?"

"Not a clue, Liv, but I'll find out soon enough. Until then, I'm really not going to worry about it." No, and she wasn't going to bother thinking about Patrick Judson's upcoming engagement, either. Still, Liv's mention of her boss's relationship with the apparently beautiful and hot Angelise Marsdon was a solid wake-up call, a smack upside the head, Darcy thought. What had she even been thinking about noticing the man's eyes and getting all gooey just because he had a deep voice and a nice smile?

"Breakfast first," Darcy said, forcing herself to stop dwelling on her boss's ability to make a woman feel hot even when she was holding the refrigerator door open. "I am not going to let you get stuck with extra chores just because I have to leave the kitchen for a few hours. Let's get started."

But she had barely managed to get the coffee made when she felt a presence at the door and turned. Patrick Judson was just entering the kitchen, and the way he was studying her...

Over the past few years Darcy had grown to expect and dread the pitying looks people sometimes sent her way, or worse, the way they glanced away self-consciously, but this was different. There was genuine interest in his gaze. And something else that made her feel like blushing when she was just not the kind of woman who blushed.

Anger sluiced through her. She liked this job. She needed it, too. Romantic or lustful thoughts were off-limits, and not just because the man was practically engaged. It went deeper than that. She'd already had a man destroy her heart when she was at her lowest. Her career had been snatched away. She'd lost her baby and more. Everything she'd dared to reach for was gone, so she no longer risked dreaming. She grasped only for the attainable. And Patrick Judson? He didn't even come close to being attainable. The man might as well have had a big, flashing Not For Darcy light on his forehead. Only a self-destructive fool would risk being attracted to him, and she was a survivor, not a fool.

Life had boiled down to the practical, the doable, and even

if she had still been the type to indulge in romantic dreams, this man was way out of her league and would have been even before the accident.

"Excuse me for invading your kitchen before you're done, but what can I say? That is one of the most incredible scents in the world," he said, glancing at the coffeepot. "A man would do a lot for a cup of that. Is it ready?" he asked with a smile that would have coaxed a snowman into a sauna.

Darcy couldn't help smiling back just a little. "It's ready. Coffee is a major food group, you know."

He grinned and that darn snowman melted a little more. "I see we share an addiction."

Darcy's body turned to fire. That deep voice and the way he breathed in the aroma of the coffee she handed him before he took a sip…Darcy could so easily imagine him nuzzling a woman's neck, breathing in her scent and telling her she smelled wonderful.

Darn it, no, where had that thought come from? Instantly she tried to blank out her thoughts. Some men could home in on a woman's attraction. She prayed that Patrick wasn't one of them. "Breakfast will be ready in mere minutes," she said, the words coming out in a rush. Thankfully the act of promising results "in mere minutes" was enough to get her back on track. The meal would have to be something uncomplicated. Omelets, she decided, with fresh vegetables and herbs and cheese.

"Sounds great," he conceded. "And after breakfast, you and I have things to do. Would you dine with me?"

Mind reading men became the least of Darcy's worries as she thought of sitting across a table from him. There was something about a meal that suddenly seemed very intimate.

"No," she said, too hastily. "I mean, thank you, but no thank you. Work to do, you know. Olivia is on her own today.

I need to…" To what? Olivia was more than capable of managing on her own when Patrick wasn't around to be fed. When Darcy had arrived, the young woman had been relying on a cache of frozen casseroles the former cook had made up. There were still plenty of those.

But this is my kitchen now, Darcy reminded herself. And she didn't like falling back on the former cook's meals. So, there. She *did* have a good excuse for not eating with her boss. She wasn't a coward.

"Work," she repeated.

"Coward," he said with a smile. "As your employer you know I'd give you a pass on the work, but…maybe work isn't the problem? You told me that you don't like being the center of attention. You must have thought I would grill you."

Darcy blinked. "Would you have?"

He smiled again. "Not until after breakfast." Then, he picked up his coffee, turned and left the kitchen. "A few minute's reprieve, Darcy," he called back. "Then you and I begin."

Silence filled the kitchen after he had gone, but Darcy's mind wasn't quiet at all. Begin what? she thought.

Less than an hour later, Patrick stood outside the house looking down at Darcy and reminded himself to tread carefully here. Darcy was his employee as well as a resident of Able House, and both of those facts made him responsible for her. It wasn't right for him to notice those warm brown eyes or the way her hair caressed her jaw when she moved. His unexpected interest in her wasn't acceptable. Especially since he would soon be leaving the country.

"Are you ready?" he asked, holding out his hand.

Those brandy eyes widened and she looked at his hand as if it was some sort of harmful weapon.

"I'm sorry. Have I…offended you?" he asked.

Quickly she shook her head. "No, not at all. And yes, I'm ready." Then she tilted her head slightly. "You just caught me off guard, that's all. People generally don't hold out their hands to me."

He nodded. "Because you need them to operate your wheels, I assume."

Darcy hesitated. "Yes, that's probably why."

But it wasn't, he could tell. What kind of people had she been dealing with? "If anyone at Able House has been unkind…"

Instantly she went on full alert. "No! They're wonderful people, all of them. I love that place! No, the handholding…I think it's just that the metal gets in the way in people's minds. It's like having one of those force fields around you from a sci-fi movie. For the record, I don't think it's an intentional snub, just an oversight."

"Good, because you would tell me if there was a problem at Able House, wouldn't you?"

She laughed. "And rat on my friends? Not a chance."

He shook his head but smiled. "You're an interesting woman, Darcy. I have the feeling there's a lot more to you than great food."

"Well, there's great coffee, too."

Patrick chuckled. "Absolutely. Now, are you really ready?"

"Not really. Last night you told me that you needed me to let my light shine. I assume that means you want me to be an ambassador for Able House. But, as I tried to explain, I'm a pretty private person. I don't think I'll ever be ready for the spotlight."

That complicated things. Could he let this drop? Not when there was so much at stake.

"I respect your desire for privacy," he said. "But Able

House hasn't had nearly enough time to prove itself to the world, and now I'm leaving. The timing isn't great, but it can't be helped. My overseas project has been in the works for five years, long before the opportunity to create Able House came about. Before I go, I have to make sure Able House's standing in the community is solid.

"That's a necessity. The people in the neighborhood have to grow comfortable with the residents of Able House, to think of them as contributors and assets. And yes, it's unfair that Able House should have a higher bar than the other locals do, but fair or not, you and your fellow residents have to show the community that the project wasn't a mistake."

The hurt, angry look in her eyes got to him. How many times had she been forced to prove herself to others?

Patrick could see the strain this conversation was having on her. Her face was pale, her body rigid.

"I'm not the only resident," she told him.

"No, but you're going to be my connection to everyone else."

"The directors?" she asked.

"Are directors. They don't have an in like you do. Caring as they are, they're outsiders. They don't live your life. They don't really know what it's like to *be* you. And neither do I. Besides, didn't you tell me that you were a police officer, a public servant? Darcy, you can still do something like that, but instead of chasing bad guys, you'll be serving Able House and this community."

While the kitchen clock ticked away, she sat there, looking angry and rebellious and sad all at once.

"You don't exactly fight fair," she said.

"My sisters would agree with you."

She tilted her head. "Were you a tough guardian?"

"A total bully."

"And not very truthful," she said with a small smile.

"Ah, the lady wants truth? All right, I let them twist me around their fingers all too often, but not when their well-being was at risk. You'll help?"

Slowly she nodded. "I don't really have a choice. Able House is special. In the short time it's been here, most of us have bonded. It's our home."

He held his hand out in a gesture of acceptance. "I promise I'll fight for you while I'm here."

This time when he held out his hand, she took it. Patrick had meant it to be a symbolic gesture, a joining, the beginning of a pact, but as she lay her slender hand in his and the pads of her fingers slid against his palm, every nerve ending in his body switched on. He was aware of her in a way he hadn't been only seconds earlier. She was no longer just a compelling, interesting woman and a great cook, no longer just his bridge to the residents of Able House. She was a flesh and blood woman who drew him in ways he didn't want to acknowledge.

He let her go as they began to move down the path toward the gardens.

"So, what do you want me to do?" she asked.

"Fill me in on your background and what life is like for you now. Give me a tour of Able House. I've been there, of course, during the building stages and at the opening ceremonies. But I've stayed away since the residents arrived. It's your home, not an institution. I haven't wanted to intrude.

"I *am* aware that some of the neighbors haven't been welcoming, and…now, after meeting you and given my upcoming departure, I'd say I dropped the ball."

"We're fine," she said.

Not true. There had already been problems with a couple

of neighbors who didn't seem to understand or to want to understand how great a barrier their parked cars posed when they placed too many vehicles on the driveway so that they stuck out over the sidewalk. Or that sprinklers that overshot the grass and hit the walkway would soak anyone rolling past. They'd been parking their cars like that for years. They'd never had to think about the impact of how they positioned their sprinklers and they resented having to change their habits for people they hadn't wanted in the neighborhood in the first place. Patrick had heard their complaints many times, and he was beginning to think that what might originally have been unconscious rudeness and laziness had become, to some extent, a form of harassment. There was still a sense that Able House would drag down property values and decrease the elite atmosphere of the neighborhood. That kind of resentment wasn't easily overcome.

"Darcy, the plan was to integrate you so deeply into the neighborhood that you become a necessary part of the whole. That would help Able House become a springboard for similar residences. But, to achieve that you have to be visible, not flying under the radar. I'm sorry if we didn't make that clear when you moved in."

"People in wheelchairs often fly under the radar."

He held up his hand. "I would never say that I understand your life, your experiences or how you feel. I don't and I can't, because I haven't lived your life, but I know this much. Your legs may not work the way they used to, but other people with functional limbs lack your talent. Hiding that talent would be a mistake."

She frowned.

So did he. "A mistake," he repeated. "Living at Able House comes with strings attached. It isn't a retreat. Retreats are fine.

They have their place, and we all need to hide away now and then, but Able House is your job as well as your home, and your job requires you to go forth and be visible. All right?"

Darcy nodded, but he could see that she wasn't happy. No wonder. She had just told him that she was a private person and here he was digging into her life.

"Has anyone ever told you that you're a stubborn man?"

Patrick chuckled. "Yes, as well as bossy and arrogant. So, are you still in?"

"I'm still here, aren't I?" she asked. "And please don't make some lame joke about how I couldn't get away. I could totally leave you in the dust if I wanted to."

"I'm sure you could," he said, and he wasn't lying. He had watched her deftly and seamlessly maneuver her chair over a place where a tree root had forced the sidewalk up a good four inches. And given her current pace, he was already taking long strides to keep up with her.

When they reached the fountain surrounded by yellow roses in the middle of the gardens, he motioned for her to stop and sat down on a bench facing her. "All right, here comes the part where I'm not only stubborn but pushy and nosy as well. So, how did you end up at Able House?" he asked.

"Don't you already have all that information?"

"I don't intrude on the residents' lives."

She gave him a wide-eyed look of disbelief. Given all that he'd told her and the demands he was making on her, he could understand her incredulity.

"Okay, I didn't *intend* to intrude. I carelessly assumed everything was going as well as could be expected, given the neighbors' initial reluctance. I didn't realize that there might be any other complications until you told me that you didn't want to be visible. And, okay, that stuff about not butting in?

I'm making an exception in your case," he agreed. "But I'm not digging through your files or asking one of the directors to break trust with you—which they wouldn't do, by the way. I'm just…asking you. I won't know if you leave something out."

Darcy frowned. "So, I could lie to you…"

"And I'd be clueless."

"That wouldn't be very helpful, though, would it?"

He laughed. "No, it wouldn't."

"So, you're trusting me?"

"Looks that way." He waited.

She gave him an incredulous look. "That is so lame. How did you ever grow up to be such a success? In the part of town where I grew up, you would have been taken advantage of on a daily basis."

He gave a casual shrug and continued to wait.

"I hate that you're trusting me. It means I have to be honest. I do have a code of honor."

Now, he couldn't contain his grin.

"You knew that, didn't you?" she asked.

Patrick tipped his head. "The directors spent a lot of time choosing the residents. Honor would have been important and they would have gone over every detail of your situation, your personality and your accomplishments. They probably know things about you that you don't even recognize yourself."

Her frown grew. "I doubt that very much, but…all right. I'll give you the abbreviated version of how I came to be where I am. I wasn't always in the chair, only for the past couple of years. Actually I was born in a very poor part of the city and ended up in an experimental suburban school program where a group of us with meager means but a decent stash of brains were thrown in with the cream of the elite. We were *not* welcomed or popular, as you might imagine, but the leaders of the program patted themselves on the back for helping the disadvantaged, the elite parents patted themselves on the back for allowing us to mingle with their children, the teachers patted themselves on the back for having to put up with our presence—the administrators hated the extra paperwork. Knowing that we were unwelcome charity cases, we had chips on our shoulders and bad attitudes, and the other students barely tolerated us. In addition, the district had budget cuts and the following year we were sent back to our own neighborhood schools where we were considered to be uppity for having mixed with the rich kids. The whole experience left me with a bad attitude about certain types of philanthropy."

"And you think Able House is like that?"

"No, but I don't like to be held up as an example or a poster child."

"Understood."

She gave him a small, resigned smile. "But we're still going forward with this."

This time he couldn't smile back. "Darcy, I was nineteen when my parents died and I was left to raise my three sisters. If I've committed myself to a cause or to individuals, I don't want to be like those people who dropped your project after a year. I intend to follow through and make sure that Able House will survive whether I'm here or not."

"Well, then, you've got your woman. Survival is something I know all about." Her smile and her attitude practically blew him away. He had a feeling it would be dangerous to underestimate Darcy Parrish. Or his reaction to her.

CHAPTER THREE

WELL…this was certainly stressful, Darcy thought as she and Patrick continued on, proceeding down the path toward Able House. She was constantly aware of the man by her side. In a physical way. In an emotional way. She hated losing control of her emotions, but her unexpected and completely feminine and foolish reaction to Patrick Judson was leading her to do just that, and now he wanted her to—

"All right, here's the rest of my story," she said, rushing ahead in the hopes that reliving those bad old days would smack some common sense into her. "After that wonderfully humiliating experience I told you about, I turned into a rebel, got in trouble, but quickly realized that was a road to disaster. Eventually I somehow got my act together enough to get into and graduate from the police academy, but just as I was about to achieve that dream, I ended up in a one-car accident that left me with some sensation but minus the ability to walk and chase down the bad guys. And then…a few things happened and I ended up here. So there, now you know everything about me."

His smile was warm, even as he shook his head. "I said that I was going to trust you. I didn't say I was a fool. *Some things happened, and you ended up here?* All right, I won't ask for the details, but it's obvious even from that brief introduction that you're a much more complex woman than you care to admit. So no, I don't know you."

"And *I* don't know you."

"Touché. I'm asking you to share, but not reciprocating?"

"I'm not complaining. You're not really my business, are you?" she challenged.

"Maybe not, but I'm asking a lot of you. So, what do you want to know about me?"

"Why did you fight to get Able House into the neighborhood? Why does it even matter to you?"

Patrick stopped walking. "Partly selfish reasons. My life has been taken up with my sporting goods business and my sisters, and when Lane—who is eighteen and heading off to college—was in a serious accident and we didn't know what condition she would be in six months down the road, I had to wonder what her life would be like if I weren't a rich man or if I weren't around. How would the world treat her? What opportunities would she have? Who would she become? Would the world even realize what a gift she was? And, when I mentioned my concerns to a physician friend and heard that there had been interest in starting something like Able House for several years, it was an easy choice to donate the land and the money. But, I would never have thought of getting involved at all if my sister hadn't had the misfortune to have a skiing accident." He shrugged.

But Darcy wasn't about to let that pass. "Lots of good things wouldn't happen without a catalyst or a defining, life-changing moment. I haven't run into her, but I assume she recovered."

"Completely."

"I'm glad." Without thinking she reached out and touched his hand. Instantly awareness of him as a man kicked back in full force. Warmth, pulsing energy, a frisson of excitement ran through her. Was she insane? She'd barely been able to sit still when he'd been holding her hand earlier. Now, *she* had initiated contact? The instinct to jerk away was strong, but she couldn't let him know that one totally innocent brush of her fingertips against his skin had affected her this much.

"Almost to Able House," she managed to say. As if he didn't know that.

"Lead on. You're the expert here." His low voice resonated through her body. Darcy kept moving, hoping none of her friends would notice how flustered she was.

"Hey, Darce, why are you back so soon?" someone called out as she rolled within view of the center. "Aren't you working?"

"Detour of duties today. We have a visitor," she said, happy that her voice sounded reasonably normal. As they neared the building, which was surrounded by deep green lawns, winding walkways, fountains, flowers and sculpture, more people appeared. All were in wheelchairs.

"Is that Mr. Judson?" one older man whispered to the man next to him, loud enough to be heard.

The other man smiled. "Sure is," he said. "You've seen his pictures in the paper and he's been here before."

"But he's with Darcy," the man said.

"Edward, you know I work for Mr. Judson," Darcy said, raising her voice a bit because Edward's hearing was less than perfect.

Still, everyone looked a bit perplexed and concerned. "I know what you're thinking. I didn't mouth off and get fired. He isn't here to return me for a better product."

Patrick chuckled and everyone turned to look at him.

"She's an excellent product," he said to Edward. "Not the

type to be returned as unacceptable. A great cook. Have you
eaten her chocolate mousse?"

"Oh, chocolate," Maria said, her voice worshipful. "I love
that stuff. But ask her to make you a lemon meringue pie next.
It's better than sex."

Instantly Darcy felt uncomfortable—and hot. She was
afraid to look at Patrick but she did it, anyway.

"Better than sex? Well, I wouldn't want to miss that." he
said with that lazy tone that made Darcy feel shivery. For
some reason the fact that she even felt that way when he talked
made her angry.

"People think that a person stops thinking about sex when
they have a spinal cord injury, but we don't," she said defiantly.

"Why should you?" Patrick asked. "Sex is complicated. It
involves the mind, not just one or two body parts."

Darcy noticed that Maria was looking at Patrick with lust
in her eyes. In fact, she was looking very much like a woman
on the verge of propositioning the man, and Maria was a
beautiful redhead, an intelligent and capable woman.

"Now that we're all settled in, Mr. Judson is here to learn
the ins and outs of Able House. He wants to make sure we're
well established when he goes overseas soon, and he might
be expecting us to go out in public and do some promotion,"
Darcy said, a bit too primly.

"Hey, okay by me. Whatever Mr. Judson wants," Maria
agreed.

Patrick looked a bit uncomfortable. "For starters, I hope
you'll all call me Patrick," he said as Darcy made the introductions and Patrick shook hands all around. Later, when
they were alone and back at the house, Darcy repeated the
details he wanted.

"Edward is an electrical engineer. Maria is a computer

programmer. Cerise was an Olympic swimmer who now teaches and coaches at a local fitness center. Laura is a fashion designer. Aaron is a dentist. If this weren't the weekend, most of them wouldn't be here. They have jobs." Her tone was a bit defensive, she realized.

"I'm not the enemy, Darcy," Patrick said, sliding to the floor beside her wheelchair.

"I know you're not the enemy," she said. "But I—I feel as if you want something from me that I'm not sure I can give and I don't even know what you want from me yet. Do you?"

"Not exactly. I want to know that you're fine."

"I am. It's been rough those first two years, but I've learned so much."

"Like what?"

She got a sly look on her face. "Well…I can pop a wheelie." She did so with ease. "And I can move from my chair to a standard chair in record time." She pointed to a chair normally used by one of the staff and transferred herself back and forth quickly from one chair to the other and back again. "If I have to, I can get this puppy up a step if it's not too high," she said, patting the bicycle tires she favored on her chair. "In short, I can be a real person, Mr. Judson, and get along without help. I'm fine."

But his green eyes were stubborn. "I want better than fine. Don't get me wrong. I'm awed by the fact that you can manage in ways most people couldn't, but those reluctant, inconsiderate neighbors of ours…"

"They want celebrity," she said. "Ceremony. Pretty wrapping paper with all the trimmings. If I were a rock star who just happened to be in a wheelchair, they'd welcome me."

He didn't look away from her direct gaze. "You're right and I'm not about to apologize for them. They're wrong."

"But you still want me to…to what?"

"I want you to make them envy you, to show them that the community would be diminished by the loss of all of you."

"We shouldn't have to do that."

"You're damn right about that," he said, angrily. "But if I get overseas where I'm not in easy reach and someone hires some legal eagle team and tries to do some workaround scheme to close down Able House…I'm trying to prevent them from even wanting to attempt that. That's all. All right?" he asked.

Darcy pursed her lips and gave a reluctant nod. "If you put it that way…if we're gearing up for a fight of sorts…" Her words ended on a harsh laugh and she looked up and blinked, trying not to show her frustration. Sometimes it felt as if she'd been fighting all her life. For money. For respect. For the right just to exist.

"I'm not trying to punish you, Darcy," Patrick said, and he cupped her jaw with his palm, kneeling next to her chair. "Really. It's not like that at all."

His hand against her skin produced an instant reaction, an awareness of him as a man. Darcy struggled to think to continue breathing. "I know you're not trying to punish me," she managed to say. "I'm so…grateful for Able House. All of us are. Couldn't you hear it in their voices when they spoke to you today?"

"I don't want you to be grateful, although I appreciate the thought. I want you to…not have to justify having your home here."

"But we will, won't we? Just by having to take the extra steps other people don't have to take, we'll work for the right to stay."

"Yes, and it's not right," he said with a groan, sliding to the ground beside her.

"What are you doing?" She looked down at him.

He looked up at her and smiled. Her heart thumped. "Making myself short," he said. "Do you mind?"

She laughed. "Well, I've gotten used to looking up people's noses, but no, I welcome the chance to look someone other than my friends at Able House in the eye."

"I'll remember that."

No, don't, she wanted to say. *Don't be too nice to me. Don't make me want things I can't possibly have.* Because she had once had things she wanted and had them taken away. Love had been one of those things.

She tried not to think of the other thing, the unborn baby she had lost and that terrible day afterward when she had lost that last sliver of faith that she could ever try to become a mother again. Darcy fought not to remember all of that…and failed.

"So, why are you going overseas?" she asked, wanting to change from the subject of loss to something more positive.

Patrick shrugged those big, broad shoulders. "It's time. I've been running the company for years, raising the girls. Now, they're grown and I have things I've put off that I want to do. I'm twenty-nine, still single, I run a major international company that sells sporting goods, but while I love adventure sports and risk-taking, I haven't taken any risks."

Darcy gave him an "are you kidding me" look. "I thought you said you raised three sisters. Sounds like risk-taking to me."

To her consternation, he moved closer, resting his arms on the side of her chair so that he was very close. "Are you teasing me, Darcy?"

No, she was torturing *herself*. But she wasn't going to back down. "I'm just saying it couldn't have been easy."

He moved away and went back to leaning against the wall. "I loved it, totally, but…you have no idea."

"No. I've never had any children." And never would now. Not after losing her baby in the accident, not when she wasn't going to get married, ever, and not if she couldn't be the kind of mother she wanted to be. So much for avoiding that heart-constricting pain.

She looked up and saw that Patrick was studying her closely. So, she dove into survival mode and forced a smile. "So, tell me more about your upcoming trip."

He continued to study her for a few more seconds.

"Please," she said.

He nodded. "It's one of those trips that's the result of too many years of daydreams. Probably too long and too expensive and too monumental in scope, but I can't wait. Several months spread out over a number of continents. Part of it will be spent on business and part will be a series of charitable fund-raisers built around adventure sports. We're hoping to draw big crowds and really make a difference."

He held out his hands. "It's a very meaty venture, a long time in the making, and yeah, I'm pumped, even though I feel just a little guilty. It sounds as if I couldn't wait for the girls to grow up so I could have a life."

Darcy leaned forward, closer to him. "Why should you feel guilty? You've worked hard, everyone knows your company is a success. You raised your sisters and…how old are they?"

"Twenty-five, twenty-three and eighteen. Cara and Amy are married and have children of their own."

"Well, then, there's no problem, is there? They're grown, and they're not going to care what you do."

Patrick gave her a look of disbelief. "You haven't met my sisters."

No, she hadn't. But that changed a few hours later when the doorbell rang, and she heard the sound of footsteps in the hallway. Lots of footsteps. She'd been told to prepare food for a few extra mouths, but it sounded as if an entire army had arrived.

She and Olivia exchanged a look. "It's them," Olivia offered.

As if she knew who "them" was. "Who?" Darcy asked. "You've been here longer than me. I don't know the code yet."

Olivia rolled her eyes. "The sisters," she whispered as the voices grew closer.

Darcy barely had time to panic before the kitchen was filled with tall, dark-haired, gorgeous women and…a dog? A big dog?

"Fuzz, get down," one young woman ordered as the dog pounced, setting his paws on Darcy's lap. Startled, Darcy dropped the stainless steel bowl she was holding. It rolled around on the floor, clanging.

Immediately a cacophony of high-pitched feminine voices began. One of the beauties screeched.

"Oh, no," another one said.

"Patrick is going to have a cow," the third one said.

"Fuzz. Down now." Patrick's voice broke through the noise. The sad-looking, big-eyed mutt backed off of Darcy.

"Later," she told the dog, winking. "Steak."

"No steak," Patrick said.

"Tyrant. He's just a big puppy."

"Who doesn't belong in the kitchen," he insisted.

We'll see, Darcy thought with some amusement. She'd spent a lifetime being told she didn't belong here or there. She and this dog had something in common. But Patrick had turned his attention away from the dog who had wandered out of the room.

"Cara, Amy, Lane, what were you thinking?" he asked, crossing his arms.

"We thought you were in here," one of them said. "We didn't think about Fuzz. Come here, big brother. We have a secret to tell you." She looked down at her abdomen and smiled.

"Cara? Another baby?" Patrick's voice was soft. He folded his sister into his arms.

"And she's such a baby when she's having a baby," another sister said. "Mark my words, she'll be calling you whenever there's a crisis."

"I will not!" the other sister said.

"You did when you were pregnant with Charlie."

"That's because I was looking for an excuse to come over and give Patrick a hand with you, Lane, sweetie," Cara said. "*You* are a handful."

"At least I won't come running to Patrick when I have a husband the way you two do," the youngest beauty said.

Immediately the two older sisters began to protest and the ensuing sounds was nearly earsplitting, but Patrick calmly broke in. "Enough. You haven't said hello to either Darcy or Olivia yet. Or apologized for letting Darcy be attacked by Fuzz."

Darcy started to open her mouth to tell him that Fuzz hadn't hurt her, but Patrick shook his head.

The trio of beauties greeted Olivia and turned to Darcy. "We were out of line," Cara said.

"We weren't thinking," Amy agreed.

"And we really are sorry," Lane agreed. "You're new, aren't you?"

"As new as they get," Darcy agreed with a smile when Lane held out her hand.

"What happened to Elaine, the last cook?" Amy asked.

Patrick gave her a look that clearly indicated that was an off-limits topic.

"Ah, the usual," Cara said.

Darcy raised one brow, but she said nothing other than what she felt needed saying. "I hope you'll enjoy what I've prepared for dinner."

"I'm sure it will be great," Amy said.

"Yes. Absolutely," the other women said.

"All right, we've disrupted Darcy's kitchen long enough," Patrick said. "If she's going to work her magic, she needs us out of here."

"Magic?" Lane asked.

"Darcy is a veritable genius in the kitchen," he clarified, winking at Darcy.

The sisters exchanged a look. Not a happy look, either. "Is Angelise coming?" Cara asked. It was clear that she wanted the answer to be yes.

"I didn't invite her," he said.

"Why not?"

Patrick frowned. He didn't answer. Now Darcy was as curious as his sisters were, but it wasn't any of her business, was it? Besides, if he wasn't going to share with his sisters, he certainly wasn't going to tell his cook his secrets.

But as the sisters and Patrick left the kitchen, Darcy was certain she heard one of the young women say, "Be careful about how you praise Darcy, Patrick. You know how many members of your staff have fallen in love with you? One word of praise and they're writing Mrs. Patrick Judson in their diaries. It's not fair to hurt them or lead them on."

"I have no intention of leading Darcy on." Had Patrick really said that or was that simply what Darcy thought she heard? His voice had been muffled and low.

"Olivia?" Darcy asked. "Is that how I got this job? The last cook went off the deep end over...um...Mr. Judson?" No matter what Patrick had told everyone at Able House, this was not a good moment to start calling him by his first name.

"Afraid so. They *all* fall in love with him. I would, too, but he's too old for me."

"Well, you don't have to worry about me. I'm not falling

in love with anyone, least of all my boss. I don't go looking for trouble anymore."

"Yes, but my mother says that sometimes trouble just finds us."

"Not me."

Olivia shrugged. "Whatever you say, but I've seen it happen over and over. That last cook—Elaine? I liked her, but she was practically stalking Mr. Judson. He had to let her go."

A sick feeling ran through Darcy. She knew all too well what rejection felt like. "We'd better get the meal on the table. We have four mouths to feed."

"Six."

"Who else is coming?" Darcy asked.

"The baby-sitter is on her way over to drop off Mr. Judson's nephews, Charlie and Davey. They're just four and five and so cute you just want to pick them up and hug them. They're the light of Mr. Judson's eyes. He loves children."

"Children?" Panic attacked Darcy's senses. She fought against it.

"Yes. Like I said, two of them. You'll see."

Darcy shook her head. "No, I'll be in the kitchen. You'll be serving."

Olivia gave her the look. "You know Mr. Judson might want you to put in an appearance."

Darcy wanted to say no, but she couldn't do that. She had had her one reprieve. He wouldn't allow her another. Like it or not, panicked or not, she was going to have to enter a room filled with women who were wondering whether she had a crush on Patrick, she was going to have to face those babies she couldn't bear to face and she was going to have to do it all while trying to pretend that Patrick had absolutely no effect on her at all.

CHAPTER FOUR

TWO HOURS LATER, Darcy blew out a long breath. She had made it through the evening. Barely. Every time she'd entered the room, she had had to decide where to look. Those two gorgeous little boys were at one end of the table. Just one glance had nearly made her heart break and made her wonder…would her child have had those chubby little elbows, those huge, innocent eyes? The pain she thought she'd conquered had hit her like a sledgehammer, dredging up emotions she'd learned to suppress.

Darcy only hoped her hastily pasted-on smile had hidden her distress. Her inability to face children was not something she wanted to discuss.

After that, she had avoided looking toward the boys and had concentrated instead on doing her job and on the adults. Whenever she'd entered the room, Patrick's sisters had seemed to be talking about women. Specifically, Patrick and women. More specifically, Patrick and Angelise Marsdon. Apparently the lovely Angelise was quite a catch. And no question about it, Patrick was…he was…

An image of smoldering green eyes and dark hair assailed her. Sudden, unexpected heat suffused Darcy's body, and as if her physical reaction was like some sort of magic beacon, she heard Patrick's telltale masculine steps nearing the kitchen. Caught off guard, she felt the plate she'd been holding slide from her hands, and she had to practically throw herself from her chair to catch it before it hit the floor.

"Darn it!" she said, hugging the expensive piece of china to her chest.

"Are you all right?" Patrick's deep voice was laced with concern as he came through the doorway. Darcy braced herself for the physical reaction she felt whenever he was near. Not a surprise. Probably every woman on earth had that same reaction. It was meaningless, she reminded herself as she nodded at him.

"I'm fine. I just nearly broke a plate that probably cost more than a Mercedes."

He frowned.

"It's all right, though," she said, holding out the plate to show him.

"I don't care about the plate," he told her. "That's not what's worrying me." But obviously something was.

Patrick was angry. At his sisters but also at himself. It had been obvious all through dinner that Cara and Amy and Lane had an agenda where Darcy was concerned. Angelise's name had been mentioned several time in Darcy's presence, and while the food had been melt-in-your-mouth perfect, his sisters had offered only the most rudimentary of compliments and they had maintained a distant air.

"I'm sorry," he told Darcy when everyone had gone home. "They're grown up and yet despite two of them being married and mothers, they're still young in too many ways. I'm sure I made some mistakes and indulged them too much to make up for their lack of real parents, but their manners are usually much better than this. I'll talk to them."

Darcy shrugged. "What did you expect them to do? Faint over my apple tart?"

"A few oohs and ahs wouldn't have been misplaced. It was the stuff men have killed for, and that cinnamon scent wafting off of it…" He groaned.

Darcy's eyes opened wide as if she was startled, as if he had done something sexual. Well, maybe he had. There was something very sensual about a woman who smelled like cinnamon and vanilla and could create masterpieces with those talented hands of hers.

Abruptly Patrick shut down those thoughts. What in hell was he doing? Darcy was his employee. As such, there were barriers he wouldn't cross.

"Your sisters were perfectly polite. They said the food was very good."

They had, but these were the three sisters who had been born speaking in superlatives. Something was amiss. He had the feeling he knew what it was. Darcy was prettier and more talented than any of his other cooks had been.

"My sisters have decided they're going to choose a wife for me, and you're an attractive woman. I think they see you as a potential wrench in their plans."

And that blush did amazing things to her skin. Dammit, he had to stop thinking like that. Where were his principles and his self-control?

"They were disappointed that Ms. Marsdon wasn't invited," she said.

"I know. Angelise tops their list. They've been trying to match me up with her for years."

"Are you going to allow yourself to be matched?"

He raised a brow.

"Sorry," she said, looking sheepish. "Cop training. Be direct, get to the point. Wade in and ask the tough questions."

"Do you miss it?" he asked, then shook his head. "No, don't answer that. None of my business."

She laughed. "I just asked you if you were going to get engaged to a woman I've never met. You're my boss and I'm asking you personal questions. And you're apologizing to me for being nosy?"

"All right. I'll be nosy. Do you?"

She looked him straight in the eye. "I wanted it very badly. I was good at it. It meant getting respect. I was going to do something important. I was going to save the world. But that's all done now."

"Don't make the mistake of thinking that what you do now isn't important."

"I cook."

"You feed people, you nourish them."

"Oh, you're good. No wonder your sisters are worried that every woman you hire is going to fall in love with you."

He gave her a look, tried to think of what to say, tried *not* to want her to be a little bit interested in him so that he could get closer to her so he could taste that sassy mouth.

No.

Had he thought that or had she *said* it?

"No, don't worry. I'm not going to fall in love with you," she said. "When I had my accident I was engaged to be married."

She hesitated.

"I see," Patrick said. Or at least he was beginning to. Who was that guy, he wondered? What kind of an obtuse idiot had he been?

"This isn't something I talk about," she said, her voice dropping to a mere whisper.

"You shouldn't have to. Your privacy is sacrosanct, Darcy. I promise you that. I won't ask."

She looked up and stared directly into his eyes. "If this is going to cause your sisters even one moment of concern, that can't be good for anyone. I don't want there to be strife between you and your sisters or concern about my role here, so they—*you*—need to know that I'm not some starry-eyed romantic looking for love. After my accident, my fiancé…well, suffice it to say that I'm not stupid enough to start down that road again." Her body was rigid. Her pretty brown eyes were troubled, and it was obvious how uncomfortable she was discussing this, but she had done it to reassure him.

Patrick had to work hard to control his anger. "It sounds as if your fiancé was the stupid one. Some men don't deserve what they're given."

She sat stone-still for several seconds. Then she sucked in a long, visible breath. "So, are you going to marry Angelise Marsdon?" she asked, catching Patrick off guard. Clearly she wanted to change the subject. Only a total jerk wouldn't take the hint.

"I don't know. Maybe. Eventually. Now that the girls are grown I'll eventually marry someone and Angelise and I have been friends for a long time. We grew up in the same world. We have similar interests."

"Does she like risk-taking and adventure sports, too?"

"She likes to ski."

"Well, then…"

"You sound like my sisters. Your next words should be 'why not?' And my answer is not yet. I have things to do."

"That trip. *Your* dream."

"Yes, although…I feel a bit guilty putting it that way. That makes it sound as if I begrudge my sisters the time I gave them. I don't. I love them. I love my nephews, too, but…I apologize if they made you uncomfortable. I know they stared at you when they came in, and I can see their presence unnerved you."

She shook her head vigorously. "Don't. They're perfectly adorable little boys. Beautiful children. And of course they stared. They're children faced with a new person and a new situation," she said, indicating her chair.

"But you could barely look at them, and it's not acceptable for them to make people uncomfortable with their curiosity. Young as they are, they need to learn that."

"I—do *not* do that."

"What?"

"Make your nephews feel guilty about staring at my chair, or apologize or anything like that. It's not them. It's me. I'll admit that…I'm just not very comfortable being around children."

He nodded. Lots of people weren't comfortable with children, but it was clear from the look in her eyes that her reaction was something out of the norm. It was also clear that Darcy didn't want to discuss the details, and he had no right to push.

"All right. I won't make them feel guilty. I never intended to do that, anyway. They're far too young. But Charlie and Davey and I might still have a bit of a man-to-man talk. Guy stuff."

She sighed, then smiled wearily. "They'll probably wrap you around their tiny little fingers."

"That's a good possibility," he admitted.

"And you'll love every minute."

"That, too."

Finally she smiled, and Patrick felt as if the sun had emerged after a long, gray day. "Come on, I'll walk you home," he said.

He could have sent for the Able House van. It would have been the wise thing to do, given his current mood, but he didn't want the evening to end on this somber note.

Still, in the dusk, as the sun began to set and the stars began to glow, the darkness closed around them and he was aware of the woman beside him in ways he didn't want to be. Her scent drew him.

"I shouldn't have told you any of that stuff about myself," she said quietly. "I don't usually open up that way but I guess it was only right that I spill some of my own secrets since I was being so nosy myself. So…here's a question. I made an appearance outside the kitchen tonight. Are we done yet?"

Her voice was low and husky and warm, she was only inches away from him as they walked along.

Suddenly he stopped.

She did, too, and without even thinking, he dropped down beside her. Her toughness, her fragility drew him, scalded him. He knew she was amazing, complicated in ways he hadn't even begun to discover. She had layers he couldn't even imagine yet, but she was breakable, too. That toughness was a cover. Now that he knew that, he…

Patrick looked down at her and the pale starlight lit up her brown eyes, that beautiful face. She was so very alive and warm…and waiting for his answer.

"We're not done yet," he said. "And without allowing himself to stop and consider the inadvisability of his actions, he leaned in and touched his lips to hers.

Her silken hair brushed his fingertips as he cupped her jaw. Her lips were enticingly warm, achingly moist and she tasted of cinnamon and something uniquely her. Patrick wanted to come back for more. Instead he pulled abruptly away.

"I'm sorry. That was a mistake," he said. "I don't harass my employees."

She shook her head. "I don't feel very harassed," she whispered.

"What do you feel?"

"You don't want to know, because you were right. It was a mistake. You and I—no—not even for fun. You've got your trip, your business, the freedom you've been waiting for, all those adventures you're going to have and those kids that Olivia says you want someday. My plans are completely different. I'm definitely not going for the husband and children. And crowds? No, thank you. No spotlight of any kind for me after we finish saving Able House."

He leaned back and crossed his arms. "Still, you should have a full life. More than just cooking for some rich guy who lives alone."

"Hey, I like cooking!" she protested.

"Shh," he whispered, smiling down at her. "It wasn't the cooking I was objecting to, just the audience you have. You may not like crowds, but you should at least get more exposure than you get working for me.

"Attracting some additional exposure would be a good starting place. Able House needs to build a reputation, and you've got an extraordinary talent. We need to find an alternate workplace for you, anyway, so…let me do a little homework. Then we'll take on the world."

It was a good idea, he thought as he headed for home. He'd rather take on the world than risk wondering why he kept wanting to kiss her again.

And he did want that very badly. Her skin had been so soft, her lips so warm…

Patrick groaned.

"Wrong time, wrong place, buddy," he told himself. He and Darcy were headed in opposite directions.

In a few weeks he would leave and might never see her again. But he would remember the taste of her and her take-no-prisoners spirit for a long time.

When Darcy arrived home two days later, she realized immediately that something was different. There was a buzz in Able House that she hadn't felt before. Not that the atmosphere here wasn't positive. It was the most homey place she had ever lived. Even when she'd been able to walk around on two legs she hadn't experienced the energy that existed in this place. But this morning something was happening. She knew it. Her gut instincts, the ability to feel a change in the stratosphere, in the mood of her surroundings that she'd honed on the street and at the police academy took hold. And pretty soon the reason for that change, that extra energy became apparent.

Cerise came rolling up to Darcy. "Hey, Darce, we're expanding our horizons."

"What do you mean?"

"Classes, training, public speaking."

"I still don't understand," Darcy said.

"I don't, either, but it has something to do with your Mr. Judson."

"Not mine," Darcy said automatically, but even as she said the words she remembered how his lips had felt against hers the other night. She'd felt…claimed. She'd felt…dominated, but in a good way. She'd always hated being dominated. It made her claustrophobic and rebellious, but when Patrick had touched her she'd just sat there, enjoying the tingle and the closeness and the warmth and the man. His hand had lightly cupped her jaw and she hadn't even objected.

Which was downright scary. She remembered what Olivia had said about the cooks that had come before her, and she didn't want to follow in their footsteps. Letting herself wish for things or reach too high was a recipe for disaster. Especially given the fact that Patrick was her benefactor.

Every time she had wanted something badly or been a recipient of someone's good ideas, she had always lost. That ill-fated school experience had severely damaged her pride and made her a target. Her abandonment by her fiancé, an instructor at the academy who had encouraged her to apply and claimed he would love her forever had made her question her ability to judge people. And her baby...oh, her baby who had never known life...

Darcy closed her eyes. With that tragedy she'd lost her sense that life was mostly good even if some of it was bad. If she even thought about Patrick as anything other than her boss...disaster was a certainty. If she knowingly did something so stupid, she risked her self-respect and her last chance to find happiness and purpose.

"Darce, are you okay?" Cerise was waving her hand in front of Darcy's face.

"Perfect," Darcy lied. "What do you mean by classes?"

"Not the usual kind," Cerise said, rolling her eyes sarcastically. "Patrick—you *know* it was him—called up Mr. Baxter here in the office and grilled him on some enrichment possibilities. He's set up some tutoring opportunities with the best in their field. Dancers, elite chefs, experts in new technological advances, wheelchair racers, swimmers, designers...you name it. If one of us wants to take a class—and Mr. Baxter said that he really hopes that as a gesture of faith in what Patrick is trying to do, we'll all devote ourselves to studying one new thing—an expert will be found to teach us, at no charge to us. But, that's not all. The two of them are also arranging some charitable ventures."

"I don't understand. This is already a charitable venture, and you just said…"

"This second part isn't charity for *us*. It's charity given *by* us. We're supposed to take our gifts and our expertise out in the world and use it by volunteering to teach, to aid, to make a difference. Twice a month if our schedules allow for it. Patrick will arrange for the initial contacts and once he's gone, Mr. Baxter will be our liaison. I'm not sure I understand all this, but it's very cool."

"He's trying to make us examples," Darcy said.

Cerise frowned. Darcy didn't blame her. Being held up as a poster child to enlist sympathy and oohs and ahs was a two-edged sword.

"I didn't mean that the way it sounded," she quickly told her friend. "He wants us to show the people in this area that losing us would leave a hole in their community. He wants us to be contributors, accomplished public figures."

By now a few other people had gathered round. "That's never going to happen," one person said. "Patrick practically had to cram Able House down people's throats. Now that we're here, the demonstrations may have stopped but very few people are really welcoming us. They don't criticize. They'd feel too guilty doing that, but they don't want us here in their elite neighborhood, either. We're an island cut off from the rest of the community by a wall of silence. Patrick can't change that."

Darcy wanted to object, but she didn't. Because she was sure the man was right, and this lingering conflict wasn't fair to Patrick. He had sacrificed all of his adult life and had earned the chance to be unencumbered. When he went off on his trip he shouldn't have to be worrying about Able House.

Darcy didn't know how to change that situation, but she knew how to change her part.

"Let's take a look at those classes. If Rick Bayliss of Frontera Grill is teaching a class," she joked, "I am so signing up right now."

To her surprise, he was and she did, but…that wasn't really pushing her boundaries, was it? She had to do more, to show Patrick that she could be bold and fearless and fine once he had gone. Closing her eyes, she gathered her courage. Then she took her pen and signed on the line next to the class that frightened her the most.

Wheelchair ballroom dancing. She'd been a heck of a bad dancer back when she had legs that operated smoothly.

"Sounds like fun," she told the person next to her. Although it didn't. It sounded scary. Darcy hated being in situations where she might look foolish, where others might stare at her, but…this was all about pushing limits. She had always been about pushing limits.

Besides, if she wanted to administer a knockout punch to the fear that she was becoming too attracted to her boss, she had to replace it with an even bigger fear.

"There's a recital at the end of the class," she muttered. Panic attacked her, and for one whole hour she didn't think about Patrick at all.

But then she did. And why not? She was on the way to his house where she was to spend more time with him. He'd left a message on her voice mail and asked if she would be available. He had news about the plans they'd discussed the other day.

Available? I'm feeling way too available. Darcy hated even admitting that, but it was true. "Please let Patrick leave town soon," she prayed.

CHAPTER FIVE

PATRICK looked up from his desk to see Darcy in the doorway of his office. "I got your message, so here I am. Is this about…the other day you said we were going to take on the world," Darcy said.

Her chin was high, her lovely hair falling back to reveal a long, slender neck that drew his attention, reminding him that in some ways he was no different from any other red-blooded male. There was a look of bravado plastered on her pretty face, but Patrick could tell that it was a show. Her hands on the wheels of her chair were white-knuckled.

His heart went out to her. "I might have been hasty in demanding that much," he said, wanting to give her an out. They could start more slowly.

She shook her head. "What day does your trip begin?"

He named a date just a few weeks away.

"The world it is, then," she said. "No point in mucking about and wasting time."

He smiled and shook his head. "All right, then. You win."

She grinned. "Sweet. I like winning."

Patrick couldn't help laughing, then. "I'll bet you were a handful growing up."

She shrugged, avoiding the comment. "Um, Mr. Judson?"

"Patrick," he said. "In spite of our employer-employee status, I think we've moved beyond formalities."

For a minute she look flustered. He probably shouldn't have reminded her that he had kissed her or that she had revealed heart-deep secrets to him, but he hated having her call him Mr. Judson.

"All right, then. Patrick," she agreed. "What exactly are we planning to do? What does taking on the world mean?"

"Dinner party. Big. Some names you'll recognize from the news and the society pages. I want you to prepare the 'meal of your heart.' Then I want you to put on your best clothes and cruise the room, let people chat you up."

She went rigid, her lips practically turned blue, she fanned herself with her hand. "I have to tell you that I stink at the chatting me up bit."

"Darcy," he drawled. "You'll do fine. Just be yourself."

"You have got to be kidding. I was going to be a street cop, dealing with hardened criminals. Decorum is not my strong suit."

"But chocolate mousse is. Rich people love their food, and above all, they like discovering the next new thing. They'll love you."

She rolled closer. "I'll bet you were a good big brother. Did you always encourage your sisters this way?"

He sat down in a chair right next to her, staring straight into her eyes. "I was flying by the seat of my pants every step of the way with my sisters and I didn't have a clue what I was doing. Even though I tried to be a good parent and to be encouraging, I don't even want to think of all the mistakes I made. Somehow they survived."

"Oh…but they love you. I heard the way they talked about you."

He laughed at that. "They certainly had their moments when they hated me, too. Trying to discipline a fifteen-year-old when you're only nineteen doesn't exactly make you popular."

"I can imagine it doesn't. But you did it, and you stayed."

"Of course, I did. I'd do it again. I wouldn't even leave now if I thought they needed me to stay, but they don't. They're all grown up." Patrick couldn't keep the pride from his voice.

"You're such a dad," she teased. "So…adventure sports? What does that entail?"

"Rock climbing, paragliding, white water rafting, snow-boarding, that kind of thing."

"You can do all that?"

For a second he thought he heard a wistful tone in her voice. "I attempt all that," he said.

"Sounds dangerous."

He grinned. "You sound like the girls. They don't exactly approve of me risking my neck, but since the entry fees and other monies raised from the events go to promote extracurricular sporting programs for kids in disadvantaged areas, they understand."

"So, in a way you're just substituting being a dad for your sisters to being a dad for a whole lot of other kids."

"Ouch! Don't nominate me for sainthood yet. Yes, this is a great cause, but I also love pushing my limits and I haven't allowed myself to do much of that for a long time."

"Now you can," she said softly.

"Yes." But he realized that *she* couldn't do most of those things. Not anymore. But the things she *could* do were amazing, like fighting back from a serious injury, creating meals that were out of this world delicious, feeding people, sassing a man when he needed sassing…

Aw, don't go there, Judson, he warned himself. *Next step you'll be staring at those lips again.*

"Let me tell you the basic elements of the party," he said, trying to take his mind off those lips. "I'll leave the details up to you."

"Are you sure you want me to put in an appearance?"

"I want other people to experience the Darcy Parrish taste."

He'd meant food, but now he *was* looking at her mouth.

She nodded, but then she froze. "You *do* have a reason for this dinner party other than me, don't you?"

Okay, he could lie, couldn't he?

Patrick wanted to groan. How could he lie when she was looking at him like that? "Sorry. This is strictly a coming out party for your talents. A job audition," he said, leaning in and crowding close to her. "And don't get that mutinous look in your eyes, Darcy. When I'm gone, you need a new position. I want you to have a good one."

"Patrick Judson," she said, poking him with her index finger. "I may not be ambulatory and I may have to occasionally rely on the kindness of others, but I do not want to be a charity case. I don't want to do this like some pitiful contestant in a cooking contest in the hopes that someone might like me well enough to choose me."

He caught her hand, enclosed it in his palm and brought it to rest on his heart, cupping her gently, keeping her still. "Not you, Darcy. Them. *They're* the contestants. You're the judge."

She shook her head, looking up at him with wide, worried eyes that glistened with her anger and frustration.

"I'm sorry," he said. "I'm so sorry. I thought you understood. You're not the one on display. They are. Any one of them would be lucky to get you. All you have to do is talk to them, see who you might feel comfortable working with and make your choice."

She closed her eyes. Was she going to cry? What a jerk he was. What an idiot! "Darcy," he coaxed gently. He brought her hand to his lips and kissed her fingertips.

Her eyes flew open wide, and he saw that she wasn't crying at all. "You," was all she said. "Oh, Patrick," she went on, laughing. "You—only you would think that I would be the one making the choice. Don't these rich people have cooks already?"

He knew he should let her go. Instead he leaned closer. "Oh, that isn't going to matter. You are the best. Believe me."

She sat there gazing at him and then she leaned forward and kissed him on the cheek. She raked her palm across his cheek, so that he wanted to turn his head and kiss that palm, make love to that soft skin. "I do believe that you're slightly crazy, Patrick," she whispered. "I should call your sisters and tell them how crazy you're talking, so they can get you some help, but I won't. I—it seems I have a dinner party to prepare."

"Darn right you do." He released her and she moved away, headed toward the door. "My guests are going to fight for the privilege of hiring you." The end result would be a new employer for her, he hoped, but at the same time there was a hollow feeling of loss deep in his chest.

"It's nothing," he whispered to himself after she had gone. He was just imagining things. Because he really wanted this trip he'd been planning for so long. He wanted freedom and a life he'd chosen, not the one that had been thrust on him. And then when that was done, he would settle down with a wife, someone who understood his world and welcomed it. They'd have a house full of children and a nice normal life. That would be perfection. Wouldn't it?

* * *

Had she actually kissed Patrick on the cheek when they had already agreed that any kind of touching would be a mistake? That was far too risky. The man was her boss! Enough of this being attracted to him already, Darcy told herself the next week as she planned the party, attended her first ballroom dancing lesson, discovered that she loved it and attended another.

She wondered if there would be dancing at the party. Patrick had said that she was planning it, but he had been talking about food-related details, not the rest. She wondered who would be there. Patrick had given her numbers. He'd handpicked most of the guests but allowed his sisters to invite some of their friends and acquaintances as well. Undoubtedly she would know no one other than the Judson family, but given Patrick's social standing, there would probably be people she'd heard of.

Darcy tried not to think about being introduced to people who would consider her either inferior or worse, an object, the token disabled person. She'd been that too many times, but…she shook off the bad feeling.

And yet…what should she wear? Oh, no, how could that little detail have skipped her mind? She hadn't concerned herself with her clothing in years. Expedience and comfort had been paramount, but now…

"Olivia, help!" she said. "What should I wear to this dinner? Do you know anything about style?"

Olivia turned to Darcy with a sly smile. "Darcy, does ice cream make my butt look big, and do I eat it anyway?"

Darcy blinked.

"The answer is yes," Olivia said, grabbing her arm. "And right after work we're going to go through your closet, your jewelry box and your makeup kit and then we're going shopping. You are going to knock Mr. Judson and everyone at that party on their wealthy…um, behinds."

Uh-oh, she'd released a fashion monster, Darcy thought. Her question had been innocent enough. She hadn't expected so much enthusiasm. "I was thinking of something a little less major than knocking people on their behinds," she volunteered.

Olivia gave her one of those "don't argue with me" looks. And Darcy had to admit that even in the kitchen Olivia strutted her style.

"Okay, you win," Darcy said. She hoped she wasn't making a mistake.

Two days later on the eve of the dinner party, she was sure she had made a mistake. The kitchen was under control, the extra staff members were following her directions. The tables, the silver, the candles, the china, the linen…everything looked perfect. But Darcy, having just emerged from an Olivia-style makeover, glanced into the mirror in front of her and wondered what she had been thinking.

The dress was perfect, a pretty slate-blue with a portrait neckline. A single wide gold chain framed her neck, and her hair had been styled into a chin-length breezy, swingy style. Unaccustomed to makeup, she had blush on her cheeks, lipstick on her lips, eyebrows that had been plucked and shaped, eyelids that had been tastefully shadowed. She felt elegant in the dress, but glancing in the mirror and then down at herself, she had one thought.

"They'll notice the chair first," she said.

"So what?"

Darcy had no answer for that. Olivia couldn't possibly understand.

"Yes, so what?" a deep male voice asked. A voice that went right through her and made her ache.

Darcy turned to face him. "You're making me meet them. I'll meet them. I even understand why and I'm grateful, but…the chair…"

"It's a great looking chair."

She frowned.

"Darcy," he said slowly, and he gave a brief nod, a signal that sent Olivia out of the room with a smile. "Maybe Olivia and I can't ever really understand completely. Neither of us can be in your shoes or know what you're feeling or what it must be like to be you, but for people who didn't know you before your accident, the chair is a part of you. And since it helps you do all the things you need to do, it's a good part."

"I know that. But—"

"What?"

"I don't want people to give me a pass because of the chair, to be easier on me because of it. The meal has to stand on its own. I don't want anyone waxing effusive because they think I need to hear pretty compliments."

He thought about that for a minute. "I can understand that. So…"

"So, I don't want anyone to know anything about me until after the meal. And if the results aren't positive—such as someone saying that my bouillabaisse sucks, then I stay in the kitchen."

"Darcy," Patrick drawled.

"Patrick, please."

"I get to make the call," he said. "I know them better than you and I can read their reactions."

She hesitated.

He waited.

Okay, fair was fair. Patrick was, after all, doing this for her. "Agreed," she finally said, feeling the butterflies starting to form.

"And Darcy," he said, as he turned to leave. "Your bouillabaisse is fantastic."

"I know," she said with a grin. "Too bad I'm not making that tonight."

"You'll pay for that," he warned with a sexy smile.

She waggled her fingers and shooed him out of the room…and waited.

He was magnificent. Darcy had heard snippets of the conversation from her station in the kitchen where she had thrown on an apron and was personally making sure that the meal was perfect. Some of the names Darcy had heard were household names, yet their deferential tones told her that they looked up to Patrick.

For his part he was gracious to everyone. And he had kept his promise. Once the meal had begun and everyone had been escorted to the dining room, Darcy had been left to do her job in anonymity. Of course, that meant that she didn't have a clue as to what was going on in the other room. The servers seemed to be good at their jobs, but they were keyed in on their work. It wouldn't be right to try to get them to spy or to pump them for information.

The strangest thing was that while Darcy knew that the exalted of Chicago society were eating her food, she was more nervous about how Patrick reacted to the meal than any of them did. And she'd been cooking for the man for several weeks now! That alone told her that she had stepped over a line she didn't want to cross.

But how to stop caring what he thought?

"Just stop," she muttered.

A server passing by looked up startled.

"Oh, no," Darcy said. "You're doing fine. You're doing great. Go on."

"Darcy."

She glanced up, fear gripping her as she heard Patrick's voice. The moment of reckoning was here, and there wasn't any way to put some positive spin on this. Either the response had been tepid and she would have to live with the knowledge that Patrick was disappointed or it would be positive and she would have to roll into the other room and meet that sea of faces.

"It's time," he said and he held out his hand.

She moved forward, stopped and took his hand.

"You're sensational," he told her.

"Patrick, I can't—not like this. It's too—I'm too—people will stare at me." Suddenly every humiliation of that long-ago day when she had walked into that exclusive prep school came rushing back at her. Her gym shoes had been on their last legs, because her mother hadn't been able to afford new ones yet. Her clothes had been the best she owned but still thrift shop specials. As she had moved past that sea of squeaky clean kids with their designer clothes and their expressions that told her that curious as they were, they would not be inviting her to any parties, she had wanted to run, to get out from under the microscope. She'd wanted to beg them not to look at her, but…

Those old, bad memories broke into pieces as Patrick dropped to his knees in front of her. "Darcy," he said. "I would never knowingly humiliate you. And…"

He frowned, that chiseled jaw growing harder. "Dammit, I don't have any real right to play God with your life or to presume to know what you're about or what you've been through, but I know this much. You have an amazing talent and a skill that no one else in that room possesses. I watched them, Darcy, while the meal was going on. They were in gastronomical heaven."

Darcy gave him a skeptical look. "That's pushing it, don't you think, Patrick?"

He shook his head slowly, his eyes never looking away from hers. She wanted to reach out, to frame her palms around his face, to feel his skin as he spoke.

"Not far enough," he said. "I know it's true, because I was so intent on catching their expressions and their comments that I almost missed the meal myself."

"Were you worried that I would mess up?"

He grinned and reached out and took her hands in his own. "Not even remotely. The scent of your cooking, Darcy…"

He groaned, a sound that made Darcy hot, then cold, then hot again. She snatched her hands away for fear she would do something stupid. The man certainly had a heightened olfactory sense, didn't he? And wasn't there just something incredibly…sexy about that?

Don't think that. Don't ever think that, she ordered herself. She tried to turn her attention back to the mundane.

"Your cooking was one of the hot topics during dinner," Patrick continued. "You may not recognize all the names, but everyone in the room has a reputation for discriminating taste in food. Yet I have it on good authority that Donovan Mintner rated your vichyssoise six stars on a five-star scale and Eleanor Givelli went off her diet for a half hour so that she could have a second helping of your lemon plum cake. Michael Brisbin asked me where I'd found my chef and wondered if there were any more where you'd come from. The point I'm trying to make, Darcy, is that they're already half in love with you."

"With my cooking."

He got that stubborn frown that she was beginning to recognize. "I have a feeling that your cooking comes from your soul. It's definitely more than a skill you've learned, which means that yes, it's *you* who has captured their hearts."

"Stomachs," she said just as stubbornly.

Without warning, he reached out and stroked his palm down her cheek, smoothing back her hair. "Didn't anyone ever pay you any compliments?" he asked. "You seem so unwilling to accept them, even when they're the truth."

Darcy fought against closing her eyes to drink in the sensation of his caress. The answer to his question was yes, she had earned compliments over the years. Just not like this. Not from someone who had opened a window to her soul. Not Patrick.

Save yourself, a little voice inside her whispered. *Run away.* And because she'd spent a lifetime relying on her instincts and had been part of too many situations where her feelings had been out in the open and ruthlessly trampled, she did just that. Darcy rolled backward just a touch. Just enough.

Patrick lowered his hand. "I'm sorry. I didn't even ask before I touched, did I?"

"I suppose it was kind of a big brother thing. You know, once you're in the habit of nurturing, you can't turn it off." Darcy desperately needed to believe that, because thinking of his touch any other way, even beginning to daydream was…preposterous, potentially heartbreaking. Unthinkable.

His brows drew together. "No, it wasn't like that," he said, as if half to himself. "Not remotely like that." He rose and took a step backward. "But you're right. It probably should have been. Dammit, we don't have time for me to get remorseful and apologetic right now. I can hear rumbling in the other room. They're probably wondering where I am and if I've bundled you off somewhere so they won't get a chance to steal you. I told them I would bring you."

"Oh, no. Are you saying that there's a sea of people waiting to meet me? I thought we were just going to quietly slip in and you might introduce me to a few people and then I would leave. This sounds like a big production."

"Nothing wrong with doing things big."

Of course, she should have expected that. This was a man who ran an international company, who had taken on the gargantuan task of raising three girls when he had not been much more than a child himself. This was a man who was organizing a global charity venture which entailed him jumping out of airplanes, rocketing down mountains on a tiny board and who knew what all else?

"Big? If I weren't so grateful for your help, I would roll over you with my chair." The words just popped out before she could think to stop them. Immediately she pressed both palms to her mouth. "I didn't just say that, did I?"

But Patrick had tipped his head back and let out a hearty laugh. "Oh, yes, and I'm not forgetting it, either." He laughed again, and Darcy heard sounds coming from just beyond the door.

"They must wonder what we're doing in here."

"I'll bet they'd never guess that you're threatening me with bodily harm," he teased. "Come on, we'd better go. And Darcy?"

"Yes?" She barely got the word out. She was a mess, a complete mess.

"It's probably best to watch your temper. I want them to hire you, not run away for fear you're going to trample them." His smile was broad and teasing and…just too darn sexy. That wasn't fair, not fair at all when he was as unattainable as the moon and stars.

"Don't you even see the chair?" she said in frustration.

His teasing grin faded. "Of course," he said. "I also see your eyes. You have the most amazing, expressive eyes. I'm pretty sure I saw a few sparks fly from them a few seconds ago."

Warmth puddled in her heart. Nonsensical desires and questions racketed through her brain. She had to ignore them, but…no one had ever spoken to her like this before. No one had ever made her feel like this. "What else do you see?" she asked, knowing it was the wrong thing to ask.

"Oh, so much more," he said, his gaze skimming down her. She felt heat everywhere he looked. Her face, her throat, her breasts. "But it wouldn't be a good idea to mention those things when other people might hear."

For a second she thought she saw frustration in his eyes, but then he turned and moved toward the other room. "Your fans await, Darcy," he said.

CHAPTER SIX

WAS he making a mistake doing this, Patrick wondered as Darcy entered the room. He knew how much she disliked being the center of attention. He also knew that she would be weighing every stare, analyzing every comment. What on earth had the world done to her? And that guy she'd been engaged to, what kind of a man would walk away from a woman like this just because her legs would no longer support her?

Idiot, he thought. But he didn't have time to pursue that train of thought and, anyway, it wouldn't be wise to even go there. Darcy's beauty haunted him, her frankness enchanted him, the fact that she didn't seem to be even remotely impressed or in awe of his money and social standing made him wild to get to know her better. And her body…well, as he'd told her it was better not to think those kinds of thoughts. It was best not to think of her in any way other than as a talented woman he was committed to promoting. Because he was leaving.

He had to leave. He'd waited all his life to leave. He'd put off everything for the girls' sake. And now that the trip was near, he had made commitments, big-time commitments. His company, his reputation and the future of a whole host of charities that were relying on his help were tied up in this venture.

It was his pleasure to go, but also his duty, and he had learned about duty at an early age.

Besides, he had no business bringing Darcy too closely into his world. It was one thing to handpick a group of guests, tactful, good-hearted people with deep pockets, who would treasure her and be careful with her. It was another to subject her to the public scrutiny she would face if anyone ever thought that she was anything more than just his chef.

The public and the media were often unkind. They peeled back the outer layers to expose the vulnerable stuff beneath, and…he had no idea what all Darcy had gone through in her life, but he knew that she was vulnerable beneath that tough exterior. A person didn't develop a tough exterior unless that person had been forced to protect herself. No doubt anyone who had to go through the harrowing experience of losing the use of their limbs and muscles and all that that entailed, who had had the rigors of excruciating physical therapy forced on them, developed strength, but Darcy had holes in her armor. If it was up to him, he wasn't going to let anyone near enough to expose those holes.

And he certainly wouldn't allow himself to do anything that might harm her…including letting the world know that he was attracted to her.

But he couldn't ignore her, either. That would be worse. And it would be suspect, as well. He had brought this group here tonight to meet his prize chef, whether they knew it or not. Then, he had taken it a step further and promised them an introduction. Darcy's future lay in the balance.

Showtime, Judson, he told himself. He gave Darcy a smile and moved forward to meet his guests who were gathered in small groups in his parlor having after dinner drinks.

He made a beeline for Eleanor Givelli. She was his first

choice, a warmhearted woman with a large checkbook. "Eleanor," he said, as Darcy moved forward. "Allow me to introduce Darcy Parrish, the woman who created that lemon plum cake you admired."

Eleanor was a short, plump woman with springy red curls. "Darcy? How wonderful to meet you. And I didn't just *admire* the cake," she said, laughing and gesturing with her hands, sending those red curls bouncing. "I attacked it and devoured it. No shame at all. It was delicious, as I'm sure you know. Not that I'm surprised. Patrick only has the best in his life. From employees to friends to…oh, everything. The girls, you know. He always had to have the best for them, to only expose them to people who met his high standards. He certainly knows how to zero in on talent."

"I—thank you. I'm so glad you enjoyed it," Darcy said, looking pleased but a bit overwhelmed by the woman's effusive charm.

Patrick began to move on.

"Oh, you're not taking her away, are you?" Eleanor asked. "I wanted to speak to you, Darcy, about an affair I need catered in two weeks. And don't get all possessive on me, Patrick. I know she's yours, but you're only one man, and Lane is a tiny woman and probably not even here all that much, given her social calendar."

Patrick grinned. "Are you telling me that you're trying to steal my chef?"

"Not yet," Eleanor said. "For now I just want to borrow her to cater this affair I'm having. And maybe one or two more."

"Are you sharing, Patrick?" Michael Brisbin seemed to appear from out of nowhere. "Because if you are, I'm first in line behind Eleanor here. My company is starting to plan its summer bash and your genius of a chef here—" he gave Darcy a smile and a nod "—is miles above the one we've used in the past. I'm Michael, by the way," he said directly to Darcy. "And you are…"

"Darcy," she said with a smile. Michael was a genius and a good man but he had the tendency to speak a mile a minute.

"Beautiful," Michael said, and Patrick gave the man a sharp look. The word hadn't sounded like a simple response to having finagled a talented chef's name. He had sounded like a man meeting an intriguing and beautiful woman.

"Hey, Patrick, don't scowl at me like that. Didn't you hear Eleanor? If Darcy isn't averse to sharing with us…do you have an exclusive right to her?"

No, he had no right to her whatsoever. Furthermore, he had arranged this dinner in the hopes of bringing about just this kind of response.

"Darcy is a free agent," he said.

"Free agent. Did someone say free agent? Are they talking about you, Patrick, darling?" Angelise asked, coming up and linking her arm through his. "Because if that's true, I'm staking a claim on you. I haven't seen you in weeks. Fortunately your sisters knew how I was pining away and invited me here."

Patrick blinked. Not in surprise, exactly. He'd known that his sisters had invited Angelise and he had spoken to her at dinner. They'd known each other for years, were good friends and he'd even occasionally—as late as a week ago—thought that after her divorce was final and she was free, the two of them might consider becoming closer. He *did* want to get married eventually, to have children, and he and Angelise had a lot in common. Similar backgrounds, similar interests. They would suit.

But tonight wasn't about him and his plans. It was about

Darcy, and his sisters had known that. They had championed
his support of Able House. He'd assumed they might have
dropped at least a hint of this night's purpose to Angelise. She
would have known that he had duties and wouldn't have time
or the inclination to flirt right now. What's more, after having
known him forever, she was aware that he preferred to do his
flirting in private.

"Angelise," he said, "I'd like you to meet Darcy."

Darcy smiled and held out her hand. "I'm afraid I'm the
free agent, but maybe Patrick is as well."

Now it was Angelise's turn to blink. "Patrick, is it?" she
said. "I didn't know that he was on such familiar terms with
his subordinates."

Patrick opened his mouth to protest, he saw Darcy's quick
blush and his sisters' startled, panicked looks. Angelise had
never been haughty.

"Darcy is an artist. She's not my subordinate," he said.

But Darcy gave him a sad, resigned look. Then he saw
her—did no one else see her?—paste a completely phony
look on her face. She laughed and looked at Angelise.

"You're right. I'm afraid I'm a bit of a rebel," she said, her
voice laced with humor even though Patrick could read
tension in her eyes. "I don't always play by the rules. Staying
in the kitchen keeps me out of trouble most of the time,
though. As a matter of fact, I have to go there now. I just came
out because…Mr. Judson requested it, and he is, as you say,
my boss." She gave Angelise a nod as if to say "you've won."

But as she turned to go, Patrick stepped forward. "You just
got here," he reminded her.

"Yes, dear," Eleanor said.

"We'd enjoy talking to you, picking your brain, getting to
know you better," Alex Torres, a young, handsome man added.

He was looking at Darcy as if she was on the menu and Patrick wondered what had possessed him to invite the man.

A chorus of those in agreement with Alex chimed in.

Darcy's smile was grateful but there was a stubborn set to her chin. "Thank you so much, but I have things to finish."

Patrick felt the first threads of anger weaving their way through him. He had cajoled Darcy into this situation, and now she had been made to feel uncomfortable. He would talk to Angelise, of course. He would apologize to Darcy, but the damage was already done. And she wanted to make her escape. He really should let her go, but—

"What do you have to do?" he asked, persisting.

"I have treats to package up," she said in a stage whisper. "Cream puffs and éclairs."

"Oh, my hips and thighs," Eleanor moaned. "Darcy, you're killing me. Let her go, Patrick. By all means, but I want your business card, Darcy. In fact, I want multiples. When Patrick leaves and you have more free time you're going to get so much business."

"Yes, me, too," someone said, and the words were echoed.

"Tomorrow," Patrick promised. "I'll make sure you get her cards."

Darcy thanked everyone and began to leave the room. Just as she was halfway through the door, he moved up beside her, touching her shoulder.

She stopped.

"We're not done," he told her. "This isn't finished. We'll talk later."

Darcy was in the kitchen, all the guests but Angelise and his sisters had gone home, and Patrick had to face the fact that there was unpleasant business to attend to. It was a fact of his life and had been for more years than he could remember. A man-boy didn't successfully raise three sisters without having had to force himself to deal with challenging or unpleasant situations from time to time.

"You three, wait for me in the study," he told his sisters. "And Cara and Amy, don't try to tell me you have to get home to your husbands and babies. I know that Lewis and Richard have a late-night game of poker, and Charlie and Davey are safe in the care of Mrs. Teniston who will care for them as if they're her own, so you've got time to give me five minutes."

"We're not children anymore," Amy pointed out, but they all came in and sat down. "And I do want to get back to Davey. I miss him when I'm gone."

Patrick sighed. He knew she meant that and he sympathized. He'd felt the same when he'd had to leave the girls with a sitter. "All right, I'll make this short," he told them. "I don't know what was going on tonight with Angelise, but I know you were at the heart of it, and I don't want it to happen again. Darcy was embarrassed, Angelise was acting out of character and you appeared to be interfering."

Lane put her chin up. "You should know that we never meant to hurt Darcy and we'll tell her so, but…we had good reasons."

"Really? I'd like to hear what they were."

"We told you. We saw you looking at Darcy the other night and especially tonight. You're attracted to her."

He didn't even try to deny it.

"Has it occurred to you that you might be leading her on? Have you thought about how disastrous it would be if she fell for you?"

"That isn't going to happen."

"Women always fall for you. You don't choose any of them. Or at least you haven't while we've been growing up.

We know it's because you didn't want to really date and lead us through a series of potential moms that might not pan out. But surprise! We're grown now. And you can choose whomever you want, but we know it won't be Darcy."

Anger began to simmer, but he controlled it. "How do you know that, Cara?"

"I'm not criticizing Darcy, but…we just know you, Patrick. You've been waiting all your life to take risks and now you can take them. Besides, I know you love us, but the weight of being responsible for us has to have gotten to you at times. No matter how independent Darcy is…you're her benefactor. You've aided her. Won't that be more of what you've been doing for us for years, the very thing you're breaking free of? Plus, if this went wrong, we—it would be different from an ordinary breakup simply because you *have* been her boss and benefactor. If you felt that you'd hurt her in any way while she was under your care…we know you, Patrick. It would kill you. You'd eventually do something unwise in a bid to make it right for her and end up sacrificing yourself."

He opened his mouth to protest, but Lane rushed in.

"Look, we know you've said you're not even going to think of marriage until after your trip is over, but you're totally free to date as much as you please. And eventually one of the women you date might become your bride. You've always said that when you marry it will be to a woman who shares your background, your interests and your ambitions, and that means someone like Angelise who's from your world and who likes climbing mountains and reckless pursuits as much as you do. And you want children. You've always wanted children, but Darcy—when we were here the other day she couldn't even bear to look at Charlie and Davey. I don't think she wants babies."

Patrick ran an impatient hand over his jaw. He didn't know why Darcy seemed to fear contact with his nephews but he wasn't about to discuss her private concerns with his sisters.

"We're sorry, Patrick, but…we just want for you what you want for us—a carefree life and someone to share that life."

"All right," he said, raising one hand. "You've made your point. Now, stop. All this worrying about Darcy…it's meaningless. She absolutely doesn't want to get married to anyone. She isn't interested in a relationship."

The three of them exchanged a look, the kind that said their sister antennae was turned on.

"I'm sorry, but we just don't believe that. At least not where you're concerned. You have this way of making women forget what they don't want and simply home in on what they do…which is you."

Patrick thought about that. Did Darcy want him? Maybe a little, in a physical sense, but…his world, the press, the attention…how long would it be before some callous idiot of a reporter wrote a story about how she was after his money or about what a great guy he was for hooking up with a disabled woman? One moment like that—and there would be many moments like that—and Darcy would retreat back into anonymity somewhere, scarred for having consorted with him. He would have harmed her just by showing her attention.

"You don't have anything to worry about," he told his sisters. "Darcy and I aren't going to get involved. I can promise you that."

Darcy was packing up to go when Olivia sidled in wearing a crestfallen look.

"Olivia, what is it?"

Olivia hesitated. "I don't know if I should tell you what I over-heard, but…I don't know if I should keep it from you, either."

But Darcy did. Whatever it was that was bothering Olivia was a burden to her. "Spill it," she said.

Olivia began, haltingly, to relate what had been said in the room adjoining the one where she had been cleaning up, in-cluding the comment about children, a topic that made Darcy want to shout that she wanted babies. She just couldn't bear the thought of not being the kind of mom she had dreamed of. She couldn't live with the thought that if her child climbed the stairs, she couldn't rush up them to prevent him from falling down the steps. "I'm sorry, Darcy," Olivia said. "I just…his sisters are great people and so is Mr. Judson, but you should know that the girls are matchmaking, that they think you're falling for him, but they don't think you're right for him."

Darcy felt sick, but she couldn't have Olivia feeling guilty for telling her something or start worrying later that what she had revealed to Darcy had hurt her. And, if there was one thing that Darcy had learned it was how to put on an act, to pretend that she was fine with the blows life sent her way, to keep her chin up so that her pride could survive. She was good at it, too. No one could tell that she was lying.

"Oh, Olivia," she said, smiling and holding out her arms. "Come here, sweetie. I can't believe you're worried about something as silly as that."

Olivia came close. Darcy took Olivia's hand and smiled up at her friend. "Believe me, Olivia, while I like Patrick, we tease each other and he helps me, he's just my boss. A great boss, but no more than that. As a matter of fact, tonight I col-lected a bunch of phone numbers for people who want me to cater their parties, so, if anything, Patrick and I will be spending less time together, not more. Gosh, Liv, he's handsome as all get out and yes, like most women I can fantasize about what his lips taste like, but heck, I feel that way about any number of movie stars, too. Don't you?" Somehow she managed a convincing laugh, and Olivia hesitated, then smiled and joined in.

"Thank goodness, Darcy," she said. "So…you really have no interest in Mr. Judson?"

"Patrick might be on my 'ten hottest men' list, but he's not on my list of men I plan to date, no."

"So who is?"

Darcy managed not to gasp. Olivia spit out the water she had been drinking. "Mr. Judson!" she squealed.

"Sorry, Olivia," he said with a smile. "I just came to see Darcy home. It's pretty dark even with the moon out. Do you have your car?"

"Yes," Olivia said. "I could drive Darcy home."

"Thank you, but I have just a few more things to discuss with her." He fished a piece of paper from his pocket. "More catering business," he said. And then he waited.

Olivia got the picture. She said a hasty goodbye and then left.

For long seconds Darcy sat there staring at Patrick as he paced. His long legs made short work of the big kitchen. He scrubbed one hand through his hair. Finally he turned in a rush.

"Olivia told you what the girls said?"

Okay, more acting. "Yes, but don't worry. I don't see what the problem is."

He raised one eyebrow, an incredibly sexy move in Darcy's opinion. "Because?"

"Patrick, I understand that your sisters are worried about you, so I'm not offended that they would be looking out for your best interests, but no, there's no problem. You and I…well, all right, yes, I do find you attractive, but I'm not interested in dating you."

"Because I'm not on your list of men to date. I take it there *is* a list, then?"

Man, had she really said that? How was she going to get out of this?

"Every woman has a list, even if it's not a conscious one." She tried to affect a teasing tone.

"And who tops yours?"

Uh-oh. What could she say? Darcy's mind raced.

"It changes. I met a really nice man in my ballroom dancing class. Jared O'Donahue. He's a former cop."

"But you told me you weren't interested in a relationship."

She wasn't. Really, she didn't want to be. She couldn't. "Who said anything about a relationship? He's just an interesting man I'd like to get to know." She wasn't exactly lying here. Jared O'Donohue was a nice man, and they shared common interests and a common background. Like Patrick and Angelise. The very thought hardened her resolve. "I'm not sure where it's going, but yes, right now he tops my list." Especially since she had just started the list five seconds ago and Jared was the only man she could think of to put on it.

Patrick was studying her intently. "Be careful," he finally said.

She nodded, regret for things that could never be pummeling her heart. She so didn't want to be having this conversation. "Your Angelise is very beautiful. Are the two of you going to marry?"

"I'll eventually marry," he said, "but I don't intend to start looking until this tour is over."

"Of course. You'll be busy, and you'll want to play the field. Maybe you'll start your own list," she said with as bright a smile as she could manage.

For several seconds he simply stared at her, his green eyes

dark and intense. She thought of him staring into Angelise's eyes. And pain that she couldn't reveal filled her soul. Then he shook his head slowly. "I've never been interested in making lists," he said. "I prefer action."

And with that he moved forward. He scooped her right out of her chair and up against his chest. His lips came down on hers, searing her, claiming her, turning her mind to a mess of sheer desire. Automatically her hands threaded into his hair. She pressed closer, kissed back.

Heat swirled through her. Need conquered common sense. She hadn't even known that she needed this, but she did. Now that she'd tasted him this deeply, how could she ever not want to taste him every morning?

But she couldn't. The truths his sisters had spoken added to her own unspoken truths, the walls she'd built so carefully, her fears of what could go wrong if…

Darcy gave a muffled cry and pulled back. "This is so…no, I cannot do this," she said. "Put me down."

Patrick pulled back, far enough so that he could stare directly into her eyes. "Darcy, I—damn, I'm such a jerk. I apologize."

That made her mad. "Do not apologize. Just because I said I couldn't doesn't mean I didn't like it."

Now, he grinned. He carefully lowered her into her chair, his arms spanning her, his hands coming to rest on her tires as he gently trapped her.

"Next time I'll ask before I touch you," he said.

Darcy sucked in a deep breath. "Next time? You intend for there to be a next time?"

Patrick shrugged. "You told me that I wasn't on your list of men to date, but you didn't say I wasn't on your list of men to kiss. In fact, I distinctly heard you tell Olivia that I was on your top—"

She reached out and placed her fingers over his mouth.

"All right, you're hot," she conceded. "But we're not going to kiss again."

CHAPTER SEVEN

PATRICK was not a man to use his fists, but right now he wanted to hit something very hard. Had he actually asked her who she wanted to date, he asked himself hours after he'd taken her home? Had he taken her in his arms and kissed her? Had he, in other words, crossed several lines he shouldn't have even thought of crossing?

No question about it, he had, and he wasn't at all happy with himself.

She'd met a man, she had said. Jared O'Donohue. Was he a good man? The right man? Darcy had said that she'd been hurt when her fiancé had abandoned after her accident. And now?

"None of your business, Judson," he muttered beneath his breath. Nonetheless, he sat down at his computer and began to work. It didn't take long to come up with a smattering of information. Jared O'Donahue. Good-looking guy, twenty-seven years old, he'd been given awards for heroism and bravery, but had had his legs crushed when a vehicle had run into him and pinned him against his squad car. He was, from all accounts, the best type of man and if the man had a heart beating in his body and any consciousness of what made a woman desirable, he would be interested in Darcy.

Who could blame him?

What's more, the man had a lot in common with Darcy. Background, upbringing, even the accident and the chair. He would understand everything she thought and felt in a way Patrick never really could.

So…she'd met someone. That was a good thing, wasn't it? Wasn't it his goal to make sure that all the residents of Able House were happy and healthy? Being in a good relationship would certainly contribute to Darcy's happiness.

"Of course, it's a darned good thing," he said to the walls. So, why did he feel as if he'd missed something, lost something?

That couldn't matter. It was selfish, and he couldn't afford to be selfish where Darcy was concerned. That kind of attitude would end up hurting her. It wasn't going to happen.

Darcy woke up the next morning and realized that she'd been dreaming about being held in Patrick's arms. She'd been kissing him, and…then he had pulled her closer, twisting so that she ended up beneath him and he was smiling into her eyes, bracing himself above her.

"Kiss me, Darcy," he'd said, and she had, betraying her good intentions in her dreams. She'd reached out, and her palms had slid over the smooth, warm muscles of his chest. No cloth barring her way. He had been warm, hard, exciting. The pads of her fingertips had tingled, and—

They'd been in bed together.

Darcy groaned as she realized just how vivid her dream had been. She reached out and pulled a pillow over her head, but that didn't erase the vision or the bereft sensation she felt now that the dream had ended and reality had set in.

Dreaming about making love with Patrick? No wonder his

sisters were concerned. She was acting like a fool. Just because he had kissed her a couple of times.

He'd probably kissed a thousand women. And walked away from every one.

Except for maybe Angelise, Darcy thought, remembering the statuesque brunette with perfect breasts, a tanned, fit body and killer legs made even more gorgeous by the lacy stilettos she'd been wearing.

"Stop it," she muttered from beneath her pillow just as she realized that someone was knocking on her door.

Immediately she sat up, shrugged on a robe, transferred herself into her chair and rolled over to slide the pocket door open.

"How was it?" Cerise asked before the door had completed its slide. "You came home so late that I didn't get a chance to ask. Did Patrick walk you home?"

He had. And as he had seen her into the house, he had slid his palm over her cheek and thanked her once again in that low, deep voice that had seemed incredibly intimate in the darkness.

Where in the world was her pillow? She had to stop the images, the memories, the longings.

Yeah, that would really decrease Cerise's curiosity. Darcy took a deep breath and managed a composed smile. "It was very successful. The meal went well, and I had people asking me to cater their parties."

"Wow, I'm impressed, but how does Patrick feel about that?"

And just like that, it hit Darcy full force. "Patrick will be flying overseas in a few weeks. He'll be gone a long time and he won't be needing my services after that."

And when he returned, Darcy thought, would he marry the beautiful Angelise and settle down to have babies? Darcy's breath caught, her throat burned. How foolish she was to have had those fantasy dreams of him. Their worlds and their lives were so different…

She clenched her hands on the wheels of her chair as if to remind herself of that.

"Did you hear that Julio's company laid him off yesterday?" Cerise asked, changing the subject.

Immediately, indignation and regret shot through Darcy. Not Julio. That was so unfair. Julio was a favorite of everyone at Able House. He had been much older than the rest of them when he'd suffered his injury and his recovery had taken longer, so just getting back into life had been more difficult. His injury had been no impediment to his job as a midlevel executive at an insurance firm and for the past few years he'd returned to his old field. But he was already in his fifties and it would be difficult to face having to start over again. Getting a new job at his age would be a challenge.

"Did you hear what I said, Darce?"

Darcy blinked. "I'm sorry. I missed the last part."

"Patrick found him a job as an apprentice piano tuner. Julio is in love with the idea!"

"A piano tuner?"

"Sure. You know how he loves to play that baby grand in the lobby."

"Yes, but…"

"Apparently Patrick noticed his skill, questioned him about it and when he heard about the problem yesterday, he made some calls, pulled some strings and now Julio is over the top. He hated the insurance business."

And who else but Patrick would have even thought to notice or to put two and two together and come up with such a perfect solution? Patrick's attentiveness to detail, the care he took with all of them made Darcy's heart fill. And break.

Patrick was the kind of man every woman wanted to know. But could a woman know this much of him and not want to know more? But to open up that way to a man who was determined to leave…could she survive the heartbreak when he left her behind?

"Still," Cerise said. "All is not well." She related her concerns to Darcy. One of the other residents had had a run-in with one of the few neighbors who continued to resent having so many wheelchairs cruising around the elite neighborhood and, supposedly, negatively impacting their property values. Words had been exchanged. There had nearly been blows. It had been ugly.

Darcy frowned. "Don't tell Patrick," she said. "And tell everyone else to keep it a secret from him, too. Patrick will only worry, and this is something he can't fix. He can't change every person's opinion of us, and I don't want him to leave here concerned that things aren't right for the residents of Able House. If he's concerned…"

She didn't want to be a responsibility to him, a loose end he hadn't tied up. Darcy bit her lip.

"Darce?"

Darcy looked at her friend. "I'll spread the word," Cerise promised. "Are we still going dancing tonight? You said we'd hit the Domenici Ballroom out in the suburbs. I assume Jared will be there?"

Jared? Darcy had almost forgotten about him. That wasn't right at all. Jared was the man she should be thinking about. They had a lot in common. He was a nice man, a handsome man. For sure, she would try to start thinking of him romantically, but for now…

"We're going," she agreed. "We'll talk more later. I have to get ready for work now."

I have to get ready to steel myself not to think about kissing Patrick when I see him this morning, she thought.

But later, when she finished setting up the small buffet she had arranged for breakfast and Patrick, the only early riser in the house, came up behind her, she turned and the first thing she looked at was his lips. And those arms that had held her, those hands that had touched her…

She caught herself and frowned.

"Don't," he said just as if she had spoken. "I'm not going to touch you again if you don't want me to."

She wanted him to. "It wouldn't be a good idea," she told him. Or was it herself she was reminding?

Darcy started to retreat to the kitchen.

"Could I have a minute of your time?" he asked.

She stopped moving and waited.

Patrick sat down in a chair beside her. "In two days time, I'm supposed to be helping out at a fund-raiser for a children's charity. It was organized before you started working for me, and since it's a brief affair, food wasn't to be a part of it. But Eleanor, who's also involved, apparently had one of those middle-of-the-night aha! moments. She asked if I could convince you to prepare some treats for the kids, but I don't want you to feel obligated in any way. I know that's not in your job description."

She looked at Patrick and saw that he was studying her intently. That dark green gaze seemed to see parts of her soul that she had been trying very hard to keep hidden.

"This is an event where there will be lots of children," he said, his voice deep and low and gentle. "And…your aversion to my nephews at dinner was more than simple dislike, wasn't it?" he asked.

Indignation and remorse threatened to overwhelm her. "I

didn't dislike them! I couldn't. They're adorable. Sweet. So very little and innocent, but…"

Patrick waited.

"It's not that simple," she finally said. "Remember how I told you that I was engaged when I had my accident?"

"Of course. Your fiancé turned out to be a shallow imbecile."

She managed a slightly wobbly smile. "Thank you, but there's more. I wasn't just engaged. I was pregnant. I lost my baby."

He leaned toward her. "Darcy…"

She held up one hand. "I'm not telling you this so that you'll feel sorry for me, but so that you'll understand. I could never dislike your nephews. I just can't—"

As if he didn't even see her hand, Patrick reached out. "Darcy," he said again, pulling her onto his lap and tucking her against him. "I'm so sorry you lost your child."

Darcy felt warm and safe lying here against Patrick's heart. She felt as if she could tell him anything. "It wasn't just the loss of my baby that made me this way," she said. "Under other circumstances, I think I might have healed a bit more than I have or maybe even tried again. As it was, not long after I finished my physical therapy when I was first learning to get around in the chair, I was in a shopping center where I'd gone to practice maneuvering. As I was moving past a flight of stairs, I looked up. Back in those days I always looked up when I saw stairs. The newness and the despair of realizing that staircases had become as insurmountable as a snow-capped Mount Everest seemed to draw my attention every time. But this time, it wasn't just the stairs. There was a little girl, a toddler standing at the top of the staircase, playing. Her mother must have moved away or looked away for a minute, and the child…she was so close to the edge and she was ungainly in the way children of that age are.

"In my mind, I can still see her taking one more step and I can still feel the horror that there was no way I could even begin to try to help her in time. I yelled, but I didn't think anyone heard. The little girl pitched forward and…just as she did, someone, another woman shot past me and caught her. She'd fallen a step or two and was banged up a bit, but she hadn't tumbled very far. I was so relieved, but also…so scared. I kept thinking, what if that person hadn't passed by at that moment? And what if I ever had a child? I couldn't chase her in that kind of a situation. I might not be able to move fast enough or to reach her if she was somewhere that my chair wouldn't go and…I just can't have children," she finished quietly, looking up at Patrick. "I can't—I don't want to be too near children. It's just so painful. The fear is always there. The loss is always there, because I wanted them…so much."

"Shh, Darcy, Darcy," Patrick said, rocking her in his arms. "I promise you I won't put you through that. I won't—I'm calling Eleanor and telling her no."

Instantly Darcy sat up. "No, that's not what I meant. You'll do no such thing."

Patrick looked startled.

"I mean…don't call Eleanor, please," Darcy said, realizing that she had, once again, forgotten that Patrick was her boss. She quickly pushed away from him and transferred herself to her chair. "I can't be *with* them, but…preparing the food…that is one thing I *can* do for a child. I can be anonymous but still give something. It's such a small thing, but it would mean a lot to me. Please let me help in this one little way," she said.

He shook his head.

Darcy frowned. "Why not? Are you telling me no?"

"I'm telling you yes. I'm telling you that you're an amazing woman, Darcy Parrish."

But she couldn't allow herself to accept compliments from him, not when she felt herself to be a coward. Had she really been so far gone that she had allowed him to take her onto his lap? She could have said no. She was sure he would have listened to her. That was the kind of man he was.

Instead she had snuggled up to him and fallen even farther into infatuation.

"Hey, this isn't such a big deal. It will be fun for me," she said, knowing that it would be a form of torture, of penance for not being more mentally tough. And staying here with Patrick any longer was only going to test her resolve to back away from what she was beginning to feel for him.

"I'd better go think of something to make." She turned away.

"Thank you. I have to get going, anyway. I'm on my way over to Able House."

Uh-oh. Her mind went on full-alert. "Something wrong?" Had he heard about the new argument with the neighbor and the heated words that had been exchanged?

"No, not at all. Just details. Eric is moving to Tennessee, but I guess you knew that."

"Oh. Sure." She smiled brightly. Maybe too brightly.

"Something wrong?" he asked, using her own words.

"No. Nothing." Darn. Definitely too bright. She'd been caught off guard with no time to don her poker face.

Patrick leaned close. He bent down. "Okay, you don't want to share?" he whispered near her ear, sending a thrill through her body. "I won't pry into your secrets."

That was good, because her darkest secret was that while she had promised herself she wouldn't be interested in Patrick, she was. She wanted to feast on his kisses.

Thank goodness she was going dancing with Jared tonight. Surely if she paid more attention to him, common sense would

kick in, she would develop an attraction to Jared, their friend-
ship might turn into something more, and this insane something she was feeling for Patrick would completely disappear.

Maybe she'd even be on the road to being over him by tonight.

CHAPTER EIGHT

PATRICK lay awake in the gathering light the next morning and cursed the reason why he had tossed and turned all last night. When he'd gone to Able House yesterday, Cerise, who taught fitness classes, had been the only resident around and she'd practically been bouncing around in her chair.

"You look happy," Patrick had told her, and she had explained to him that she and Darcy were going dancing later that evening with some friends. It had been clear from the glow in her eyes that the friends were men.

The cop, he had thought. Be happy for Darcy, he'd told himself.

He was. He was also something else, something unacceptable, and he didn't want to think about that. He had no business being jealous of Jared O'Donahue just because the man had spent the evening dancing with Darcy. And yet...

Patrick let out a growl, got out of bed and stood under a cold shower. Then, he went to the kitchen and prowled around. Darcy wasn't there, but Lane was.

"Where is she?" he asked.

Lane didn't even bother pretending she didn't know. "Cara and Amy are coming over. I wanted to have breakfast on the lawn, so I had your new gardener carry the tables and gear out. Darcy is out there with a blender and some secret ingredients making something luscious, fruity and frothy for us to drink."

Patrick nodded. He made a beeline for the French doors and continued on a straight line until he reached the semi-shaded area at the far end of the broad expanse of lawn where Darcy was working her magic.

She stopped her blender at his approach. "Bad night?" she asked. "You look grumpy."

"You're not supposed to tell your boss he looks grumpy," he said.

She peeked up at him from beneath those long eyelashes, a mischievous look on her face. "Too late. I already did."

"You seem very lively this morning. Have a good evening?" Patrick cursed himself for not being able to prevent himself from asking the question. Dammit, her private life was none of his business, was it?

Her wonderfully expressive face had grown more pensive at his question. Slightly distressed.

"Forget I asked that. Cerise told me that you were going dancing, but I shouldn't be intruding on your privacy."

"No, it's all right. Really." She waved her hand, dismissing his concern. It's just, I should have had a good time. I've loved the lessons so far. The dancing is exciting and fun and I love learning new things, but up until now the lessons have been private. Last night, at a public ballroom where we stood out so much, I felt as if I was on display. It was a small crowd, so it wasn't completely terrible, but…it was uncomfortable. I felt as if we were taking up too much space on the dance floor."

"You had as much right to be there as everyone else."

Darcy laughed suddenly, a bright sound. "Thank you for

saying that, but…I wish you could see your face. You look so wonderfully miffed on my behalf. A little bit pompous, too, as only someone of your stature can be."

Patrick couldn't help himself then. "As if you care about my stature." And wasn't that part of Darcy's appeal? She didn't care about his rank. She didn't care about…

He stopped himself cold. He'd been nearing forbidden territory again. "Was Jared there, then?" he asked, wading right in where he didn't want to go.

"Who's Jared?" Cara's voice broke into his thoughts and Patrick turned to see his sister marching across the lawn, toddler in hand.

He felt the lightness fade right out of Darcy even though he couldn't see her. Panic, sadness emanated from her. He could sense it. And—was it his imagination or did she retreat further behind the table?

"Jared is a friend of Darcy's," he said. "And none of our business."

"Oh? Sounds delicious," Amy said, following her sister. "I'm happy for you, Darcy." She sounded happy, too. Too happy.

Patrick shot her a warning look. He quickly scooped up Charlie on one arm and Davey on the other as if to protect Darcy, even though his nephews were loving little boys. "Hey, scamp," he said to Charlie.

"Me, too?" Davey said.

"Absolutely, you, too. I was just going to say hi, scoot," he told Davey. The little boy beamed.

Patrick felt Darcy's eyes on him and turned to catch a look of such pained longing, such utter sadness that he quickly made his excuses and started to carry the boys away.

"You haven't had your breakfast," Darcy said, but her voice seemed a bit broken.

"It's all right, Darcy," he said, even though it was clear that nothing was all right. "I'm fine."

She got a stubborn look in her pretty eyes. "Breakfast is the most important meal of the day. You shouldn't miss it."

Amy's and Cara's eyebrows rose.

"I know. I have a bad habit of lecturing him. I'm working on it," she told his sisters, that stubborn, unbending look still firming up that pretty chin of hers.

"I wouldn't worry about trying to learn not to lecture him," Lane said as she came outside, too. "After all, he's leaving the country soon. Then how you treat him will be a moot point since he won't even be around. By the time he comes back, who knows? He might be married and have a wife who cooks for him and lectures him."

"Lane," Patrick said sternly. It was totally clear that his sister was warning Darcy off, even though he knew that Darcy didn't need any warning because she wasn't interested.

"I didn't mean that you would leave Darcy high and dry," his youngest sister reasoned. "Because, of course, she'll go directly from here right to another job, right?"

He didn't answer at first. It occurred to him how quickly time was flying by.

Amy and Cara came closer. Patrick noticed that Lane was tugging at a strand of hair. It was an old habit and a sure sign of a guilty conscience. "I mean, you'll make sure Darcy has a good place to go, won't you, Patrick?" she asked.

"Because you always taught us that we needed to care for our employees' feelings," Cara cut in.

"And we know that you've already found at least temporary jobs for everyone else who'll be left with nothing to do when you're gone," Amy added.

"Darcy, I apologize," Lane said. "Those things I said—that

was mean of me and…not okay. I didn't mean to be so flippant. But I naturally thought that Patrick would—"

"She'll have the best," Patrick finally said. "I promise you that. I look after my own." But, of course, she wasn't his own, he thought as he carried his nephews into the house, fed them there and kept them there. He didn't want to leave Darcy alone with his sisters, but he couldn't bear to see how torn up she was when the boys were around.

His sisters did have a way of blurting out whatever was on their minds. Almost as much as Darcy did.

Maybe he should have asked them to find out if she was falling in love with Jared.

But maybe he didn't actually want to know that.

"These muffins are decadent, Darcy," Amy told her. "I—I apologize, too. We've been rude. Thoughtless. It's just that…"

Darcy turned to face Patrick's middle sister. "Thank you for the compliment. And don't worry. I know you're concerned that I might have some sort of crush on Patrick, but that's not going to be a problem."

Amy blushed.

Cara rushed forward. "What Amy meant was, yes, we're concerned about Patrick, but not in the way you think. He gave up so much for us and never, ever made us feel that he was sacrificing his happiness, not even when he got called home from the prom because one of us had gotten in trouble. But we knew he had to want more. Now he can have more, but…we're also worried that without at least one of us to fuss over, he'll be lonely. And we have female friends—not just Angelise, but others, too, who've been waiting for the chance to date Patrick. We've been making plans and—"

And. Cara didn't have to say more. Darcy Parrish hadn't

been in the plans. She almost wanted to laugh. Wasn't that just the very thing that had tripped her up all her life? Either she hadn't been in someone else's plans and had messed with their situation, or life had thrown her a curve that hadn't been in her plans. But that had to change. She didn't want to be remembered as a negative in Patrick's life, someone who showed up at the wrong time and messed things up for him and kept him from meeting the perfect woman.

Heaven knew she wasn't the perfect woman, and by perfect Darcy wasn't thinking about her legs. She was thinking about those two little boys and how right they had looked snuggled up in Patrick's arms, how he should have some children of his own to cuddle and spoil and raise and love. Her heart hurt at the thought.

Slowly she shook her head. "You don't have to worry. I'm not going to have a romantic entanglement with your brother," she said quietly.

The three of them nodded, though guilt still seemed to register in their eyes. They ate their breakfast in silence, then picked up their plates, said a subdued goodbye to Darcy and walked toward the house. As they neared the graceful white building, Darcy thought she heard them rattling off names of women.

Five minutes later, Patrick came out to where she was cleaning up the area. "I was just going to call Peter to help me get all this inside," she said.

"Will I do, instead?"

She looked up into those compelling green eyes. Yes, he would do, a small, wistful voice inside her shouted. He was the kind of man that every girl dreamed of, wasn't he? Even smart-mouthed girls from the wrong side of the tracks who couldn't possibly ever have someone like this?

"I don't know," she said, pasting on a grin to lighten the mood and hide her wistfulness. "Let me see your muscles."

Patrick raised a brow. He turned and struck a mocking pose. It was meant to be silly, but oh, he did have a fantastic set of muscles.

"Okay, I think you can handle a few utensils. At least light ones," she teased, hoping she didn't sound breathless.

"Yes, but the question is can I handle you?" he asked as they gathered some of the gear and headed toward the house.

"Handle me?" Darcy hoped she didn't sound breathless.

"Able House. What's going on there? I meant to talk to you earlier but I didn't want to have this conversation in front of my sisters. The thing is that when I showed up at Able House yesterday I could tell that something was wrong. People kept looking at me and whispering, but when I asked them to tell me what was happening, no one would say anything. Eventually I heard someone whisper your name, but by then I knew trying to get information from them wasn't going to work. So, I'm taking my questions straight to the source. What's going on with you, Darcy?" They had entered the house and he had put the things he'd been carrying down. He leaned closer.

She stopped breathing. What was going on with her? Him. This. This ridiculous, silly, unacceptable longing she felt whenever he got too close. After she'd just told his sisters—

"Nothing's going on with me," she said solemnly. And she meant it. She willed it to be true.

"Then what's wrong at Able House?"

Darcy considered ignoring the question or lying, but now that he had asked her directly…

"Tell me," he said, his voice a rough whisper. "I can help. I'll try to help."

"No, you can't, Patrick. You can't fix everything for us. You've done so much, but…"

Darcy flung her arm out. "You can't make everything right for us. All of us know that. Some battles can't be won. We know it. We live it, and…we're so incredibly grateful to you for what you're doing, but…"

"I don't want your gratitude," he said, his voice low and dark and husky.

"But you have it," she told him. "I can't stop that."

He was close now. So very close.

"I hate it that someone might have wronged you in a neighborhood where I set you up."

"It's just one or two people."

"But it wouldn't have happened somewhere else."

"You don't know that."

"I think I do. I've lived here all my life. There are always a few people who don't like young children or dogs that don't have pure enough bloodlines or—"

He didn't have to finish. There were two neighbors who just weren't happy about Able House and probably never would be.

"I'll talk to them again," he said. And he would come away frustrated and feeling guilty, because Darcy knew the kind of person they were dealing with. She'd dealt with them in that school and on her job from time to time. She'd seen the lack of acceptance in her former fiancé's expression.

"Don't do it," she said, reaching out to catch Patrick's wrist. "It just isn't worth it."

"Darcy."

"Promise me," she said.

He stared into her eyes for so long that she was afraid she would lean toward him, signal him, show him how drawn to him she was.

Instead he looked down to where she clasped his wrist. He covered her hand with his, turning her hand so that her palm was up. Then he brought her hand to his lips and kissed that most sensitive center of her palm.

Desire shot through her so fast she couldn't contain it.

He kissed her palm again, his lips soft and warm.

"Don't let me do more than this," he said. "I want to kiss you, but if you tell me no, I won't."

Darcy sat there just a breath away from Patrick. He had replaced his lips with his thumb and was tracing long, slow circles on her skin. She could barely sit still, could barely keep from moaning.

When more seconds than she could count had passed and she still hadn't spoken, he turned to her, leaned toward her. His lips were close. If she leaned forward just slightly, she would be against him. She could kiss him, feel him, feel right.

"Tell me no," he told her again.

She reached up and threaded her fingers through his hair. "No," she said, even as she pulled him down to her and touched her lips to his.

She kissed him greedily, tasted him, savored him.

He didn't touch her. Only a low growl escaped him, but his body was rigid, hot, tense.

Darcy kissed him again. She wanted more. She wanted… she wanted…

"Please," she said. "Please, yes. Just one kiss."

"Thank you," he said on a groan and pulled her to him. He dropped to his knees so that he was slightly below her and he nuzzled his mouth against hers. Then he covered her more fully, licking at the seam of her mouth, exploring her carefully, hotly. He was making her insane.

He cupped her face in his palms and replaced his lips with

his thumb, discovering the shape of her mouth, making her shiver with his light, teasing touch. His hand drifted lower, to her chin, her throat. Wherever he touched, he followed up with a trail of kisses that left her aching for more.

"I—Patrick—I—"

"I love the way the scent of cinnamon and vanilla clings to your skin. I want to breathe you in. Deeply. You make me want things," he whispered against her skin. "Things I didn't even know I wanted before. And I know I should stay away. I want to stay away, but—"

As he spoke, his lips continued on their fiery path until his mouth was against that oh-so-sensitive line where her injury had occurred, where sensation was always more intense, a line of demarcation that—

Patrick kissed her there and Darcy's mind went blank, then turned hot, needy and—

Oh, he'd just said that he wanted to stay away. She'd just promised his sisters that she wouldn't do this, want this, be this way and yet…

Patrick kissed her, his touch shaking her to the core.

His sisters would bring other women. Angelise. More. He would do this with them, too, she thought and knew that it was true.

Something broke inside her. Something hurt. What was she doing? "No more."

Her voice barely ranked as a whisper, the sound was so soft, but Patrick stopped. Immediately. He was breathing hard, his green eyes were glazed with desire so heated that Darcy could barely look for fear she'd reach out and grab him again, but he stopped. Completely.

"We can't," she said, biting at her lip. "I'm sorry. I keep doing this, but—I have to be whole when this is over. So do you. And you—I—this might leave a scar, unfinished business. I don't want any unfinished business in my life. It's more than I can handle."

Slowly he nodded. He reached out and gently righted her clothes, even though she hadn't registered till now just how disheveled she was.

"I'll try not to let this happen again," he said, "but you must know by now that you have a tendency to make me lose my self-control."

"You might have noticed that I was the one who grabbed you."

"But you didn't want to."

"No."

"As I said, I'll try to make sure it doesn't happen again." Just as if he could control the whole thing. And maybe he could. He'd been put in charge of the care and feeding and rearing of three sisters when he'd only been nineteen. Control had been a part of his life for so many years.

And wasn't that part of what his trip was about? Do some good, do some business and let loose of all that stunning control?

Yet, here he was, promising her that he would take care of things once again. He would police himself and her as well. And he would take the blame if anything went awry.

His sisters were right. Entirely right. He needed lightness and fun and a woman who wasn't going to always be making him feel the heavy responsibility of maintaining control. With the right kind of woman, he could let loose. He could give one hundred percent and he could be happy.

"You don't have to make sure it won't happen. I'll do that," she said.

He had risen and the quick frown he cast her way, the rigid line of his jaw, didn't bode well for her power grab. She needed a distraction, a change of topic.

"Got to go."

"We're not done yet, Darcy. Things aren't settled."

"Yes. They are. And I have to figure out what treat I'm making for that benefit for the children tomorrow. No time to waste. I've got lots of work to do. Things to decide. Supplies to purchase."

He let her flutter a bit. Then he stared her down until she stopped.

"It wasn't a whim," he told her. "Not something I do lightly. I want you to know that."

She didn't want to know that. She didn't want to think about it. Thinking meant longing, and longing meant admitting that he was just one more thing she couldn't have. No, not that. Not *just*. He was so much more than just one more thing. He was major.

"If things were different. If I weren't your benefactor and if—"

Darcy let out a small, fierce cry. She reached up as if to press her fingertips over his lips. No, she so didn't want to hear that. If things were different and they tried to make this something more than it could ever be, then…

I'd be another responsibility to him, she thought. He would never have that carefree time he craved and needed. He would never have that easy fling with a woman, because much as she liked herself, Darcy knew that nothing about her was easy.

"Things aren't different," she said carefully, trying not to look too deeply into his eyes. Then, as quickly as she could go, she escaped.

A part of her wished that he would follow her, but he didn't. And she knew that it was for the best. Sometimes doing the right thing felt…wrong. This business of training herself not to want Patrick's touch was going to take some time.

* * *

The next time Darcy saw Patrick was the next day when he came to load his van and take her to the fund-raiser.

"Have you spoken to Eleanor?" she asked, trying for some light conversation.

"Yes. An hour ago."

"Oh, things must be taking off, then."

"Yes, I think so. She did tell me to let you know that a few more children than she had originally told you about had been added."

Was that an evasive look on his face?

"Oh," she said. "How many more will there be?"

For a second Patrick looked uncomfortable. "Let's just say that Eleanor was a bit distraught and Eleanor is pretty much unflappable."

Darcy felt panic creeping through her chest. "So...how many exactly did you say?"

"I didn't."

"I know. Patrick," she drawled, trying to look stern.

"Let's just say...too many."

The panic grew. She gave him an exasperated look. "Let's just be really exact. I need to know if I have enough supplies and if I made enough to go around."

Patrick swore beneath his breath. "All right. I was trying to save you from panic. Fifty more."

Fifty? There had already been two hundred on the original list, and—

"Okay. All right. I can handle that many," Darcy said, trying to convince herself. "I'm not panicking."

Liar. Panic was beating at her like a bird's frantic wings. It was speeding up, taking over. *What was she going to do about that?*

"Okay, let's see. Well, fifty more? Hmm, Patrick, I'm definitely going to go throw up now. You might not want to stick around for this. I can guarantee that it won't be pretty."

And just like that, he was on his knees in front of her, smiling up into her face. "I'll help you," he said. "I'll stay beside you all the way. You're going to be so great. They'll absolutely love you."

"You're a very brave man kneeling in front of a woman who just told you she was going to be sick."

"Well, what can I tell you?" he asked with a wink as he rose. "I'm a risk-taker."

He was. She knew that. She knew about the skateboarding and the bungee jumping and the skydiving. He loved the challenge.

And she was not a risk-taker. She might have a smart mouth, but that was all a self-defense move, a mask to hide behind. She admitted it, and Patrick probably knew it as well.

He also knew something else. He knew how to distract a woman perfectly. She was no longer feeling sick or worrying about how she was going to come through for two hundred fifty children.

Instead she was worrying about how she was going to manage to get through the afternoon. Patrick had said he was going to be beside her the whole way.

Darcy pressed her palms over her chest and concentrated on breathing in and out. And she began to count to two hundred fifty. By the time she reached that magic number, she was hoping common sense would have returned and her panic would have subsided.

There was, after all, nothing to worry about. This was a totally public event. She wasn't going to drag Patrick down and kiss him again. What could possibly happen?

CHAPTER NINE

DARCY was amazing, Patrick thought, watching her at work. The fund-raiser was in a big, beautiful new building and she was closed up in the kitchen, secluded from the area where hundreds of children had gathered. Eleanor had been more than willing to transfer this to a venue with an open-air kitchen so everyone could watch Darcy work her magic. Instead this place was totally utilitarian and sterile, and probably most people would have found the setup a bit boring. Demanding. Not at all fun or energizing. But Darcy was glowing.

Just an hour earlier, the countertops had been groaning beneath the weight of what had seemed like thousands of finger sandwiches decorated with colorful cream cheese frostings, various pitchers of pink and green and blue smoothies and fruit cups topped off with whipped cream and star sprinkles. There had been home-baked potato chips and a dinosaur centerpiece surrounded by a wall of cheese cubes.

"So, what do you think?" she asked him, holding out a tray of cookies shaped like cars and airplanes, unicorns and stars and various other shapes. Each cookie had a child's name swirled on in a contrasting color.

"I think you must be totally insane," he told her. "Insane, but very cute with that frosting on your nose." He gently wiped it off with an index finger, then licked his finger.

Bad mistake. She blushed, and he felt heat swirl through him. He ignored it. "Two hundred fifty individualized cookies, Darcy?"

"Well, all of them but the last fifty were made in advance. I had Eleanor give me a list of names. Olivia was there to help me with the first two hundred, and, as you know, she was here earlier until she had to leave."

He knew. He had positioned himself at the door to make sure that no one intruded, so she could have the privacy she needed, and be out of sight of the children whose presence clearly brought her pain. Now, the event was almost over except for the finale, those amazing cookies she'd whipped up and tirelessly decorated.

Patrick signaled the last of the students he'd hired to go ahead and distribute the cookies. Then, he looked around at the kitchen. It was almost immaculate, even though he'd watched Darcy destroy the place during her preparations. The food and the kids, not the state of the hospital white kitchen had clearly been her priorities, but now she and her crew had worked a miracle cleanup worthy of a magician.

"Almost done," she told him as she took a few last swipes at a table with a damp cloth. "We can leave soon." But, he saw her gaze shift toward the door where children's voices suddenly rose higher. Obviously Eleanor had planned some sort of exciting grand finale.

"Are you sure you don't want to go have a look?" he asked.

She gave him a wary, tired and very tight smile. "No, I'm okay right here. Do you think they liked the food? Not that kids pay that much attention to food, I know, but…"

"Darcy," he said, cutting in. "You made every item so kid friendly that they would have had to be asleep not to have loved it. In fact, I saw two munchkins comparing those cream cheese faces you had put on their sandwiches. I think they were striking a deal, a trade, and both of them looked immensely pleased with themselves." Which was, in fact, the truth.

"Good. Eleanor told me that some of them end up eating the same thing every day because they can't afford anything but the least expensive items. I remember what it was like not to have variety. Oh well, let me just finish putting away one or two more things."

He nodded, just as a voice sounded behind him. He turned to tell the person approaching that this room was a private area, but before he could do that, a woman with a camera came barreling past him. She flashed a badge dangling from her neck, some sort of press ID or something, but she kept moving, making a beeline for Darcy.

"Suburban Gazette," she said. "Just a few quick questions, Ms. Parrish. You *are* Ms. Parrish, aren't you? The one who did the catering?"

Without asking, she stuck her camera into Darcy's face and clicked off several rapid shots.

Patrick didn't even hesitate. He stepped between Darcy and the woman. "She's off-limits," he said.

Darcy's groan was almost imperceptible, but he heard it and knew what she was thinking. She was right. He should have known better. His statement had just made Darcy much more interesting than she had been a moment before. A talented chef in a wheelchair was intriguing. One who had a bodyguard was doubly intriguing, and when that bodyguard was one of the wealthiest men in the city, well...

"What Mr. Judson meant was that I'm off-limits because I'm

in the midst of the creative process. We're planning his sister's surprise going-away-to-college party, but if word gets out…" Darcy blew out a frustrated sigh so big that her bangs lifted off her forehead. "We would just have to go back to square one and plan something else. There wouldn't even be any party," she said, pointedly staring at the reporter.

"So…I would be writing about a nonexistent event?" the woman said.

"Exactly."

"But you have to know that I don't care about the party. I came here to interview you."

"Another time, perhaps," Darcy said, pasting on an angelic smile that Patrick had never witnessed. "Ms.—I'm sorry, I don't know your name, and the print on your name tag is pretty small and above my line of sight and—well, it's hanging right over your…um, your chest."

"Ms. Compton," the woman said.

"Ms. Compton, you're a writer and a photographer, clearly a creative individual. Were you ever in the middle of creating something and had the process interrupted? I just—it's so— it's difficult to explain to someone who doesn't make their living using their imagination, but—"

The woman smiled. "Okay, you win. Interrupt the process and the best ideas may be lost in the ether and never return. I understand and…all right, I'll go." And she turned to do just that. Just before she left, she turned back. "Is it all right if I use the picture?"

Darcy's angelic smile disappeared. It was replaced with a look of anguish. "I really need people to know me for my talents, not for…other things," she said. "Would it be all right if you skipped the picture and just mentioned my name as the chef? I'm starting a catering business, and that would be a big help."

The woman considered the question. "The photo might bring in business."

"Not the kind I want. Let me put it this way…if this were an earlier era, would you want to be hired because you were a female reporter and, therefore, a curiosity or would you want to be courted for your talent?"

The woman considered that. "Okay, you win again. Just a one or two sentence mention of you and those great smoothies. I had one," she confessed. "I could live on those things."

And then she was gone.

Patrick sat down on a chair across from Darcy. "Are you okay?"

She nodded.

"I'm sorry," he said. "I nearly messed things up for you there."

Darcy shrugged. "I would have weathered the gossip."

As she had weathered the taunts of her old classmates and the desertion of her idiot of a fiancé and the loss of her baby.

"I'm supposed to be helping you engineer your success, not rocketing you into the tabloids."

Her mouth tipped up slightly. "The tabloids? Good thing Ms. Compton didn't hear you refer to her newspaper that way."

He grinned. "I wanted to say worse."

Darcy studied him, tilting her head. "Do you really end up in the tabloids?"

"Not usually. My life is too dull."

Her laugh was delicious. "How can it be dull when you have three sisters all trying to marry you off? I've seen the photos of all those gorgeous women Lane's been leaving on the breakfast table for you to chance upon, and I've heard about all those luscious women drooling over you."

But he didn't want just any woman drooling over him.

"Drooling isn't high on my list of admirable qualities in a wife."

She laughed. "What is?"

He stared at her. She blushed, then licked her lips nervously, making him want to groan, to snatch her up, to touch her, taste her, know all of her.

"Because," she rushed on, "maybe I could guide your sisters, point them in the right direction."

Anger rushed over Patrick. Darcy so clearly wasn't interested in him, not for the long-term, anyway.

"Do *not* start matchmaking with my sisters," he said, his voice rough and uneven. "I would hate that. You know I'm attracted to you." He got up and began to pace the room, shoving a hand through his hair. On his fourth trip back across the room, he noticed that she was holding a paper napkin that she was shredding, the pieces falling on her lap and to the floor.

Immediately he stopped pacing. "I'm being a total jerk. I'm sorry."

She looked up at him with those big, beautiful eyes. "Do you think I'm not attracted to you, too? You know I am, but I can't—this—this thing that keeps happening between us— it's just one of those benefactor, beneficiary situations. We're attracted because we're thrown together so much, it's…circumstantial, and it's not real. It's not—I don't want it."

"Shh, I'm sorry." He took the remains of the napkin from her and kissed her fingertips. "I'm sorry. What do you want?"

"I want to go home now, please."

"Absolutely. It's as good as done."

"And Patrick?"

He looked down into her eyes.

"I told that reporter I was planning a surprise party for Lane."

"I'm not putting more work on you. You're already

swamped with business. I saw Eleanor bringing you all those business cards and she told me that you were booking up fast. There will be a discreet notice placed in the newspaper that the Judsons dined privately for Lane's last day at home. The reporter will simply think that we've changed our plans."

As the last word fell from his lips, he realized that he had veered from his own plans. He'd been thinking about Darcy more than his trip lately, but she was right. This was circumstantial. She had things she wanted and needed, and he had dreams he'd wanted to pursue all his life. It was time to turn those dreams, hers and his, into reality.

In two weeks time, he intended to be in France, with Darcy a distant memory. But before that happened, he was going to take care of a few things for her.

He was going to create some opportunities. The fact that those opportunities would only create more of a chasm between them…well, that was a good thing, wasn't it?

Well, she had officially turned into a liar, Darcy thought, later that evening. She had said that she didn't want whatever it was that she felt pulsing between her and Patrick, and that was a flat-out lie. She wanted all of it. Every second.

And if she grabbled for it, then when he left…

A garbled moan escaped her lips.

"Something wrong?" Olivia asked.

"Nothing." Everything. Except…even though she'd been talking off the top of her head when she'd mentioned that benefactor, beneficiary concept, maybe, hopefully that *was* a big part of the attraction. Patrick was attracted to her because she was a novelty, and she was attracted to him because she owed him so much. He was a man who had been kind to her in ways she wasn't accustomed to.

Instantly an image of Jared came to mind. Jared had been kind. He was a friend.

She shook her head. This was different somehow.

"Darcy, what is going on with you? You're muttering and shaking your head," Olivia said.

"I've got lots of work. Just look at all these events Eleanor has snagged for me."

"You love work," Olivia pointed out.

Darcy gave her friend a deadpan look. "You're far too smart and intuitive for someone just out of high school."

"It doesn't take intuition to know that work makes you happy when you practically shriek every time you come up with a new way to serve artichokes or when you spend hours practicing your plating skills and go home with a grin on your face. Or the way you practically float on a cloud when Mr. Judson follows his nose to your coffee."

Okay, that was getting just too personal. But…

"I want to do something for Patrick before he leaves," she said.

"Kiss him?"

Darcy gave Olivia an evil glare. "That was not funny."

"But you know you want to. Everyone does."

"Not you."

"He's too old for me, and anyway, I have a boyfriend, but you…"

"I have Jared."

Olivia studied her friend. "Do you really feel that way about Jared?"

"What way?"

"Oh…like you daydream about kissing him, like you wonder what he looks like naked."

She had never even thought of Jared naked.

"How do you know I haven't *seen* him naked?"

"Have you?"

Darcy wrinkled her nose.

"I thought not," Olivia said. "You don't have 'the look' when he's around. When he came to pick you up to go dancing the other day, it was as if he was just the mailman delivering your mail."

"We have a nice mailman."

"Exactly. Your Jared is nice. But if I asked you about Mr. Judson, you wouldn't say that he was nice. Not in that way, anyway."

"What way would I say it?"

"Your voice would get all soft and kind of choked up, as if you were weak or something."

"I'm not weak."

"Weak? My Darcy? Never."

Darcy squealed and turned around. "Patrick!" she said, and her voice did, indeed, come out in a rather weak whisper. She cleared her throat and tried again. "You have got to stop doing that."

"Doing what?"

Being you, she wanted to say. Proving Olivia right.

"Sneaking up on me. At least stomp around a bit before you enter the kitchen. Or growl or shriek or something. Maybe a trumpet."

His laugh was warm and delicious and just the way a man's laugh should be.

"Sorry," he said with a wink. "I just…I needed to ask you something." He looked up at Olivia and Darcy knew he was going to ask Olivia to leave. Then she would be totally alone with him, and given the way she was feeling right now she didn't trust herself one bit. If she wasn't careful, she might do something terrible like think of him the way Olivia had suggested that she might. To Darcy's consternation, she noticed that Patrick's shirt was open at the neck, the sleeves of his white shirt were rolled up. He had the most wonderful arms, the most amazing hands. Her breathing kicked up.

"Olivia stays," she said.

He raised a brow.

"Please," she added.

"Olivia stays if you like. I just wanted to ask you if you would have any objections to Jared moving into Able House. There's an opening and the directors asked for my input. But your input is much more valuable and valid than mine. I know you like him. Would you want…"

He glanced at Olivia again.

"I'm out of here," she said, ignoring Darcy's panicked look.

"I wasn't sure what the situation is," he told Darcy. "I don't like interfering in your more personal affairs and this feels very much like interference."

What should she say? If she said yes…people already thought that Jared was romantically interested in her, and if she recommended him for this slot even Jared might begin to wonder if she was interested in *him*. Still, he was a friend, no matter what. Able House was an opportunity. Could she deny her friend this chance just because there might be complications she didn't want?

"Give the spot to Jared," she said.

He gave a tight nod. "It's done," he said, and he was gone just as quickly as he had arrived.

Darcy felt an urge to scream, to punch something. Patrick was putting up another barrier. That was a good thing. He was trying to do one more favor for her when he'd already done so many.

"This being a beneficiary all the time is making me insane," she said out loud.

*So...turn the tables. Do something for Patrick. Then you'll
be the one doing the giving and you might be free of this hero-
worship stuff, because you'll be the heroine, the benefactor.*

The idea she'd been toying with solidified. That was it. Flip
their positions and she would lose that warm, heartbreaking
gratitude tinged with desire that she always felt for Patrick.
She would be the warrior-giver; the strong, stolid one.

Nice thought, too, except...what could she possibly do
that would benefit Patrick? What did he care about? What did
he need most?

The answer wasn't long in coming. It was a decent idea, a
sound way to end things and to free both of them, too.

By rights she should have been dancing around the kitchen.
Happy that she had found a solution for her aching heart and lips.

As it was...well, life didn't offer too many perfect skies,
and this solution wasn't a totally guaranteed winner.

But at least it was something to sink her teeth into and at
least if she was thinking of some way to help Patrick she
wouldn't be thinking of kissing him.

At least when she was awake. Dreaming at night didn't
count, did it?

CHAPTER TEN

PATRICK was nearing Able House. This was the day Jared was moving in, and he wanted to be there to—

"To what?" he said out loud. To meet with the man who might be the one to make Darcy happy, the man she might fall in love with?

No, I want to make sure he isn't going to hurt her, he told himself. He couldn't really even claim that he was here to make sure that Jared was a good fit for Able House, since he already knew he was. The guy taught self-defense to the disabled, a tremendously important task since opportunistic thieves sometimes targeted them.

Jared was also, Patrick had been told, outgoing, energetic and engaging, perfect for Able House. Maybe perfect for Darcy, too.

The thought left him grumpy and distracted, so he was caught off guard when he heard a commotion just ahead of him.

"What are you doing?" That was Darcy, but she wasn't speaking to him. One of the two troublesome neighbors, the one who had apparently shot his sprinklers over the sidewalk to discourage Able House residents from rolling past his house, was facing her. The man, Cal Barrow, was on the sidewalk while two men were shoveling dirt, making a terraced area on either side of the walkway. Cal's purpose was obvious. When he'd been running the sprinklers that day, Karen, the woman who'd been passing by and had been dressed for her job at a downtown office, had been forced off the sidewalk onto the grass. But the terraces and rocks the two men had piled up would prevent that.

Right now, however, Cal's future plans weren't Patrick's concern. The man was leaning toward Darcy. "Keep working," Barrow told his men. "I need more dirt right around here." And he picked up a handful of dirt and threw it where he wanted it, but some of it fell on Darcy.

"Oops," he said. "My apologies." But his tone sounded anything but apologetic. Instead he seemed…smug and satisfied.

Patrick was still fifty yards away. "Barrow!" he yelled as he charged toward the man. "Back off. You go near her again and you'll be missing your head."

The man whirled toward Patrick. "Back off, yourself, Judson. This is my property."

Patrick crossed his arms and looked down at the shorter man. "You are such a boring, sadistic creep, Barrow, and you're also wrong. The sidewalk and the parkway are public property. Darcy has every right to be here," he said, moving closer to the man, crowding him.

"But those kinds of technicalities don't matter to jerks like you, do they? I wonder what does matter to you. Those shops you run? So what would your customers think about your bully status? I can get that information to them in a matter of hours."

"Judson," the man said with a sneer. "You social snobs who have roots going back two hundred years think you're better than the rest of us, but…look at this woman. She doesn't have a pedigree. I've checked out every single person who lives in your pet project. Most of them are human mutts, too, so don't use that high-horse tone with me."

A red rage formed in Patrick's brain when Cal called Darcy a mutt. He drew back his fist. The man was lower than dirt and he was going to pay.

"Don't. Patrick don't hit him. Do *not*, under any circumstances, do that." Darcy's voice was soft. She spoke in a low command, not a yell, but her words effectively stopped Patrick's forward movement.

He turned to her, and Cal Barrow faded from his view. "Darcy, I'm not letting anyone hurt you."

"Then don't hit him. You can't. If you do, you'll make the news. Able House will receive bad press. Right now, other than the dirt, he hasn't done anything he could be charged with. His insults are protected by the First Amendment."

Of course. All that police academy training. She would automatically assess whether or not a crime had been committed.

Cal laughed, an ugly sound. Patrick tensed as hot anger flowed through him, but he didn't hit the man. "Listen to the little lady," Barrow told Patrick. "I haven't done anything wrong."

Patrick's anger escalated. Violence had never been a part of Patrick's life, but right now he wanted to let this guy have it in the worst way. He felt his control shredding. "Stay away from her," he said again.

"Patrick," Darcy said, and once again he forced control on himself. He focused only on her. "I want you to know this," she continued. "If he had touched me, I could take care of myself. I'm trained as a police officer, and knowing that my chair might hamper my ability to control the situation in case of an attack, one of the first things I did was bone up on self-defense."

Doubts assailed Patrick, and now—with this instance—and with the knowledge that he would soon be leaving her alone, he had to know. Had to hear it again. Would she say something just to keep him from getting hauled off to jail, to protect him?

He was pretty sure she would, but—

"You're sure?" he asked.

"I could have him on the ground if I needed to."

"Did Jared teach you that?"

"No, I learned this skill before I met him."

He was staring straight into her dark, expressive eyes now. He was going to have to believe what he saw there.

Cal laughed again, but Patrick wasn't laughing. He turned to Cal. "I wouldn't push it with Darcy. If she says she could take you down, it's true."

"I'd like to see her try."

"Then you'll see it. No complaints if I win?" she asked.

"Hah, you can't win!"

"Swear that you're inviting this," she ordered. "That this is an agreement, not an assault on my part."

Barrow laughed. "Like you're really gonna hurt me. Yeah, try it."

"Your call." She rolled forward. "Just try to knock me out of my chair. Go ahead."

Okay, that was enough, Patrick thought. He believed in her, but he wasn't going to let her mix it up with this guy. Even if she won, she still might get knocked about some.

But maybe nothing was going to happen, anyway. Barrow was looking sheepish. "No."

"Yes. Try it. Do it." She motioned for Cal to "come on."

"Hell," Patrick said. He hadn't thought it would get this far. "Darcy…"

Without warning, several things happened in quick succession. Barrow swore, something about stupid females. He roared and made a quick feint her way.

Darcy yelled, "Back off!" Then she slammed the heel of her hand hard against his face, snapping his head back. When he reeled, she hit him in the groin with her other fist.

Patrick barely registered what had happened, it took place so fast. But Cal was down on the ground, in the dirt, groaning, rolling, swearing, holding himself, trying to call Darcy names and keep from retching at the same time. "I'll sue!" The words he choked out were barely recognizable as words.

"Too late. I have your agreement on video," she said, pulling her camera phone from where she had slipped it into a loose pocket. "You have to pay attention when you're angry, Mr. Barrow, and not let yourself be distracted. You might miss something…like a woman holding a camera phone like this." She demonstrated how she had held the phone low at her side so that it was barely visible, but obviously effective. "Yeah, the picture's a little crooked, and it might not stand up in court, but I doubt a jury would convict me. What's more, do you really want anyone to know that I knocked you down? That would be *sooo* bad for your tough guy reputation, wouldn't it?"

Cal's response was to simply glare at her.

"Can we go now, Patrick?" she asked with a tense smile.

Without another word, they moved away together. They were almost to the front door of Able House and well out of Cal Barrow's view when Patrick stopped. He dropped his head for a full three seconds and let the blackness and fear that had enveloped him when he'd seen Barrow come at her take over. He counted to ten. Then, slowly, he straightened and looked her right in the eye. "If you ever do something like that again—Darcy, my heart completely stopped. If it hadn't worked and he had hurt you—"

"If he had hurt me, then, you could have hit him and I

wouldn't have stopped you. Then, it would have been a case of you protecting me from actual harm, not from his nasty words. You wouldn't have gone to jail for that or had your reputation damaged."

They had resumed their slow, forward movement, but now at the entrance to the building, Patrick leaned against the bricks and looked up to the sky. "You were protecting my reputation?"

"Someone had to do it. Heavens, Patrick, you were going to slug the guy over a little dirt and a bit of name calling."

"Darcy." He slid to his knees and took her face between his big palms. "You amaze me. Constantly. It wasn't just a bit of name calling. His words were ugly."

Her smile was tremulous. "Oh. You." As if that meant anything at all. "I've been called worse than that."

Which totally slayed him. He couldn't bear to think of her being subjected to that kind of thing, having to swallow insults. But…how could he tell her that? That he wanted to, needed to protect her if that ever happened again. She valued her independence so much, and heck, she had just knocked Cal Barrow on his rear end. What's more, she had been totally right about Cal not wanting the world to know about his humiliation, but Patrick still didn't trust the guy. Cal knew how to make nice when it suited his purpose. He had no problems lying in order to win people over and make Darcy and Able House a target if he had a good enough reason. Now he had a real reason.

Concern washed over Patrick, and still framing her face, he brushed his thumbs over Darcy's soft skin. Her silky curls twined around his fingers.

She was so close. He was so worried about her. Patrick had one thought. He wanted to tumble her onto his lap, he needed to kiss her silly and hold her tight so that he could—finally—

convince himself that she was safe and secure. Once he had her up against his heart, no one could touch her. He was on the verge of putting his thoughts into action when the sound of a slamming car door halted him.

Patrick looked up. He rose to his feet. Jared was sliding from his car into his chair. Had to be Jared. Up until now, Patrick had only seen pictures of the man. They didn't do him justice. His hair was California sun gold, his skin tanned, his biceps were the biceps of a man who worked out long and hard and often.

The man rolled toward them, but Patrick's focus was on Darcy, not on the man he was meeting for the first time. She was smiling, holding out both hands. "You made it," she said.

Jared gave her a long-suffering look. "Of course, I made it here, Darcy. Why wouldn't I?"

"That car…" she said. Patrick gave the car another look. It was long and sleek and black and obviously expensive. "That's the kind of car that makes you a target and you know it as well as I do. If someone tries to take that car from you, they just might—"

"Darcy, no mothering," Jared said.

She winced a bit at the word, and Jared looked as if he'd hit a bird.

Patrick ground his teeth. "Darcy," he said, but she held up her hand.

"Hell, Darcy, I'm sorry," Jared continued, "I know better than to use that word with you, but your…your nurturing when you know I can take care of myself…"

"I know," she said. "You're right. It's your car, your choice."

"And if you were the one with the expensive car…" Jared continued.

"You're right again," she agreed. "I wouldn't let you caution me about driving it."

"You'd bust my teeth out if I even suggested you couldn't protect yourself or your vehicle." Jared swung his head toward Patrick. "He must be the man who makes all this possible," he said, gesturing toward the building.

Darcy rushed forward to make introductions.

Patrick shook his head. "I supplied the start-up money and a little more. Everyone here supplies the work."

Jared nodded. "Sorry about losing my temper there, but Darcy gets a little overprotective. That's hard to take when she won't let the pendulum swing the other way."

"Tell me about it," Patrick said.

"So, you've tried to protect her, too?" Jared asked.

"Hello," Darcy said. "I'm right here, you two. You don't have to talk as if I'm not in the vicinity when I'm a living, breathing person, and I can hear you perfectly."

Patrick gave her a sheepish grin. Jared didn't even look slightly ashamed.

"So…maybe we should go inside so Jared can get settled in," Darcy continued.

"Bossy," Jared added as he followed her in. "But very cute," he told Patrick. As Darcy moved ahead, Jared lagged behind a bit, so Patrick waited.

"Too bad she doesn't want a relationship, right?" Jared asked. "Oh, but I'm gonna keep trying. You can't blame a guy for that, can you?" His tone was teasing, but the fact that he had made such a statement at all…

Patrick wasn't sure if Jared was merely being overly friendly or if he was trying to find out if Patrick would be a vindictive landlord if he shared Jared's interest in Darcy. Either way, it didn't change the score for Patrick. Dating Jared or not, Darcy was still off-limits. And after that episode with Cal Barrow, Patrick was even more worried about her.

"I can't blame you, but I'm sure you already know that Darcy's her own woman who makes up her own mind," Patrick said. Even so, he was definitely going to have to take action and make sure she was protected from volatile, hostile and possibly vindictive people like Cal. But if he did that…knowing how much she wanted, no *needed* to be in charge, would she hate him? Her need went beyond a mere desire for independence. It was a desire to be seen as a person who had overcome all those bad things that had happened to her. Single-handedly. If he took that from her, she might hate him.

And he might have to live with that…thousands of miles from her. His departure for France was less than two weeks away.

Darcy was in the kitchen alone three days later when Patrick came in suddenly. The expression on his face was so strange, so unreadable, so not like Patrick that—

"What is it?" Darcy asked. "Is it one of the girls?" Already her heart was breaking for him. She rolled forward.

Quickly he shook his head. "They're fine."

"Then what?" She was afraid she didn't want to know. But she had to know.

"It's nothing," he said. "I'm going."

"I know. In less than two weeks."

"No. The day after tomorrow. Change of scheduling. I just found out." And without another word he dropped onto a nearby chair, pulled her onto his lap and dragged her up against his chest. She looped her arms around his neck as he kissed her.

Desire and sadness and panic filled Darcy's heart as she tasted him, as he consumed her. Hungrily she kissed him back.

"Why so soon?" she asked as they came up for air.

"There's a gathering of government officials and community groups taking place in Madrid. Our project is being hailed as a good way to promote tourism and philanthropy and they want to know more. My presence has been requested."

Darcy tried a tremulous smile. "Publicity for your cause? That's…wonderful. It's what you've wanted."

"Yes. It's what I want."

But still he held her. He kissed her throat. He stroked her skin, his thumb brushing her breast, making her ache.

"It's what I've *always* wanted," he said, and now his voice sounded vaguely angry.

"Patrick?"

"Darcy, look at me. I'm sorry I'm manhandling you like this. I didn't even ask your permission. Again," he said as he eased her back into her chair. "I hope you know that I would never ask you to do anything that made you uncomfortable."

"I could have made you stop if I wanted you to."

He rested his forehead against hers. "Yes. You could have, but still…I don't want you to believe—I'll try not to let it happen again," he repeated.

No. There wouldn't be a chance for anything to happen between them, even if she wanted it to, Darcy thought with tears clogging her throat. Because he would be gone.

Somehow she had to live with that. She had to get past it, to make his last day here special and happy. A celebration.

It was time to put her plan in action. The only problem with the plan was…she had no time to plan.

CHAPTER ELEVEN

PATRICK was going slowly insane. This was the day he had been anticipating for years, and now that it was here, all he could think about was Darcy.

He'd run out of time with her, and…tension suffused his soul. That tension wasn't personal, he told himself. No, because that would be crazy. He and Darcy were polar opposites. They wanted different things. He was finally getting his freedom, a chance to fly free and explore his wild side. That would bring him and his company lots of attention, but it wouldn't be good for someone like Darcy. She hated attention, and this kind—it would be worse than what she was used to. It would involve celebrity. People wouldn't just be curious about her chair. They would want to know everything about her. They would dig up the school story, the fiancé story, the miscarriage story.

He frowned at that. He could never subject Darcy to that. He didn't want to hurt her. He didn't want anyone else to hurt her, either, he thought, remembering Cal Barrow.

Darcy might have bested the guy this time, but what about the next time or the next Cal Barrow?

"I'll take care of that," he promised himself. Already a

plan was in motion. That plan didn't make him feel any better about leaving Darcy tomorrow, but it was the best he could do on such short notice.

But his departure was still hours away. And Darcy was somewhere in the house. He could at least talk to her one more time.

Patrick opened the door of his study and stepped into the hallway.

The scent of sage and thyme and something roasting drifted to him. He breathed in and followed the aromatic trail. Cinnamon, nutmeg, coffee. Oh, yes, coffee. He would know that particular blend that Darcy brewed blindfolded.

He turned the corner.

And there they were. His family. All of them, his sisters and his brothers-in-law, seated around the table in front of a sumptuous candlelit meal. A small table had been set up for Charlie and Davey far away from the threat of candles and burns. Someone had put out little plates decorated with farm animals for them, and Charlie was leading Davey in a game of "what sound does this animal make?"

A banner hung over the doorway. It read, Happy Adventures, Patrick! Another one in the other doorway said simply, We'll Miss You. On the wall a long ribbon had been strung with photos of him and the girls over the years.

A large lump formed in Patrick's throat. "Well," he said. "What's all this?"

"It's your going-away dinner, big brother," Amy said, her voice a bit thick and teary. Patrick went to her and gave her a big brotherly hug.

"It's not forever," he said.

"It feels like forever," Cara said. "You'll be gone for six months and when Lane leaves in two weeks…nothing will be the same."

"I'll miss you, too," he told his sisters. "Like mad. Now, who's idea was this? Lane?"

"No. Not me. Cara and Amy and I were too upset to think straight. We might have managed a meal at a restaurant, but— this was all Darcy. She dug out the photos, and she handled all the decorations and the food. She wanted us to have one last special night together."

Someone entered the room then, but Patrick had grown so used to Darcy that he could feel her presence. This wasn't her. Olivia stood in the doorway with a bowl of food in her hands.

"Darcy?" he asked.

"In the kitchen."

Of course. "Would you ask her to come here, please."

Olivia gave a nod, and in moments Darcy was in the doorway.

She was dressed in pale blue with a silver clip in her hair and a snowy-white apron around her pretty, slim form. He wanted to simply stare at her, but that would have called attention to her and made her uncomfortable. "Thank you," he said. "Come sit with us."

Darcy's eyes opened wide. She twisted at the ties on her apron. "Oh. No. Me? Here? No."

"Yes. You did this," he said, moving toward her.

She shrugged. "It's just a simple meal. You were rushed. I thought you'd probably say private goodbyes, but I wanted everyone here for your last day. And anyway, I'd been planning it before that so it wasn't much work. Mrs. D. helped me find the pictures last week. I got help with the banners, of course." She seemed to run out of steam then. He could tell that she was ready to turn and run back into her safe little kitchen.

"Darcy," he said.

"Please. Stay here with us this time." That was Lane.

"Yes. Please. We mean it," Amy said.

"Really," Cara agreed. "You—everything is so nice. And you know that we're all on the verge of tears. None of us would have had the presence of mind to do this nearly as well as you have. You even made a special place for the boys and I know—well, thank you. Please, don't go."

"Mommy?" Davey's wavering little voice broke in. Patrick's younger nephew looked around as if he had just noticed that Amy wasn't at his side. Tears hung on his lashes. He looked so terribly sad and tiny.

Patrick heard a gasp. He turned to see Darcy looking at Davey as though her heart might break. She moved forward toward Davey half an inch, such a small amount that no one else probably saw, but Patrick did. Then, her hand flew to her throat and she slid backward, again just a touch. He couldn't help wondering and worrying if she was thinking of her baby. Her child would have been younger than Davey, but not by much.

"Come here, sweetie," Amy said, holding out her arms as Davey ran to her and she gave him a kiss. Darcy's expression was unreadable.

"Darcy?" Lane was asking. "Please. We meant it. Join us. It would make the evening complete."

Everyone seemed to be waiting for a response, and Darcy hesitated for a second. Then she gave a small, swift nod. "Thank you. I just have to do a few things. We can't—there's food to be finished. We can't eat our fingers."

The mood lightened. Lewis laughed and slung an arm around Cara, who managed a smile. Amy looked more at ease and so did Lane.

"Davey, boy," Richard said. "Mommy's going to sit here, not far from you. You be good and go keep Charlie company and he'll keep you company, too."

Davey hesitated. He chewed on one fat little finger, but

finally nodded. "Char," he said, pointing to Charlie and wandering to the smaller table. The two little boys hugged and went back to their game.

Everyone laughed, and only Patrick saw that, though Darcy smiled, too, her expression was still tinged with sadness. She turned, moved off and was just entering the kitchen when the doorbell rang.

"Who could that be?" Lane wondered.

Darcy halted. "I invited Angelise," she said. "But I didn't think she was going to make it. I thought—you said she was an old friend."

For several seconds there was silence.

Patrick stared straight into Darcy's eyes, but she looked away and he couldn't read her expression. What was this about?

Then, Cara nodded. "Thank you for thinking of her."

Mrs. D. came in, escorting Angelise. Angelise greeted everyone. Then she turned to Patrick. "I hate you," she said in a teasing tone, which had everyone turning their heads to see Patrick's reaction. "You're going to go away and take all the fun with you."

She came and sat beside him, pressing close. Patrick greeted her, but what he really wanted to do was march into the kitchen and ask Darcy a few questions. He wanted her beside him at the table. Now.

"You know, I've been thinking. I might take a trip to France soon, too," Angelise said. Which evolved into a discussion about foreign travel. In the meantime, Olivia and Darcy moved in and out with food. Olivia carried in special treats for the boys, but Patrick knew that it was Darcy who had thought of them.

The conversation swirled around him. He tried to pay attention to what his sisters and Angelise were saying. What he was noticing most, though, was Darcy.

When she came through the door the next time, she was carrying a wand lighter. Olivia had a dish. "Darcy's extra special peach flambé," Olivia said as she lit the concoction.

The glow from the flaming dish was reflected in the eyes of those sitting closest and a chorus of satisfied "ahs" added to the ambiance. The scent from the warm dish and the rum was spectacular.

Patrick looked up to voice his appreciation to Darcy, but she wasn't looking his way. She had turned toward the table in the other room. Suddenly a small cry left her lips.

"Davey, no, honey!" she cried, quickly maneuvering toward the child, who, Patrick realized, had found the cigarette lighter inside Angelise's purse.

Patrick stood, throwing off his napkin and interrupting Angelise midsentence as he shouted and charged toward Davey.

But Darcy had lifted the lighter from the little boy's hand already. "No, sweetie, I'm sorry, but it will hurt you," she was saying, rolling backward from the frightened face of the child.

"Charlie, stop!" Patrick yelled, but it was too late. Charlie had been rushing to see what the commotion was all about and had come up behind Darcy just as she was trying to back off and give Davey some space. The wheelchair bumped him. Charlie fell, and Darcy's wheel caught the edge of his foot.

He screamed in the high-pitched way only a terrified child can scream.

The world turned to slow motion. Every adult at the table rose and moved toward the area where Darcy and the children and Patrick were gathered. Tears started streaming down Davey's frightened face. Charlie crawled over to his mother, his arms reaching up to be held as she cried out.

And Darcy—the look in her eyes was the saddest thing Patrick had ever seen. She had raised her hands to cover her face, but those eyes…those stricken eyes that condemned herself completely…

Patrick could already see that Charlie was okay. He was cuddled against his mother and still whimpering and snuffling loudly, but beginning to move on to the next smile the way kids do.

"Darcy…" Patrick said.

She shook her head, hard. She closed her eyes. She broke his heart as two tears trickled from beneath her lashes. "I hurt him," she said with such anguish. "I hurt a—a baby. It was all my fault. I hurt a baby."

And Patrick realized in that moment that Darcy's fear of children, her unwillingness to cut herself a break went much deeper than that day with the little girl and the staircase. She was punishing herself for the loss of her own baby. She blamed herself for the miscarriage.

"Don't," he said. He realized that everyone at the table was starting to look at the two of them. He didn't care, not for himself, but for Darcy—

"I'm sorry," he said. "I know I promised not to do this again, but…"

He reached down and plucked her from her chair, pulling her into his arms. She was air, she was light, she was in pain.

"I'll call all of you before I leave," he told his sisters, and he strode out of the room, not even knowing where he was going.

As if Darcy suddenly realized what was going on, she tensed. "You can't leave. It's your farewell dinner."

"Watch me," he said. "It was a beautiful dinner, by the way, but I have something else I need to do now." He dropped a kiss on the crown of her head.

She looked up at him. "Patrick, please, you have to go back." But the anguish was still in her eyes.

He slowly shook his head. He climbed the stairs. As if his feet knew what his mind didn't, he found himself in the doorway to his bedroom.

Patrick stopped. He shifted Darcy in his arms. "Look at me, Darcy. He'll be fine. Children are very resilient."

"Not always, Patrick. No, they're not, and—I didn't even see him. He's so small. If he had been just a few inches closer and the tire had rolled over him, he would have been…I would have hurt him so much more…I…Patrick…"

Another tear slipped from beneath her lashes, and Patrick swore. He toed open the door and carried her in, sitting down on the bed with her on his lap. Slowly he rocked with her, shushing her and kissing her temples.

"I don't want to leave you," he said.

She froze. "You have to. Angelise is here. Everyone is here."

He hadn't meant that. "I don't care about Angelise."

Darcy looked up at him, a solemn expression on her face. "All right, maybe I made a mistake about her but someone else will come along. Someone like her."

"Darcy…"

"I *want* you to have someone like her," she said. "You have to do it, Patrick. You're used to family. You're going to miss all of that now that Lane is leaving home, and it's going to be difficult for you. I don't want you to be in this big house all alone when you come back. Do you understand?"

He understood. She wanted him to marry someone else, because she wasn't available.

"We'll see," he told her.

"You should get back," she told him again. "Would you mind—could I stay here just for a while? I can't go back down there."

"I'll stay with you."

She started to shake her head. "No, you have to…"

That did it. He turned with her, depositing her on the bed and sliding both of them down so that he was leaning over her, braced on his elbows while she was beneath him. "I have to kiss you," he said, finishing her sentence. "I'll never get the chance again. All right?"

Her response was a whimper as she reached up and pulled him down to her.

He slid his hands into her hair, loosening that fine wheat-colored silk from its bonds and fanning it out around her. When his lips met hers, he tasted salt from her tears followed by sweetness that was just…woman, all Darcy.

Heat rushed over him as he claimed her and she claimed him right back.

His gut instinct was to tell her that he didn't want to hurt her, but he'd heard Cerise complaining that she hated it when men treated her like a china doll, so he didn't say the words. Instead he told her what he was feeling.

"I want all of you," he said.

"Yes, I want that, too. Touch me," she told him.

He kissed her lips, her eyelids, her chin. He sipped at her throat, found a spot behind her ear that made her breath catch which made his pulse pound. When he reached the neckline of her apron, he reached behind her to untie the sash, pulled it from her and released the buttons that ran down the front of her dress. When he was done, he parted the lapels and kissed his way down her body. He stroked his palms down her sides.

She gasped, and he stopped. "Darcy?"

"I'm sorry. It's just that the line where the break was tends to be very sensitive in people with spinal cord injuries. It's the line between feeling and, in my case, less feeling and it… when you touch me there…"

He touched her there. She arched against him. He stroked her again, put his lips on her there.

She tore at his shirt, so he removed it.

She tugged on the waistband of his pants, so he disposed of them. Somewhere along the way, he tossed aside her dress, but his attention was on her, not on the clothes, not on the actions, just on her, on the expressions on her face, the sighs that escaped her lips.

He was on fire for her. And then, he was touching her in the places he had already learned made her burn. Her throat, her breasts, that wonderful, sensitive line she'd mentioned.

"You can love me," she said. "I want you to."

Her words nearly drove him right over the edge, and he had to close his eyes and concentrate not to leave her behind. That wasn't going to happen. He would be patient. He would wait forever, hold off forever.

"Patrick, touch me again," she whispered. "Touch me more."

He groaned. "Oh, yes, I intend to do that, but we are *not* rushing this. If this is the only night we make love, we're going to make it last."

Patrick slid his hand down her torso.

She gasped and mimicked his movements. Heat ripped through him.

He stroked. She caressed. He kissed. She nuzzled.

Then slowly, carefully—so carefully that he could barely stand it—he entered her and they began again. In aching slow motion he loved her. And the fire began to build.

Darcy's fingertips on his flesh were driving him insane. He moved in her. She welcomed him against her satiny skin. Touches. Caresses. He was losing control, trying to hang on.

"Patrick? I'm—I'm—" Her voice was breathless, strained.

"Yes," was all he could manage to say.

He brought her close, kissing the side of her neck and sliding his fingers over the exquisitely sensitive line of skin he'd discovered earlier as he joined their bodies again.

She cried out and wrapped her arms around him as his world teetered on the edge of bliss. Then everything turned to heat and stars and sun, and he fell apart.

When he returned to earth, and his breathing returned to normal, Patrick was disoriented. He looked down and realized that he held Darcy firmly at his side. He'd never had that happen before, that total loss of self. Thank goodness he hadn't crushed her.

She was gazing up at him and she brushed his lips with her fingertips. "Thank you."

"I think that's my line."

That brought a blush to her pretty body and she looked away. "I want you to promise me that you'll have a good time. Don't worry that I'll be remembering this night like some sort of pathetic novice who doesn't know anything about reality."

Patrick frowned. "What's the reality?"

She rested her arms on him and leaned in close. "That I want you to find an Angelise substitute and go shushing down mountains with her. Don't make me worry about you, and…"

"And?"

"And I meant what I said. I'm going to be really angry if *you* worry about *me*."

"Then I won't," he lied, "because you're a successful businesswoman with lots of friends." Which was the truth.

"You're darn right." She smiled at him, and then a wistful look came over her face. He tilted her chin up and gently kissed her lips.

"What?"

"I meant what I said," she repeated. "Thank you. You didn't

make me feel awkward or self-conscious. You made me feel wonderful. You were my first."

Later, when he'd taken her home and he was alone staring into the darkness, Patrick thought about that statement. He knew she hadn't meant that he was her first lover ever. She had been pregnant once before. She'd meant that he'd been her first since the accident, but…something was bothering him.

She wanted him to find another Angelise and date, maybe marry, and—and he had been her first.

That meant he wouldn't be her last.

A sharp pain whipped through Patrick. "Hell," he said to himself. "Don't go there." But he did, and he forced himself to accept it, because he wanted her to be happy, and it was clear that she wouldn't find happiness with him.

Maybe she would find it with Jared, or with someone else. Surely there would be someone else. But *he* had been her first.

And that wasn't a damn bit of consolation to him. He missed her already.

CHAPTER TWELVE

Two weeks later, Darcy sat in the kitchen. She held a bowl on her lap, stirring the contents.

"Are you going to beat that to death that, or will we eventually do something food-related with it?" Olivia asked.

Darcy looked up at Olivia, then down at the bowl. She shifted it in her lap and kept stirring. "It's going to be a cake. This is for Lane's "week of goodbyes.""

"Oh, yeah, she's having different friends over every day. What cake is it tonight?"

Again Darcy looked down at the batter and tried to concentrate. "Chocolate. I think. Yes, it's brown. Chocolate."

The look in Olivia's eyes called her back to attention. "What?"

"You never just say chocolate. It's always chocolate surprise, or hot fudge delight or too-good-to-be-true caramel. You are in bad shape. We need to do something. Fast."

That got Darcy's attention. "I'm fine. What are you talking about, Liv?"

"I'm talking about Mr. Judson."

Immediately Darcy flashed hot, then cold, then hot again. An ache so deep she could barely stand it took hold and she wanted to moan. Patrick was gone. He had kissed her and loved her, and it had been wonderful beyond anything she could have imagined, but now he was gone.

"You need to call him."

"What?" Darcy froze in midstir.

"I said, call him."

"What for?"

"Because you love him, you idiot. And you miss him."

"I do not!" But she did. Not that that could matter. He needed to be free, to fly, and she wasn't built for flying. More than that, though, was the other. He'd spent his life helping women, and just when he'd been on the verge of being free of that duty, she'd come along and he'd had to leap in and help her. Well, enough of that. She refused to be another duty holding him back.

And when he finally settled down, she wanted it to be with the right kind of woman: socially elite, accomplished, poised, beautiful and fully capable of giving him and caring for a houseful of precious babies.

"Not calling," she told Olivia stubbornly. "I've got things to do."

Olivia walked over and took the bowl out of her hands. "Now you don't."

"Hey!"

"I know how to make a cake," Olivia said. "You, pick up the phone."

"And say what?"

"That you love him."

"No."

"That you miss him, then."

Darcy thought about that. "No, he would worry."

"Then at least ask him who those people are that have been hanging around you lately."

"I know who they are. They're bodyguards. He's trying to protect me and the others at Able House from the Cal Barrows of the world."

"Well, then, you could at least thank the man. I'll bet you haven't even done that yet. Some appreciative woman you are."

Darcy opened her mouth. "I can't, Liv."

"He would call you if the tables were turned. Mr. Judson always treated everyone the same. He was always fair and polite and courteous to the lowliest of his employees."

"That's so not fair of you to remind me of that."

"Yeah, but it's true. Go in the other room. I won't listen."

It wouldn't matter. Darcy intended to make this very polite and extremely short.

But in the end, her plans went awry. The person who answered the phone was a woman who said that Patrick was unavailable. She was going to give him a massage, as soon as he woke up.

Patrick lay facedown on a table in the room adjoining the team locker room. He was exhausted. He'd fallen asleep waiting for Tanya, the team masseuse to finish with another competitor, and his unintentional nap had forced Tanya to wait for him to wake up. Now, Tanya was going to try to beat life back into his body, but his heart wasn't in the process. Because his body wasn't really the reason he felt so rotten.

"Your cell phone rang while you were out. I carried it into the other room and answered it so you wouldn't wake up. You need rest," she said, handing him the phone.

He needed a lot more than that, but Patrick was trying not to think about why he felt so miserable, especially since there was no solution to the problem.

Now, as Tanya began to pummel his muscles, he looked at

the record of received calls on his cell phone. The one that Tanya had told him about had come straight from his house.

His heart leaped just before reality set in. Probably Lane. Like Cara and Amy, Lane had called him several times already. He missed them, too, but he especially missed—

"Dammit," he said.

Tanya slapped him on the shoulder with her meaty hand. "Do not swear in my presence. I cannot unkink your muscles if you don't lie still and cooperate."

"That's okay. I'll keep the kinked muscles. Right now, I have to call my sister. Thank you for the massage."

"I barely began."

"I know. Bill me for the full session."

"You're going to be sorry, Mr. Judson. Your body has taken a beating these past two weeks. You look, if you don't mind my saying so, like heck."

"Like hell. I look like hell."

"Exactly." Tanya left.

Once she had gone, Patrick sat up and hung his head. He ran his fingers through his hair at the temple. He felt worse than he looked. No question why. He was in love with Darcy, who had made love with him, but had told him to marry someone else. Because she wasn't available.

"So, do it," he told himself.

Maybe he would. Maybe tomorrow. Right now he had to return Lane's call. He hoped that Darcy wasn't around. If she was, he just might do something stupid…like saying how he really felt about her, and that would make her feel guilty and unhappy. "No, I'm not doing that," he said to the empty room.

Darcy was wrestling with the centerpiece she was creating and trying not to envision what Patrick might be doing when Lane and Cara and Amy came into the room. Amy put Davey down and he gave everyone a big smile, then ran over to where Charlie was pulling things out of his toy bag.

"Charlie," Davey said. "Me, too."

Charlie gave his cousin a sigh and handed Davey a truck.

Instantly, Darcy went on full alert. For several reasons. The three sisters had never shown up in her kitchen all at the same time, they'd never looked at her in that strange way they were looking at her now, and…this was the first time Darcy had seen Charlie since the day she had run over his foot. What if he was afraid of her now? The thought of scaring a child…

"That looks great, Darcy," Amy said, indicating the arrangement of red and white candles, crystal glasses of cinnamon red candies and white mints and the cardinal and white University of Wisconsin-Madison logo. A small photo of Lane wearing her new red and white jacket was front and center.

"Love it," Lane agreed. "But I was wondering…"

"We were all wondering," Cara said, plopping down in a chair. "Have you heard from our brother lately?"

Darcy's panic antennae switched to full power. She felt as if she'd been hit by a sister sledgehammer. Not wanting them to see her face, she turned away and started rolling toward the other side of the room, trying to pretend she was intent on a task. "Not at all. Why do you ask?"

A small giggle sounded to her left and she saw that Davey was trying to play peekaboo with her from behind a chair whose rungs in no way hid his face. Against her will, she smiled, but the tension still gripped her as she heard Amy's next comment.

"He just called Lane, and…I spoke to him two days ago via video phone. He doesn't look well at all."

Darcy's heart stopped. Trying to hold on to her composure, hide her concern and not disappoint a child all at the same time, she cupped her palms over her face, then separated her fingers and peered out at Davey. "What do you mean, he doesn't look well?" she asked just as Davey giggled again.

"He looks positively ill." Lane's voice was choked, and Darcy turned slowly to face her.

When Davey came over and approached her, Darcy didn't even stop to think. She reached out and plucked up two plastic ladles and two plastic bowls and handed them to him.

"Two bows," he said.

"Two bows, indeed," she agreed, but her hands clenched. And not because she was speaking to a child.

"Patrick's sick?" Her voice came out too thin, slightly high-pitched.

"We don't know," Cara said. "That's the problem. He isn't saying. He isn't saying anything of substance."

Darcy fought not to let her feelings show. Panic. Fear. Love. More fear. She needed to see Patrick, to talk to him, but...

"I've tried to pry info from him," Amy said, "but he insists that everything is perfect. We're not sure if he's keeping things from us because he's still playing the guardian-brother who wants to protect his younger sisters from bad news or—we're beginning to think that maybe we're just too close to him to be objective. This is the first time Patrick has gone away for any length of time, and maybe we're just letting the fact that we miss him get in the way. We could be reading him wrong or just somehow selfishly hoping everything isn't perfect so that he'll come home sooner. We need someone more rational and sane than us to offer some perspective."

Oh man, were they really talking about her?

"You seem to have gotten to know him pretty well in the

weeks before he left. We just…I'm going to call him," Lane explained. "You talk to him and tell us what you think."

"No!" Darcy said, but as she said it she glanced to the side to see that Charlie had sidled up to her. He was holding out his hands and looking at her with big solemn eyes that quickly filled with tears. His lip was trembling in that way that little children's lips trembled, the way that made your heart break.

"Oh, Charlie, I wasn't yelling at you, sweetheart," she said. "Did you want some dishes, too?"

He nodded and she wasn't sure which one of them was going to cry first. "Here," she said, rolling back a bit and digging into a drawer. "Here's a whole set of measuring cups and spoons. Okay?"

Charlie nodded and ducked his head. He took his toys and retreated to a corner while Darcy's throat closed up. For so many reasons.

She looked up to see the sisters staring at her. "Will you do it?" Lane asked. "I'll get a video line going."

Would she do it? Yes. Her heart filled with tears and fear. Patrick was ill. She loved him and she was going to kill him if he wasn't taking care of himself.

"Yes, please call Patrick," she said, and she prayed that his sisters didn't know just how much this meant to her.

Patrick's nerves were strung tight. This was the second time in an hour he'd spoken to his sisters. Something was up. Lane had put the call through, but now she was being evasive, claiming that the other girls wanted to speak with him, but he had spoken to Cara and Amy only yesterday.

"Hey, big brother, how's it going?" Cara asked.

"Yeah, how's it going, Patrick? What did you do today?" Amy asked.

"I'm fine. I was paramotoring." But then she already knew that. He'd told her that yesterday. And…Lane had set up in the kitchen. It was the first time she'd placed a call there.

His head began to pound. The camera didn't take in all of the room. He studied the perimeters of the viewing area and frowned. Where was Darcy? He tried not to think about the fact that she might be with Jared…or someone else. Maybe she was dancing. Or maybe Eleanor had sent her off on a catering job or maybe she was wheeling down the sidewalk from his home to hers. She'd have to pass Cal's.

Patrick scowled.

"What?" Lane asked. "What's wrong?"

"Nothing."

"Good. That's good. I—Darcy's here."

Now his heart began to thunder. He cursed the limits of the video linkup. Where was she?

She came into view, moving closer to the camera. "Patrick." That was it, just that soft sound, like a caress. "Your sisters were right. You're not taking care of yourself."

"I am." A total lie.

Now that cute, stern look he loved came over her face. "I'm not your sisters. I'm not going to treat you with kid gloves or lie to you. You look like you've been staying up all night and day and not eating right."

He held his hand up. "I'm fine, just brilliant. But you…are you getting out of the kitchen?"

She smiled and his whole body ached. "I'm a cook. I'm supposed to be in the kitchen."

"But not all the time. And those neighbors…have they given you any more trouble?"

"Nothing I can't handle."

"Dammit, Darcy. You look as if you've lost weight."

She blinked and looked slightly evasive. "Didn't anyone ever tell you not to ask about a girl's weight? That's not like you, Patrick. You've usually got that etiquette thing down pat."

Ah, she was teasing him. He loved it when she teased him, but not when he couldn't be there with her or touch her. This damn video connection wasn't nearly three dimensional enough. You'd think that a man with his money could convince someone to invent a device that captured the essence of Darcy.

"You're right. No weight questions. Are you...enjoying life, then?"

She nodded. That was it? Just a nod? No details?

"And..." He frowned. "Everything is all right at Able House, isn't it? I get reports but they don't really tell me the half of it."

"We're okay," she said quietly. "You shouldn't worry."

All right, there was a loaded sentence. "I could have post-poned this trip, done more before I left," he said, hating the feeling that he wasn't there to control things.

"Patrick, look at me," Darcy said. So quietly. Her voice was almost a whisper, but it mesmerized him.

He looked at her, he connected with her. "*Don't* worry," she said.

"You know I'm going to."

She frowned. "Are you...what are *you* doing?"

He rattled off a list of activities he'd taken part in during the past two weeks in various stops in Italy, Spain and France. Skydiving, bungee jumping, white water rafting in Chamonix. But he didn't want to talk about himself. "Have you and Jared gone dancing anymore?" Did that sound jealous? "And Cerise," he added, just in case he had sounded jealous.

"Once." Her answer told him nothing. "Are there...are there a lot of parties?"

"I suppose there are quite a few. The company arranges events during the day and entertainment for the evening."

As he spoke, he saw Charlie appear at Darcy's side. Where were his sisters? Why weren't they taking care of Charlie? Didn't they know how difficult this was for Darcy? No, of course they didn't. He had never told them about her past, and Darcy wouldn't have told them, either.

"Is Cara there?" he asked suddenly.

Darcy blinked and slid back. Cara moved into her spot, but he didn't want to discuss this in front of everyone, not even his other sisters. Charlie was Cara's and it should only be her. "I have something to ask you, but…take the call in the other room, all right?"

Cara's expression turned to alarm, but she clicked off the monitor. When her voice resumed, they were audio only. "Patrick, what is it? What's this about?"

"Darcy. It's all about Darcy." In as brief a manner as he could, he explained that she needed to be careful with Charlie and Darcy.

"Charlie is the best," he told her. "I love him to pieces, but Darcy is fragile. Especially after that dinner, she'll be…don't make her take care of him."

"I didn't know, Patrick. I didn't ask her to take care of him and now that I know, I wouldn't. I—"

"I'm not blaming you, Cara, but I just…" He rubbed the back of his neck. "I don't think I did well by Darcy. I want her to be happy, and it's driving me nuts that I don't have the power to make sure that she is."

Cara hesitated. "Is that why you look so beat-up? You're worrying, the way you used to worry about us when we were growing up."

No, it wasn't like that at all.

"Something like that," he said.

"We'll look out for her," she told him. Cara was, he knew, a woman of her word. Her promise should make him feel better, so why didn't it?

Because he wanted to be the one. Even as the thought formed, Patrick realized that there was more than one meaning for that statement. He wanted to be *the one*.

But that wasn't a choice that was open to him.

"I'll want a full report next week, sweetheart. On all of you."

And if things weren't all that they should be, he was going to do something drastic.

CHAPTER THIRTEEN

DARCY looked up when Cara came into the room and found the other woman studying her intently.

"What?" Darcy asked.

Cara shook her head. "So, what's the verdict on Patrick?"

"He looks...tired."

"Worse than tired," Lane said.

"He doesn't look like Patrick. It's as if something's missing from him," Amy said.

"It's as if someone turned off the light inside him. His essence, the thing that makes him Patrick has been dimmed." The second that Darcy uttered the words, the girls turned toward her.

"Yes," they all agreed.

"He's worried about you," Darcy offered.

But the sisters exchanged a look. "He asked an awful lot of questions about *you*," Amy said.

"He knows that I have Lewis and Amy has Richard and Lane has school, but it's Darcy he's worried about," Cara agreed.

Darcy's heart hurt. "That's so unfair."

The sisters looked startled and Darcy shook her head. "I don't mean that what you're saying was unfair to me. I meant that it's unfair that Patrick should be worrying. He's done all he could for me. He's even hired bodyguards to watch over us at Able House."

"Yes, but that wouldn't be enough for him. Patrick's very hands-on. Not being able to prevent our parents' deaths ate at him. I think that colored his life, so when one of us got hurt and he couldn't keep it from happening or cure us, he walked the floor and pestered the doctors even though he knew they were doing their best. He did the job of two parents, so no, hiring a bodyguard wouldn't dispel Patrick's concerns."

Cara shook her head. "It's you. You're the one."

Darcy bit her lip. Her throat felt tight. "He's supposed to be playing, not worrying about me. I told him I wanted him to find a wife. That and all those fun things he wants to do should be all he's thinking about."

Lane raised one brow in a gesture that was so like Patrick's that Darcy had to swallow hard to keep from remembering. "A wife? I wish, but despite all our attempts…apparently not likely yet. I've heard from friends over there that there are plenty of women falling over him, but when he attends functions, he goes alone and leaves alone."

Darcy tried not to react to that. Relief and distress warred within her.

"Look. Darcy," Cara said. "Patrick is obviously worried sick about you. How can he enjoy himself when he's so concerned?"

"I don't think he's sleeping right, either," Darcy said. "He really will get sick if he doesn't take better care of himself. I'll call him back and reassure him. I'll tell him I'm just great."

"You already did. We did, too. Numerous times. He's asked about you every time any of us has spoken to him. I don't know exactly what's going on between my brother and you, and maybe it's none of my business. Or it wouldn't ordinarily be my business, but if neurosing about your well-being is affecting his health and well-being—well, whatever your relationship is, it's…"

"It's my fault," Darcy said. "From the beginning he knew I had issues." She launched into a brief explanation of her past. When she got to the part about children, Cara nodded sadly.

"That's why he was so worried just now that I was letting Charlie crawl all over you."

Darcy bit her lip, thinking about how she had scared Charlie, but also about how he had been so quick to forgive her. What a charmer he was and…he was Patrick's nephew. Her heart swelled, thinking of the two little boys and their uncle. She took a deep breath and nodded. "Patrick knows where I'm vulnerable. I wish…I should have done more to show him that I can be strong. I hate the fact that I haven't made more of an effort to show him how much of a difference he made in my world. He brought me out of myself."

There the three of them went, exchanging those secretive looks again. Darcy wondered what it must be like having sisters so close to you that they could read your expressions.

"You could still do that," Amy said. "Show him that you're strong, I mean."

"Yes, Amy's right," Lane said. "I can guarantee that telling Patrick you're fine is never enough. It never was with any of us. He always needed to see proof."

Darcy blinked. She and Lane studied each other. "So, you think that if I show him that I'm moving on with my life and that I'm capable of going it alone without his assistance, then he'll be able to move on, too?" She frowned. "Do you really think that's why he looks so ill? Maybe it's something worse, something else."

"I don't know. Patrick drives himself. He demands more

of himself than any man I know. It's as if he thinks he should be able to work miracles. Remember when Lane was in the hospital with a concussion and we didn't know if she was going to come out of it?" Cara asked.

Amy nodded. "Patrick looked just like that, then. As if he had aged ten years in a day. I came across him when he thought he was alone and the devastated expression on his face scared me to death. Darcy, I—Cara and Lane and I—Patrick's more like our father than our brother, but we can't do anything for him. You're the key. You have to be the one to help him."

Darcy wanted to do that. She needed to be with Patrick and see for herself that he was safe and strong and happy. "But, he's in France," she whispered. "And I'm here."

Cara didn't hesitate. "That's the one thing the three of us can do. We can get you there and we can get you in, but you have to do the rest."

"You have to have a plan," Amy added. "If you go over there and whatever happens increases Patrick's anxiety about you…"

"Maybe we should just ask him to come home and see how she's doing for himself," Lane suggested.

"No," Darcy said. "This is his trip of a lifetime. He's put heart and soul into this. And it's important. Think of all those children his charities are going to help. I'm not asking him to cut his trip short or take time away just to come check me out."

"So…you're going over there then?" Amy asked.

For ten seconds Darcy allowed panic to overtake her. To get on a plane and travel around the world chasing a man she was in love with in order to convince him that she *wasn't* in love with him and that she had conquered all her fears when she hadn't done anything of the sort was taking a major chance. Not only with her own heart but with Patrick's health and well-being. Because if she messed this up and came across as needy in any way, he was going to blame himself for her vulnerability. Everything she knew about him and everything his sisters had told her pointed to that.

She took a deep breath. "Anything I do or say has to be realistic and utterly convincing. Patrick has a way of seeing through me."

"Can you act?"

"No."

Lane opened her eyes in alarm.

"I can't act well enough," Darcy clarified. "I'm not good at playing a part, so if I'm going to show Patrick that I've moved on and made a new life for myself, it has to be real. I have to believe it, too. So…if you'll give me two weeks and set up the travel arrangements, I'll just head home and…quietly try to reinvent myself."

"Who will you be when this is done?" Olivia asked, entering the kitchen.

"I haven't a clue," Darcy said, trying to keep the despair and concern from her voice. She just hoped that the woman who would emerge from the cocoon in France would not be in love with Patrick.

She wanted to set him free. It would be so much easier to do that if she didn't care about him so much.

Patrick paced the floor of his hotel room. He was supposed to be getting ready for a meeting and then attend a dinner, but he had just received an e-mail from Lane telling him that Darcy would be arriving within the hour for some sort of event she had been asked to cater. What was that about? And why hadn't Darcy contacted him herself?

A part of him didn't care. He just wanted to see her and hear her and touch her.

"You're not touching her, buddy," he told himself.

But he damn well was going to ask her a lot of questions. He whipped out his phone and called the number Lane had included in the message.

Two rings. Three rings. Four. Darn it, the voicemail was going to kick in. He didn't want to leave a message. He wanted to hear her voice and he wanted...*intended* to meet her at the airport. What airline was she flying? Lane hadn't said. He was on the verge of calling Lane when the telephone in the room rang. He picked it up.

"Patrick?" Darcy's voice slipped right through his body, soft and sexy and—

"Where are you?"

"In the lobby. May I come up?"

Yes, yes, yes. Hurry. But she would need to find someone to help her with her bags and direct her to his room and—

"Stay there."

He barely waited for her assent before he sprinted out the door and down the hall, ignoring the elevator for the much faster stairs. Emerging from the stairwell, he bolted into the lobby and saw her.

His heart turned three somersaults. She had done her hair differently and the soft tendrils brushed her cheeks, accenting those phenomenally expressive eyes. She was holding out her hands to him and a gorgeous smile lifted her lips and lit up her eyes.

"Patrick, I'm so happy to see you," she said. He had never seen her more lovely. A glow seemed to emanate from her. She looked healthy and happy.

He walked straight toward her, took her hands and bent to kiss her cheek. That wonderful woman and lemon scent he remembered filled his senses and nearly brought him to his knees. He wanted to inhale her. "Are you staying here?"

"Um, on the fourth floor. Amy made the arrangements."
Then, she frowned slightly. "That is, I would have made them
myself, but I had so many things to do before I left that I
just…let her."

"My sister made hotel arrangements for you?"

"Yes, and the flight arrangements, too. Your sisters are
pretty efficient, Patrick. Someone must have trained them well.
I wonder who." She wrinkled her nose and laughed. Patrick
wanted to groan. She was the most incredibly, sexy, exciting
woman he'd ever met. How could he have forgotten that?

"I see you're just as sassy as ever."

"That's a good thing, right?" she asked. For just a second,
he thought he saw her hesitate. Then she rushed on. "You're
probably wondering why I'm here."

"Lane said something about an event you were catering.
International stuff, Darcy?"

She shrugged. "I know. Isn't it crazy and great? I was
talking to Eleanor one day and she told me about some friends
she had who liked to throw parties, and the next thing I knew
they were offering me a job! A brunch for a big gathering of
friends and family they were having. How could I turn that
down? It's not like I get invited to France every day."

A bellman arrived at that moment. "Mademoiselle Parrish?"

Patrick looked at Darcy. "What's your room number?" he
asked, preparing to give the man directions and a tip.

But Darcy was already talking to the man. "Guillaume, is
it?" she asked in somewhat halting French, tilting her head up
to see the man's name tag in a way that emphasized her lovely
neck. "How do you do, Guillaume? It's my first time to France,
I'm afraid, so I apologize in advance for speaking French so
poorly." At least that was the gist of what she said. There were
also a few extra words in there that made no sense whatsoever.

Patrick cleared his throat, planning to help out. He spoke perfect French, and Guillaume knew it. They'd had numerous conversations in the hallway this past week.

But Guillaume was clearly charmed. He gave Darcy an intimate smile. "I speak *un peu*, I mean, a little Anglais," he said, his accent almost as bad as Darcy's command of French. "You—tell me whatever you need. I'll help you. Anything."

Darcy looked at the man with a teasing twinkle in her eye. "Guillaume, you're not giving me special treatment because of my chair, are you?" she asked, motioning toward her wheels.

"Maybe just a very little," the man said, "but mostly because you are polite about the language, you have a nice smile and because you're a very beautiful woman. I like you."

Her soft laughter rang out, and Patrick wanted to lean closer. He wanted to push Guillaume aside. "I think I like you, too, Guillaume," she said as she gave him her room number and he headed off with her bags.

She clearly liked Guillaume. She had practically been flirting with the handsome Frenchman. Okay, Patrick thought, for a man who wasn't prone to violence, he definitely wanted to *hit* the man now. No, that was wrong, and it wasn't fair, except…he'd seen Guillaume flirting with the maids. He was pretty sure he was dating several of them. He had an urge to tell Darcy to be careful with men like that, but that wasn't right, either. Darcy was an intelligent woman with a good head on her shoulders and she had spoken to Guillaume, a total stranger, in a completely uninhibited way that was unusual for her. She had even called the man's attention to her wheelchair. What was going on here?

Patrick looked down. Apparently what was going on was that Darcy was looking at him as if wondering what the holdup was.

"You probably want to go to your room and rest," he said, wishing he had more time with her but not wanting to exhaust her.

"Are you kidding me, Patrick? I'm in France, it's late and tomorrow I have to get up at the break of dawn and get ready to prepare a brunch. Right now I want to…I want to do lots of things."

He grinned. "Lots of things?"

She blushed. "Yes."

"Like what?"

"I—I well I guess I don't have a clue. What do people do in France?"

Patrick laughed. The excitement on her face delighted him. She was playing with the wheels on her chair and he could see that she was ready to be off. "They live. They shop, work, go to museums, they eat. You are going to love that about Paris. The food is…"

"An orgasmic experience?" she asked with a wicked smile, and he remembered the first day that they had met.

"Well, nothing surpasses your chocolate mousse, but you'll love it."

"That's it. Take me on a tour of restaurants!"

"A tour?"

"I don't have much time."

Ah. The emptiness that had disappeared completely when he had heard she was coming returned. "How much?" His voice was a bit too clipped. Had she noticed? Would she guess how much it mean to see her?

"Two days. Not quite that. More like forty hours before I have to head back to the airport. I have to get back to—to help with some—an event." Darcy got that old nervous look in her eyes, she licked her lips, but then she shook her head as if to get rid of something that was bothering her. She smiled again.

"Another event? You're a busy woman."

"You have no idea. I don't have a moment to myself. Busy all the time, night and day."

"Your nights, too, Darcy?" What did she mean by that?

She blushed, which only intrigued him more. "Oh, you know, dancing, partying, stuff."

"Partying?" he said. But it was the word "stuff" that caught his attention. Did she mean men? Unbidden the memory of Darcy in his arms, her delicate skin beneath his questing lips invaded his thoughts.

Patrick took a deep breath. He didn't have the right to ask her about men. She was free to date whom she pleased, and…darn it, she was only here for two days. For tonight anyway, she was his.

"I'll walk you to your room and you can get changed. Then we'll go have a movable feast."

She nodded, but neither of them moved. Her gaze locked with his. And somehow his feet took him closer to her. He took her hands and kissed the palms. "I've missed you, Darcy Parrish. No one else plays it as straight with me as you do."

For half a second he thought he saw something dark and sad in her eyes. Had he pushed her too far? Had he let his feelings show too much?

"I'll find my room," she said. "And I'll meet you back here in twenty minutes."

Darcy broke into a cold sweat on the way to her room. What was she doing? How had she ever thought she could handle this?

The girls had given her a crash course in French. She'd done all kinds of crazy things to throw this together fast. The whole situation was surreal. The energy involved in making this happen had kept her from panicking.

But, when she had seen Patrick, her heart had flipped over completely and when he'd touched her—she stopped right in the middle of the hallway and sat there, her hands crossed over her chest as she counted to ten and fought for composure.

Thank goodness she had insisted that this trip be kept short. She couldn't keep up this charade with Patrick for long. Smiling and pretending that all she felt for him was friend-ship when…well, what else could she do? While they had been talking several gorgeous women had entered the lobby and looked as if they intended to approach him. They had looked as if they knew him, as if they wanted to know him very intimately, or maybe already did. But they obviously wanted the chance to get him alone because none of them had actually come close enough to speak to Patrick. And now…

"Get hold of yourself, Darcy," she muttered. "You can do this. You can see that he's feeling more at ease already. And when this is over, there's only one more thing you have to do and then he's free and clear. You'll have done one good thing for him and ended it right. Don't blow it."

No, she refused to mess this up. If she appeared in any way lost or in love or needy—it would hurt Patrick so much to have to let her down easy.

"Never going to happen." She took a deep breath, plastered on that air of confidence she'd been practicing, changed into something attractive but not provocative and went down to meet Patrick. This was going to be so hard…and so wonderful.

CHAPTER FOURTEEN

THE evening passed more quickly than Darcy would have liked. She was incredibly tired now that jet lag was setting in, and she had to get up early to prepare for the brunch, the job that she had all but begged Eleanor to help her secure. The people who were hosting the brunch hadn't even been planning anything at all until Eleanor called them up and raved about how she knew this simply marvelous chef who would be passing through Paris for a couple of days and would like to try her hand with some of the local produce, wines and cheeses. Now, Darcy had to live up to the billing.

But tonight there was Patrick, if she could just keep her eyes open and her mind on the task at hand and off the fact that she wanted to kiss him in the worst way.

"There?" she asked. "I'm not so sure." They were headed for their last restaurant of the evening. He had chosen ones that were known for fine dining, and she had done her best to come out of her shell, to be witty and open with the staff and even with total strangers who were simply dining there as well. In short, she had acted totally unDarcylike. Because that was what Patrick needed to see, that she was making progress and healing. That he had no reason whatsoever to worry about her.

"You don't want to go there?" he asked. "I haven't been there yet, but it's gotten great reviews."

Maybe, but at the moment the crowds had thinned. There was a sterility to the chrome and glass. And the tables were big. She would be many feet away from Patrick. And tonight...oh, just tonight she wanted one more chance to be close to him.

"That one," she said, pointing to a small, intimate looking place on the corner across the street.

"You're sure?"

She laughed. "It's kind of plain, isn't it? I'll bet you never eat in ordinary little places like that."

Looking up, she saw that Patrick was looking a little sheepish, but he was smiling, too. "You don't do you?" she asked again.

"I do tonight. I have it on excellent advice that it's a place I should try. My favorite chef tells me so."

"What if it's awful? You'll never trust me again."

"I trust you implicitly. You're always honest with me, and you'll admit if you've made a mistake."

Honest? She wasn't being honest with him now. At best she was leaving lots of things out. But she was never going to tell him that she had come over here to do a snow job on him.

She sighed. Oops. Major error, that sigh. "Sorry, I'm a little jet lagged," she said.

"You should be in bed."

"No!" She didn't want to give up this time.

"Alone," he clarified. "I wasn't implying that you should be in *my* bed."

"I would like to be in your bed." Okay, all this playacting and being totally open and outgoing was having a bad effect on her. "Forget I said that."

"Not in this lifetime."

"It was the lack of sleep talking. I probably couldn't do much, anyway."

"I could do all the heavy lifting."

Excitement rose within her. But oh, why had she even started this conversation? She couldn't survive making love with Patrick and leaving again. Look at what one night in his arms had done to her. She was pathetic and needy, all the things she had fought not to be for years.

"Let's go in," she said, but then she realized something.

So did he. "Those are very narrow aisles." No room for her chair.

Embarrassment flooded her face. These were the kinds of things that made her feel as if she didn't belong. If she sat here long enough someone would notice and realize the reason they were milling about outside. That was when the pitying looks or the averted faces would begin.

And she knew that Patrick realized her distress just as sure as she knew that darkness fell every night. Once that registered with him, the man was going to go into all-out, full protective mode. He would be worried about her; he'd try to save her. That was the very thing she had come over her to put a stop to.

"Pick me up, please," she said.

"Darcy?"

"Well, it's totally clear that I'm not going to roll or walk in there, isn't it? And I'll bet you're almost strong enough to carry me." She said this rather loudly as a couple was passing. When they looked at her, she smiled and waved as Patrick was lifting her into his arms, holding her against his heart.

"Do they have good desserts here?" she called out in her very bad French.

"*Oui, mille feuille,*" the woman said.

"Ah, *merci*," Darcy said with a big smile. She waited until the couple had gone. "What did she say?" she asked.

Patrick laughed and pulled her closer. "She implied that they had good Napoleons here," he whispered near her temple.

Darcy fought to keep breathing. "I love Napoleons. Let's go inside." Oh, she needed to get inside. She needed Patrick to put her down. If he didn't do it soon she would grab him and press her aching lips to his.

But the little shop was closed when they tried the door. The man was just locking the door. *"Demain,"* he told them. "Tomorrow."

Which only served to remind Darcy that there wouldn't be a tomorrow with Patrick. She had already asked him what was on his schedule tomorrow and he had a ball he had to attend. The day after that she'd go back to Chicago.

By the time they got back to her room she was so weary that she could barely keep her eyes open. Patrick saw her to her door. "I'll see you bright and early tomorrow," he told her.

She blinked.

He smiled. "I'll bring the Napoleons. And coffee."

Then he kissed her on the forehead and left her.

Dratted man. Now she would never be able to sleep.

Patrick stood back and watched Darcy work the room. He had been with her since early morning and she was still going strong. She was simply amazing. And different. In a sassy, sexy way that he found incredibly tempting.

Was this the same woman who normally hid in the kitchen? Couldn't be, because she had been roaming the room for the past two hours, making sure dishes were replenished and that everyone got a taste of each dish. She even talked with apparent ease about the preparations and the history of some of the dishes. She supervised the staff she'd made arrangements for and stayed until the last dish was cleaned and put back on the rental truck.

Then she said an affectionate goodbye to the hosts.

"You are adorable," the woman said.

"And a fantastic cook," her husband agreed.

"And a good judge of men," the woman went on. "Your husband is very handsome." Just as if Patrick wasn't there.

For the first time Darcy looked flustered. "We aren't married," she said.

"But he desires you. I see it in his eyes when he looks at you," the man said.

"And you look at him the same way," His wife added.

Total panic filled Darcy's eyes. "Desire isn't nearly enough," she said. And didn't that say everything he needed to know about how she felt about him?

He should just let her go about her business, and he should go on to his affair tonight. "Come with me tonight," he whispered as they neared the hotel.

She looked up at him with confusion. "I can't."

He gave a curt nod. "You have things to do."

"Not a thing, but…" She looked down at herself.

"Not a problem," he told her. "I have to warn you, though. There will be a lot of people there."

"Angelise?" she asked. "I—Cara called me today to check in, and she said that she'd heard Angelise was here."

Cara had called Darcy and not him? What was that about?

"Angelise gets around."

"She wants to marry you."

"We're friends."

"But there are other women here who wouldn't mind wearing your ring, either. I've seen them. They're like you."

What the hell did that mean? Was she talking about her wheelchair? Her social status? Patrick wasn't quite sure he cared. Darcy had told him that he should marry. She'd made it very clear over and over that she wasn't interested in marriage.

"I'll be dancing with you tonight," he said. It was a dare, a claim. He wanted her last night here to be spent with him.

"I'll take you up on that," she said.

"I can't wait." And that was no lie.

Focus, focus, focus, Darcy told herself. She had come here with a goal in mind, to demonstrate to Patrick that she was a woman on the move, a woman who had her life together and who no longer feared being the center of attention, so tonight she had to make her case. Cross any t's and dot any i's she hadn't managed to cross or dot yet.

But she also had another goal: to grasp this last chance to soak in as much of Patrick as she could. When she got home she had one more very important task. She had to make sure that everyone at Able House was committed to Patrick's plan for them. Then she was going to leave Able House and set out on her own. She couldn't stay connected to Patrick and have any chance of happiness.

Tonight really would be their final goodbye, at least in person, so Darcy rolled into the ballroom prepared to act her heart out and make as many memories as possible. That strange sensory trick that made her instantly aware of him helped her locate him almost immediately. He was surrounded by men, but there were also a number of beautiful, willowy mobile women with perfect hair and makeup and shoes crowding close to him. Lots of them sported bare shoulders, cleavage and dresses to die for whereas she was wearing a very simple and inexpensive red gown. No cleavage. Not that she had much in the way of cleavage.

Don't think that way, she told herself. Remember, you have to be the new Darcy for Patrick. Paste on a confident smile.

The magical thing was that the second he saw her and smiled at her, her smile became real, too. She looked up and down that tall, broad-shouldered form. She remembered how that dark hair had felt against her fingers, how those green eyes had gazed into hers as he caressed her, how that mouth had felt against her skin.

Nothing could have stopped her from entering that crowd then. For once Darcy was happy that her wheelchair attracted attention, because the sea of people parted to let her pass.

Patrick met her halfway. "Darcy, you look amazing."

"So do you. You look…hot," she said as the people closest to them laughed. Darcy blushed. "Sorry," she said to everyone. "I have a big mouth."

"Don't apologize. Who are you, beautiful lady? Judson, introduce us," some man said.

Patrick looked askance at her, and Darcy nodded.

"This is Darcy, a wonderful chef and a wonderful friend. If you ever need a caterer—"

"I'm your woman," Darcy said, dipping her head in a mock bow.

"Interesting," another man said.

"Where has Patrick been hiding someone as gorgeous as you?" another male voice called out.

"In his kitchen, but I'm a free agent now," Darcy said, remembering that conversation with Angelise.

"Well, then—"

"Time to go," Patrick said. "Didn't you promise me a dance, Darcy?"

She smiled up at him and was surprised to see that he was

frowning at her. She'd thought that conversation had gone pretty well. It took some deep breathing to put herself out there in such a public way, but no one had seemed to be offering pity. The banter had been light.

"I hope I didn't embarrass you with that comment about you being hot," she said, as she and Patrick left the crowd behind.

He shook his head. "I think you just made my reputation," he said with a chuckle. "Every guy who heard that is going to be envious. I walked away with the girl in the red dress with the wild, wicked mouth. Half those guys want to sleep with you now."

"What do the other half want to do?"

Patrick laughed. "They want to sleep with you, too."

"My, your friends certainly have one track minds. How do they get any business done?" she teased.

"I haven't a clue. They're total boneheads. Don't even look at them," he teased right back, and when she looked up into his eyes and saw him smiling at her, Darcy's heart felt as if it was expanding so much that her chest wouldn't be able to hold it.

"I wouldn't think of it," she said. I've missed you, she thought. "I don't have time to look at them. You and I are going to dance, aren't we?"

"Absolutely."

"You'll be okay with the wheelchair?"

"I can't believe you're even asking me that. By now you ought to know me better. I want to dance with you, and your wheelchair is how you get from place to place. If anything, you'll be the one having a problem with me. You know what you're doing, while I don't have a clue."

"Don't worry. I'll be gentle with you," she teased.

"Then there's no problem, is there?" he asked. "I'll trust

you to give me cues. I did watch a few wheelchair dance videos on the Web in anticipation of this moment."

"Then you do have a clue."

"Seeing isn't doing," he quipped. But in the end, Darcy decided that Patrick must have either watched those videos carefully or he was just a fast learner. All that natural athleticism of his was unleashed, and when the music began and he took her by the hand, everything clicked.

She twirled and swooped and he met her. He became her shadow, her other half, her mirror image. They touched, then broke away and returned to meet each other again.

The music swelled and, at one point, Darcy realized that people were watching them, but she didn't care. Patrick was totally focused on her, and she couldn't take her eyes off him.

When the music rose to a crescendo, he took her hand, twirling her around three times, then pulling her toward him in one fast, fluid movement. She rolled into him, pressing her palm and forearm flat against his chest in a controlled, sensual movement as she slid closer into his body, then pushed off of him, rolling backward and motioning to him in a come-hither gesture. He followed her, sliding on one knee to meet her and drawing her to him for a slow, swirling embrace as the music faded away.

The applause was instantaneous, and Darcy blinked. Her heart was pounding, and she looked at Patrick, not at the gathered guests.

He had stood and he was staring down at her, his hair falling over one brow, his green gaze intent.

"Let's get out of here," he whispered and she nodded.

"That was wonderful," someone called.

"Beautiful," someone else added.

"The sexiest thing I've ever seen between two people who are fully clothed," another person said.

"Oh, come on, take a bow," someone finally said.

Patrick looked askance at Darcy. "Your audience," he said.

"And yours." She tipped her head to him. "All right."

"Thank you," she called to the crowd as Patrick twirled her around one last time and nodded to his friends.

"Hey, you're not stealing her away, are you, Patrick?"

"Sorry, Cinderella and I need to rest," he called.

Out of the corner of her eye Darcy saw Angelise watching them, but she didn't come close. Then, Patrick opened the door, and the two of them moved out into the darkness beneath the stars. "That was amazing," Darcy said.

"*You* were amazing. You astound me. Constantly."

They wandered farther into the empty gardens, down a lonely trail lit only by small solar lanterns. The roses were dark shadows in the night.

"I astound you because…I'm not hiding from the world anymore?" Okay, she was pushing him, but that was the thing she wanted him to key in on, that she wasn't hiding. He didn't have to be concerned about that aspect of her life from now on.

His chuckle was incredibly sexy in the darkness. She couldn't see him clearly and the sound slipped through her bones, touching her and turning her to fire.

"When you decide to do something, you don't do it in a small way, do you?" he asked.

She smiled, but then realizing that he probably couldn't see her, either, pulled up short. He dropped to a bench on the path and she drew up beside him. "It wasn't so much that I decided," she whispered. "It was that you made it easy for me. You never treated me like an oddity."

"Why should I? You're a beautiful, intelligent and talented woman. That's not odd. It's pretty darn great."

"Thank you, but...even before you knew much about me, you saw me in a different light than other people had."

"You underestimate your ability to impress," he said. "I always knew that you were special."

Darcy closed her eyes. She wanted nothing more than to tell him that he was special, too, that she had loved him for longer than she had even realized, but that was the opposite of what she needed to do. She had come a long way to make a point and she wasn't trying hard enough, so she took his big hand in both of her own. She faced him in the darkness.

"You've given me so much, Patrick and I'm so...so incredibly grateful, but I want you to know that I'm much more confident now than I was when we met. I owe you for that, but you don't have to champion me or protect me anymore. I can do that on my own." Even as she was saying the words, she knew that this was her farewell to him, the last time she would see him. Angelise—or someone like her—was waiting in the wings, and that was as it should be, but that didn't make the pain in Darcy's heart any less powerful.

"I don't want you to be grateful."

"But I am." She could barely get the words past the ache in her throat. "Thanks to you I'm ready to proceed on my own. I don't have to have you beside me anymore."

"Dammit, Darcy." He leaned forward and framed her face. He brought his lips to hers.

The fire was instantaneous. She twisted closer, looping her arms around his neck.

"I've missed you," he said, and he kissed her again. Darcy's consciousness began to retreat. In a minute she was going to beg him to make love to her. She should stop now.

Instead she pressed into him. I missed you, too, she thought, but somehow she managed not to say the words. If she said them, if she even let him discern one tiny inkling of how she felt about him, he was going to feel so guilty eventually. Because he had that damned innate sense of duty.

Closing her eyes, Darcy breathed him in. She pushed back.

"I—I have to go. This is—" Heavenly, wonderful, everything I want. "It's wonderful," she said, deciding for honesty, "but not the right thing for me."

He stared at her, his chest heaving. "Of course," he finally said. "I'll see you to your room."

All right, she had to say it, to do it. She had to make the break.

"By leaving, I didn't actually mean my room. I'm going home. It's a bit early, but—" And there she stopped. Her throat began to clog with tears and she couldn't proceed. She had meant to tell him that she would be leaving Able House, too, but—she couldn't tell him. Nor could she stay at Able House waiting for him, knowing that she was going to turn into one of those many women who followed Patrick with their eyes, hoping for a few kisses and wishing for things that could never be.

She should at least tell him of her intent to find a new home in another part of the country. She owed him that much, but the words would have to wait for an e-mail or a letter. As it was, she was barely able to retain her faux composure.

"Say something," she said. "Tell me goodbye. Wish me a— a great flight home."

"You're leaving because I kissed you again. I took things for granted and pushed you," he said.

"No. I wanted you to kiss me."

"And now you want to leave."

No. She didn't want to leave at all. "I just need to leave." And it was all she could do not to beg him for one last kiss.

He stood, and she realized that this was the last walk they

would take together. Her heart hurt, her throat ached, her eyes…she would never make it back to the hotel without crying.

Dammit, yes, she would. She wasn't coming this far only to mess everything up at the end. So, they moved in silence to the door, he rode up to her room with her in the elevator. "When is your flight?" he asked.

"Tonight," she said. "I have a limo booked to take me to the airport." Both lies. Her plane left in the morning, so there was no limo tonight. But there would be. If she had to, she would sleep at the airport, because she didn't trust herself to stay in the same hotel as Patrick and not do something that would spoil all the progress she'd made.

Now, she had only one more thing she had to do before she severed her ties with Patrick forever and looked for a job in another town.

"I have a favor to ask of you," she said, forcing the words out. "I have an—an event planned for next Saturday. It's a bit different in scope from my usual, and you've always given me good feedback. I'd like to ask for your opinion on this, too."

He cleared his throat. "Ask." His voice was like a bullet, fast and hard and devoid of emotion.

"We'll have a live feed. If you're willing, I can set up a transmission. I'll send you a message with the details."

"That must be some event if you're transmitting it."

She nodded. "It's the biggest thing I've done yet."

He nodded. "I see. Yes, of course. You're moving up and on and this will be your big break. I promise you I'll watch, and I'll contact you afterward."

No. Don't contact me, she wanted to say. Don't tell me you'll call. If you do, I'll wait for the phone to ring. I'll die every time it rings and it isn't you, and if you call and I hear the sound of your voice…

The unthinkable might happen. If she didn't make the break clean, she'd be begging him to come back and let her work in his kitchen again, and she would suffer far too much when he finally settled down and started looking for a bride.

It was time to go. This was it. The last time she would ever see him.

"Patrick."

He knelt by her side.

"Are you making yourself small for me again?" she whispered.

"No, I'm bringing myself close."

"I'm glad." She threw caution to the wind and risked eternal heartbreak as she reached for him and kissed him with all her heart. Then, without saying goodbye, she let herself in her room.

One hour later, she left the hotel. Her heart stayed behind.

CHAPTER FIFTEEN

PATRICK had been in a bad mood for days, and he wasn't sure why. Or…maybe he *was* sure why, and that was the problem. He'd just discovered something about himself. He was in love with a woman he couldn't have.

That brief visit of Darcy's should have reassured him and helped get her out of his system. She was well, she was beyond well. She was vivacious and outgoing and sparkling and…she had absolutely no need of him anymore. Her life had moved beyond him. He should be happy for her.

He was. He also missed her like crazy.

And as the day for her televised event came close, he turned into a ragged fool, forgetting to sleep or eat. He forgot duty. He missed an appointment for the first time in his career.

Now, he sat in the dark, private auditorium and waited tensely for Darcy to appear on the screen.

And then she was there. But…what was she doing?

Patrick sat up straighter. He leaned forward in his chair.

Darcy moved to the center of a makeshift stage. She held a microphone, and while she was getting ready to speak, the camera panned over the crowd in front of the stage. The area dead in the center was crowded with people in wheelchairs, far more than the Able House residents could account for. But beyond that, Patrick made out his sisters, what looked to be most if not all of his neighbors, friends and even some politicians. Camera crews from local television stations were in evidence.

The camera zoomed in on Darcy again. Dressed in pale yellow with that smile, that incredible smile he loved, she was riveting. Patrick couldn't have looked away if the roof of the auditorium had caved in. A banner behind her came into view. It read, The First Annual Patrick Judson Able House Festival.

Patrick swore beneath his breath.

Darcy cleared her throat. "First of all, let me welcome all of you and thank you for coming. Today is a day that heralds what will, hopefully, become a new tradition in the city and in this neighborhood. In a few moments, we'll begin a day of competitions, classes, food, fun and togetherness, and all of that has been made possible by Patrick Judson who spearheaded Able House and served as an intermediary between us and the community.

"Unfortunately Patrick can't be with us today. He's in France but he's watching us and I know that he's here in spirit. It was Patrick's idea to have those of us at Able House share our skills with the community, and as a result, we're now involved in a community education program teaching evening classes as well as participating in an enrichment program at the local grammar schools twice a month. Patrick's idea has proven to be so successful and popular that we've decided to take it to the next step. We don't just want to live in this community, we want to be a vital part of it, so to that end, for the past two weeks we've fanned out into the community to approach our neighbors and invite those who were willing to come here today to share their talents with all of us. The result is this community festival. In addition, we'll be opening our doors one weekend and one weeknight a month so that we can all join together for classes, book discussions and a meal.

"All of this has been made possible by those on both sides who have been willing to reach out to each other. When we first came here, many people were skeptical and nervous, but you've welcomed us and now we welcome *you* into our home. We're so glad to have you here."

The crowd broke into applause. Someone called out, "Way to go, Darcy!"

She waved and held out her hand for silence. "And now, I have just one last thing I want to add before we begin and that is this: "Patrick, wherever you are, we're—we miss you."

Patrick had moved from his chair and was standing directly in front of the huge screen now, staring into a larger than life Darcy's eyes. Those beautiful eyes were filled with unshed tears and her voice had broken.

She had never been more beautiful. His heart had never hurt this hard.

"We miss you," she continued, "and all of us here at Able House want to thank you for…for enriching our lives, for championing us, but mostly for helping us and the world to realize that each of us, every one of us in the world, whether on two legs or four wheels, have gifts to give, and those gifts are meant to be shared with others. I'll—*I'll* miss you," she finished. Her last words were barely a whisper.

Were those tears streaming down her face? Undoubtedly.

Patrick moved closer, but—dammit—this was just a screen. The real Darcy was a continent away. He heard her whisper, "I—I need to make the sendoff announcement, but— I—would you please do it for me?"

A gruff male voice said something Patrick couldn't understand. Then Cal Barrow appeared on stage and took the microphone from Darcy. She moved out of view.

Outrage filled Patrick's soul. What was that guy doing forcing Darcy off the stage?

Patrick whipped out his cell phone. He started to call his sister and had hit the first three numbers when Cal cleared his throat.

"It's time to get started, folks," he said. "The schedules are on the table, the food is in the dining room, events are in the rooms, in the lobby, on the stage, in the pool and out on the lawns. Go to it and have a great time. Oh, and—could we please give a cheer for Darcy and Mr. Judson? She's made me crazy and I've been a total ass. Me and Billings—who has, thank goodness, decided to move—were the lone holdouts and were pretty mean to Darcy and everyone here, but…what can I say? She knows how to win a guy over and make him feel like a stupid heel and now she's got me teaching wood-carving, so…let the games begin!"

The crowd exploded in applause.

People were starting to file out to wherever they were going, cutting in front of the cameras and such when Cal fiddled with the mike again. "Oh, and Judson? If you're wondering how a little bit of a woman who took me down and punched me in the unmentionables managed to make a believer out of me…she got me with her brownies. Came over every damn day for nine days and brought a different kind every day. I cursed her up and down and all she would say was, 'Cal, don't make me hit you again. Do you want a brownie or not?' So, the fact is…I don't know how you can stay away from her. She's a hard one to ignore. She's a total bully and a sweetheart, too. Makes me want to beat *myself* up for what I did to her and all the fine people here."

Then the mike went dead.

The screen broke into four areas, each one covering a different event taking place on the grounds. Every thirty seconds the areas would switch in a round robin random kaleidoscope. There was a group of knitters, a film discussion group, Cal's woodcarving, relay races with teams alternating a racer on foot with a racer in a wheelchair, a photography group, swimmers, a homemade miniature golf course and numerous other activities. Patrick was impressed, but despite the ever-changing footage and the fact that he had seen almost everyone else, his sisters waving to the camera as they assisted at the races and in the pool, the woman he wanted most to see eluded him.

Patrick cursed the cameramen who didn't seem to know what was important. Once again he took out his phone. Surely one of his sisters could remedy the situation. This time he got Lane.

"I miss you. I love you. Where the hell is she?" he asked.

"Whoa, Patrick," Lane said. "Who is *she*?"

"Darcy."

"Ah."

"Don't ah me, Lane. I need help."

"Sounds like you need Darcy."

"Yes."

"I might tell you if you stop being so cranky. Darcy and Cara and Amy and I have bonded while you've been gone."

"That's great." He meant it, too.

"She knows you almost as well as we do."

"You might be right about that, but…*where is she?*"

"How's Angelise?" Lane suddenly asked.

"I don't know. I don't care. Where's Darcy?"

Lane chuckled. "Right answer, big brother. She's been cooking and other stuff. I'll get a cameraman over to her."

"Thank you, Lane. I do love you."

"Me, too. Just…be careful. I don't want to see you get hurt."

"What do you mean?"

"Darcy's leaving soon. She's moving to Seattle. She told me last night."

Patrick's heart fell right onto the floor and shattered at his feet. He clicked off the phone. He ignored the ringing when it began. He watched as the camera zoomed in on Darcy. She was sitting on a couch reading a story…and she had a toddler on her lap. Davey and Charlie were snuggled up beside her. She was surrounded by children. As she read the story, something about a bunny, she smiled at something Davey said and leaned over and dropped a kiss on his head.

Patrick felt as if he was going to collapse. His Darcy had mastered her demons. She was happy.

She was leaving. And she hadn't told him.

For a long time he sat there. The screen flickered as the cameras switched from room to room, except the one on Darcy never moved.

His phone rang again. He answered it.

"Patrick?" Lane's voice was worried.

"I'm all right," he said. But he wasn't.

"You didn't know that she was leaving, did you?" she asked.

"I know now."

"Do you care?"

"Lane, let's talk later. I have something to do now." He was already starting to move by the time he clicked the phone off. Within hours he was flying over the Atlantic.

Darcy awoke with a headache and a deep sense of sadness and distress. Yesterday had gone well, but she hadn't heard from Patrick. Lane had mentioned that she spoke with him briefly, but that was all.

So, there was nothing left to do but make her final arrangements to depart. Patrick's new life had obviously taken hold. She had to make her own way, too.

That's what she should get started on. Definitely. It would be the height of stupidity hanging around today hoping that he would call so that she could say goodbye to him.

"You call him," she told herself, but she knew that she wouldn't do that.

Listlessly she took a shower and got dressed. She opened her door and went out into the hallway.

Patrick was leaning against the wall opposite her room, his arms and ankles crossed. He didn't smile when he saw her.

Her heart leaped, then fell.

"What's wrong? Why are you here?" she finally asked.

"When were you going to tell me?" he asked, pushing off the wall.

"Tell you…"

"Lane said that you were moving to Seattle and…dammit, Darcy, not a word? Not a hint? Why?"

"I—I thought you might worry about why I was going." But, of course, that was only part of the truth.

"You're darned right I'm worried. Did we run you off? Did something happen? I know it wasn't Cal, because he seems to have fallen totally under your spell. What happened?"

You, she wanted to say. Just you. Love.

"I—well, I'm not so scared of being out and about in public anymore and I—"

"That's no reason." He ran his hand through his hair. "Or…maybe it's a perfectly good reason. I shouldn't be badgering you. It's your life. You're free to live it the way you want to."

No. No, she wasn't. Darcy bit her lip.

"You're supposed to be in France," she said.

"I was. Now I'm here."

"Why?"

"I had to see you. I was afraid you would leave and I wouldn't be able to find you. I had to tell you…thank you for yesterday. You were magnificent. You've accomplished so much. Seattle is going to love you."

He crossed the hall, reached out and gently touched her face. "Not half as much as I do, but they'll adore you."

Darcy froze. Yearning swept through her and she looked up, his fingertips sliding across her jaw. His touch was heaven. Love? Had he said love? Did he mean—?

No, of course not. He'd meant it in a generic way, like "I love cookies." Not "I love you so much that it kills me to be apart from you."

That kind of love and hurt was what she was feeling right now. The kind that made your throat hurt and your eyes sting. She was staring into those green eyes that did awful, wonderful things to her and she felt herself falling apart.

"Don't go," he said, in a ragged, broken voice.

She closed her eyes. "I have to. I can't stay here."

"Why?"

Again she looked into his eyes. "You have a plan for your life. You've had it for years. It's a good plan, a great plan, a totally wonderful plan. You have things to do overseas. There are people counting on you. You're the center of everything happening there. And you want it. You've always wanted it, and I want you to have it, too. More than anything." She bit her lip, fought the tears.

Patrick dropped to his knees in front of her. "That plan of mine? It *was* a good plan, Darcy, but plans change. You came into my life and changed everything."

"No!"

"Yes. I can hire people for France and Spain. I have money to pay people to take my place everywhere but here. With you."

"You wanted to be free. I want you to be free."

"I love you, Darcy. Being apart from you taught me that freedom is so much more than being alone. Being *with* you frees me. You opened my eyes to pathways I hadn't even imagined. All those years ago when my parents died and left me alone to raise my sisters, I thought I needed my freedom, but what I needed, what I wanted, was someone to share my life. Someone to talk to and love as an equal. What I wanted, Darcy, was you."

"Patrick…"

He placed two fingers over her lips. "You don't have to let me down easy. Just tell me if I have any chance of convincing you to stay, yes or no."

He opened his mouth to say something more, but she leaned forward and placed her fingers over *his* lips this time.

"I love you, Patrick," she said. "Just in case it isn't shining through in my eyes." She leaned forward and wrapped her arms around his neck.

"Is that a yes, you'll stay, Darcy?"

"It's the loudest yes you'll ever hear. I've missed you so much. You complete me. You make me want to do more and be more than I've ever been."

Patrick drew her close and kissed her. "You don't have to be more," he said. "You're already everything I want and need."

EPILOGUE

Six months later, Patrick came in to find Darcy baby-sitting Charlie and Davey. She gave them each a hug, then sent them over to Patrick for more hugs before they ran off to find Olivia in the kitchen.

"They're so precious," she said. "Your sisters have let me hog them lately. I wonder what Amy and Cara and Lane will think when they find out there's a new Judson on the way." Darcy looked down at her still flat abdomen.

Patrick kissed her. "I suppose they'll be just as happy to hear about the baby as they were when they found out you were marrying me. And then they'll probably take turns filling in the calendar so they can baby-sit."

Darcy looked up at him, a slight trace of concern in those lovely eyes. "I hope I'll be a good mother," she said.

Patrick did a double take and raised one eyebrow. "Have you ever found anything you're not good at? Since we got married, you've mastered downhill skiing and wheelchair tennis and probably a few other things I've forgotten about. If I hadn't begged you to consider my heart and not take up skydiving you probably would have excelled at that, too. Do you seriously believe you won't be a good mother?"

She reached out and slid one hand around his neck, pulling him close for a quick kiss. "I'm so glad I met you."

Patrick smiled. "Me, too. From the minute I walked into the kitchen and found you defying me, I was lost."

"I was, too, even though I didn't think I'd survive you. I didn't think I'd ever want to have a child, either, but…do you think we might have more than one?"

What did I ever do to deserve this woman? Patrick thought. "Yes," he said. "Absolutely."

He laughed.

"What?" she asked.

"You," he said. "You have so much energy, so much love, so much life. I can't imagine why I ever thought I needed to go looking for adventure when living with you is the greatest adventure of my life."

"What a catch you are," she said with a teasing smile.

"Does that mean I get to kiss you again?"

"It means a whole lot of things. I'll show you later," she said. "After everyone has gone home. It's going to take a little while."

"Hours?" he asked, raising one eyebrow.

"Years," she said with a mocking smile and love in her eyes. "At least fifty. Now, kiss me, please."

He did. Then he smiled against her lips.

"What?" she asked.

"Kissing you has to be a whole lot better than flying," he confessed.

She kissed him again. "Let the adventure begin, love," she said.

Oh, but it already had. And it was so much better than he'd ever dreamed.

72 Hours

DANA MARTON

Author **Dana Marton** lives near Wilmington, Delaware. She has been an avid reader since childhood and has a master's degree in writing popular fiction. When not writing, she can be found either in her garden or her home library. For more information on the author and her other novels, please visit her website at www.danamarton.com.

She would love to hear from her readers via e-mail: DanaMarton@yahoo.com.

With many thanks to Allison Lyons and
Denise Zaza.

And to Susan Mallery for being the
wonderful friend that she is.

Chapter One

August 9, 21:11

A good spy had many tools at his disposal. One of them was the instinctual knowledge of when to run. Parker McCall was running for his life, toward the Tuileries on Rue de Rivoli that stretched parallel to the River Seine.

When he'd been on jungle missions, running for the river was a good idea most of the time, and often the only way out. But right now he was on a street dense with tourists. Jumping into the Seine would do nothing but draw attention to himself and bring the authorities.

He hated Paris. It was the city that had taken Kate away from him.

"Excusez-moi." He slipped between two business-men deep in discussion, blocking the sidewalk.

The chase scenes they showed in action movies, where seasoned professionals madly scrambled from their pursuers, knocking over vendor stands and causing all kinds of commotion, were nonsense. When you were hunted, you went to ground. You went quietly, did everything you could to blend in and become invisible, part of the usual tapestry of local life. You ran in such a way that nobody looking at you could tell you were running.

He glanced at his watch again, deepened the annoyed scowl on his face and smoothed down his tie as he moved briskly through the crowd. He was a businessman late for a dinner. And the throng of people who'd seen hundreds of late businessmen rushing through identified him as such and parted in front of him, paying him scant attention. He was swimming through people and he had to be careful not to cause any ripples. Ripples would be noticed.

And his enemies were watching.

He figured at least four men were after him. He had caught glimpses, but mostly he operated by instinct.

They, too, were professionals. Professional killers who moved through the city the way the lions of Africa moved forward in the cover of the tall grass, in a well-coordinated hunt, invisible until they were but a jump away from their prey.

"Excusez-moi." He stepped around a twin stroller and glanced up at the large *M* sign a few yards ahead— Le Métro, Paris's famed subway system. He could try to disappear there or go for the Tuileries and see if he could deal with the men in the garden.

The subway would be packed. This was one of the busiest stations, the one closest to the Musée du Louvre. He could get away without confrontation.

But he wanted more. Information was the name of the game. And right now, the information he needed was the identity of the man who had sicced his henchmen on Parker. He had too many enemies to take a blind guess.

Like New York, Paris never slept. Especially not on hot summer evenings. Tourists and locals filled the streets.

He moved forward and could see the garden at last. He crossed the Avenue du Général Lemonnier and hurried to the nearest entrance. The sixty-three acres of mostly open landscaping that lay before him was enough to make anyone stop in wonder, but he didn't have the time to enjoy the sight. He planned and calculated.

The lions that hunted him were hidden in the tall grass. At least he didn't have to worry about the approaching darkness and not being able to see. They didn't call Paris the city of light—in addition to love—for nothing. It was lit up like Methuselah's birthday cake.

Head for higher ground. Get a good vantage point. But there weren't many of those in the garden, so he strode toward the Ferris wheel.

Too late.

A blur of movement caught his attention by the pedestal of a large statue. They'd gotten in front of him. Or at least one of them had. But hunters as good as these four didn't reveal themselves by accident. Parker had a feeling that he'd been supposed to see that. They wanted him to run in the opposite direction. They were trying to herd him someplace out of sight where they could take him out.

He strode to the statues instead, feinted in one direction and went around the other. He didn't take the time to look or evaluate. His fist connected with a man's face in the next second. He caught the guy as he staggered back, then looped the man's arm around his shoulder, holding his gun against his side, and dragged him off into the stand of trees nearby, away from the curious gazes of passersby. Nobody would be walking off the paved paths today. The ground was muddy from this morning's rain.

"Who are you?" He was disarming the man as he spoke, confiscating first his gun, then the near-microscopic communications device attached to the guy's ear. "Who sent you here?"

The man—in his mid-thirties, around six feet, cropped hair—had a swarthy skin tone and that wide Slavic facial type that marked him from somewhere around the Black Sea. He pressed his thin lips together and went for the knife that had been hidden up his sleeve. Parker turned the blade and drove it home. No time for a tussle, to subdue him then get him to talk, although he could have made him talk, given some time. But the others could be here any second.

He lowered the body to the ground and searched the man's clothes, found no identification. He hadn't expected any.

One down, three to go. He headed out of the woods.

He'd come to Paris on the trail of Piotr Morovich, a slippery Russian mercenary who'd been discovered to have connections to a Middle Eastern terrorist group his team had been watching. But he'd run into something bigger than he had anticipated. Good thing that handling the unexpected was his specialty.

He moved through the strolling tourists and children playing and reached the Ferris wheel. His tie was off now, his jacket swung over his shoulder, his body language the same as all the other casual sightseers'.

"One ticket, *s'il vous plaît.*" He scanned the tourists already on the ride. *"Merci,"* he said, then boarded the Ferris wheel.

The giant wheel turned slowly, taking him higher and higher. But while the others oohed and aahed over the sights, he was watching the people below.

There. One of the men he was looking for was coming down the central walkway. Parker looked even more carefully and spotted another by the fountain. Where was the third? Where would *he* be in the same situation? Every hunt had a pattern; he just had to find it.

He watched the two men as they looked for him and for their lost teammate who wasn't checking in over the radio. The four would have formed a U originally, trying to get him in the middle. He looked in the direction of the river. And he found the third man.

He was impatient now for his cart to reach the ground again, keeping his eyes on the men. He would get them one by one, would get some answers.

His phone buzzed in his pocket. He pulled it out and glanced at the display, intending to return the call later. Then he saw the coded ID flashing on the small screen—the Colonel.

"Sir?"

"This evening at 21:03 hours, Tarkmez rebel forces overtook the Russian Embassy on Rue de Prony," the head of the SDDU, Secret Designation Defense Unit, one of the U.S.'s most effective covert weapons against terrorism, said.

The hundred-plus-member unit did everything from reconnaissance to demolition, personnel extraction, spying, kidnapping and assassinations. Parker himself had done it all. He glanced at his watch—21:25.

"The Russians haven't made it public yet. They haven't even notified the French authorities," the Colonel went on.

He didn't have to ask how the CIA, from whom the Colonel had no doubt gotten his information, would know this fast. They'd had the Russian embassy bugged for decades. Well, on and off. The Russians were as efficient at sweeping out the bugs as the agency was creative at placing them.

"The U.S. consul was at an unscheduled, informal dinner with the Russian ambassador and his wife. She is in the building, but we don't have an exact location on her."

While ambassadors represented the head of their country and there was only one of them, consuls handled visa applications and all the various problems of U.S. citizens abroad, representing their country in general, the position more administrative than political. The U.S. had about a dozen consuls in France.

But Parker had a bad premonition, cold dread settling into his stomach. "Kate?"

"Affirmative."

The single word slammed into his chest with the force of a .22 bullet.

"Is she okay?" Tightly locked away emotions broke free, one after the other, tripping his heartbeat.

"We don't know. The Russians are not good at asking for help. It's possible that they'll keep the situation secret for several hours, unless the rebels themselves make contact with the media."

His cart was approaching the ground. Ten feet, nine, eight, close enough. There were times for blending in, then there were times to break all the rules, even if it did draw attention. He lifted the safety bar and stood, eliciting a warning cry from the operator and loud comments and gasps from bystanders. He jumped and landed in a crouch, staying down so the next seat wouldn't knock him over the head, then sprinted into the crowd.

"What do the rebels want?" he asked, scanning the park for the men. His business with them would have to wait.

"Don't know yet. Probably autonomy. We can't offer help to the Russians until they tell us about the problem. Saying anything now would be tantamount to admitting that we have their embassy bugged. Considering the current political climate, the last thing we need is to cause an international incident," the Colonel said. "Be careful. This has all the makings of a disaster."

Pictures of news reports flashed through Parker's mind: the infamous Dubrovka theater siege and the Ossetia school-hostage crises. The Russian elite Alpha counterterrorism troops and their Vymple special forces, like their U.S. counterparts, were known for not nego-

tiating with terrorists. Unfortunately, they were also
known for getting their enemies at any price, even at the
cost of innocent lives. In the theater siege, 115 hostages
were killed, in the school standoff, over 300, many of
them children.

Parker popped his earpiece into place, tucked away
his phone and broke into a flat run. The men who hunted
him would have to wait. The embassy had been taken
only minutes ago. There was a small chance that the
entire behemoth of a building hadn't been secured yet
by the rebels. The sooner he got there, the better his
chances were for getting in.

"Of the few men we have in the area, you're the
closest," the Colonel said. "And you know the most
about the Tarkmezi situation."

And Parker suspected that the Colonel had also taken
his private connection into consideration, knew he
would want to be involved. Not that the Colonel would
ever admit to personal favors.

"I appreciate it, sir," he told the man anyway.

Rain began to fall again.

"Do try to remember that this is a minimum-impact,
covert mission," the Colonel said in a meaningful tone.

Which meant that he was to make as little contact as
possible, remain close to invisible as he searched for
Kate and got her out. He was to change nothing, interact
with no other aspects of the situation but those strictly
required for the extraction.

"And the other hostages?"

"As soon as their country asks for our help we'll give
it. Our hands are tied until then."

That idea didn't sit too well with him. He hated when politics interfered with a mission of his, which happened about every damned time.

"Parker?" The Colonel's tone changed to warning. "Don't make me regret that I tagged you for this job."

"No, sir."

"Just get Kate Hamilton out."

"Yes, sir."

That he would. Yeah, he was still mad at Kate for leaving him. Mad as hell, but he wasn't going to let any harm come to her. Any Tarkmez rebel bastard who laid a hand on the woman he'd once meant to marry was going to answer to him.

August 9, 23:45

"Do you have visual?" The question came through his cell phone. His battery was at twenty-five percent so Parker was rationing his calls to the Colonel. But he had called in to report that he was inside.

He tapped the phone once in response. He was trying to speak as little as possible, wasn't sure who could overhear him as he docked in the vent system that had openings to the various rooms. One tap meant no, two taps yes.

At least four of the gunmen who had overtaken the building were talking in the room below him. He could hear no one else. If there were hostages in there, they were kept quiet.

"I'm scrambling to get you some backup, but I can't pull anyone who's near enough," the Colonel said.

He understood. His team was specifically created for undercover missions. A lot of the members were built into terrorist organizations, rebel groups around the world or sleeper cells. To pull one at a moment's notice before his or her job was done would ruin months or years of undercover work.

"I'm going to get someone else in to help as fast as I can," the Colonel went on.

Parker tapped *no*. He'd snuck in before the embassy had been fully secured. Anyone trying to get in now would have to fight their way in. And that could mean disaster for the hostages. He could bring Kate out on his own.

Muted pops came from somewhere behind him. He immediately reversed direction.

"Gunshots. Two," he whispered into the phone.

"I'll check it out. Contact me if there's anything else," the Colonel said and then he was gone.

Those bugs hidden throughout the embassy were still transmitting. From his CIA connection, the Colonel should be able to get some information on what was happening. Parker backed through the vent duct as fast as he could. Since the weather was cool and overcast, the air-conditioning wasn't on; there was nothing to hide the noise he made. So he didn't make any.

He had a rough idea of the building's outline. The Colonel had briefed him on the way over. Since Kate had last been heard near the kitchens, he'd been heading in that direction, surveying all the rooms he could see as he went. So far he'd seen or heard a dozen or so rebels but no hostages.

The gunshots changed everything. There was a better-than-fair chance that the hostages were that way. His phone vibrated. He opened it without halting his progress.

"Bad news." The Colonel's grim tone underscored his words. "To prove how serious they are, the rebels just shot Ambassador Vasilievits."

Parker went faster, crawling with grim determination, one hundred percent focused on the job. Kate had been with the ambassador and his wife at the time of the initial attack on the embassy. He hoped she had somehow been separated from them and had managed to escape the rebels' notice.

Because if she hadn't, if the rebels figured out who Kate was, she would be next. They hated Americans as much as they hated the Russians.

He wished he had prepared for more than surveillance before he'd left his hotel late that afternoon and then run into the four men who'd seemed hell-bent on taking him out. He had nothing but his gun and his cell phone with its dwindling battery. Right now he would have given anything for the full tool kit that waited hidden behind the ceiling tiles of his hotel room.

"Any publicity on this yet?" he asked, able to talk more freely having gotten into a section that didn't have any openings to rooms.

"Nothing. The Russians might not break silence until morning. Their counterterrorism team is on its way. We don't think they asked the French for permission, but once the team is in place there isn't much the French can do. That's all I have."

They ended the connection, and he kept crawling. When he reached the next vertical drop, he lowered himself inch by inch, stopping when he heard voices ahead. The men were talking in Tarkmezi.

"And if they gas us?" The speaker sounded on edge.

"That's what we have the masks for," came the calm reply.

"What if they have something new and nasty? Kill us before we get the masks on."

"Get it on and keep it on, then," another guy snapped. "Maybe it'll shut you up."

"What do you think's going on?" The worrywart on the team didn't seem to be able to stop himself. "I wonder if they are negotiating?"

"When there's something to know, Piotr will tell us."

Parker picked his head up at the mention of the name. What were the chances that this was his Piotr? It was a common name, the Russian equivalent of Peter. But his instincts prickled. Could be that this was why Piotr Morovich had come to Paris. And if that was the case, then he hadn't come alone, something that U.S. intelligence had failed to detect.

"I could go check," Worrywart said.

"You stay the hell here."

The men fell silent just as Parker reached the vent hole.

Three Tarkmezi fighters, armed to the teeth, stood among two dozen tied-up hostages who were sitting in the middle of the floor in some sort of a gym, probably set up for embassy staff. He zeroed in on Kate and his heart rate sped up.

Hello, Kate. How have you been? He'd pictured, on too many occasions, the two of them meeting up again after all this time, but he had never imagined it would be under these circumstances.

She looked unharmed and calm. The spring that had been wound tightly in his chest since the Colonel had called now eased. Her hair was different from when he'd last seen her—a classy, sexy bob. He felt a ping of annoyance. Why had she changed? For whom? He had loved to run his fingers through her long, honey-blond hair. She had lost weight, too, but not much, still had those curves that used to drive him mad.

Memories flashed into his mind—hot, sweaty and explicit—and his body tightened. For a second he was transported back to the past, with Kate under him, her back bowed, her silky hair fanned out on the pillow, that soft moan of hers escaping her full lips as she looked at him the way she had always looked at him during their intense lovemaking, straight in the eyes. Man, it used to turn him on.

Not much had changed since, he realized ruefully and shifted in the tight space.

Keeping control with her in bed had always been a challenge. One of the many things he had loved about her. A single touch and all he could think was fast and hard, now, now, now. Slow and easy took superhuman effort. Pleasurable, highly gratifying effort. He pushed that thought as far away as he could. He couldn't go back there now. Not now, not ever.

One of the rebels moved and blocked her from view.

Come on, get out of the way. Parker gritted his teeth until the man finally moved again.

Kate stretched her long legs without getting up. In her dark slacks, white top and a cook's jacket, she blended in with the other half dozen kitchen staff among the hostages. Where were the rest? He didn't see any of the security team that would have guarded the embassy.

He focused on the three rebels. They would have to be distracted and neutralized before he could go in to save Kate. He surveyed the room, noting every detail, including the position of the doors and windows and their distance from each other, every piece of exercise equipment that could be used as a weapon or for cover. He swore silently at the floor-to-ceiling mirrors that lined the walls and made it impossible to sneak up behind anyone.

The easiest thing would be to go in predawn when the guards were ready to nod off, exhausted by their night vigil. But he hated the thought of waiting that long. He wanted her out before the Russian counterterrorism team got here.

He preferred planned and coordinated operations where nothing was left to chance. But those took time. And Kate's life was at stake. To save her he would do anything.

"Hang in there." He mouthed the words as he pulled his gun and screwed on the silencer, preparing to make his move.

The Colonel had asked him not to leave any signs— meaning a string of dead bodies—that he'd been there, if he could help it. Well, looked like he couldn't.

August 10, 00:05

SHE HAD Parker on her mind and that annoyed her no end. Kate Hamilton stared at the floor, not daring to make eye contact with the rebels.

They left the hostages alone for the most, but gave orders now and then that they expected to be followed, a problem since Kate didn't speak Russian. All the embassy staff did, even the French employees; it was a condition of employment here, just as fluent knowledge of English was a condition of employment over at the U.S. embassy. She was smart enough to copy whatever the others did in response to the commands. It had worked so far, but she wasn't sure how long her luck would hold out.

"Try something," Anna, a slightly built, petite young woman whispered barely audibly to her left. She was French and the personal secretary to the ambassador's wife.

Try something. Brilliant idea. Except that her hands were bound and three nasty-looking AK-47s were pointed in her general direction.

Parker would know what to do. He spoke a dozen languages. And he could always handle tough situations. The way he'd handled an attempted mugging when they'd gone down to Florida for a long weekend came to mind. She supposed he'd had to learn. He visited dangerous parts of the world as a foreign correspondent for Reuters. His continued absence had driven her nuts during their engagement.

She refused to let the memories hurt anymore. She was better off without him.

She pressed her lips together and looked around the room for the hundredth time, trying to figure out a way she could make a break for it and not be shot within a fraction of a second. *Okay, Parker. What would you do?* The gunshots they had heard earlier didn't fill her with optimism.

Several embassy guards had been killed within the first few minutes of the attack, as well as the sole civilian-dressed bodyguard who had escorted her over from the U.S. embassy for an unofficial visit with Tanya, the Russian ambassador's wife.

Tanya had left the dinner table for just a moment to take her two young girls to their nanny when the rebels had rushed in. Maybe they'd been able to escape. The rebels had taken her husband, the ambassador, immediately and herded the rest of the people in here, along with other staff they'd found around the embassy that late in the evening.

It was Anna who had begged the white coat off a cook's assistant and given it to Kate, warning her not to speak English, not to reveal who she was. And Kate had kept quiet, although she wasn't sure if it was the right thing to do. Being a U.S. consul came with a certain amount of respect for the title and the full backing of the American government. Maybe if she'd spoken up, the rebels would have decided they didn't want to tangle with the U.S. and would have let her go. She shifted on the hard floor. Maybe she should tell them now.

Or maybe not. She still wasn't over the shock of

seeing the bullet rip through her bodyguard's head. She swallowed and squeezed her eyes shut, trying not to think of Jeff as he'd lain there on the dining room floor in a pool of his own blood. He and the sole Russian guard who'd been inside the dining room were badly outnumbered when the rebels had poured in.

"Pochemu tu..." One of the armed men launched into a tirade.

She wished she could understand what he was talking about, what they were discussing. The lanky one seemed to be whining a lot. The oldest of the three ignored him for the most part. The short, pudgy one kept snapping at him, then finally gave up and shrugged with a disgusted groan.

The whiner swung his rifle over his shoulder and walked out the door, letting it slam behind him.

"Two," Anna whispered.

They were down to two guards. This could be the best chance they were going to get to try something— disarm them, maybe, and get to the phone on the wall by the gym's door, call for help. Breaking out of the embassy didn't seem possible. Too many armed rebels secured the building.

She tried to establish eye contact with the chef who appeared to be in good shape, then with two other guys, tall, beefy and Slavic-looking with hard features and dirty-blond hair. They looked alike, possibly related. They seemed to be the largest and strongest men in the room.

Come on. Over here. She fidgeted and managed to get the attention of one of them. She wiggled her eyebrows toward the guards. The guy looked back non-plussed.

Since her hands were tied behind her back, she couldn't make any hand signals. She kept wiggling her eyebrows and nodding with her head. The guy smiled.

Probably thought she was coming on to him. Did she look like a complete idiot? Apparently so, because he wiggled his eyebrows back.

She stifled a groan and rolled her eyes in a *never-mind* look she hoped translated. And felt a hand on hers.

She turned slowly toward the other side and met Anna's gaze. The woman glanced toward the guards then back at Kate with a questioning look in her large blue eyes. Kate nodded. *Yes, yes, that's what I've been trying to do.*

"Now," Anna breathed without moving her lips. She took a deep breath then started to cry.

The pudgy guard yelled at her immediately. Anna stifled her sobs and leaned against Kate as if for support. She tugged on the nylon cuffs that held Kate's hands behind her back. Then came heat. Under the noise of her crying, apparently she had lit a match or a lighter that must have been hidden in her pocket.

Every snarly thought Kate had ever had about smokers blowing smoke in her face at the cafés that supported her French-pastry habit, she took back.

Ouch. Even a small flame could be pretty hot this close. But the pressure of the nylon eased on her wrists, and in the next second she was free.

"Hurry," the girl whispered into her shoulder and dropped a lighter into her hands.

But then the door opened and the whiny guard was back, carrying a large box, leading with his back. Or maybe it wasn't the whiny guard. This one looked bigger. But familiar.

The pudgy rebel barked a question.

"Da, da." The newcomer mumbled the rest of his answer and kept advancing into the room, groaning, bent under the weight of whatever he was carrying. But the next second the box flew at the older bandit, knocking his weapon aside while the stranger took out the pudgy one with his gun. He had enough time to shoot the other one, too, before that one gathered himself.

Her hands were free, but all she could do was stare at the man dumbstruck, unable to believe her eyes.

Parker?

She pushed to her feet and stepped toward him, but he shook his head slightly and severed eye contact as if he didn't want anyone to know that they knew each other. He spoke in Russian as he cut the plastic cuffs off people then distributed the rebels' guns to the hostages, who were asking questions at the rate of a hundred per second.

He answered before he pointed at her, said something else in Russian and ripped the gas mask off Pudgy's belt, then shoved it into her hand. He dragged her out of the gym, closing the door behind them.

"What's going on?" She followed him down the corridor since he wouldn't stop. "What are you involved with now?" He looked even better than he had in her frequent dreams of him. Whoever she'd been with in the two years since they'd broken up, her dreams brought only one man to her: Parker.

He couldn't be here on assignment. That wouldn't make any sense. "If the press could get in, why isn't the rescue team here?"

"Later." His whole body alert, the gun poised to shoot, he moved so fast that keeping up was an effort. He looked like Parker's action-figure twin: eyes hard as flint, body language tight and on the scary side. Even his voice sounded sharper.

She'd never seen him like this before. Pictures of the last few minutes flashed into her head, the way he had shot those men. He sure hadn't looked like a reporter back there. She struggled to make sense of it all. Then, as they rushed forward, her gaze snagged on a security camera high up on the wall—not pointing at the row of antique oil paintings but at the hallway itself.

"Can they see us?" She looked around, bewildered, expecting to run into rebel soldiers any second.

"They're not working. The rebels took out the security system when they broke in. Phones are disabled, too. I already checked."

Where? How? She didn't have time to ask.

Voices came from up ahead. *No, no, no.* A fresh wave of panic hit just when she thought she was already at max capacity for fear. They were in a long, marble-tiled hallway with a single, ornately gilded door they'd just passed.

Parker pulled back immediately and reached for the knob. Locked. He looked around, searching the corridor.

Why didn't he just kick the door in? She was about

to ask when she realized they couldn't afford to make noise. Good thing one of them had a clear enough mind to think.

The voices neared. Parker let go of her and hurried to an ornamental cast-iron grid low on the opposite wall, pulled a nasty-looking knife and began to unscrew it.

They were never going to make it. She looked back and forth between him and the end of the hallway. *Hurry, hurry, hurry.* "They're almost here."

He got the heavy-looking grid off and laid it down gently, without making a sound. Then he climbed in, legs first. She was practically on top of him. But he didn't move lower to make room for her. "Get on my back," he said.

"What? I can't. It's—" She didn't have time to argue. The rebels were coming.

She went in, legs first like he did, feeling awkward and uncomfortable at having to touch him, having to hang on to him, being pressed against his wide back. He was all hard muscle just as he'd always been. She snipped any stray memory in the bud and kept moving. When she had her arms around his neck and her legs around his waist as if he were giving her a piggyback ride, she stopped, barely daring to breathe. She wasn't crazy about dark, tight places.

And they weren't in some storage nook as she had thought, but in a vertical, chimneylike tunnel with a bottomless drop below them.

But just when she thought things couldn't get more dangerous, he let go with his left hand and reached for the cast-iron grid to lift it back into place. Boots passed in front of their hiding place a few seconds later, people talking.

The men stopped to chat just out of sight. *Oh God, please just go.*

They didn't. They stayed and stayed and stayed. Her arms were aching from the effort. She could barely hold herself. She couldn't see how Parker was able to hold the weight of two bodies with nothing but his fingers.

An eternity passed. Then another. She distracted herself by organizing her half-million questions about his sudden appearance and his complete personality change.

"Hang on," he whispered under his breath and moved beneath her.

She barely breathed her response. "I think we should stay still." No need to take any unnecessary chances, make some noise and draw attention.

"Can't. We're slipping."

All her questions cleared in the blink of an eye, replaced by a single thought. They were going to die.

Chapter Two

Kate braced a hand against the wall and realized at once why they were slipping. The brick was covered with slippery powder. She could make out some cobwebs in what little light filtered through the metal grid. She didn't want to think of the number of spiders that would be living in a place like this. She put the hand back around Parker's neck.

He slipped another inch.

Oh God, oh God, oh God. Please, please, please. She held her breath, expecting a fall any second. How high were they? And what was waiting for them at the bottom? Too dark to tell.

"Parker?"

"Relax," he whispered; he could probably feel the tension in her body.

She loosened the death grip she had around his neck. Whatever he was doing to save them, he could probably do it better if she didn't cut off his air supply.

He was slipping even though he had both hands and

feet braced on the side walls. But they had a slow, controlled descent; he was able to achieve at least that much. After the first few moments of sheer panic, she unfolded her legs from around his waist and stuck them out, hoping to take some of her weight off him and help to slow them even more. The less they slipped, the shorter their climb would be back to the opening once the rebels moved away.

She succeeded, but only marginally. They were still steadily going down.

At least they weren't crashing. She concentrated on the spot of light that was getting closer and closer, coming from the next cover grid on the floor below them. An eternity passed before they reached it.

Hanging on to the cast-iron scrolls, Parker was able to halt their downward progress temporarily.

They listened, but could hear no voices from outside.

"Can we get out?" she whispered.

"Maybe." He waited a beat. "Looks deserted out there. We still have to be careful. I'm sure they secured every floor."

"They can't have people in every hallway." At least, she really hoped they couldn't.

"They don't. They're set up in strategic control positions." Parker pushed against the grid, his muscles flexing against her.

The metal didn't budge.

"Want me to get your knife out of your pocket?" she offered, although his pocket was the last place she wanted to be moseying around.

"Screws are on the outside. Can't get to them." He

made another attempt at rattling them loose without success. "The offer is tempting, but I'll pass for now."

She bit back a retort at his teasing. She could and would let things go. She had learned over the years. "What do we do now?"

"Get to the bottom and find another way up." He didn't seem too shaken by their situation.

She, on the other hand, was going nuts in the confines of the tight space. "What is this place?" Her muscles tensed further as they began sliding again.

"The building used to belong to some nobleman back in the day. This is where the servants pulled up the buckets of coal from the basement for the tile stoves that heated his parlors."

"And you know this how?"

He couldn't shrug in their precarious situation, but made some small movement that gave the same effect.

Their shoes scraped on the walls that were less than three feet from each other, but the old coal dust muted the sound. She let go with one hand again and tried to find support. Carrying their combined weight had to be difficult even for a man as strong as Parker.

"I think I can do this on my own." She'd seen rock-climbing done at the gym before, how those climbers supported their weight with nothing but the tips of their fingers and toes.

"We came from the second floor. With the twenty-foot ceilings these old palaces have, the drop to the basement could be fifty feet or more," he said. "You stay where you are. If you slip, you die."

She was perfectly clear on the hundred and one ways

she could die in their given situation. She was trying hard not to think of them, thank you very much. "What can I do to make this easier?"

"Stop moving."

She stilled and kept silent for a while before she realized she could probably move her lips.

"How did you get in here? Don't tell me it's for a story."

"I quit that job. I work for the government now."

He always had been dark and mysterious, something that had drawn her to him at the beginning of their relationship but had ended up driving a wedge between them eventually. Mysterious was fine in a sexy stranger. But when you were trying to build a life with someone, there were things you needed to know. There had come a time when she had realized that he was never going to let her in fully.

"You're a marine?" The U.S. embassy was protected by marines. She had expected them to come after her eventually. But Parker wasn't part of that team. He was probably too old for enlistment at this stage. She thought the age limit was twenty-eight. He was four years older than her, which made him thirty-six.

"Something like that," he said, and in typical Parker fashion, wouldn't elaborate.

She had a few guesses as to why. So her ex was some kind of special commando. "Something like" a marine. A picture was beginning to take shape in her mind. "Did you know I was here?"

She made sure to hold her elbows in, and her knees, although that wasn't an easy task since her legs were wrapped around his waist for support. She couldn't hold herself up by her arms alone any longer. On second thought, her brilliant idea of going down on her own might have been overly optimistic.

She tried hard not to think of the countless times her legs had been wrapped around his waist from the other side. Slow breath in. Slow breath out. The stifling air of the stupid coal chute seemed unbearably hot.

"I've been briefed," he was saying.

He? What about the rest of the commando team? And in that moment, she knew without a doubt that there were no others. The embassy wasn't being liberated. She was. Through some crazy plan, he was here to rescue her, and they were about to leave all those other people behind.

As if she would ever agree to anything as insane as that.

They were just reaching the landing, had to get down on their hands and knees to crawl out, touching each other way more in the process than she was comfortable with. He had always had an instant, mind-melting effect on her. There should be a vaccination against men like him, something that would give the recipient immunity. She'd be first in line at the clinic.

A dim security light burned somewhere, enough to see that they were both black, covered in hundred-year-old soot. He looked like some Greek hero, sculpted from black marble instead of white. She glanced down at her own clothes, stifling a sigh. She looked like an Old West horse thief, tarred and waiting to be feathered.

"Come on, we don't have much time." He moved

forward, gun in hand. "I came in through the roof, but we'll see if there's a way out through here. Maybe some connection to the neighboring building. Like a secret emergency tunnel for the embassy staff."

She thought of Anna, who had risked her life to melt the cuffs off her, and the kitchen staff who'd risked their lives to conceal her identity. She thought of Tanya and the two small children, and Ambassador Vasilievits, who had been separated from the others by the rebels.

"Did anyone make it out of the building?"

"No," Parker said without turning around.

He was a dozen feet ahead before he realized that she wasn't following and turned around. "What's going on?" His eyes flashed with impatience.

She had a feeling he was about to get even more unhappy with her. "I'm not leaving," she said.

WHAT in hell?

"You're leaving, babe, believe me. You're leaving if I have to carry you." His blood pressure was inching up. For some unfathomable reason, she didn't comprehend that every second counted. Odd really, because Kate Hamilton was one sharp woman.

"I'm not leaving the rest of the hostages to die. As soon as someone goes into the gym and realizes what you did, they'll be massacred." She was shooting him an accusing look, standing tall like some movie heroine.

Oh, man. She had that stubborn determination in her fine eyes, the same rich green color as the highland forests of Scotland. And he knew from experience that meant nothing good.

"I left them armed."

No way was he going to stop to have a fight about this with her. He scanned the basement instead, which seemed closed to the outside, the only exit being a staircase that led up to the ground floor. He could see a few spots on the brick walls where at one point in the past there had been basement windows to the street, but they were walled in. And since the building was an old one, the outer walls were close to three feet wide, solid brick and mortar. They couldn't even dig their way out.

"They are admin staff and people from the kitchen." Kate wouldn't let the subject drop. Her full and delicately shaped lips were set in a strict line of displeasure.

"The rebels won't kill them. They need someone to negotiate with." He eyed the stairs and calculated.

"They can negotiate with the ambassador," she countered, backing away from him as he began stalking her. "The rebels have him someplace else in the embassy. He was taken away from the rest of us at the beginning."

He stilled.

"Parker? What happened to him?"

And when he didn't respond, she asked with horror in her eyes, "They killed him? That's what the gunfire was about, wasn't it?"

He said nothing.

Her tanned hands flew up to cover the lower part of her face until only her big, luminous eyes showed, glinting with moisture. Her shoulders drooped with defeat.

"Tanya…" Her voice sounded as if she was fighting

for air. "How about his wife and the—" She didn't seem to be able to take in enough air to finish the sentence.

"No idea." He felt remorseful, but undeterred. "We are leaving. Now."

"No. It's *my* life."

And his breath caught, because that had been the last thing she had told him before she'd left. *It's my life, Parker. I'm sorry. I have to do what's best.* And he had stood there, without a word, without trying to change her mind, and watched her walk away.

Letting her go had been the single most selfless thing he had ever done in his life. He knew she was better off without him. He was darkness and she was light.

But it had still hurt like hell.

He blinked hard, waited for the tightness in his chest to ease. "What are you doing here, anyway?"

"None of your business," she snapped at him. "I'm not going. I'm serious."

So was he.

"Kate." The word came out in a low growl of temper. He hated how quickly she could make him lose his cool. He was frustrated that she wouldn't give him her full cooperation.

She hesitated another long second. Damn. There had been a time when she had told him everything, had laid her soul bare and shared it. Well, the trust was gone now. He should have expected that.

"I am considering adopting a child from Russia. Tanya has two adopted children. I had some questions about the process and the orphanage she used," she said with a defensive set of her chin and a hint of vulnerability around her.

That wasn't the answer he had expected. The words cut him off at the knees. There had been a time when he was looking forward to Kate having *his* children, although he had tried to tell her that the time wasn't right just yet, that they would probably have to wait a couple of years. He didn't want to miss anything. He didn't want to be an absentee father on active duty. Not that he'd been able to tell her that. He'd had to cook up some stupid story about how he needed a lot of time at that point because he was fighting hard for his next promotion.

A tidal wave of regrets slammed into him. He couldn't think about all that now. He had to get her out of here.

But she wasn't done fighting yet. "Listen to me. Chances are they would have let the hostages go at the end. Now that you shot their men, they are going to kill the people we left behind. *Because of me.* I can't live with that. I'm not that kind of person. I can't." There was urgency and desperation in her voice. "Please," she added with her unique mix of vulnerability and determination.

She wasn't a delicate woman. She was vivacious. She had lively eyes, a full mouth and a stubborn jawline. She laughed from the heart and cried from the heart.

He still had a crush on her. The realization caught him off guard. That rush of attraction, the magnetic pull. A crush—that was all it was. He imagined there wasn't a man who could go within ten feet of Kate Hamilton without developing a little crush on her.

He could disarm a nuclear warhead. He should be able to neutralize some leftover attraction.

"Parker?"

She wouldn't give up. She wasn't the type. When someone needed help, Kate Hamilton was your gal. She'd charged to the rescue of neighbors, friends and coworkers alike, making time to find homes for strays she picked up on the street. Which made her a fine consul, he supposed, since part of her job was to assist U.S. citizens who ran into trouble here in France. She could manage a problem like nobody's business.

"Please?"

Those eyes were going to be the death of him. Oh, hell, when had he ever been able to resist her?

He drew a deep breath, recognizing himself for the fool he was. "Okay. I'll get you out. Once you're safe, I'll come back to see what I can do for the others." And the Colonel was probably going to fry his ass. A freaking barbecue.

"How can you even think about taking only me?" She was outraged and not bothering to hide it.

"Because that is precisely the order I got." He kept his voice deceptively low, although his blood was fairly boiling.

"From whom?"

He stayed silent.

"Some orders need to be questioned."

She'd never met the Colonel. "Maybe you question too much," he said.

"We should go back for them right now." Her voice had a lot of steel in it.

Something told him Kate had toughened up a lot since he'd last seen her. Or maybe that core of steel had been there all along, and he'd just never seen it because he'd been too busy running from one mission to the next, never having enough time for her, always leaving her behind.

No wonder she had walked out.

He watched her in the dim light and fought against the tide of emotions. *No regrets.* Not now. He walled off the memories. They could reminisce once they got out of this hellhole.

But first he had to placate her and gain her cooperation. Her cooperation! He was here to save her, dammit. She was supposed to jump into his arms, misty with gratitude. If he'd had more time, he would have spent a moment or two enjoying that fantasy.

"How about this? I'll neutralize as many rebels on our way out as I can, evening the odds for the hostages whom we are *temporarily* leaving behind." Even though a silent exit would have been by far preferable and had been specifically requested by the Colonel. "I'll do whatever I can for the hostages on our way out as long as it doesn't put you in jeopardy. That's non-negotiable."

She looked around thoughtfully, as if taking stock of the basement, then back at him. "We bring the hostages down here. They can barricade themselves until help comes. There's only one entrance to the basement. The rebels might not even find them down here by the time the building is taken back. Nobody gets killed because of me. That's non-negotiable."

She was managing the problem.

She was insane. And yet, the plan did have some merit. And damn, but he liked her pluck. Always had. He'd always liked everything about her.

All they had to do was go back up to the second floor where the gym was and make sure the hostages got to the coal chute without being seen. The hostages would come down, Kate and he would go up the two extra floors to the roof. They had to pass through the second floor anyway. Once they were at the gym, they'd be halfway to their destination.

Lightning cracked outside. He thought he heard rain.

"Deal," he said.

August 10, 01:57

"How did you get in?" Kate asked half an hour later— they'd searched the basement inch by inch to make sure there really wasn't another exit—pretty happy about getting her way. It wasn't every day that Parker McCall yielded to someone.

"Through the roof." He stood at the top of the stair-case, pulled out his cell phone, opened it, then swore briefly. "Doesn't work down here."

He looked a lot cleaner than ten minutes ago. They had spent some time brushing soot off their clothes, off each other. That had been a picnic and a half. She'd just about jumped out of her skin when he touched her. It had taken everything she had not to let him see that he could still affect her with as little as a brush of his knuckles.

"Through the roof how?"

"From the next building. The rebels heavily secured the main entrances. Can't get in or out through there without a major fight. They were focused on that when I got here, hadn't gotten to securing the roof yet. I'm sure that has been done by now, but we'll fight our way out if we have to."

Fight. Oh God. She was scared stiff. Although if anyone could get her out of here, it was Parker. Especially this new, military version.

"How many are there?"

"Two dozen, tops. They're spread out over the four floors. Have to keep the whole building secured. They can't spare more than a handful for the roof. And up there, it's pitch-dark—a definite advantage."

For Parker. She, on the other hand, was afraid of the dark, especially when it hid murderous rebels. Parker looked…almost excited, as if this was nothing but a game.

"Are you going to tell me who you really are?" she asked.

He was Parker, but not *her* Parker. Not the man she had fallen in love with. This Parker was a lot darker and infinitely more dangerous. He moved with feline grace and constant preparedness. He had shot people without blinking an eye. She still couldn't process that.

He shrugged.

He'd always been darkly mysterious in a brooding-but-gorgeous kind of way, but now… "You—"

He had his hand over her mouth the next second, his
hard body pushing her against the wall, into the shadows
as he towered over her. But she didn't feel threatened,
not for a second, never with Parker. She felt protected,
but she wouldn't admit to herself just how much she had
missed that. Voices filtered down from above.

They stood motionless, although since the stairs were
made of stone, they didn't have to worry about creaking
wood giving them away. But she barely dared to
breathe, feeling paralyzed all of a sudden, and unsure
if it came from the proximity of danger or the proximity
of the man who had the power to liquefy her knees.

Parker ran a calming hand down her arm, which she
didn't find calming in the least.

His skin still smelled the same—well, almost, plus
hundred-year-old coal dust. On him, it smelled sexy. His
body was still incredible, his lips still just as sensuous.
He could still arouse her with a touch. The full-frontal
contact was wreaking havoc with her senses.

And she panicked, because in her perfect little world,
she had managed to convince herself that she was over
him, that if they ever met again, she could walk by him
without batting an eye. And here she was, assailed by
such a sharp sense of longing it stole her breath away.
It took all her willpower not to bury her face into the
base of his throat and lap at the warm, smooth skin she
knew she would find there.

The voices faded.

He didn't move.

And she didn't want him to.

No. Not again. She couldn't fall for him again. He

had never truly loved her. He couldn't have. He had left her every chance he'd had. He had lied to her about things. She was pretty sure about that. She didn't want to think how many nights she'd lain awake wondering about where he was.

The two of them together spelled disaster, she reminded herself and pushed him away. Maybe with a little more force than was strictly necessary.

"Easy," he said, watching her with his usual unsettling intensity, as if trying to puzzle out her thoughts.

Not if she could help it. She stepped away from the wall. "Let's go."

He moved away from her with some reluctance. "I'll pick the lock, you see what else you can find here that we could use."

She moved around him and set to the task.

The opposite wall of the staircase was lined with metal shelves. He already had a length of inch-wide nylon rope twisted around his waist that he had found, and a small screwdriver in his hand that he had gotten from the giant four-feet-by-four-feet toolbox near the bottom of the stairs.

The basement was used by the Russians as a storage facility. It held everything from broken office furniture to security supplies and crowd-control posts, even a crate of sea salt in one-kilo bags.

She opened an oil-stained box and rummaged through it. "What are we looking for exactly?"

"You'll know it when you see it," he said. "Grab anything you think we can use."

A lot of help he was.

But he was right. When she spotted the flashlight hanging from a peg behind the box, she took it. She was pleased to notice its metal case was heavy enough to be used as a weapon in a pinch. She flicked it on and grinned at the circle of light that appeared on the wall. "Even the battery works. Doesn't get better than that."

"Here we go." He straightened.

The door stood slightly ajar. He had obviously worked some magic on the lock.

"I don't even want to know where you learned that."

"Of course you do." He flashed a flat grin. "You want to know everything."

"Fine, I do. But I'm not asking. You wouldn't tell me, anyway."

His mouth twitched. "Wish we had time to look around some more, but we should probably head out." He bent his sinuous body into some SWAT-team pose.

Where had he learned that? Of course, she wasn't about to ask that, either. Trying to pin Parker down was futile. She ought to know.

He pulled the door a little wider, peeked out then closed it again, pulling his gun up and ready to shoot.

She could hear footsteps come their way then fade into the distance.

"Is your name Parker?" she whispered, unable to take her eyes off the weapon.

He tossed her a don't-be-stupid look that got her dander up, but then he nodded.

"You never were a foreign correspondent, were you?" Bits and pieces fell into place; a lot of things that had bewildered her in the past were making terrifying sense now.

He held her gaze. "No."

Oh God. "I've been so stupid, haven't I?" She looked away, embarrassed that she had never figured it out. He must have thought her incredibly gullible. She'd been blinded by love and lust. She would have believed anything of him. Not until the very end had she begun to see the chinks in his armor.

"You're one of the smartest women I know. One of the reasons why I fell in love with you."

Her heart, her stupid, gullible heart, turned over at his words. But had he really? Had he fallen in love with her, or had he been using her as some kind of a cover? He was a spy or a secret agent or something. He would probably say anything to have her cooperation so he could carry out his current mission successfully. She'd do well to remember that.

But it was difficult to remember anything when he put a hand on her shoulder. She shrugged it off. She didn't need to be further confused by the way his touch had made her feel. She hadn't been able to forget that, or anything else about him. Not for a single day, not even when she had dated other men.

"We'd better get going," she said, trying hard to shake off the sharp sense of unreasonable longing that hit her out of the blue.

She needed to think about the hostages instead of Parker. They had to get to the gym before some rebels decided to check on their buddies stuck watching over the embassy staff. Every minute counted. Every minute could save a life.

He nodded slowly before he took his eyes off her and pushed the door open again. This time, the hallway must have been clear, because he stepped outside.

She followed. She had been a guest at the Russian embassy a half dozen times, but had never been in this part, wasn't sure of the way.

After a moment, Parker glanced back at her and parted his lips as if to say something, but was prevented by the sound of gunfire coming from somewhere above.

Above and to the left. They were just coming to a T in the hallway. There had to be a way to get up there. Kate turned left and took off running.

More gunfire. It lasted longer this time. Long enough to have killed every man and woman in the gym.

"Oh, God, no." She held the flashlight as tightly as she could, the only weapon she had, and ran faster, her heart beating its way out of her chest.

They had spent too much time arguing over what they should do. And now it was too late.

Chapter Three

Kate resisted as Parker caught up with her and pulled her in the opposite direction.

"You promised to help." She tried to tug her wrist from him in vain.

"This way." He dragged her farther in the wrong direction, away from the sound of gunfire.

So he wasn't going to help the others. He had lied. The thought hurt, but she shook off the pain. She didn't have time for it. Of course he had lied. Just as he had lied to her about everything else. The only surprise was that she was still stupid enough to believe him. She would have thought she had grown wiser than that. Apparently not.

She had no idea who he was anymore, what he was capable of. Yes, he had promised to help, but he had promised other things before.

She dug her heels in, aware that if he decided not to listen to her, there was nothing she could do. He could and would take her out against her will. He'd always had a powerful physique and was in the same top shape now as he'd been two years ago, if not better.

In great shape, but in a terrible mood, not at all amused that she would stand up to him. Tough. He'd better get used to it in a hurry, because she wasn't the same woman he remembered. "We can't leave them to their fate."

He looked at her hard, harder than he'd ever looked at her before—scary hard. She couldn't breathe.

"I said we wouldn't. I don't go back on my word." He was practically growling.

But she obviously wasn't as smart as she had always thought herself to be, certainly not smart enough to take heed.

"Since when?" The question slipped out before she could have stopped it. He'd sure gone back on all his promises of love in a hurry.

And how embarrassing that after two years, she still wasn't over him, was still hung up on the past. Better make sure he didn't figure that out. "Sorry, this isn't about us." She tried to dance away from the subject.

He watched her with those laser-sharp, gunmetal-gray eyes of his for a moment. "Some of it *is* about us. But we'll have to get to that later. And we will."

His words sounded more like a threat than a promise.

"I'm sorry, Kate," he said then, and his face softened marginally before he looked away from her.

And damn him, her heart softened, too, which was the last thing she needed. She had to keep her wits about her.

"Why are we going in the opposite direction?" She was still suspicious.

He dragged her on. "We can't start an open battle where we're outnumbered twenty to one. If we do anything, it has to be guerilla warfare. Once again, here is what we are doing. I'm taking you out. Through the roof, if possible. We are going up. The hostages are on our way. I'll get them free of their guards and help them to the basement, where they have a chance to hide out until this is over. Even if they're found by the rebels again, they'll have a well-defendable position and I'll make sure they have some guns. That's the best we can do. The two of us sneaking out of here is going to be difficult as hell. Twenty people sneaking out is impossible. If we try, everybody dies. Do you understand?"

That made sense. She gave up resisting. He looked as though he knew what he was talking about, not that she was over the shock of his commando persona yet.

"I would appreciate if you didn't question every move I make," he bit out as they stole along the corridor in a hurry. "Our lives could depend on split-second decisions and your split-second responses."

"You think I'm putting us in danger by not following you blindly like some robot? Like you've given me reason to trust you and your almighty judgment in the past? Hardly."

His eyes flashed thunder. "Do you really want to get into all this right now?"

Okay. No, not really. She bit her tongue. Not at all. She would just as soon see their past buried if not forgotten. "What do the rebels want, anyway?"

"Probably troop withdrawal from their republic. They've been fighting for autonomy for the last seven years." He seemed to calm a little. "The violence slowed lately, since their leaders were captured, but apparently someone else has taken the helm." He thought for a second. "Strange, really, when you think about it. Their ethnic leaders are pretty divided. Some are turning into outright warlords. Mashev and his bunch." He shook his head.

"How on earth do you know all this?" She worked for the State Department and the Tarkmez struggle was barely a blip on her radar screen.

"CNN," he said, bland-faced.

"Yeah, right."

The corner of his mouth turned up in a grin.

"Not funny," she said, breathing a little hard since they were moving at a fair speed; it had nothing to do with his smile. Nothing whatsoever. "You have no idea how much I hate it when you lie to me."

His grin melted away, his face growing somber. "You have no idea how much I hate having to lie to you. Do us both a favor and don't ask me any more personal questions, okay?"

He was asking a lot.

"Are they going to get it?" She asked something he wouldn't consider personal. "Their independence?"

"Not anytime soon," he said.

She didn't like the sound of that. It didn't bode well for the hostages. "How desperate are they?"

"Over a hundred thousand have been killed so far in the sporadic fighting. Women and children included."

His gaze hardened. "Carpet-bombing is not an exact science."

God. She'd nearly lost it at the sight of Jeff going down, and the two dead rebels back there in the gym. She couldn't picture a hundred thousand dead. She blinked hard.

"They have nothing to lose," he added.

"I get it." When it came to fighting, which would probably come soon enough—either the French or the Russian government would try to get the hostages out— the battle would be savage. "Why isn't help here yet? Didn't anyone hear the gunshots? Didn't anyone call the police?"

"It's not a residential district," he said. "Nobody is here at night. And even if they were, the weather is drowning out most of the noise."

They turned down a hallway and rushed to the end, flattened themselves against the wall as Parker checked around the corner to make sure they wouldn't run into anyone that way. Then they were off again.

"Where is the rest of the embassy staff? The security?" he asked.

"Some of them were killed when the building was taken. I don't know about the rest. You think they were murdered, too?" She didn't even want to think about that.

"Probably. The rebels wouldn't want to leave anyone alive who might prove to be a danger later. They have the office and kitchen staff for bargaining. They would want to neutralize anyone trained to fight." He paused for a moment. "But if we knew for sure that some of the security staff are still alive, it would be worth spending time on finding them. We could use help with the hostages."

"If some of the security was still alive, where would they be?"

"Anywhere," he said after some thought, never slowing down. "There could be a man or two who had avoided capture, hiding out. Or there could be a few of them in the custody of the rebels, held in a different location from the rest of the hostages. Or they all could be dead," he added on a somber tone.

And since they were talking about missing people, another thought popped into her head, and she couldn't believe that she had let it slip her mind earlier. "Where are the children and Tanya?"

He looked at her as if she'd gone off her rocker. "What children?"

"The ambassador and his wife have two girls. One's five, the other's seven. They were at the dinner. Wasn't that in your briefing?"

He swore under his breath. "My briefing was rushed. It focused on you and on the weak points of the building. When did you see the kids last?"

"At dessert. Then Tanya took them to some rec room to play. The nanny was supposed to watch them. The whole family was supposed to go home together later," she said miserably. But her mind was finally settling down enough to take stock of the situation. "I'm going to need a weapon." She eyed the rifle that hung from his shoulder and the handgun tucked into his belt.

"You have the flashlight," he said without looking

back. "So there's a nanny, too? That's at least four civilians missing."

"I can shoot."

That gave him enough pause to slow and stare at her, his dark eyebrows sliding up his forehead. "Since when?"

"Since I decided to take the consul position. U.S. embassies have been known for being attacked in the past. I've taken some firearm courses and a few months' worth of self-defense lessons."

Mostly she'd done it to set her mother's mind at ease. The consulate was in Paris, France, not in some third-world country. The worst crisis she had expected was an overdrawn credit card from too much uninhibited shopping.

For the first time, she was actually glad that she had a mother who saw doom lurking everywhere, and who had forced her to take extraordinary precautions. The only time, ever, when her mother's paranoia had failed was with Parker. She loved the man to death. Not a word of warning there, just when Kate would have needed it most.

They came to a row of doors and he tried the first. Locked. Tried the next one and the next one, too, before he found one that was open. He moved in low, the handgun held out in front of him.

"All clear."

She went in behind him and closed the door. They were in a large storage room with nothing but boxes and boxes of what looked like reports and printouts.

"What are we looking for?" she asked when he began stacking some boxes by the wall.

"That." He nodded upward. "If we stay out in the open, sooner or later we're going to get caught."

She followed his gaze to the vent opening high up on the wall and swallowed. Another tight, dark place. She tried not to think of her great-grandmother's tiger-maple hope chest her cousins had locked her in for two terror-stricken hours on a hot summer afternoon when she'd been six.

"You'll be fine," he said.

Did he remember her telling him that story? That came as a surprise. He hadn't spent enough time at home during their year-long engagement to notice much about her. He certainly hadn't noticed that the relationship was falling apart. But, apparently, here and there on the odd occasion, he had actually paid attention.

"I'll be fine," she agreed, because she had no other choice. Whatever happened, she wasn't going to freak out, mess things up and jeopardize the lives of others.

Parker climbed his stack and had the cover off in seconds. He pulled himself up, half disappeared inside, then slid back out and dropped to the top of the boxes again. "Come on." He extended an arm to her.

She took it and ignored his hands moving lower on her body as he helped her to inch higher and squeeze in. The space seemed insanely small and devoid of air. She closed her eyes for a moment to calm herself. Parker's shoulders were much wider than hers. If he fitted, she had no reason to fear that she would be stuck. And there was air, there really was, she just couldn't draw it as long as fear constricted her lungs. All would be well as soon as she relaxed.

She inched forward, fighting the instinct to back out. And a few moments later Parker came up behind her. A barely audible rattle told her that he had put the vent cover back in place.

She swallowed, sweat beading on her forehead. *We aren't really locked in. We aren't locked in.* There had to be a hundred vent openings all over the building. A good kick and they could come out anywhere. She fought her panic with cold logic and won after a few seconds, then moved on, appreciating the fact that Parker hadn't said a word, hadn't rushed her.

"I'm going to be fine," she said again.

"I know." His hand came up from behind, pushing something her way. "Here, you take this."

The handgun.

She made sure the safety was on then slid it into her waistband. So he was going to treat her like a partner. That was certainly new. Maybe he had changed since they had parted ways. Yeah, and maybe pigs flied. In formation. At the Millville Wheels & Airshow he was so fond of.

She flicked on her flashlight, illuminating the dark passage ahead, not wanting to contemplate a new and possibly improved Parker. The old Parker had been enough to make her fall head over heels in love, had been enough to break her heart. She didn't want to think what damage he could do the second time around.

They hadn't crawled a full minute before Parker said, "Incoming call," behind her.

She stopped.

"Sir, we heard some shots from the north end of the building about five minutes ago. I also have information that the ambassador's children are in the building. Can you give us a location for the rec room?" he asked the caller. Then he listened before he swore under his breath. "The Colonel would like to speak to you," he said at last and handed the phone to her.

"This is Kate Hamilton."

"Glad to hear that you're well, Ms. Hamilton," a deep voice said without identifying himself. "I have my best man in there. You just do what he says. He's going to get you out as fast as possible."

Parker was the best man on his team? Well, he always was good at whatever he did. Except for the whole commitment thing.

"He'll take care of you," the man on the other end of the line continued.

"What is your plan for the other hostages?"

"The other hostages are not our responsibility. We have to trust them to the Russian forces."

"Who might be too late?"

"Ms. Hamilton—"

She cut the man off, not liking the tone he was taking. He might have been some military expert, but he wasn't here, hadn't seen the faces of those hostages. "If I see people about to be killed and there's a chance I might be able to help them that makes them my responsibility."

"Ms. Hamilton—"

"I do appreciate your sending Parker, though. We'll be out as soon as we can." She closed the phone and handed it to Parker, who was grinning like a kid at the circus, his face partially illuminated by the flashlight.

He looked breathtakingly gorgeous when he smiled. Not that the new Parker smiled all that much. But his smiles and those eyes had a way of breaking down her defenses.

"I can't believe you hung up on the Colonel." His grin widened another full inch. "I'm sure he can't believe it, either."

"You barely have any battery power left. We can't waste that on pointless arguments. So what did this Colonel tell you?" Whoever he was, she wasn't impressed. What kind of cold-hearted person would leave a group of defenseless people to their fate? *Politics.* She pressed her lips together.

"The Russian rescue team is here."

Her heart sped at the news. "Is that what the gunfire was about?"

"Their Alpha troops are in the process of securing the building from the outside. They are already on the roof. We have to get out before they storm the place and we get caught in the cross fire. A few of their Vymple special forces are coming, too. They won't be far behind."

"Can't we just all go to the roof? Then they can save us all?"

"To reach the Alpha troops, we'd have to get through the rebels. I'm not taking anyone into the cross fire. The roof is out. We have to find another way to escape. Before the Russians turn up the heat and attack full force. I don't want them to shoot any innocent people by accident."

She was trying hard to maintain a positive attitude about this whole mess, but it was slipping away from her as she listened to Parker. Sneaking out of here was already an impossible mission. Trying to help the other hostages while doing it added another level of difficulty. They really didn't need a timeline. "How soon will they attack?"

"They'll try to negotiate first. That can go on for as long as a couple of days, or they could lose patience with it in a few hours. We need to operate expecting the latter."

The whole prepare-for-the-worst thing. Made sense. She nodded, recalling a number of Russian hostage crises that ended badly for the hostages. "They'll probably shoot at everything that moves."

"I'm afraid so," he said.

"Okay, so we can't go to the roof."

"We'll find another way out after we get the kids and the hostages to safety in the basement."

"But we get the kids first?"

"Yes. We are on the same floor. It shouldn't take long if they are still where we expect them to be."

He didn't say, *and nothing has happened to them,* and she didn't dare to think it. She focused on the next step instead. "And help the other hostages."

He gave a low growl. "Would you like to save the ice cream from the freezer, too, so it won't spoil in case the Russians cut the power?"

"What? There's ice cream? Head to the kitchen first," she said, because she desperately needed a moment of lightness in the taut atmosphere.

"Tell you what. I'll take you for ice cream when we get out."

She couldn't see him, but just *knew* he was rolling those gunmetal-gray eyes. She didn't dare linger on the thought that he meant to take her anywhere after this was over.

"The Colonel said the rec room is in the west corner of the building," he said.

"Which way?" Inside the vent ducts, she was completely turned around and disoriented. Directions like east or west were beyond her.

"Turn left up ahead."

Not the best of news, since the sound of a small explosion had just come from that direction.

August 10, 05:40

WHEN THEY were in sections that opened to the various offices, their progress was excruciatingly slow; they stole forward at the rate of an inch a minute, never knowing who might hear them. But now they were finally in a section that had no openings to the outside, and could go faster. Kate kept the flashlight on. He didn't mind, knew she was uneasy with tight spaces and outright scared of spiders. The light reflected back toward him, however, did outline her body as she crawled in front of him. He didn't even try not to admire her curvaceous bottom.

He couldn't help the flashbacks of that round bottom straddling him, images of Kate naked above him, the way he felt as he pushed into her soft heat, rising up to bury his face between her generous breasts.

"Parker?"

The insistent whisper brought him back to the present, although he noticed ruefully that one part of his body still lingered in the past and was bound to make the crawling more difficult. His body's reaction to her was instant and powerful. It had always been like that with Kate. "What is it?"

"Can you hear them?" She turned off the flashlight, but they weren't left in complete darkness, as some light filtered in through a vent cover up ahead.

Despite their situation, she was cool and collected. Almost as cool as she'd been when she had walked away from him two years ago, telling him that she had gotten a chance for the consul post in Paris and she was going to take it. She hadn't felt that what they had was enough to keep her with him.

And now for the first time, he wondered if he shouldn't have done something to stop her. *Stupid idea.* She was too nice. He was too dark. His life was— She was better off without him. *Safer.* The only mistake he had made had been asking her to marry him in the first place. That had been irresponsible, given his position. And yet, he couldn't regret it.

He took a few slow, controlled breaths and focused on the task at hand.

Men were talking up ahead, but he couldn't make out what they were saying. "Move closer. Careful."

But getting closer proved to be difficult, as the duct narrowed ahead. The building was an old one. Whoever had put in the system had had to adjust to some restrictions, he supposed, going around existing beams and structural elements.

Kate was nearly at the vent opening when she stopped. She looked back at him without saying a word. He could clearly hear the men below now, which meant they would hear Kate if she spoke. The best they could do was to communicate with hand signals. He did that, motioning forward.

Kate shook her head.

Okay, so she was stuck. Damn. They had to crawl back and look for another way. But first he wanted to take a look at the men below, see how many there were, how well they were armed. He listened. They were talking about Russian politics, not terribly useful to him at the moment.

He signaled to Kate to press herself to the side then moved up, parallel to her body. His face was in line with her ankles, then with her knees, her thighs. *Her hips,* heaven help him. He couldn't get as far as she had, his shoulders being wider. He got stuck with his nose about buried in her chest.

Her scent, her being, her energy surrounded him and filled him with a sharp longing that stole his breath.

She stayed absolutely still. Frozen. The men chatted on below.

He filled his lungs slowly and reached for his cell phone, set the camera on Record and handed it to her, pointing toward the vent cover. She only hesitated a moment before holding it up to a slot. Her breasts lifted as she stretched her arms.

He felt sweat bead on his brow. *Don't think about it.* He motioned to Kate to move the camera around a little. She did so, then when he signaled a minute later, she passed the phone back to him so he could view the file she'd just recorded.

He selected Play, then Mute.

Six men, their rifles propped against the wall, hand grenades and handguns clipped to their belts next to their gas masks. One of them left, then came back in a few seconds. End of recording. Parker turned off the video as talk in the room switched to the expected harvest at the men's village. They cursed the Russian tanks that had destroyed half their fields.

He doubted he was going to find out anything important here in the near future, and they didn't have time to wait around and hope that the men decided to chat about more important things, such as where the rest of the rebels were and what their plans were for the siege.

He pocketed the phone and moved back a little, but she did, too, at the same time. And she had moved faster, bringing them face-to-face. The duct gave a low popping sound as both of their weights centered on the same spot.

The conversation stopped below.

He could see the sudden fear and questions in Kate's eyes. He put a hand on her arm. They just had to stay still for a while.

Touching her was a mistake.

The heat of her body seeped into his skin. He could smell her skin, her body lotion, which she had changed since they'd lived together, her shampoo, which was the same.

The men in the room resumed talking. He wasn't listening.

He could remember, as if it were yesterday, massaging that shampoo into her hair—she had worn it long back then. The two of them in the shower. Water sluicing over her curves, followed by his hands as they slicked over her soft skin, his mouth on hers, then on her neck, then everywhere.

"You're a maniac. We're going to break the stall." She had laughed, an indulgent look on her fine-featured, delicate face, water glistening on her long dark lashes.

"It'll be worth it." He'd reached under her buttocks and lifted her, pushed her against the tile wall then wrapped her legs around his waist.

She'd been ready, had always been ready for him, and he had pushed into her hot, tight, welcoming body, losing himself to the insanity of needing her more than the next breath he took.

Her low gasp brought him back to the present and he realized he had gripped her arm harder than he had meant to. Also, a part of his anatomy was pressed against her, making it pretty obvious what he'd been thinking about.

He was grateful that they couldn't talk so he couldn't be expected to explain. The pull of chemistry between them had always been unexplainable, anyway.

He couldn't see much in the dimly lit duct, but it sure looked as if her eyes were throwing sparks. Well, hell, as long as she was already mad at him…

He dipped his head forward and took her lips. She was soft and sweet, as mind-bending as he remembered. He had been craving this reunion from the day she had walked away. He liked to think that now and then she had thought of him, too.

So it came as a surprise when she put a hand to his chest and pushed, not even whispering, but breathing the words, "No. Parker, no," against his mouth.

And like the bastard he was, he kissed her anyway. Because he could.

And felt immensely gratified when in the next second she melted against him.

Chapter Four

She'd had this dream too many times, always woke with her body and soul full of aching and yearning. Except, this was no dream, as every cell of Kate's body attested. This was the real McCall.

Surprise had her resisting for an embarrassingly short moment, then pure gut reflex, body reaction, took over and all she could do was feel, all blood flow to her brain cut off. Minutes passed—not that she was aware of anything as mundane as the passage of time—before she could think again and pulled away. Breathing hard.

He came after her, but she turned her head—the small movement requiring an inordinate amount of effort— and those sensuous lips of his landed on her cheek. She became aware of his large hands that gripped her waist and had been inching upward. They stopped. Fell away.

I don't want this anymore, she wanted to tell him, but they couldn't talk, and even if they could, the words would have been a lie. She wanted him still. Her body throbbed with need from head to toe.

But her mind was emerging from its pleasure-induced stupor at last, and it reminded her that as spell-binding as the pleasure had always been with Parker, the pain of their breakup had been too devastating to bear.

She had given him her trust, her heart, her body and soul. She had believed with everything in her that he was *it,* the one for all time, the man to grow old with. Their breakup had caused her to lose not only her faith in him and marriage, but in herself, as well.

She bit her lip and squiggled down, anxious to separate their bodies. When her head was in line with the strong column of his throat, she tried not to think of how much she used to like to kiss that spot. Then came his wide chest and she blocked the memories of it rising above her, of how she would rest her head over it at other times and listen to that strong, steady heartbeat. The space was tight, but she managed to turn her head when she reached his flat stomach, hurried on as she moved lower, ignoring the all-too-obvious signs that he still wanted her.

Jason. She thought of one of the administrators at the embassy who had taken her out twice now to dinner. *Jason, Jason, Jason.* He was the same age as she, but with the heart of an old-fashioned gentleman. He was soft-spoken and into the arts. Had promised her tickets to Bizet's *Carmen,* the most popular French opera of all.

Jason left her pleasantly entertained and always looking forward to their next meeting. There was none of the mind-spinning heat that confused her and scared her so much with Parker, that had her acting out of character. Jason had not even asked for a goodnight kiss when he had escorted her home. And she found his patience and his European good manners admirable.

Focusing on him got her through crawling over Parker's body. For the most part. She drew her lungs full of air when there was finally a foot or so of distance between them.

She crawled in silence, up to the nearest intersection of ducts.

"Left," Parker murmured.

And she went that way, as fast and as quietly as she could. Until she felt his hand on her ankle, his hot palm on her bare skin. Her pant legs had ridden up from crawling.

She couldn't deny the jolt. Did he— Then she heard footsteps from outside. She held her breath as men passed by them. When Parker removed his hand, a signal that she could move again, she resumed crawling until he told her to stop.

She reached a vent cover that looked out at a hallway and a door opposite. She crawled a few feet farther so he could look out, too. His bulk coming toward her in the narrow space should have made her feel more claustrophobic, but instead, she found his presence comforting.

"That's the rec room," he said.

She wasn't surprised that he'd been able to go right to it. He had a near-photographic memory. If someone had told him the building's layout, he would be able to navigate it as well as if he had a map in hand.

She drew a deep breath. The girls. *God, let them still be there and unharmed.* She pressed her lips together, forgetting everything else for a moment but the two sweet little girls with the big silk bows in their pigtails. "How do we get over there?"

But Parker was already laying down his rifle and reaching for the vent cover. He pushed it out, handed it to her. "I need the handgun."

He tucked the weapon into his belt, then squeezed through the hole, right arm first, then his head, then the left shoulder. She could barely hear the small thump when he dropped to the ground.

"Hold the cover back in place in case somebody walks by," he whispered when she stuck her head out to look after him.

She did that while watching him cross the hallway in two long strides and listen at the door. He had his gun in his right hand now, inching the door open with his left after a long second, keeping low to the ground. She wished she could point the rifle at the door and cover him if necessary, but since they were in a narrow section of the duct again, she couldn't turn the long weapon, couldn't aim it to where she should have.

Parker opened the door another inch. He could see in now, but she couldn't. She held her breath, desperately wanting to know what he'd found, but his body language gave away nothing. Then he turned a fraction and she could see the thunder on his face and the way his lips flattened into a grim line. Her heart stopped as he disappeared inside and closed the door behind him.

He wasn't going to say anything? He expected her just to sit there? She stared after him, stunned, and waited—not too patiently—a full minute. When she heard no sound of fighting, she eased the vent cover out of place and pulled it back in, slid it out of the way.

She considered the rifle for a second. She couldn't climb out with it; she needed both hands to manage that, and it was too big to stick into her belt. If she swung it over her shoulder, it would get caught and stuck in the small vent hole, and tossing it out ahead of her would have made too much noise. And she couldn't reach it after she slipped out. The vent holes were too high on the wall. Parker had to help her each time she had to get up there. She left it, knowing Parker wasn't going to be too happy that she'd abandoned one of their only two weapons.

She went out feet first, dangling from her fingertips soon and still a four-foot drop between her and the floor, thinking of her bad ankle, her most recent tennis injury. Putting out her ankle would be disastrous. She wasn't going to think about that. If she focused on something going wrong, for sure it would. She visualized landing with the grace of a ballerina then let go, tilting her weight so she would fall on her behind rather than on her knees if she toppled over.

She made more noise than had Parker, who was there the next second and dragged her into the room behind him, shutting the door quietly. A thunderstorm was brewing in his eyes.

"What do you think you are doing?" he asked through clenched teeth, the expression on his face making him seem a foot taller and much wider in the shoulders. He had looming down to a science.

Not that he could have scared her. Not Parker.

She was about to tell him to cut it out when her gaze caught on the body on the floor. "Oh my God." Her hands flew to her chest from where cold was spreading through her.

Tanya lay in a limp heap a few feet behind Parker, her throat cut, blood everywhere on the geometric-patterned carpet. Even in death, she had a determined look on her face.

Kate blinked as her stomach roiled, getting ready to reject the gourmet dinner she had eaten a few hours ago. Then Parker stepped in her view, blocking the gruesome sight, his hands coming up to her shoulders.

"Hey, take it easy." Concern replaced the earlier annoyance in his voice, the angry lines of his forehead smoothing out as he watched her. "You know her?"

She swallowed again. "She's the ambassador's wife. She was going to come back to dinner as soon as she handed off the kids to the nanny." Just a few short hours ago. Sure seemed as though a lifetime had passed since. "Where are the girls?"

She had hoped that they would find the children here with their mother and their nanny, had counted on it. Maybe under rebel guard, but here. It seemed a logical assumption since they hadn't been brought back to join the rest of the hostages at the gym. Every extra minute Parker and she spent wandering around the embassy, searching, decreased the chances of any of them making it out of here alive.

"Could have been taken someplace else. There are sixty-eight rooms and offices in the building, not counting storage closets," he said.

Her brain scrambled to come up with an idea as to where the girls might be, thinking of every area of the embassy that she had seen before. She tried not to think of how scared they probably felt, that there was a good chance that they had seen their mother killed. She absolutely refused to consider that the children themselves might not be alive.

The rebels wouldn't do that. They couldn't. These were innocent little girls, for heaven's sake. She wouldn't allow herself to remember the Russian school-hostage crises when hundreds of innocent children had died. She held Parker's gaze and believed with all her heart that he would find the children and save them. Because she had to.

She sank to her knees next to Tanya and raised a hand to the woman's face, gently closed her eyes. "You don't know how nice she was. She was so helpful with everything I asked. Just open and forthcoming and…" Her voice broke.

She reached for her top button, meaning to take her borrowed kitchen jacket off and cover the woman's face at least, but Parker put a hand on her shoulder.

"We can't. Have to leave everything the way we found it. If the rebels come back this way and figure out that there's someone loose in the embassy, they'll come looking for us."

Her hand fell away. "You think they have the girls?" she asked, but hoped with all her heart that the kids were hiding someplace with their nanny.

"They could still be here," he said, and squeezed her

shoulders briefly before he let her go to look around again. He pointed at Tanya. "No defense wounds."

How could he tell with all that blood? She couldn't make herself look that closely. She shook her head as she got up, not understanding what he was getting at.

"Don't you think she would have defended the children? I would expect the body to be in the farthest corner, where she would have drawn back with them, shielding them behind her, fighting to the last drop of blood. But she was cut down right in front of the door, without defending herself."

"Almost as if she stood here, waiting for the rebels." She swallowed hard. "Trying to draw their attention to herself."

"Right." He was going for the armoire already and throwing open the doors. Not much there but video games, board games and books.

"But still, why wouldn't she at least go out fighting?"

He waited a beat before he answered. "She wanted to get it over with as quickly as possible. If she had the children hidden, she wouldn't want a prolonged fight. She wouldn't want to risk that the girls would cry out, or come out to help her. She wanted her attackers to spend the least amount of time in here."

His words painted a vivid picture she could only too easily imagine. She rushed to the built-in closet and found a hundred or so paperback novels in a messy jumble, her gaze returning over and over to Tanya. Where else could she have hidden two small kids? Her heart was pounding as she scanned the room, her gaze halting on the TV stand that had one of its doors slightly ajar. The piece of furniture was small and low to the ground, just large enough for a DVD collection.

The next second, she was crossing the room. She opened the door slowly and stared into a pair of round eyes that watched her, frozen with fear. The older girl. There was movement behind her.

Kate drew the first full breath of air since Parker had dragged her into the room.

"It's okay, Elena," she whispered as the tension eased in her chest. They'd found them. The girls were here, unharmed. "Do you remember me? We had dinner together." According to their proud parents, the girls had an English nanny and a French babysitter who popped in when the nanny wasn't available. They spoke both languages, in addition to Russian, fluently.

Elena nodded slowly. Kate opened the other door and found the younger one, Katja, curled up asleep, her tear-streaked face squinched up as if she was anxious even in her dreams.

Then Elena looked behind Kate and screamed, waking the smaller girl, who started to cry immediately, repeating a single word, something that sounded like *matj,* which Kate thought meant *mother* in Russian.

"Shh." She reached forward to pull the girls out.

But Elena pulled back, holding back her little sister. "Mommy said we can't come out until she told us."

She couldn't force them, not even for their own good. They had to cooperate and do it quietly. "Your mom told me to come and get you if she got hurt."

Elena nodded. She understood that her mother was injured. "Did the bad people hurt her a lot?"

"Just a little," she said. "We have to go before they come back."

Elena eyed Parker.

"I'll move back," he said.

He had probably scared the girls; no wonder when they had witnessed a brutal attack by men in uniforms just like his.

"He is a friend." Kate wrapped her arms around the girls, who burrowed against her body, just about melting her heart.

Parker was talking in a calm, low voice a few steps away, in Russian. After a moment, that set the children somewhat at ease and the younger one peeked over Kate's shoulder at him.

"He's not going to hurt you. He is my friend. He is a very good man. He is going to take us from here so we'll be safe." She didn't let them go for a second, knowing that they needed the comfort of her touch.

Frankly, she needed theirs. She was a lot more freaked out than she let on.

But being responsible for someone else now gave her extra strength. Whatever came their way, she was going to tough it out for these girls. Strange how that worked. She wished she had the rifle Parker had left with her, and she knew that she would use it without hesitation when the time came. Nobody was going to hurt these kids while she was breathing.

"Do you know where your nanny is?" She tried to remember the name. "Have you seen Mrs. Baker?"

Elena shook her head. Katja was staring at Parker.

"She wasn't here when your mommy brought you up?"

The girl shook her head again.

"We have to go," Parker was saying.

And in a hurry, Kate thought. They couldn't be sure that nobody had heard Elena's scream.

"Let's go," she repeated to the girls, and stood, holding their hands, holding them close to her body.

"To daddy?" Katja asked, her incredible blue eyes still fringed with tears.

"Yes," she lied, her throat growing tight. They couldn't tell the girls the truth now. They needed them as calm as possible and moving fast. "We have to hurry so we can find him."

"What's wrong with mommy?"

Although Kate held the girls away from the body on the floor, they must have seen it already from their hiding place.

"Did she die?" Elena asked.

And Katja's eyes were already filling up with tears all over again.

"She's just a little tired. We have to leave so that she can rest for a while," she lied again. They had to move in absolute silence. She had to make sure the children wouldn't cry and draw the rebels' attention. The girls would have to wait for the terrible truth until they were safely away from this place.

Elena was watching her doubtfully, but Katja nodded, and held her hand a little tighter.

The small gesture from the little girl who didn't know yet that she'd been orphaned and was all alone in the world again squeezed Kate's throat, sending moisture to her eyes. She glanced at Parker, caught a soft look on his face as he watched her. The same regret that clutched her chest swam in his eyes. He nodded as he went to the door and looked out. "Okay, hallway's clear."

Up until now, she had made sure that she'd been between them and the body on the floor, as had Parker. Now she turned them as they walked, talking about how quiet and fast they had to be to keep their attention on herself as they hurried out of the room.

Parker was standing below the vent cover. "You go back in. I'll take them to the basement."

The girls tightened their hold on her.

"I'll go with them. You can't just leave them alone while you come back up for the rest of the hostages."

"They've been alone for the past couple of hours. The basement is much safer than being up here. In another half an hour the rest of the embassy staff will be down there with them."

The girls pressed against her legs, one on each side.

He looked at them, and must have realized that he would need a crowbar to pry the kids away from her, because he shook his head, threw her a dirty look, then unfolded his fingers that had been waiting for her to step up to the vent hole, and jumped for it himself. He caught the edge on the first try, pulled out the rifle and then the vent cover and put it back into place.

"Are we going to stay out in the open now?" As much as she hated the ducts, she wasn't too crazy about the idea of wandering around in plain sight. "Where are we going?"

"Can't crawl in the walls with kids. They make one noise, it's game over."

And with a sinking heart, she knew he was right. "How far are we from the gym?"

"It's two corridors over and one floor up."

"We'll take the kids."

"They would have been safer sitting in the basement."

"Then I'll go and sit there with them."

"You are taking the shortest way out of here. I'm not letting you go in the opposite direction." And that was that, the look on his face said.

Fine. "Where is the staircase?" They'd taken so many turns in the ducts, she had no idea where they were anymore.

"That would be guarded by the rebels. And the elevators were taken out at the beginning, shut off along with the security system."

She tried to stay calm for the kids' sake. They were stuck out in the open, still with no clear plan on how to get out, two children in tow, no knowledge of where the main rebel force was hanging out and no way to get to the other hostages. Oh, yeah, and time was running out, too.

She didn't think things could get any worse.

But then a door opened, without any warning, not twenty feet down the hallway from them, and a scruffy rebel soldier stepped out.

SURPRISE FLASHED across the young man's face, but he was aiming his AK-47 already. Not fast enough. A barely audible pop, not louder than a person smacking his lips together, came from Parker's gun first. He loved the new silencer that the SDDU had been testing over the last couple of months.

One of the advantages of being a part of the Special Designation Defense Unit was that they got to try out all the latest gadgets first. He loved that part. And he loved knowing that he made a difference in his job. But he hated that a particularly gruesome mission in Southeast Asia had cost him Kate two years ago.

She gasped as the rebel soldier folded to the ground, but Parker was there already, catching the man's rifle before it could have crashed to the marble floor. Then he pushed through the door with his gun raised.

Nobody in there, he registered with relief.

He stepped back out, glancing at Kate, who had the kids behind her, protecting them with her body, blocking the sight of the fallen man. The girls were crying again, but at least quietly. She was talking to them in a soothing voice.

He grabbed the body by the boots and dragged it inside the room, scanned the place for all possible hiding spots and decided on a metal supply cabinet. He had to remove a shelf to get the guy in, but he managed, locked the door and pocketed the key. He didn't want the rebels to find the body and realize that there was someone inside the embassy who wasn't under their control. He didn't need them to organize a hunting posse. The man whose uniform he had taken earlier was safely stuffed into the vent duct near the gym.

Parker brought out the guy's gas mask and handed it

to the older girl, hoping he could get his hands on another for the little one. Kate had worked her magic on them, it seemed, because they were no longer crying, just watching him with large blue eyes fringed with tear-soaked lashes.

They were cute and tough. Followed directions well. He supposed their life in a Russian orphanage hadn't been a bed of roses before their adoption.

"Everyone okay?" he whispered.

They were still too scared of him to talk to him. But Katja whispered something to Kate.

"She has to go to the bathroom," she said.

He tried to think when the last time was he'd seen one. Damn. Not anywhere nearby. He took in the kid's scrunched-up face. "Okay."

They found a bathroom without any problems. But then they spent an hour jammed into the same stall, balancing on top of each other as rebels came in and out. The girls kept as quiet as mice. He was simmering with impatience by the time they got out. Time, they'd only lost time, he reminded himself. They could have lost much more.

He moved ahead and glanced around the corner. All clear. He signaled them to follow. The elevator he'd been heading for stood a little over twenty feet away and was unguarded as he'd hoped. He'd figured nobody would care much about it since it was out of commission. Perfect for his purposes.

He walked up to the stainless-steel doors and pried them open with the knife he had gotten away from the first rebel he'd taken out. He pushed the panels aside enough for his head to fit in and looked around. The elevator car was stuck on the ground floor below them.

"Come on," he said as he stepped back and forced the door open another few inches, enough so he could fit in sideways. "We'll be going up through here."

Kate looked in and up at the metal ladder, holding the kids even closer. "Can they do this?"

He thought back to his own childhood. "Are you kidding? Kids climb like monkeys. Right?" He grinned at the girls and Katja smiled back shyly. She had a dusting of freckles across her nose and a very direct gaze that looked a lot like Kate's.

He lifted Elena first and placed her on the nearest rung of the ladder, wouldn't let go until she had a secure hold on the metal bar and started moving up. Kate went next so she could help the girl if needed. Then he helped Katja up and stepped in behind her, closed the elevator doors when they were all in, enclosing them in darkness. It lasted only a split second. Kate's flashlight came in handy.

He kept his attention on the three people in front of him as he climbed, careful not to rush them, although the pace was excruciatingly slow. But he didn't say anything, letting them pay attention to each handhold, each step. The drop to the top of the elevator was about twenty feet—probably not fatal, but enough to break a bone or two, injuries they could not afford. He watched them, all three, ready to catch whoever needed his help.

An old memory floated up from the dark recesses of his mind. His father teaching him how to climb a tree in the park. He couldn't have been more than four at the time. It'd been well after midnight. Then the picture switched to the last time he'd seen his father. He hadn't thought about his old man in a while, hadn't had that nightmare in a decade or more. He pushed those thoughts away.

When they reached the door that led to the second floor, he motioned for them to go a little higher until he was level with it. He pressed his ear against the metal panels. No sounds came from outside. He eased them open an inch, looked out, but couldn't see anyone. He opened the doors wider, stuck his head out first then his body. Luck was still with them. He helped the others out.

"Which way?" Kate asked once the doors were closed behind them.

The girls didn't look too shaken by the climb. They were more excited than anything else at this point, actually, and he was grateful for the short attention span of kids that age.

"We're going to sneak around a little," he told them.

"Like Super Spy Girls on the Cartoon Channel?" Elena's face was glowing.

He had no idea what she was talking about. "Exactly," he said.

He shut his eyes for a second and pictured the hallways they had taken on the floor below. Where did that put them in relation to the gym? "This way," he said and they followed without another word.

This hallway was not decorated with paintings and even the light fixtures were utilitarian, a stark contrast to the antique chandeliers of the main areas of the embassy. He glanced at the row of doors on each side. Maybe these were the back offices where visitors weren't allowed. He tried a door. Locked. Not that he wanted to go in there, but he wanted to make sure nobody would be coming out and getting behind him.

Then, at the next door, he heard a small noise and he froze with his hand on the doorknob. He motioned for Kate to stay back and stay down with the children. Since the embassy was furnished mostly with antiques and had kept the old style, he wished they had kept the antique hardware, too, with keyholes instead of security locks. That way he could have taken a look. Going into a situation he knew nothing about was dangerous, but he had no other choice. If there were rebels in there, he had to neutralize them.

Kate was holding the rifle in front of her. The girls were crouched behind her, peeking over the side, watching him, wide-eyed. He'd better not make a false move. Whatever waited for him behind the door he would deal with it. Whoever was in there and however many of them there were, he would not allow them to reach Kate and the kids.

He tried the knob silently and wasn't too surprised when it gave. He opened the door a millimeter. He was ready to shoot at anything that moved, but nothing did. A dozen bodies covered the floor. They weren't wearing the camouflage militia outfits of the rebels, but the official Russian dress uniforms. The embassy security force, all dead and piled on top of each.

He stepped in carefully but stuck a hand back out the door to signal to Kate to stay where she was with the girls. They didn't need to see this. He spotted a man in civilian dress, too, with a different style of military haircut and typical Midwest good looks, ruined only by the hole in his head. He figured him for Kate's body-guard. The muscles tightened in his face. He stepped farther inside and grabbed as many guns and gas masks as he could for the hostages, then drew back in surprise when one of the men he touched groaned. Parker had his gun aimed at the guy's head the next second.

"Help," the man begged in Russian, his unfocused eyes fluttering open.

He had blood on his face, but Parker couldn't see an open wound. The guy had plenty of blood soaking his pant leg, too.

"Can you stand?" Parker asked and held his left hand out, keeping the gun handy in the right.

The man rubbed the back of his head. "Give me a second. I got knocked out." But he was scrambling to his feet anyway. He looked at the carnage around him, his eyes and the set of his mouth hardening.

"What happened?" Parker asked.

"I don't know. I was at the back gate. We got ambushed." Anger seethed in his words. "They must have thought I was dead and brought me here." He pressed a hand to his leg and limped over a body, stared at the carnage. "They killed everyone."

The man eyed Parker's uniform warily. "You're not one of them. Alpha troops?" he asked with suspicion. "Did they take the building back?" He seemed angry at the thought. Probably because he had missed the action.

Protecting the embassy was his duty, and here he'd lain the whole time, out cold.

"I'm a friend of the ambassador. I was here for dinner. The Alpha troops are on the roof, negotiating."

The man looked him over, glancing at the rifles slung over his shoulders. "I'm Ivan. Let's do what we can from in here." He reached for a rifle.

Parker pretended that he didn't see the move as he kept surveying the room.

"Can't take offense, I suppose," Ivan said good-naturedly, seeming to marginally relax at last. "I don't trust you, either."

Parker kept an eye on the guy as he turned to leave, switching to English when they were out of the room. "I have the ambassador's children and their nanny."

The man took in Kate, hesitated for a moment. "She's not the English nanny."

A tension-filled moment passed.

"She's the new one," Parker said. "She came today to start training to replace the other one. She hadn't been introduced to the staff yet." He didn't trust the guy with Kate's true identity. He didn't trust anyone just now.

Ivan accepted his explanation with a nod. "Where are we going?"

"The other hostages are in the gym."

At least he hoped so. He had told them to stay put when he'd left them. The liberating forces were on their way to them. Even if the rebels came looking, the hostages could defend a barricaded room a lot easier than they could defend themselves if they were caught out in the open. And breaking out of the embassy wasn't a possibility for a large group like that, even with the guns they had. Too many rebels secured all the exits of the building.

The sound of gunfire came from the roof, a short burst, then silence. Both Ivan and Parker pulled back into a protective position around Kate and the children. A moment later, when nothing else happened, they both stepped away, ready to move on.

"How do you plan on liberating the hostages?" Ivan asked.

"I have a plan," he said simply.

"I can help."

Yes, he could. Parker watched the cautious expression in the man's eyes. It had been this guy's job to keep the embassy safe and he had failed. That had to burn him. He would probably do anything to redeem himself. And Parker had to trust him because he needed help, badly. He handed him one of the handguns.

"We are taking the hostages to the basement where we can barricade ourselves until the embassy is taken back." He felt no need to mention his other set of plans for Kate and himself. His orders were to get Kate out.

The man considered his words for a moment then nodded. "I'll go ahead and make sure the way is clear."

But Parker had another idea. He'd been uneasy about having the children around, taking them into a potentially explosive situation. There was a chance that the hostages had been recaptured in the short time he and Kate had been gone. There might be a fight waiting for them. Better to have the girls as far from that as possible.

"How are your arms?" he asked Ivan.

"Fine." The man pulled himself up straight, wanting to prove that he was capable, probably desperate to look strong enough for whatever Parker had in mind.

"Can you take the girls to the basement and barricade the door down there?"

The man only hesitated a moment before he nodded. "But if I barricade the door, how will the rest of the hostages get in?"

"Same way you will." They reached the coal-chute grid and Parker pulled it off then began to unravel the length of rope from around his waist.

Kate threw him a questioning look, but didn't argue with him for once. She knew as well as he did that the longer they had the kids out in the open, the more likely it was that they would run into some rebels who wouldn't care who got killed when they opened fire. He hated to let the girls go as much as Kate did, but it would have been insane to drag them along on this dangerous mission.

She bent to the children and began explaining to them what was going to happen and what they needed to do. They seemed okay with it. The sight of the security uniform seemed to have set them at ease with Ivan. They probably saw men in the same uniform every day and knew they were with someone who would protect them.

Kate hugged and kissed them both before lifting Elena onto Ivan's back and Katja into his arms. "Hang on tight. Super Spy Girls, remember?" She gave them an encouraging smile.

They didn't exactly smile back, but at least they weren't crying. They went in, Ivan hanging on to the ledge while Parker screwed the grid back into place then tied the rope to it. Then Ivan could finally move over to the rope and begin his descent.

"They'll be fine, right?" Kate's emerald gaze searched Parker's for reassurance.

"The basement is the safest place for them right now. And they have an armed guard, a professional." That was as good as he could arrange under the circumstances. "I'll go keep watch. Let me know when he yanks on the rope." He strode to where the corridor turned, keeping lookout.

"Okay," Kate called in a whisper a few endless minutes later.

Parker glanced at his watch. Ivan had made good time. The embassy guards obviously kept in top shape. He walked back to Kate, untied the rope and looped it around his shoulder, then they headed toward the gym together. They were almost there when he heard footsteps from around the next bend.

Grateful that the girls had gone, he stopped and listened carefully. Only one man, he registered with relief. That was the good news. He glanced around the corner quickly. The bad news was that the guy was heading for the gym. But it wasn't the worst part by far. Parker swore under his breath. The man had a belt of explosives strapped around his midriff.

And if the rebels had *one* guy walking around as a human bomb, they probably had others.

Chapter Five

August 10, 08: 15

Kate held her breath, knowing there was someone in the corridor in front of them, knowing Parker was about to confront the man. They had managed to stay alive so far. She prayed that their luck held out.

Then she stared as Parker pulled his knife, but instead of lunging forward and around the corner, he cut a line across his left palm, pumped his fingers a couple of times to get the blood going. He lifted his right index finger over his lips to tell her to be quiet before he smeared blood on his face, covering his features almost completely, and staggered out into the open.

He moaned something in Russian or Tarkmezi—she couldn't tell the two languages apart—and an urgent response came. Then there was silence.

"All clear," Parker said next.

By the time she peeked out, he was wiping his bloody face on his sleeve. Then he cut off a strip from the dead man's shirt and bandaged his self-inflicted wound with speedy efficiency before she could even think about offering help. Frankly, at this point, she wouldn't have been surprised if he'd got out some commando first-aid kit and sewed himself up.

"Stay in cover," he mouthed as she caught up to him.

She didn't like the idea. She had a rifle and she knew how to shoot. She wanted to help, to even the odds a little. They were in front of the gym's door.

"What are we waiting for?" she whispered back.

He tapped his index finger to his ear.

She didn't hear anything. Then she got it, that was exactly what he was worried about. Everything was quiet inside. Either the hostages were dead, or under guard again and forbidden to speak as before, or they had heard the exchange of words outside and were preparing to shoot the living daylights out of the rebels they expected to enter any second.

"Vents?" She pointed down the hallway where there was a vent cover. They could climb up and take a look inside the room without its occupants noticing. She couldn't believe she was suggesting crawling back into the dark, tight place. But it seemed a better solution than to walk into a situation blindly.

Gunfire sounded from the roof again. Or maybe closer. Could be the Russians were inside already.

"No time," Parker told her, probably thinking the same, then called out something that she figured was the Russian version of, "Hold your fire."

He tried the doorknob. Locked. He shouted something else. A response came, then more conversation back and forth, followed by the sounds of something heavy being dragged away from the door. Then it opened, the barrel of an AK-47 poking out.

April 10, 10:15

"YES, COLONEL." Parker spoke into the phone.

He was back in the vent system with Kate again, having seen the hostages safely to the basement through the coal chute. With Ivan to organize them and the guns and gas masks he'd been able to give them, they should be able to defend themselves if everything didn't go according to plan.

He still had about ten percent battery power left in his cell, and he'd figured he'd better check in with the Colonel since the location of the hostages had changed. He wanted someone to be aware of that, in case the information could be passed along to the Russians.

"They should be as safe as possible. They are armed and hidden in a well-defendable position. They have a Russian security guard with them."

"You're sure about the explosives?"

"I can be sure only about the one I've got here." He carried the belt of TNT slung across his shoulder. "But my gut instinct says there's more."

"Get her out of there."

"Yes, sir." He sure was working on it.

"There's a press conference called for noon. I expect the Russians will come clean about the embassy crisis to us before that, then the CIA can offer help. Not that they'll take it, dammit."

The Colonel wasn't a swearing man, even frowned

on the practice among those who reported to him. His frustration was a reminder of just how dire their situation really was.

"What's your next move?" he asked.

"I'm gonna try to get into the security office and bring the security system back online for a few minutes. If I could figure out what positions the rebels are holding, I could map a way out."

"I have a brand-new blueprint of the embassy in front of me that just came in. Where are you now?"

"Second floor, a hundred feet or so east of the gym, in a vent duct that's running parallel to a hallway to some inner courtyard."

"Okay," the Colonel said. "As soon as you can go down, do it. The security office is to the southeast of you, one floor down."

"Roger that," Parker said and signed off. He was coming to a passage where the duct narrowed again and he needed his hands stretched in front of him to wiggle through. He pushed his guns and the TNT belts in front of him.

"Can you make it?" Kate asked from behind him. They were once again in a section where there were no openings to the duct so they could talk a little more freely as long as they kept their voices down.

"Squeaking by."

Silence stretched between them as he got through the tough parts.

"This is what you've been doing all along, isn't it?" she said out of the blue as she eased her smaller body after him without any trouble.

He knew she wasn't talking about worming through ventilation systems. She was talking about his job. Hell of a time to bring up the issue.

He could have pretended that he didn't know what she meant, but he would only insult her intelligence and tick her off. Kate didn't take well to being patronized. "I can't discuss my job with anyone. Not even with my fiancée." He glanced at her.

"Ex-fiancée," she corrected tartly.

There was a hardness to her now that hadn't been there when he had met her, and he regretted that most likely he had brought about the change.

"I'm sorry," he said, and found that there was a long list of regrets behind that sentiment, a list he had no time to detail or even think about right now.

"No, fine. You're right. It doesn't matter. None of what happened matters, anyway." She sounded tired and maybe a little defeated.

He wanted to protest that it did matter, hating the dejection in her voice even more than he hated the hardness of her words. And he couldn't even see her face because she was behind him. He couldn't grab hold of her shoulders and make her look at him, make her listen while he explained everything, because he could not give any explanations.

He had requested permission, back when he had first realized that he was falling in love with her. His request had been denied. Their life together had been based on lies. He had thought that the fact that their love was true would be enough, that it would cover everything. It hadn't.

He reached a three-way junction in the vent system with one branch going to the floor below them. "I'll slide down. Give me a minute before you come after me," he said. He wanted to make sure the route was passable before both of them got wedged in.

He'd had a friend when he'd been in the army who was into caving and had taken him and a few others spelunking. This place had reminded Parker of that, the tight spots and turns, the semidarkness, the seeming lack of air. Except that in the caves you could make all the noise you wanted without having to fear you'd be shot at.

He cleared the bend. "Okay," he whispered back to Kate.

They were coming into a stretch with a number of openings so they wouldn't be able to talk. He stole forward to the first, eager to be able to look out.

An empty office.

He moved on and tried the next. Damn. "Found the nanny," he whispered.

"Alive?"

He shook his head, looking at the stout Englishwoman sprawled on the floor. Looked as though she had put up quite a fight. The room's antique secretary desk had been reduced to kindling.

He moved up to the next room. Empty. Same with the next and the next. He was nearing the end of the duct and a sharp turn he wasn't sure he would be able to navigate by the time he finally found what he was looking for—the security office.

But of course, since everything that could go wrong

on a mission usually did, this room wasn't empty. A rebel soldier sat in front of the rows of darkened monitors, snoozing. Parker focused on the familiar-looking wide canvas belt around the guy's waist. Another human bomb. Just what they didn't need.

"Someone's in there," he breathed the words toward Kate, couldn't be sure if she heard him or even saw his lips move as she had the flashlight turned off.

He kept his attention glued to the room, couldn't see all of the space from his vantage point, couldn't see if there was anyone in there with the man, so he waited. No sounds of anyone moving around. Gunfire came again from somewhere far above. Didn't seem to be any closer than the short bursts they'd heard before.

Didn't look like the Alpha troops were making much progress. Or could be that they were engaging the rebels up there only as a distraction and were working their way in someplace else entirely. That was what Parker would have done. Machine-gun fire peppered the silence again. The man slumped in the chair didn't wake, didn't even stir.

Parker turned on his cell-phone camera and stuck it out through the vent cover's slots, tilted it down as best he could without risking dropping it, careful not to scrape against the vent cover and make noise. Then he pulled the cell back to look at what he got. Nothing. Perfect. Their man was alone, which he indicated to Kate by holding up his index finger in the spot where the light coming in from the vent hole made it visible.

He could barely see her silhouette in the darkness, but thought she nodded.

He pulled his handgun and slowly pushed the silencer through the slot, took careful aim. He couldn't give the man a chance to shout out. They had no way of knowing who might be nearby. So he aimed for the head, knowing it would make the hit messy, but unable to think of another solution that would take care of their problem as quickly and efficiently.

A small *pop* came first, then a louder thud, as the rebel hit the floor. Parker waited but there was no sound of any commotion from outside, no sign that anyone had heard. He pushed the vent cover out, held on to it so it wouldn't clang to the floor, and squeezed his shoulders through the opening, then helped Kate.

"Don't look," he said, too late.

Her face was already white, her eyes round with horror. Head shots were always messy and this was no exception.

"It had to be done. Him or us," he tried to explain, fearing that she was beginning to see him as some sort of a monster, unsettled by the thought that if she did, she might be right. If it had just been him, he would have killed the man without thought. Only because she was with him had he hesitated at all.

"I know." Kate reached a hand to his arm in a brief touch of reassurance.

What did she know? He looked at her and saw the understanding in her eyes, was humbled by it. Yeah, she knew.

And he found he breathed easier all of a sudden. "Why don't you check on the computers?" He pushed her toward the nearest desk gently, wanting to turn her from the gruesome sight and give her mind a chance to be busy with something else.

He checked a smaller door in the back. "There's a bathroom in here." He looked around to make sure it was safe and nearly got knocked over when Kate whizzed by him, then shut the door in his face.

He allowed a small smile before he walked back to the man and removed the TNT belt. When he was done with that, he tugged off the guy's camouflage jacket and covered his head with it. He didn't take the man's guns, only his ammunition. They might need serious firepower on the way out.

He used the bathroom after Kate was done and had returned to the computers. Then he came back out for the dead man, got him into the chair and wheeled him inside one of the stalls and closed the door. When he was done, he washed his hands and face, drank.

Most of the PCs and monitors had bullet holes in them. She was rebooting one of the unharmed computers by the time he came out. He watched as a gray screen came up. Password-protected, of course. He swore under his breath.

He wasn't bad at cracking security, but he wasn't a whiz, either—it wasn't his specialty—and he figured the security PCs at the Russian embassy had to have some pretty fancy systems. He had no time to waste by fooling around on a prayer of a chance. Instead, he dialed the Colonel.

"I'm going to need a computer expert on the line," he said. "Is Carly available?" Carly Tarasov was a new member of the SDDU team, the wife of one of Parker's old buddies, Nick, who'd met her on a mission and promptly recruited her. With good reason. She was a genius when it came to encryption codes.

"You got it. Give me a second to reach her. I take it you got in?"

"Yes, sir. Found more explosives, too."

Silence at the other end.

"One more thing, sir."

"Whatever you need."

"I need permission to disclose."

Longer silence this time.

"She has security clearance, sir," he reminded his superior officer.

"Not this high," he said. "Her boss's boss doesn't even know that the SDDU exists." The Secret Designation Defense Unit was normally used in clandestine missions that skirted Congressional approval, running operations where to take out a dangerous enemy, they often had to bend the rules of the game.

"With all due respect, sir, her boss's life is not on the line."

The Colonel grunted. Another moment of silence followed. "The most bare-bone basics only," he said finally. "Just what she's likely guessed on her own by now. Nothing but what she absolutely must know to cooperate and survive."

Parker's chest expanded, and his gaze locked with Kate's. She was watching him and listening with interest. "Yes, sir. Thank you, sir," he said.

HE WAS finally going to tell her what was going on, was finally going to let her in. She didn't know whether to be relieved or scared. Scared that she would find out that she had made some bad decisions in the past and had judged him unfairly.

She spoke before he had the chance to. "You didn't just start this job, did you? This is what you did, even back when we were engaged and living together." Nobody got to be this good without years of experience.

She waited, afraid now that she'd spoken that he would dodge the question, as he had dodged her questions in the past.

But he nodded.

She drew a deep breath, her mind going a mile a minute. Here it was, the truth coming out, finally. She owed him her own part.

"You know those times when you were gone and I couldn't reach you? Sometimes I thought that you had somebody else."

Thunder came into his eyes. "You thought I was cheating on you?" His voice was dangerously low.

She nodded tentatively, licking her lips in a nervous gesture.

His eyes flashed. "You said you loved me. How could you not trust me at all?"

Was that hurt in his voice?

"You said you loved me. How could you lie to me the entire time?"

That gave him something to think about. He held her gaze, a storm of emotions simmering under the surface.

"What was I supposed to think? You were moody a

lot, you know, when you came back from assignment." Her voice choked. "And your shirt smelled like perfume sometimes."

"I work undercover. Sometimes I work with others. There are a few women on my team." His voice was husky, toe-curlingly sexy.

She wrapped her arms around herself. "Why not tell me at least that? That you worked some law-enforcement job you couldn't tell me more about. I could have accepted it." At least, she thought she could have.

"I had no authorization. When we met, I was investigating an information leak that had some clues pointing to the State Department—where you worked and still work," he emphasized.

That gave her pause and brought up more questions than answers. "Did you ask me out to get information from me? Was I your cover or something?"

He stepped closer, his eyes holding her in such a stark bind that the room around them seemed to disappear. She couldn't look away.

"When you backed into my car—" He paused and her heart sank.

She remembered the accident clearly. She'd been distracted, leaving the parking lot of the Harry S. Truman building, that is, the headquarters of the U.S. Department of State. A few blocks from the White House in Washington, D.C., it was in a neighborhood called—no joke—Foggy Bottom.

"I was there watching someone. I couldn't be sure

that you didn't make me miss my man on purpose," he said.

She felt cold. He had only asked her out that night to investigate her. And she had been completely taken in by him. The attraction, on her part, had been instant. There he was pretending and, oh God—she had *slept* with him. Anger and embarrassment swept over her.

"I'd run a background check on you by the time we met for dinner. I knew you were clean. I could have skipped," he was saying. "I went— And you were—" He shook his head. "I didn't see *that* coming."

She was still angry, but she wanted to hear him out. She wanted to be fair. It seemed she might have made some rash judgments in the past. They had cost her. She didn't want to make the same mistake now—didn't want to be ruled by her rush of emotions.

"I wanted you from the first second I saw you," he said, carefully enunciating each word. "When I found out where you worked, I told myself I had to walk away from you. But I couldn't."

Judging by the harsh intensity on his face, she didn't think he was lying. Some of the tension inside her chest eased.

"But don't you think you should have told me at least some of the truth after the engagement?" She wasn't ready to give in yet to the dizzying pull that drew her to him, had always drawn her to him.

"I wanted to. I didn't get the authorization. I wanted to put off asking you to marry me until I could come clean. It just— Things got away from me."

Yes, she remembered. Things had gotten away from

both of them. They had been explosive together from day one. Dynamite. They couldn't get enough of each other's company, bodies. From their first date, she could think of no other man.

"You let me go without a word." That had hurt. Even at that point, she had still hoped that something could be worked out if they both wanted it enough. She had expected him to try to keep her, had hoped he would heed the wake-up call. Instead, he had let her go without a fight. Which she took as a sign that he hadn't really loved her at all.

"What did you expect from me?" he asked, tight-lipped, going very quiet.

Parker in quiet mode wasn't a good thing.

"I expected you to give me a reason to stay."

He turned away before she could have caught the expression on his face, walked to the blank computer screen and stared at it.

"Remember Jake Kipper? He stopped by one night with some car parts for me."

She did. "Yes." There hadn't been too many people in Parker's life it seemed. His parents were gone and he had no brothers or sisters. Only a handful of friends stopped by now and then, and out of those, she had only met Jake that one time. He had an infectious grin and had brought his wife along, a woman who clearly adored him.

She'd been insanely young—too young to be married, early twenties at the most—beautiful and happy. The same happy Kate had hoped to be in her own marriage with Parker. Well, *that* didn't happen.

And Jake and Elaine had died in a car accident a few months after that, the news sending Parker into one of his dark moods for weeks.

"The group I work for—" Parker drummed his fingers on the desk, his muscles tight, his face hard. "Nobody's cover had been broken before. Jake was the first and so far the last."

Her breath caught. "Are you saying—"

"It was a car bomb, Kate, not an accident." Pain and regret swam in his gaze. "Elaine was pregnant."

Her hand flew over her mouth. "You didn't tell me."

"It was still early. I don't think they'd told anyone yet. It came out in the autopsy."

Other things clicked into place. How Parker had said it was too early for a baby when she'd told him she'd like to start trying as soon as they were married. She had taken that as yet another rejection.

For the first time, she had to consider that maybe he'd just been scared. Hard to think of Parker like that. He was never scared of anything.

She shifted toward him. He waited, not moving a muscle, so still she thought he might be holding his breath. She stepped close, then closer, putting her arms around his torso and burying her face at last into the crook of his neck, inhaling his scent, the warmth of his body. And then his strong arms wrapped around her and held her tightly.

Moisture gathered in her eyes. God, she had missed this. Missed him.

"I was scared to death that I couldn't keep you safe." His voice sounded scratchy.

"Looks like I found plenty of trouble without you," she said ruefully.

"I'm here now." He lifted a hand to tuck her hair behind her ear, put a finger under her chin to tilt her face to him. "I'm not going to let anything happen to you, Kate."

She knew. And her heart leaped against her rib cage because she also knew that he was going to kiss her. His gaze was dropping to her lips already.

"Parker, we…" she started to say, but then changed her mind and rose to meet him halfway.

He kissed her so sweetly, so tenderly, as if he had put all the longing of their separation into that one kiss. Her body responded on autopilot. Nobody had ever gotten to her the way Parker did without half trying. He was the only person that she had ever slept with on a first date.

Her hands crept under his shirt. She needed to touch his skin, needed to feel the familiar landscape of his abdomen and his chest, needed to feel that he was still the same. Her Parker.

The thought pulled her back from the haze of pleasure and she untangled herself from him shakily, finding the strength somewhere to step away.

He wasn't her Parker. He was no longer her fiancé. And if things were the same, they wouldn't work, anyway. They hadn't worked in the first place. Truth was, beyond the physical, they had failed to make their relationship a viable union.

Now she knew what he did for a living. But she didn't know yet how she felt about that. She wouldn't be any happier with him being gone half the time now than she had been before. And he could never tell her everything. There would always be secrets between them. That wasn't her idea of marriage.

"Kate." He reached for her.

She drew back. "I'm sorry."

He gave her a rueful smile. "Let's call a moratorium on apologizing to each other, okay?"

She nodded.

"Do you have any more questions about me? There are at least a few things now that I could tell you."

But she shook her head. She knew enough. And what she really wanted to know, anyway, was whether he still loved her.

Did she still love him? Hard to say when the need for his touch still hummed through her body. For the moment, the physical pull still obscured the emotional side of things.

She didn't want to love him. She knew that without a doubt. She didn't want to open herself up to a world of hurt again. She had found out enough about him now to give more meaning to the events of their past, lay it to rest somehow and hope she could finally bury her regrets along with it.

"I think—" She didn't get to finish what she was saying. They were interrupted by his cell phone.

"Okay, go ahead." Parker put the phone on speaker then laid it next to the keyboard as he dropped into a chair.

"Hang on for a second." It was the Colonel. "Before I hand you over, you should probably know that the rebels have made another demand. In addition to troop withdrawal, they also want some Tarkmez war leaders released. There's a trial coming up soon at the international court at The Hague. All right, here's Carly."

"Hey, beautiful," Parker said with a half smile and Kate's stomach clenched.

"Sucking up right off the bat, huh? Must be in a lot of trouble, McCall."

"Nah. Just wanted to hear your sweet voice. How's the baby?"

"Intent on kicking his way out. As stubborn as Nick. You know what I'm talking about?"

"Hear you about that," he said, then briefly ran through his problem. "You think you can help me?"

"I have to, don't I, if I want a godfather for this kid," she groused good-naturedly.

And Kate relaxed.

She was beginning to suspect that Parker had a slew of friends she hadn't been allowed to meet because they worked for the same group or organization or commando patrol or whatever it was he belonged to.

"I'll stand guard by the door," she whispered, not wanting to interrupt.

Parker nodded. They set up a voice connector on the computer to save his cell-phone battery as much as possible, then started the work with Carly, and between the two of them, a grainy image flickered onto the screen after a couple of hours. Kate had spent that time listening at the door, peeling her ears for any noise that might indicate that rebels were coming their way.

"How about the rest? I can only see with one security camera," he said toward the phone.

"We have to reroute the feed from the others to the one working monitor you have. Then you should be able to scroll through the images," Carly told him, and they got working on that right away.

Three more nerve-wracking hours passed before they got anywhere. Some of that time Kate spent by taking a sponge bath in the bathroom sink, with the dead body locked in the stall behind her. She tried not to look at the feet in the mirror.

But finally they did have the pictures, one hallway after another, the front entrance, the back, Parker flicking through them one by one.

"Thanks. Does Nick ever tell you that you are as brilliant as you are beautiful?"

"Not enough. He's barely home," she said then went on with some admonitions about Parker proceeding very carefully.

So she was very pregnant, close to birth from what she'd said, and her husband, who seemed to be on the same team with Parker, was obviously off on some mission. Yet it didn't seem to bother her. There had been humor in her voice when she'd brought it up and an enviable amount of love.

And Kate wondered if she could ever be like that, if what Carly had would ever be enough for her. Carly seemed happy. She was still giving some last-second instructions to Parker.

"What if the rebels try to contact those two you took out in the gym? If they get no response over their radios, they might go over to check that out. They'll see that the hostages are gone and start a search. Won't they figure out that someone got in to help?"

"They'll probably figure that the hostages overcame the guards themselves."

"But—"

"Look, even if they do realize that the hostages are gone, they can't afford to send too many men after them. They need all the muscle they have to fight off the Russians. Ivan and the hostages we've given guns to should be able to handle a rebel or two."

"You're right. I was just…"

But he didn't look as if he was listening to her anymore. He was leaning toward the screen, narrowing his eyes at one of the grainy images.

"Damn. That is the dead-last thing we needed," he said.

Chapter Six

Their situation was getting wilder by the minute. Parker stared at the screen. He shouldn't be surprised. Nothing that had to do with Kate had ever been easy.

He was only here to save her, but would she come willingly and speedily? Hell no. Always had to save the whole world and then some. *Easy* was not in the woman's vocabulary. Still, he could probably have handled it all, except for what—or who—appeared on the computer screen: Piotr Morovich.

He could have done without that complication. "What in hell is he doing now?" he hissed through his lips.

"Know him?" Kate asked.

"Yeah, and it gets worse. He knows me."

"Nice friends. Who is he?"

"A known anarchist and mercenary. His father was a Russian spy who was assassinated after defecting to

France. He hates the Russian government and blames the French for not protecting his father well enough."

"Is he Tarkmezi?"

"Russian. From Kiev. But lately he's been hanging around with one of the Tarkmezi warlords."

"How do you know him?"

He stayed silent.

"I thought the Colonel said you could tell me things." Her emerald eyes flashed with impatience.

"On a need-to-know basis."

Her chest expanded as she drew a deep breath, getting ready to singe the hair off the top of his head. He braced himself for it.

"He is part of a group that has taken me hostage." She drew herself to full height, and even being several inches shorter than he was and much more slightly built, she did manage to look intimidating. "I'm stuck in an explosive-riddled building with him. My life is in danger. I *need* to know." The last words were said in a seriously pissed-off diplomat voice.

He drew an uneasy breath. She was right—to a point. And he was only too aware that this was the very issue he had lost her over in the past. "Piotr was looked into as a possible liaison."

"For what?"

He clamped his lips, aware that he had probably said too much already. He was walking a fine line here. But she was a smart one and, after a moment, put it all together on her own.

"You tried to recruit him to spy for the U.S.?" Her eyes widened.

"I evaluated him. A long time ago." Recruitment wasn't his territory. The SDDU had a handful of selected people for that—a task that had to be handled with the utmost delicacy. Since the group was top secret, before they approached anyone and revealed even the slightest information, they had to be a hundred percent sure the possible recruit would say yes.

"And?" She still had that dazed, Alice-down-the-rabbit-hole look on her face.

Made him want to kiss her senseless. Just about everything she did or said made him want to do things he could not, under any circumstance, do. And not all of them had to do with sex. Some had to do with turning back time. Good luck with that.

Or becoming the kind of man that she could love. *Don't go there, McCall.*

"Too unstable," he said, focusing on Piotr. An understatement, really. Piotr was one scary son of a bitch. But, God, what a relief it was to finally be able to level with Kate, at least about some of his work.

She pinched the bridge of her nose and squeezed her eyes shut for a second, visibly gathering herself before drawing herself straight and shaking off any momentary discouragement. "Great."

He kept an eye on the screen as Piotr moved along the long corridor, all alone. The man looked around then pulled a small package from his shirt.

No, no, no. Let it be a sardine sandwich. Parker's fingers tightened on the computer mouse, all of his attention focused on the man.

"What is he doing with the Tarkmezi rebels?" Kate was asking.

"That's the question of the hour, isn't it?" He watched the man step up onto an overstuffed, antique armchair and pry off a vent cover, shove his package in there.

"What is that?"

He wasn't exactly sure, beyond that it couldn't have been anything good. And if his gut instinct was right, Piotr's little package could be something downright disastrous. "We'd better check it out."

He scrolled through the screens again, noting the rebel positions, how many of them there were at each spot, mentally mapping an escape route. The basement was completely closed off to the outside world, the roof occupied by Alpha troopers. He had to find a way out somewhere in between the two. And it wouldn't be easy. For one, all the windows had bars on them. Then there was the distinct chance that if he stuck as much as his head out, the Russians would shoot from the roof without stopping to ask questions.

They would need a distraction. He hefted the two TNT belts onto his shoulder as he stood, running all the possibilities through his mind one more time.

"There are two balconies," he told Kate as he headed for the door, weapon drawn. "The large one is on the second floor and it faces the front." All ornately carved stone. This was where the Russian flag flew. "The smaller one in the back is on the third floor and overlooks the yard." It was used for private dining for the ambassador and his visitors in the summer. "We'll try that one. We might be able to get over to the garage roof." Embassies had their own fleet of cars, a number of them bulletproof.

Since there were most likely no rebels in the garage or any of the outbuildings that belonged to the embassy, it was unlikely that the Alpha troops focused any serious manpower on those, after having swept them initially.

For a moment he considered getting Kate safely inside one of those bulletproof vehicles and sitting tight until the embassy was liberated. But he didn't much like that idea unless he had no other choice. Ideally, he wanted her far away from here by the time the serious fighting started.

They made their way over to the elevator shaft without trouble and he got them inside one more time. He was halfway up the ladder behind Kate when the Colonel called.

"The State Department is trying to work with the situation. The Russians know that our consul is in there with a bodyguard. All offers for help have been refused. They assured us of Ms. Hamilton's safety."

Which they both knew meant exactly squat.

"The media is camped outside the building," the Colonel went on. "There's a live feed to most TV stations. Special news break and all that."

Great. That would make it that much harder to get out without drawing attention. He could not afford to have his picture pasted all over television as he was dangling from a rope down the side of the building with Kate Hamilton, the U.S. consul, in his arms.

"Piotr Morovich is here," he reported.

"For what?" The Colonel sounded as surprised as Parker had felt when he had spotted the man.

"He hates both the Russian government and the French. Beyond that, I have no idea. I guess this is why he came to Paris." They had figured he was here to put into place some weapons-exchange deal. Someone had passed on incomplete intel. On purpose? He needed to look into that once they got out of here.

"I'll check into it." Apparently the Colonel was thinking the same thing.

"Appreciate that, sir."

"Any change of status?"

"There are twenty-two rebels left as far as I could tell from the security cameras." Not all areas of the embassy had cameras, unfortunately. "I neutralized five so far. Had to be done, sir." He felt it necessary to defend his actions since the Colonel had asked him to get in and out with a minimum of interaction with anyone.

"Well done," the man said, not sounding upset by the news.

"Do we know who's leading the rebels?"

"Not yet. Wouldn't be Piotr, though."

Right. He wasn't Tarkmezi. Those fighters might have worked with him if he had something they needed, like information on the embassy, but they wouldn't follow a man not their own.

If he knew who the leader was, the most likely way to end the conflict quickly would be for him to locate the man and take him out. But with Kate by his side, his main goal was to avoid the rebels and not to go charging among them. More than anything, he wanted to keep her safe.

"How is Ms. Hamilton?" the Colonel asked. Didn't seem like he had taken offense over Kate hanging up on him earlier.

"Holding up well, sir. I'm going to try to get us out of the building and to the garage. I plan on checking on a package on the way out that Piotr put into the vent system. I'll report in if it's something important." And it was going to be, he knew that from the sick sensation in his stomach every time he thought of it.

They exchanged a few more words about enemy positions before hanging up.

"Are we going back into the vents again?" Kate asked with trepidation. But she looked ready to do it if he asked her. That was the kind of woman she was: strong, loyal and courageous.

He'd made a few whopper mistakes in his life, but he was beginning to think that letting her go might have been the biggest of them all. He struck that thought from his mind. He couldn't let himself sink into regret or the tempting fantasies of what could have been. They needed to get a move on.

"Not if we can help it. Keep your gas mask close at hand."

She nodded and resumed climbing—they had stopped for the phone call—and even in their dire situation, he couldn't help admiring her tempting lines and long-legged grace. A man would have to be dead not to notice. He saw something else, too. The tension in her body. He needed to distract her from the danger around them.

"Remember the orange duck at Meiwah?" he asked without meaning to. Meiwah, a high-end Washington, D.C., restaurant had been the venue for their first date. Obviously, he had food and sex on his brain. Not necessarily in that order. Hey, he was a guy; he wasn't going to apologize for that.

"Parker." Her voice was a soft plea.

She remembered it, all right, but didn't want to.

He'd walked her home after that first date, still deluding himself that he was doing it for the sake of his investigation. It had begun to rain.

Why don't you come in for a second? I'll dig up an umbrella for you. She looked mind-boggling in a white summer dress that had gotten just damp enough to stick to her curves.

Couldn't turn an invitation like that down, could he? A chance to look around her place—strictly in the interest of the case.

And then, *kaboom.*

To this day, he wasn't sure how they'd ended up kissing, how they'd ended up making love on the chaise lounge. It was pure insanity that first time, then the next and the next. He had waited for the breathless feeling in his chest to go away. It never did. They saw each other every day for the next two months—he was stateside for his investigation. The day he solved the State Department case, he proposed to her. Not that he had planned to. And he could barely believe when she had said yes.

He moved in with her the day after that, thinking it

could work. Hey, there were a handful of guys in the SDDU who had families. Then, two days later, he got his marching orders to Taiwan for his next mission. For the next year or so, they barely saw each other.

He realized then that the relationship was probably torture for the both of them, but he would have married her in spite of his own judgment and the advice of his superior officer. Except that he had to lie to her the entire time, until she got sick of him and booted him right out the door.

And the hell of the thing was, he wanted her still, even now. Given half a chance, he would have found a way to make love to her in the dim elevator shaft, mark every inch of her body with his, sink himself deep into her soft heat. He wanted to hear her moan his name.

Sweat beaded on his upper lip by the time they reached the door to the third floor and she moved up on the ladder so he could get into position to open it. Better focus on the here and now if he didn't want to lose her. He opened the panels a crack as he'd done before, just enough to sneak a peek. The hallway was clear.

They got out and reached the turn in the corridor without trouble. But there was some muted noise up ahead. He used his phone camera to look around the corner, pushing it out low to the ground where he didn't think it would be noticed against the black marble tile. Five lounging rebels were doing nothing in particular up ahead, looking out the window. That portion of the corridor faced the courtyard. What were they looking at? Couldn't have been anything important, judging from their body language. Probably just passing time while their leader negotiated a deal.

They didn't look as though they were inclined to move anytime soon, which meant that he had to find another way to get around them. To reach the back balcony, he could have simply rounded the building with Kate. But he did want to take a look at what Piotr had left in the vent. That was crucial information he could pass along.

He motioned to the row of doors across the hallway. Kate followed. None of them were open. And he couldn't make much noise. The rebels were just around the corner.

He got out his knife and the belt buckle from one of the TNT belts. The blade was too wide, the prong of the buckle not strong enough on its own.

"Flashlight," he mouthed to Kate.

She handed it to him and he took it apart, popped out the spring that kept the batteries pressed to where they needed to be. He bent it until it resembled the shape he required, then tried again. *Bingo*.

"We're gonna have to go back into the vent," he whispered when they were inside. Not knowing what in hell Piotr had put into the vent system, he really hated the idea.

He was torn between telling her to stay here in relative safety and taking her with him because he didn't want to take his eyes off her.

"Put your gas mask on," he said, deciding at last, pulling the stretch band of his own mask over his face. He made sure hers was on just as tight.

He opened the vent cover and pulled himself up first before helping her up behind him. He signaled to her to keep a fair distance. Didn't have to tell her to be quiet.

He could hear the guards talking, passed by them, reached the suspicious-looking package that he'd seen on the closed-circuit monitor before. Damn. He grabbed the capsule gingerly, signaling to Kate to back up.

He didn't talk until they were back in the room.

"What is it?" she whispered, pulling her mask off, rubbing the red marks the tight rubber had left on her face.

Good, that meant she'd had a tight seal. He didn't give her time to get comfortable. He tugged the mask right back over her face with his free hand.

"Some homemade chemical weapon." His voice sounded strange through the mask. He turned the capsule over. Surprisingly well put together. Whoever had made it knew what he was doing. He didn't think Piotr had this kind of expertise.

He took in the small sensor. "Remote release. It's fine for the moment, but the second someone pushes the control button somewhere in the building…" He gave her a meaningful look.

Kate drew back several steps, her hands on the mask now, pushing it tighter onto her face. "Do you think there are more?"

"I'd be willing to bet my 1969 Camaro on it." And he wasn't the type of guy who'd say those words lightly.

He looked at Kate and considered seriously, for the first time, that they might not make it out of here.

Chapter Seven

August 11, 04:31

"How can you stay so calm with a bomb in your hands?" Kate was hyperventilating behind her mask. Not just any bomb, a chemical-weapon bomb. *God.*

And he thought there was likely more.

"Practice," he said easily.

"You're nuts. Certifiable." And what did that say about her? She was trusting her life to him.

She thought of the other hostages, grateful that Parker had thought to provide them all with gas masks, grateful that they were in the basement and so were Elena and Katja. She didn't remember there being any vent openings down there. If anything happened up here, at least the hostages might yet be safe.

She hated the sight of Parker just holding the wretched thing. If it were up to her, she would have been running the moment they'd figured out what it was.

"In how many ways are they planning to kill the hostages?" The rebels could easily have shot the embassy staff. She'd already thought the explosives were too much. And now the nerve gas? "Isn't this overkill?"

"Terrorists, in general, are not known for their restraint," he said dryly.

"Can you disable it?" She was half holding her breath, not a fun thing since the gas mask was an impediment to her breathing already.

He hesitated, then looked her square in the eye. "Not without tools."

Okay. He was being honest with her. That was what she wanted. What she had always wanted. But— *Oh God.* "What are you going to do?"

"Take it with us." He was putting it under his shirt already so his hands would remain free.

She caught a glimpse of tanned skin and flat abs. She had to be insane even to notice something like that at a moment like this.

And damn if he hadn't caught her looking. He arched a dark eyebrow. *Damn, damn and double damn.*

A hint of amusement underscored his voice when he spoke. "We can't leave it behind. We're going to have to find a way to deal with it before someone decides to set it off."

She so hoped he wasn't going to say that.

"That sounds like a good idea." Fear and anger at the unfairness of their situation bubbled up inside her, loosening something. "Why didn't I think of that?" It was hard to sound sarcastic with a mask on. "Oh, wait, I know. I must have thought that carrying around two TNT belts while sneaking among armed terrorists was dangerous enough." She was finally losing her cool, was aware of it, but couldn't do anything about it.

Morning was nearly here. She hadn't slept in two days. That and the constant danger had a way of making a girl cranky. And she wasn't even going to bring up her ex-fiancé's sudden and mysterious reappearance in her life. The kisses she was totally blocking. Indefinitely.

"I'm hoping to get it someplace where it'll do less damage than in the vents."

Okay, so there was some logic in that. The vent system was the worst possible place for a nasty-looking chemical weapon. "Like what?"

"A refrigerator or a freezer. Those doors are vacuum-sealed to keep the cold in. Not a perfect solution, but better than letting the airflow distribute all the poison through the whole building."

"The kitchen is on the first floor."

"I know. But they have diplomatic lunches on the back balcony when the weather is good. I'm betting there's at least a pantry somewhere nearby, and if we're lucky, there's a good-quality fridge."

AND THERE WAS. Unfortunately, they got very little time to spend with it, not even enough to grab some food. The rebels decided to go for a snack just a few minutes after Kate and Parker got there.

Six men were hanging out in the small indoor dining room in front of the balcony, coming and going from another room that was a pantry-slash-food-preparation station. They were eating and drinking, looking at the room's decorations and chatting as if they were on a field trip instead of a murderous mission. They had the flat-screen TV tuned to a soccer game.

Kate and Parker were hiding in a small closet behind a few dozen crates of soft drinks and some top-quality vodka. They'd been forced in there when the men came, and now they had no way out. There were no vent openings in here to crawl through.

Trapped.

She wiggled in the small space.

"Hang in there." Parker was watching her.

She focused on his eyes, which seemed to burn into hers even through the glass of the gas masks that were doing nothing to ease her sense of claustrophobia. She kept her gaze on him, trying to forget the lack of room, lack of air and the possibility that one of the rebels might get curious enough to look in there again.

The first one had nearly scared her to death. But apparently there were enough drinks available outside that he hadn't gotten excited by the sight that had greeted him in here. And, thank God, he hadn't looked too hard.

Her breath came in quick pants. She reached up to her mask. "Could we please take these off?"

He considered her for a long moment before he nodded. "Keep it at the ready."

She let it hang around her neck and took a full breath, then another.

The good thing about having no vent openings in the storage closet was that if Piotr what's-his-name activated the nerve gas and he had other capsules, the air wouldn't blow it in here. And, thank God, Parker had managed to put the capsule they'd had into the freezer in the other room before the rebels barged in, had even thought of submerging it in a bowl of water that would, she hoped, soon freeze into ice. He'd said it might mess with the remote control mechanism. She could only hope the rebels wouldn't find it as they foraged for food. They had no reason to look in there. They couldn't eat frozen food, anyway.

She rubbed the side of her face where the mask had left dents in her skin. Having her face covered so tightly added to her sense of unease. She wasn't an all-out claustrophobe, but she was very uncomfortable with small places, getting a rush of panic now and then that she fought with controlled breathing and sheer logic.

"You okay?" Parker whispered near her ear.

The TV wasn't loud enough to make out much except the roar of the crowd whenever the game took an exciting turn, but it drowned out the rebels' talking for the most part and Kate hoped it would mask whatever noise she and Parker might accidentally make in their hiding place.

They spoke in barely audible whispers, pressed against the back wall. Only a few inches separated them from each other. They were close enough for her to hear his even breathing, smell the familiar masculine scent of him.

What they said about scent being a potent trigger of memory was true. Memories flooded her. She fought back valiantly.

"I wonder how Elena and Katja are doing." She hadn't been able to get the two girls out of her head. Her thoughts cut back to them from time to time. They were tough little kids, hadn't been spoiled by life. But they were still kids. She worried about them.

"They're with people they know," Parker said reasonably.

But from the way he looked away from her, she could tell he was worried about them, too. "They didn't look like they knew that Ivan guy. Maybe he's new on the job," she said.

"I'm sure they don't know every single person who works here. But they probably know the kitchen staff. I bet they've eaten plenty of meals here at the embassy."

True. "And they would know Anna. She is…was… their mother's secretary." She couldn't bear thinking of Tanya. If their circumstances were different and their meetings hadn't been limited to a few diplomatic luncheons, they could have been friends. She couldn't think of a nicer and more warm-hearted person.

"Those poor kids lived in an orphanage for years. Then they're adopted by wonderful parents, and then— What do you think's going to happen to them?"

"They'll be saved. All of the hostages will be. They are in the most defendable location in the building. They have weapons. The rebels don't even know where they are. And the Russians will keep these bastards too busy to go looking for anything."

She sure hoped so. "I meant after that. Their parents are gone. Do you think they'll have to go back to the orphanage?"

"You can't help it, can you?"

"What?"

"You're always worrying about everyone," he said with a soft smile.

"*Worry* is the key word. Look what you're doing. You are risking your life for them." And had for countless others over the years, no doubt. "We didn't have a choice in being taken hostage. You waltzed in here all on your own, right into danger."

"They'll probably go to the rest of their family. I bet they have a boatload of aunts and uncles and cousins." He deftly steered the conversation back to the girls.

Of course they would have other family. Tanya had a large family and so did her husband. She hadn't thought of that. Good. That sounded good. Those children didn't need any more trauma.

"You didn't want children," she said without meaning to. The words just slipped out.

He looked at her in the dim space. The only light came from the inch-wide crack under the door.

"Just not right then. I figured we would have plenty of time. I wasn't in the position to take on that responsibility."

Considering the spot they were in at the moment, she could understand why he would have thought that. And this was what he did on a regular basis. It seemed almost incomprehensible. Who would do something like that?

Someone who cared deeply about others, who would risk his own life to keep others safe.

And she had thought him irresponsible when he hadn't always called to let her know he would be late.

"I assume there are other people on this team of yours, whatever it is. Are any of the others married? Nobody has any kids?"

He nodded yes with visible reluctance.

"And none of their wives know anything?" She could sympathize with the women, with what they must think, how they must feel. She'd been there.

"Some do. Some are on the team, too."

That had to make it easier for them. Or harder. They would know exactly what kind of danger their husbands were in when they left the house. If she'd known Parker was doing this while they'd been living together, she doubted she would have slept at night. She had worried plenty back when she had thought he was a foreign correspondent for Reuters.

She still felt betrayed and angry at the unfairness of life. Why couldn't she have fallen in love with a regular guy instead of some special commando soldier? But no, she hadn't fallen in love with Parker, she could see that with some clarity now. You needed to know someone to fall in love with him. She had fallen in love with the cover he presented.

This man was a lot more edgy, a lot harder, a lot more dangerous. He did things that barely bore thinking about. He killed. She'd seen that firsthand.

And he protected her. With his life.

She filled her lungs, trying to stop that thought from worming its way to her heart.

He slowly ran a hand down her arm, and she closed her eyes.

That was the same. The way his touch affected her. Nothing changed there. And how unfair was that, on top of everything else?

He pulled her against him. "Try to get some sleep. There's nothing else we can do."

He wouldn't sleep. She knew that without him having to say it. He would guard them and listen to the rebels. He would wake her when they were gone.

She did need sleep; she was seriously dragging after two days of playing cloaks and daggers. But she didn't want to sleep against him. She wasn't nearly as impervious to him as she would have liked. She moved away.

He pulled her back again. "You are going to need your strength."

The heat of his body seeped into her, his scent, the feel of his arms around her. This time, she stayed where she was.

His chest rose and fell beneath her cheek. Just like old times. She swallowed. There had been good times. She couldn't deny it. Fantastic times. She had been swimming in a surge of new love. What she'd *thought* was love. But there had been disappointments, too.

Or had she been too quick to judge? She wasn't going to go there. Hindsight might have been twenty-twenty, but it was also worthless.

He quietly moved the box next to him a few inches forward and maneuvered her deftly so she would end up on his lap, her head remaining on his chest and his arms around her.

They'd sat like this countless times before. It seemed

they'd been always touching. Except when he had disappeared on "assignments."

But her mind was, at the moment, more inclined to drift over the good times. And then into dreams. Most were about danger, but Parker was there in every one of them, always on her side. Others were about naked bodies and breathtaking pleasure. Also with Parker in the starring role.

Her growling stomach woke her up. She felt disoriented in the small, dark space for a few moments, but registered Parker's protective presence and relaxed. She pressed a hand against her stomach.

"Sleep well?"

Well, but not nearly enough. She still felt exhausted. "I really needed that. Thanks."

The TV was still going outside. The game was over. Some woman was talking now. The news? She couldn't make out her words. She sounded excited and outraged, but then again news reporters always did.

She had no idea what time it was or how long she had slept. It had been forever since she'd eaten. Her body needed sustenance.

"Here." He must have heard her stomach growl, because he was handing her a can of soda.

Not much, but it had caffeine and enough sugar to keep her going a while longer.

She could feel the phone vibrate on Parker's belt. He took the call and she pressed her ear to the other side of it so she, too, could hear what was said. He didn't protest.

"VICTOR SERGEYEVICH is heading the rescue team," the Colonel said. "He was the KGB agent who assassinated Piotr's father. He's with the Alpha troops now, the leader of their counterterrorism team."

And Piotr probably knew that. He knew that if something as big as an embassy hostage crisis occurred, Victor would come. Piotr was here to draw and take out an old enemy.

"He has nerve gas," Parker whispered into the phone. "I retrieved one capsule. He probably has one for every floor." For all his faults, Piotr was a dependably efficient guy.

"Do you have gas masks?"

"Yes, sir."

"Good. I'll pass that information along. I'll tell them that our consul managed to get to a phone for a few seconds and contacted us with information. I've been holding back until now, not wanting to appear too suspicious. But at this stage we have enough to be of serious use. I'll tell them about the location of the hostages and ask for time before they attack. I want you out of there before that happens."

"We're near the rear balcony that overlooks the utility buildings and the garage. We'll be exiting through there most likely. I'd appreciate it if you could pass along a request to hold their fire if they see movement in that area. We're stuck near the exit point. Should be able to move within a few hours at the latest. Do you think you can gain us a couple of hours, sir?"

The Colonel didn't respond. Parker waited, pulled

the phone from his ear to look at the display screen. Black. The battery was dead. They no longer had a way to communicate. The question was, how much had the Colonel heard of what he had said?

Chapter Eight

Had he been on his own, he would have broken out and to hell with the consequences. He couldn't believe they'd wasted ten hours hiding in a stupid pantry when the clock was ticking. A growing tide of frustration simmered dangerously close to the surface. Every minute that passed brought them closer to disaster. But the rebels outside the door would not leave. They seemed to be hung up on the TV and the food.

At least he'd finally caught a few winks. Kate had insisted, and he trusted her to stand guard. They seemed safe in the storage closet and he needed to be at one hundred percent capacity when they finally broke out of here.

He had no idea how many rebels there were out there at this time, but by the voices alone he figured still about half a dozen, always shifting as some came and others left. Several times he had come close to kicking the door out and charging forward with guns blazing. But

Kate was right behind him, no place to get cover in the closet. The plastic crates and soda bottles wouldn't stop any of the bullets the rebels sent his way. And he had no way of knowing if there might be one among them with a TNT belt who could set off his charge in the heat of the moment, taking out the whole room if not the whole floor.

What one considered "acceptable risk" sure had a way of getting reevaluated when you had the woman you cared about by your side.

"Parker?" She stood leaning against the opposite wall in the small space of the storage room, a foot or so away from him.

He already missed her body touching his. She had slept in his arms again. The memories of her sleeping in his arms on a regular basis seemed little more than a fantasy. A fantasy he would be only too glad to return to.

"I'm sorry," she whispered, her voice thick. "Back when—"

She stopped, and he leaned forward, waiting.

"I should have trusted you more," she finished.

His heart fumbled a beat with surprise. "We barely knew each other. And living with me is no picnic. Hey, I know that. You drew whatever conclusions you could, based on the information you had available."

Was she saying that maybe she regretted how things had gone down between the two of them?

"We still barely know each other," she pointed out as she watched him with those big emerald eyes that often haunted his dreams.

"At least now you know what I am." Maybe not the particulars, but she would have a fair idea of what he did for a living. And that probably wasn't a plus. She had seen him kill without hesitation. Two years ago, she had thought him uncommitted to their relationship and undependable. Chances were good that now she thought him a monster.

But she wouldn't sleep in a monster's arms. The thought gave him hope, more hope perhaps than he had the right to.

Her fingers fiddled with the bottom of her shirt. "You are so different from who I thought you were."

There it came. He held her gaze in the dim light, feeling as if a grand jury was about to pass judgment over him. He could have come up with a dozen excuses why he was the way he was, some pretty good ones among them. He didn't.

All he did was ask a single question. "Am I really?"

She closed her eyes for a second, drew a slow breath. "I suppose not that different," she conceded with an ironic little smile when she looked at him again. "I knew you were tough. It's just that you're tougher than I thought. And I knew that you were wild—" She paused. "But you are wilder than I could have ever imagined. I knew that you could be dangerous if someone threatened you."

He knew what she was thinking about. The small altercation down in Tampa when two lowlifes had tried to shove him out of the way to get to her purse. "I can be dangerous when *you* are threatened," he agreed, seeing absolutely nothing wrong with admitting that.

Another, longer pause followed.

"Thank you," she said. "For coming after me."

The tension in his chest eased a little, relief turning up the corner of his lips. "You bet." Then he added, "Next time you want to see me and reminisce, you can always just call."

She took her turn to smile, but grew serious again after a moment. "Parker?" she whispered, quieter than ever.

He had to step even closer to hear her over the TV outside the door. "Yeah?"

They were about toe to toe.

She drew a deep breath that lifted her breasts, making his hands itch to touch them. "I missed you," she said.

His smile widened, and he reached for her, drew her into his arms, inhaled her scent and sank into the feeling of having her body flush against his. Fear never had the ability to weaken his knees, but now he realized that there existed a profound relief that could do just that. "I missed you, too."

They held each other, just processing those two short confessions, appreciating them.

"But I don't think we can just pick up where we left off," she said after several seconds.

Considering where they had left off, how angry they'd been, then no, definitely not. "We'll figure this out as we go."

Her lips nuzzled his neck, hesitant, as if she couldn't decide whether to go with the moment or pull away.

Neither his mind nor his body was in any sort of

confusion over *his* preferred course of action. He held her tightly.

"But how far could it ever go? Until you disappeared again?" She pulled back enough so she could look him in the eyes.

"I have to disappear now and then. You understand what that's about now. But I'd always come back to you. Promise."

"Can you promise not to get hurt? That you'll be careful?"

That he could not do, not even for her, not even if he wanted to. His wasn't a careful type of occupation. "I can promise not to take unnecessary risks."

She pressed against him tightly the next second, holding him fiercely, as if she never wanted to let him go, and it made his heart sing. He ran his fingers up her arms, then neck, lifted her chin and brushed his lips over hers.

He hadn't meant to go much further than that. Okay, to be honest, he did hope to cop a feel or two. Holding her in his arms while she slept had riled his body. He tasted her bottom lip then the top one, tried hard not to think of what those lips could do to him. He was determined to remain in control.

Then she gave a little sigh that sent fire skittering across his skin. And he swept inside her mouth and forgot all about his good intentions. She was sweet and hot and she was his, dammit. And he kissed her with enough passion to make sure she knew that.

And the good thing about Kate, one of the many that he had always appreciated about her, was that she always gave as good as she got. And then some. He nearly lifted out of his shoes when she gently sucked the tip of his tongue.

His hands that had rested on her waist now crept under her white top and the silk blouse under that, reveling in the feel of her soft, warm skin, spanning her narrow waist. She had lost weight in the past two years, but still wasn't what one would call skinny. Which titillated him on every level. He loved her curves, loved that lush, passionate body of hers. Could have sculpted it from memory.

Which, he thought thankfully, he had no need to rely on right now.

"Parker." She sighed his name in a voice saturated with passion.

Having his hands on her and hers on him, her soft lips beneath his, that unique scent of her and that voice of seduction surrounded him like a spell. There was no room to escape the onslaught of sensations, and he didn't want to. He wanted more of it, more of her. He let his palms slide over what they pined for and closed his fingers over her incredible breasts, resenting the thin fabric of her bra between him and her skin.

But then his thumb brushed against the front clasp and he smiled against her lips.

"Parker?" His name was whispered not on a voice of worry, but on a voice of need.

And he had need enough inside him to match hers, enough to drown in.

Her breasts were firm, the skin soft and smooth, her nipples hard against his palm. He groaned his satisfaction into her neck and kissed her there, the gentle slope that led toward her shoulder, the spot where he knew she was extra-sensitive.

He had no plans of seducing her completely or taking this too far. He just wanted her to remember. The trouble was, once he unbuttoned her shirt and sucked one dusty-rose nipple into his eager mouth, then the other, he seemed to forget all about his original intentions.

She let her head fall back and rest against the wall, arching her back, offering herself up to him. And he took it all, took everything he could, made her his feast.

He needed her. The thought made him straighten and crush her against him, and claim her lips again. He had always needed her, he'd just been too stubborn and full of himself to know it. He had thought he didn't need anyone, that the job was enough. And maybe there had been a time like that. But not after he'd met her.

He needed her. He had her for now. Out of that came the next logical thought: There was no way he was going to let her go again.

She might have something to say about that. The treacherous voice of doubt surfaced.

He would just have to convince her that she needed him. Judging from the glazed-over look in her eyes, he was on the right path.

He wanted her. That wasn't news. He had always wanted her, from the moment she had fumbled out of her car, all apologetic, asking him with big emerald eyes swimming in worry whether he was all right.

After they had split, he had hoped that eventually the wanting would stop, or would at least fade with time to a bearable level. He'd been wrong. He knew that now. He was going to want her until the day he died.

He loved her. Now there was a thought to take the air out of his lungs. He loved her still. Maybe even more than before, although that hardly seemed possible. Then again, this time around he knew what it was like to lose her, so that added a whole other dimension.

"What is it?" She looked at him, her face flushed with passion, but concern leaping into her eyes. "Did you hear something?" she whispered.

He blinked, dazed but not confused. He knew without confusion what he wanted. But for that to happen, he had to get them out of here alive. With superhuman effort, he refastened her bra and smoothed down her shirt.

"I got carried away."

She watched him for a moment before offering a soft smile. "Yeah. Me, too. That hasn't changed, has it?"

He found it hard to focus on anything but her lips, which a few moments ago were deliciously under his. "Some things always stay the same. Forever."

It surprised him how good saying that word in connection to her felt.

She raised an eyebrow in a puzzled look that said she was aware of the undercurrents in his mood, but couldn't quite make them out.

And this was not the time to explain.

Excited shouting outside drowned out the TV. Could be the most recent game was over. He could only hope and pray that the men would leave. They had cost him and Kate way too much time already.

"What time is it?" she asked. Her watch had been snatched when she'd been taken hostage at the beginning.

He glanced at his. "Just after five. In a couple of hours it'll be dark." And the Russian forces may take advantage of that and storm the building.

The noose was tightening.

Her stomach growled, and his answered, as if hunger was as contagious as yawning. He was used to going hungry. He'd been on assignments before where he'd had to fight his way out of the jungle with no food and little equipment, foraging as he went.

Not much to forage here. He handed her another soda—the only source of nourishment they had—and grabbed one for himself, too. He was swallowing a big gulp when the sound of breaking glass came from outside, making the drink go down the wrong way. He couldn't help coughing, but stifled it as much as he could. Gunfire. More coughing came from outside, too. People swearing savagely. His instincts had been honed in battle, and they didn't fail him now. He pressed Kate's gas mask to her face before he grabbed his own, securing it in place.

He couldn't make out her expression behind the mask, but her muscles were drawn tight, her body tense. He squeezed through the crates and listened to the gunfire that came less and less frequently. He cracked open the door. Smoke swirled. The men were fleeing. One still fired backward in the general direction of the balcony as he was running away. There were three on the floor, one still living, but gasping for air. He hadn't had his gas mask handy, apparently. The other two were dead or dying from multiple gunshot wounds. He assessed them as being past the ability to pose a threat.

"Let's go." He took one last glance toward the glass doors that led to the balcony. Broken now by the gas grenade the Russians had shot in.

Obviously, the Colonel had not heard when he'd told him that they would try to exit through the rear balcony. Or he had and had passed on the message, but the Alpha troops didn't care.

Their previous plan probably still firmly in her mind, Kate did step that way, crunching glass underfoot.

He shook his head and grabbed her arm to take her in the opposite direction, the way the rebels had fled the room. There could only be one reason why the Russians had cleared this place. But he had no time to explain.

In the end, he didn't have to. Outside, black-clad men rappelled down from above and swung onto the balcony. Except for the blazing guns, the scene looked like a ninja attack. They didn't stop to ask questions or demand identification. He couldn't blame them. He was wearing a rebel uniform that marked him as a clear target.

He shoved Kate out of the room ahead of him. "Go!" And took only one glance back. He meant to get a count on how many men were coming in, but the large-screen TV snagged his gaze. It showed the outside of the embassy. The cameras were showing a man's body being thrown from the other, larger balcony at the front of the building.

Parker didn't have time to linger. The Russians were shooting at him.

He ran down the hallway with Kate, ducked around the next hallway, then the next, opposite to where he heard boots thudding on marble, rebels coming to push the Russians out.

He went for the elevator doors as soon as they reached them, forced his way in and sealed Kate and himself inside.

"Are you hurt?" Kate hung on to the metal ladder for dear life with one hand, while trying to take the mask off with the other so she could talk more easily.

"Keep it on." His voice came out muffled. "I'm fine. You?" He looked her over carefully.

"I'm okay. Are they taking over the building?" Her voice sounded shaky and weak even beyond the mask's distortion.

"I don't think so." He'd only seen three Alpha troopers come down. "I think it's another distraction. The main force is probably trying to get in someplace else. Or they could have seen the rebel's leader through the window and figured if they took him out the rest would give up."

Not that he knew who the rebel's leader was. He also had no idea what connection Piotr had to the guy. The operation was full of unknown elements. And what he did know, he really hated—like the explosive belts and Piotr's little capsules, and the fact that time was running out.

Gunshots sounded directly outside the elevator shaft.

Just a few. Still didn't seem like this was a major battle.
More like a small skirmish.

"The rebels found at least one of the hostages. Or,
best-case scenario, one of them came up to look
around." He told her what he'd seen on TV: he hadn't
been able to make out the dead man's face, but he had
recognized his clothes. He'd been part of the group in
the gym with Kate.

Then came the sound of more shooting.

Russian forces were in the building. The rebels had
started killing hostages again. And the whole place was
booby-trapped. The situation inside the embassy was as
volatile as possible.

"Where are we going next?" Kate asked.

He looked down, thinking of the hostages, wanting
to help them. But his first responsibility was to Kate. A
circle of light swooped by just above his head. He
grabbed for the door.

"Out of here."

Looked like either the Alpha troops or the Vymple
special forces had found the elevator shaft, as well, and
had their own plans for it. He hadn't seen the Vymple
team so far—he'd been wondering where they were and
what they were up to.

SHE DIDN'T think the Russians had seen Parker and her.
They didn't shoot. The elevator shaft was fairly dark and
their faces were further darkened by their masks.
Although she'd had a white top on at one point, it was
now pretty much gray from the coal dust in the chute

they had slid down and from all the dirt she'd crawled through in the vent ducts and their other hiding places.

Parker was working his magic on the door and got them out of there in a few seconds. Opening the door let light in and earned them a few shots from above, but they were already out of there too quickly to be in serious danger from that direction.

"Where can we go?"

Sounds of fighting came from the hallways around them. He motioned to the nearest vent covering. *Oh God.* She had so hoped that they wouldn't have to go back there. But the funny thing was, in the face of men with automatic weapons, having to crawl through a vent didn't seem nearly as scary as it had before.

He helped her up before coming in after her and closing them in.

"Which way?"

Gunfire sounded from their right. He went left. Didn't want to risk a stray bullet, she supposed. He moved fast, faster than before. With all the din outside, they didn't have to worry as much about making noise. She put what she had into it and kept up, tried to keep her breathing slow and controlled. Anyone who thought a tight vent tunnel was claustrophobic never tried being in one with a gas mask over her face. Under different circumstances she would have freaked out a dozen times by now, but Parker's calm presence and strength radiated over her somehow. She focused on him. He was going to get them out of this.

When they came to a section that led down to the floor below, Parker took it and she was glad for that. She was hoping they would somehow end up near the hostages and be able to help them. She wanted to make sure nothing happened to the kids.

He waited for her at the bottom. Wouldn't move forward.

"Are you stuck?"

"There's another capsule ahead."

She held her breath for a second. Would have held it indefinitely if she could.

"Your mask is on good and tight?"

She checked. "It worked before. It should work now, right?"

"Back there, they used some juiced-up tear gas. This is some sort of chemical weapon. A whole other ball-park." He moved forward slowly.

She couldn't see, but he must have reached the capsule because he stopped again.

"Is there a freezer on this floor, too?"

"I wouldn't think so. Let's find a window that looks out onto the street." He picked up the capsule.

They crawled straight for what seemed an eternity. Einstein had been right. Time was relative. Kate was fairly certain that having a chemical weapon ready to blow in your face stretched it.

"We are coming to a T in the duct," Parker said. And when she didn't respond, he added, "Could be we reached the outside wall." He moved up to the next vent cover and stopped there, looked out. He held up two fingers.

Which probably meant two rebels in the room below them that he could see from his vantage point. He motioned to her to move back and she did, then a little more and a little more as he asked for it.

She held her breath as he put the capsule down and pulled his gun, aimed carefully.

Someone shouted below them, then bullets came through the wall, three of them where she had been only moments before. Parker shot again. Twice. Everything fell silent down below.

"Okay. All clear." He was going down already, caught her in his arms when she crawled after him.

"Are you going to try to throw it out the window?" she asked, keeping her eyes averted from the bodies on the floor.

He nodded, but moved in the opposite direction instead, flicking the light off and plunging them into darkness.

"Just as soon not give them a target. I'm sure there are sharpshooters up front." He crept to the window and looked out, then stepped aside and pressed himself to the wall next to it, opening the window with one hand.

"What about the people on the street?" she asked.

"I'm sure the French have the street secured by now. Probably the whole block."

Ornate bars bolted to the walls made it impossible for a person to pass through them. But the capsule would fit.

Parker moved back and took his camouflage shirt off, wrapped the capsule in it, and was left wearing a dark-gray undershirt that stretched over his flat abs and his impressive biceps.

"I don't want this thing to break and go off," he said.

"I'm aiming for the grassy patch on the traffic island. The French terror response units out there will have someone with the right tools to disable the damned thing."

He drew the capsule above his head with his right arm, swung a couple of times like a national league pitcher. And then he went for it.

The capsule sailed through the bars without trouble. Floodlights hit the window the next second. Kate squinted against the glaring light, backing away from the window as far as possible. But not before she caught sight of Parker's arm, heavily bleeding.

"When did you get shot?" She moved toward him instinctively.

Not here. No gunfire came from outside, just the sweeping floodlights.

"Back into the vent. Up, up, up." Parker was pushing her in front of him, not taking his chances.

"DID YOU get hit in the elevator shaft?" Kate's voice was thick with concern.

For him. Maybe there was hope for the two of them yet. Parker closed the vent cover behind him, making sure to have it flush against the wall. "Grazed."

He didn't want to give her one more thing to worry about.

"You can't know that. We'll have to stop somewhere and look."

"Believe me, a graze on the skin feels different enough from a shot through flesh and bone to know." He could recall several instances clearly. "You can look at it to your heart's content when we get out of here. But I think we should get going now."

"You've been shot before?" She began crawling forward, but was moving with clear reluctance.

He followed and kept quiet. He was good at blocking pain, a learned skill most people who were in his line of work eventually developed. You couldn't let pain distract you on a mission.

"Parker?" Her voice was a whisper, but a sharp whisper. She wasn't going to let this go.

"The scar on my lower back."

"Your dog bite?"

"They're more like shrapnel holes. I'm missing a kidney there."

"Oh my God." She sounded genuinely horrified.

"Not that bad. I had a spare." He made light of it, but the truth was the injury had very nearly cost him his life. If it hadn't been for Jake Kipper's quick thinking and expert care, it would have. Jake, who was dead now, along with the wife he had loved more than life itself.

The gunfire was receding in the distance.

"Do you think the rebels beat the Russians back?" she asked.

"I doubt it. Unless that is what the Russians want them to think."

"I expected a bigger attack."

"There'll be one. Count on it. Only three Alpha troopers rappelled into the dining room through the balcony. Could be they only came in to place some hidden cameras so they can figure out how to structure the main attack."

"How soon do you think that'll come?"

"I can't remember any cases when the Russians let a hostage situation go beyond seventy-two hours. After that, it gets hairy for the hostages without food and water and medical care." And it got dicey for the Russian authorities, who didn't like to appear as though they didn't have everything under control.

She reached a point in the duct where she could go down one more floor and did, making a slight noise that he didn't think would be noticed under the circumstances. The rebels would be focused on the intruding force, distracted by intermittent gunfire.

He slid down behind her, holding his arms out to control his fall. She had already moved forward in the duct to make room.

"We're on the ground floor now. West corner of the building," he told her.

"Can we get out through here?"

"The front entrance is probably heavily secured by the rebels. The back doors to the courtyard probably have a half dozen high powered rifles aimed at them."

"Where can we go, then?" she asked.

He could hear the desperation and the panic in her voice, but to her credit she didn't show any of that in her actions. "Back to the basement."

Her shoulders relaxed. Probably from the thought of being back with the girls again. "Good. We can stay put with the hostages until the Alpha Team or whatever takes the rebels out."

"Or not. I think it's time to get out of this place."

"But you said there was no way out of the basement." She glanced back at him.

He grinned under his gas mask and lifted his shoulder to jiggle the belts of TNT. "We are about to make one."

Kate picked up speed. Looked like she was fully behind the idea.

"Keep an eye out for funny-looking capsules," he said. There were still a number of things that could go disastrously wrong. But this was the only one he wanted to bring to her attention. The others they could do nothing about so there was no sense in wasting energy worrying over them.

"You think there's more?" Her voice was hesitant, but she didn't slow.

"So far we picked up one on the third floor and one on the second floor. Piotr couldn't have smuggled in many more without his buddies seeing it."

"You don't think the other rebels know about the capsules?"

"I don't think so. Remember how he kept looking over his shoulder while we watched him place the first capsule on the security video? I think this is his private agenda. He managed to lure his archenemy into this building. He's going to take the guy out no matter what it takes. Even if it means killing the rest of the rebels or killing himself, too, in the process. Keep your mask on and be prepared for anything."

They crawled in silence for a while before she asked, "How long has it been since the rebels took over?" Then she shook her head and gave a small groan. "It's bad enough I lose all sense of directions in the ducts. Now I'm losing my sense of time."

"Happens when you don't get enough sleep. And don't get enough outside light. And when you're under attack," he added after a moment. "Combat time doesn't feel like real time. It takes a while to get used to it."

Amazing that she had held up as well as she had, that she wasn't sobbing in some corner yet, hadn't given up. She was a strong woman, something he had always loved and respected about her. He glanced at his watch. "Two and a half days."

"What about it?"

He was getting used to the raspy way her voice sounded through the mask. It didn't remove any of the sexiness.

"That's how long we've been here," he said. "Two and a half days." And he was frustrated as hell that he hadn't been able to get her to safety in all that time.

"That can't be right," she said hesitantly.

"Seems half as long, doesn't it? Time flies when you're fighting for your life."

"The fighting picked up," she said.

"The Russians are about to start a full-out attack."

"How long do we have?"

"A couple of hours at best."

If they were lucky. If they weren't, they could have a lot less than that.

But even if they did reach the basement, there was no guarantee that the hostages were still there, that any of them were still alive. He had played down the scene he had caught on TV—that man being thrown from the balcony. But he was only too aware of the implications.

They couldn't discount the chance that the rebels had taken the basement. And even if they hadn't, he had little structural information on the building. The Colonel had been more concerned with the layout when he was passing information through the phone. There was a chance that they couldn't, in fact, blow their way out.

Which meant they'd be trapped.

Chapter Nine

They had wasted hours, time they didn't have, because the ducts didn't always follow the hallways, didn't always connect.

But they were finally in the home stretch, passing by the kitchen. Even if he didn't know from the quick but detailed description of the building's layout the Colonel had given him, the smell of fried oil and spices would have given it away.

Neither of them had eaten a decent meal for what seemed like forever. His stomach was so resigned to the lack of food, it had even given up growling. Kate was definitely getting slower.

And he feared that the worst of the fighting was yet to come.

"I'm so hungry my knees are shaking," she said, confirming that she needed nourishment to face what they had to on their way out.

And that was probably how all the hostages felt.

He figured they could get in and out of the kitchen in under two minutes. "Let's see if we can grab something. I'll go first."

Kate crawled past the vent hole to make room for him. He peered out, noted the deserted kitchen that looked as if a family of baboons had looted it, food wrappers and boxes tossed all over the place. He hoped the scavenging rebels had left at least a few bites of something edible behind.

He couldn't see anyone. Wouldn't have minded checking out the wall directly under him that he couldn't see from his current position, but his cell-phone camera didn't work with a dead battery.

He waited and listened. No sound of movement or breathing came from down below. The gunfire he heard was in the distance. Sounded as though the rebels were fighting on one of the higher floors.

He pushed out the vent cover, turned it and pulled it in so it wouldn't crash to the floor and attract attention. The kitchen doors were open. There could be anyone out there in the hallway, guarding this section of the building.

"Give me a minute to look around," he said over his shoulder and stuck his head out little by little, his handgun at the ready.

A gloved hand came up from below and clamped around his neck the next second, pulling him until he crashed headlong onto the tile floor. The fall rattled his brain, the hand nearly crushing his windpipe.

Damn. Anger flooded him and a split second of fear,

not for himself, but for Kate. If he stupidly let himself be killed, who was going to get her out?

He struggled for air behind the gas mask, fighting off the man as best he could. He couldn't get the gun between them, his hands blocked by the attacker's, their bodies twisted together as they rolled on the kitchen floor, groping for hold and leverage like wrestlers. The other guy had on a gas mask, too, his face obstructed.

The man was strong. Heavy, too, and unaffected by injury and hunger. He had to get Kate out of here.

"Go!" he yelled, his bruised windpipe hurting from the effort, hoping she would heed him, and not go into her typical leave-no-man-behind routine. She would have made a hell of a soldier. She was a hell of a woman.

"Get out of here," he ordered again in his best superior-officer tone that no man had ever dared refuse. Whoever the attacker was, he must have heard him talking to Kate before he'd stuck his head out of the vent, so the guy would already know Parker wasn't alone. Would already know Kate's position. He was giving no new information away.

He finally got his gun where he wanted it as they twisted, but so did the other guy. He heaved back. Both guns discharged at the same time, neither hitting its aim, but one leaving a hole high in the wall. Right about where the ducts were.

Parker swore, his breath hitching. "Kate?" he asked without daring to take his eyes off the enemy. They rolled again.

No answer came.

He chanced a glance that way. Couldn't see anything.

Dammit.

The guy went for Parker's gas mask with his free hand just as Parker grabbed for his, and they managed to unmask each other at the same time.

"Piotr?"

They both stilled for a split second. The man seemed surprised to see Parker, but got over it fast and rolled him. He was heavier by a good fifty pounds, and strong as the proverbial Russian bear. Working out had always been his religion. That was how Parker had first gotten to him—through his gym and his steroids supplier.

They rolled on the floor, among the garbage the foraging rebels had left strewn all over the place, until they banged into the kitchen island, sending pots and pans rattling inside.

"Working for the Kremlin now?" Piotr spat at him, but missed.

The man wasn't thinking clearly. But as soon as he had time to mull things over, he would know that Parker wouldn't switch sides, that he was still connected to the U.S. government. Piotr was a serious liability. To Parker personally, to his cover, to his team, to the current operation and operations to come. Piotr wouldn't sit on a piece of juicy information like this for long.

Parker heaved and got the upper hand, rolling them against a table. Plastic storage boxes bounced to the floor. He brought his right hand between them slowly, millimeter by millimeter, grunting along with Piotr. He almost had the guy when a bullet whizzed by him and he had to roll again, letting go of the man, giving up the gained ground.

The Alpha trooper dressed entirely in black who'd appeared out of nowhere kept on shooting at them. To him, the scene must have looked like two rebels had gone fist to fist over something, possibly food. He didn't give them time for explanations, nor could Parker have explained who he was and what he was doing here, even if the chance presented itself. He fired back while keeping on the move, working to get out of the open.

Then fire opened from another point. High up on the wall. *Kate.*

Which meant the round that Piotr had fired into the wall hadn't hurt her, or at least not too badly. Parker breathed a little easier. But damn it all, she wasn't supposed to be here. And she sure as hell wasn't supposed to engage the enemy.

She had surprised the Alpha trooper and distracted him long enough for Parker to roll behind a counter as near to Kate as he could get. He sprayed the room with bullets the next second, providing her with cover until she could crawl farther into the duct where she couldn't get hit. She had gotten him out of a tight spot, but now that he had everything under control, she needed to draw back and remove herself from harm's way. He kept up the rapid fire.

And swore when she tumbled out of the vent opening head-first, rolled across the floor and was by his side the next second. All he could do was stare. Even his finger stopped on the trigger. But it didn't seem the other two men cared. They used the lull to go after each other.

He scanned the room, noticed the small Russian army issue rucksack by the wall. Probably Piotr's. Most likely, he'd been in here to put another capsule in the very vent opening Parker had popped out of. What were the chances the remote control device was in the bag and not with Piotr?

At least the man was going nowhere for the moment. The Alpha guy had him pinned.

Parker rested his weapon and signaled to Kate to do the same with hers. "Let them kill each other." He looked toward his mask that lay in the middle of the kitchen where Piotr had ripped it off.

He should get that back before the bastard decided to set his knapsack off.

Kate had pulled her mask off at one point. He reached out and pulled it back into place, caressing what little skin it left bare with the back of a finger.

She held his gaze through the glass. "Who are they?"

"Piotr put out the capsules. The Alpha guy must be Victor, the man he'd been hunting most of his life." He'd already told Kate some of the story when the Colonel had given him the information.

Bullets flew in the air as the two men sparred. Parker drew Kate next to him to protect her with his body, kept his own weapon ready. The air was filled with the acrid smell of discharged weapons and plaster dust from the bullets that had missed their targets.

"How long are they going to keep at this?" she asked above the din.

"Until one of them is dead." He was pretty sure about that. He was hoping it'd be Piotr—before he had a chance to release whatever it was that he'd put in the capsules. Probably nerve gas. Hard to tell just by looking. Parker measured the distance to his gas mask.

Too far.

The men ran out of bullets at about the same time. There was a moment of silence, then Piotr roared. They went at each other like charging buffalo. Piotr was a big man, bigger than the other guy, but that one was solid muscle. The floor practically shook from their collision.

Both were bleeding, Parker registered, but neither was wounded fatally.

He could have finished them now, was ready to do it at a moment's notice. But something held him back. The men were no danger to Kate and him just now, their attention focused on each other as they were locked in a fight to the death.

Little by little, Piotr gained the upper hand. He didn't waste the momentary advantage. He put his considerable weight into it and choked the life out of his opponent with his bare hands, held the man down until he went limp.

"Okay." Parker rose, keeping his gun at him. "Now hand over the remote. I know about your capsules. You got what you wanted. Game over."

Piotr turned slowly, as if he'd forgotten in the haze of his murderous rage that anyone else was in there. He stood, took another look at the body at his feet, then pulled a small plastic device out of his pocket.

For a moment, Parker thought he *would* hand it over. Then Piotr reached for the gas mask hanging around his neck. He didn't seem inclined to listen to reason. Or maybe he was smart enough to know that whatever happened, Parker was never going to let him walk out of here.

Parker fired at the man's wrist. He wanted to make sure that a reflex twitch wouldn't push that button as it might have if he'd gone for the heart. He hit his aim as he'd known he would, and lurched for the remote that flew out of Piotr's destroyed hand, expecting the guy to do the same.

But Piotr made a run for the door, and by the time Parker came up with the remote, the man was gone from the kitchen, leaving a trail of blood behind him.

"Put that rucksack in the freezer," he told Kate. Thank God they were in the kitchen. He grabbed his gas mask. "Then get back into the duct and stay there until I come back." He sprinted after the man without looking back.

He hated to leave her alone, even if for a moment. But he couldn't let Piotr go and he could move faster without having to watch out for Kate.

KATE SHOVED the rucksack into the freezer, into a drawer on top that said Rapid Freeze. Then she ran after the men.

They charged into the staircase. She followed them, and could hear the door open then slam shut one flight down. The main level. She wasn't sure where they would come out. The resplendent lobby? Or these could be backstairs leading someplace else entirely. The door opened again. A hail of bullets came before it slammed shut this time.

"Parker?"

Sounds of energetic swearing came from below. Then she turned on the landing and could see him, the point of his knife in the lock as he tried to turn it.

"They locked us out?"

"I'm trying to lock *them* out. What are you doing here? Can't you follow the simplest order?" He gave her that hard, military-intimidation stare that seemed to be the new Parker's default expression. "Half the rebel force is out there, dammit."

A round of shots sounded the next second, proving his claim. Thankfully the door was bulletproof. They had a staircase like this at the U.S. embassy, as well, their "safe place" where all employees were expected to gather in case of an attack until they could be rescued. It was fire- and bulletproof with a vent that pumped in fresh air, no windows, designed to be able to withstand a lot if terrorists or rioters attacked the building.

Unfortunately, this staircase didn't go below the main level; it ended where Parker stood. They had to go back up and find another way to the basement to see if they could help the hostages and bust their way out of here with the explosives they had. She was glad Parker had had the presence of mind to arm those people.

He was running up the stairs, while behind him the rebels were pounding on the door, trying to break it down.

When they were up and out in the hallway again, Parker took the lead, heading back toward the kitchen. They rushed through, keeping an eye out for food, though not seeing any until Parker came across a bag of rolls and biscuits on a high shelf and they stuffed those into their pockets, a few stale croissants into their shirts.

When the food was safely tucked away, Kate headed toward the vent opening, but Parker said, "Piotr saw us coming out of there. They'll be looking for us in the ducts." He was searching again, opening pantry doors.

"What are you looking for?"

"Service elevator. According to the Colonel, the kitchen was moved to this floor from the ground floor recently. Since it no longer has a street-level entry for deliveries, they have to get stuff up here somehow. I doubt they bring sacks of potatoes through the marble grand foyer to the main elevator banks."

Made sense. She went to help. The first door she opened led to cold storage. The second revealed a dead-end hallway. And stainless-steel elevator doors. "Bingo."

She didn't expect much to happen, but she pushed the button anyway and was surprised when it lit up. "It works?"

Parker was next to her already. "The rebels might not know about it. They might have older information on the building, without the new kitchen."

Maybe his Colonel did, too. Otherwise, wouldn't he have given Parker the location of the service elevator? She didn't have much time to worry about that as the doors opened.

She grabbed a croissant out of her shirt and shoved nearly half of it into her mouth. She was so hungry it was a miracle her brain still functioned.

Parker smiled at her and did the same. "Should have

gone back to the duct until I came for you." He couldn't seem to be able to help himself from lecturing, but did it mildly.

"Could have stayed with me."

"I need the guy."

He explained to her how serious a security risk Piotr was. Piotr knew him. Could blow his cover, which would jeopardize his team and future missions.

"Why didn't you shoot him in the kitchen while you had the chance?"

He made a strange face, his cheeks puffing out with food. He looked unbearably cute in a very macho and dangerous way. God, he was the handsomest man she had ever seen. The only man who could turn her on with a look in the middle of a hostage crisis. She was one sick puppy. Or— No, she wasn't going to consider that. She was not, under any circumstances, going to fall back in love with Parker McCall.

"The guy Piotr took out, Victor Sergeyevich, was responsible for his father's death," he said, then fell silent.

"So you gave him a chance to get justice for that?"

He shrugged.

"But you *are* going to kill him, right? I mean, that's the goal."

"I have to."

She couldn't say she completely understood the workings of Parker's mind. He was operating under his own sense of justice at the moment it seemed. "Look, his father— When my father—"

He looked away from her, as if expecting some sort of judgment.

"Hey." She put a hand on his shoulder. "Piotr is the bad guy here."

He looked up with a surge of hope in his eyes. The breath caught in her throat. She swallowed the last bite of food. So did he. He leaned forward. She held her breath. Something dinged.

The service elevator was so slow it took a full minute to go down one floor, but they were finally there.

"Stand aside." Parker pulled back and stepped in front of her with his gun drawn. The doors opened. Bullets flew in.

Okay, so the rebels did know about the elevator. They hadn't disabled it for a reason. Maybe they needed it for a part of their plan.

Parker was shooting back, and she did, too, as best as she could from behind him. He was leaning on the Close-Door button with his free hand until, after an eternity, the thick metal doors slid together again.

"I was afraid of this," he said, his mouth set in a grim line.

"Are we trapped?" She was breathing hard, her heart going a mile a minute.

He looked up. "Not quite." Then he was reaching up, dismantling the ceiling. "Keep pushing the button so they can't open the door."

And they were trying. She could hear them. She fused her index finger to the button while Parker worked on getting them out of there. He had the decorative panel off in seconds revealing a small door. She'd only seen stuff like this in movies.

He jumped for the ledge and pulled up. The next

second, all she could see were his dangling feet. Then he was gone.

"Push the button for the kitchen." He reached back down for her. "Wish the damn thing went higher."

So did she. Whatever he had in mind, they only had about a minute before the elevator reached the kitchen, opened, and the rebels who would run up the stairs to meet it realized Kate and Parker weren't inside. It wouldn't take them long to figure out that they were up on top. She didn't see what Parker's plan was, but there was no time to question his judgment. She pushed the number one button, then reached for his hand and let him pull her up, trusting herself to him.

The elevator started with a shudder and some scraping sounds.

"Come on, we're getting off," he said.

"Here?" she asked, bewildered.

But he was already stepping over to a ledge of bunched wires on the side. There was enough room in the shaft for him to fit by the elevator if he flattened himself against the wall.

It looked dangerous. She peered down as the elevator inched past him, covering him up to the knees, then up to the waist.

"Come on."

She reached for a bundle of wires and stepped over quickly, holding her breath until she found sure purchase with her feet and both hands, sucking her stomach in and cursing her breasts, which stuck out. But she made it. Barely.

Deep breath. The elevator was rising, and she found

it harder and harder to stay still as the elevator neared her head. She felt trapped, about to be crushed. Not that being spread on the wall was her only worry.

"Aren't we going to get electrocuted?"

"Only if you touch the wrong thing," he said, perfectly calm.

"What's the wrong thing?" She had to yell to be heard. She might have yelled anyway. In fact, she decidedly felt like screaming.

"You'll know when you touch it," he said.

She felt the urge to escape, but panic kept her pressed to the spot. There was an equally strong urge to strangle Parker at the earliest opportunity. Which, after a moment, she did recognize as unreasonable. He hadn't gotten her into this situation.

Well, he did get her into *this* situation, but not the whole embassy-hostage-crisis deal. He'd come to save her. He just didn't realize that she wasn't a professional and that likely he was going to kill her in the process.

For a few moments she was completely blocked in by the elevator, the heavy machinery moving inches from her ears like some horrific creature, ready to grind her up. It pushed the air around, giving her the eerie feeling that the great beast was breathing down her neck.

"Parker…" she said in a weak voice, not expecting him to hear her over the noise. But his warm hand closed around her calf and anchored her, both to the wall and to reality. So maybe she could wait a little longer before she strangled the man.

Then the elevator passed by her, and Parker tugged. She wasn't about to move.

"Let's go."

Okay. But only because she couldn't stay here forever. She tried desperately to decide which wires were the wrong ones so as not to touch them.

They lowered themselves to the bottom of the shaft about fifteen feet below, careful not to step on anything that looked as if it might give them a nasty shock. The closed doors that led out of there were about waist high.

They listened first. No noise came from outside. The rebels had probably run up to meet the elevator in the kitchen.

Parker did something to the wiring on what looked like a maintenance panel, then jammed his knife in the slim slot where the doors met and pried them apart far enough so his fingers would fit in there. Nobody started shooting outside. Encouraging. After another moment, he was able to pull the doors open enough for them to fit through. He went first, then helped her out.

"Where are we?" she asked.

"In a back hallway near the embassy's courtyard."

There were no windows, only a steel-reinforced door. He tried that. Locked.

He glanced at the TNT belts on his shoulder, then said, "The Russians probably have all the exits covered. Let's get down to the basement and check on the hostages. We can always try this if we can't get out through there."

"Which way?" She'd gotten turned around again, enough so she couldn't remember where the basement door was. She had a deplorable sense of direction, something he used to tease her about back in the day.

He took off as sure as an arrow. She rushed after him, keeping her gun at the ready. They moved as fast as possible. It wouldn't take long for the rebels to figure out what had happened and come back down to look for them here. This was the only other exit from the elevator shaft.

They were in the back areas of the embassy, nowhere near the marble-tiled grand foyer and its twenty-foot-high ceiling. The hallways were narrow and the flooring the same heavy-duty tile usually used in hospitals. When they finally reached the basement door, they flattened themselves to the wall outside it, one on each side, stopping to listen.

No sounds came from downstairs. It could have been that the door was heavy enough to block any sound.

Parker reached out and turned the knob silently. It gave. That didn't bode well. Ivan was supposed to have barricaded the door.

She thought of Elena and Katja, her heart beating in her throat.

Parker looked at her.

"I shouldn't have let them go," she mouthed the words miserably.

He cocked his head and raised his eyebrows.

Okay, fine, so they'd been in a hairy spot or two since she'd sent the girls to what she'd thought was a safe place. So maybe they wouldn't have been better off with her. She was going to reserve judgment until she found them.

Parker went first and after a moment or two she followed.

They took the stairs one step at a time, careful not to make noise. Nobody was talking below, but there were some odd sounds and clothes rustling, so they knew there were people down there.

Had to be the hostages. *Alive.* She relaxed marginally. The rebels wouldn't just be hanging out down here when there was fighting going on upstairs. Instinct pushed her to rush forward, but common sense held her back.

Then Parker stopped and held up a hand, staring intently at something out of her range of vision. She stayed motionless for a minute, then took the few steps that separated them, using extra care not to make even the slightest noise.

A pair of feet came into sight first, then the torso of a man, lying on the ground at an uncomfortable angle, motionless. Then she could see the top of the chest, covered in blood, and knew, even before she could see the cook's vacantly staring eyes, that he was dead.

PARKER MOVED lower on the stairs, signaling to Kate to stay where she was, hoping this time she would listen. "Be careful," he mouthed, a last admonition before turning his full attention to what waited ahead.

Something had gone terribly wrong down there. The tension was so thick in the air he could smell it over the musty scent of the old brick walls that drew cold moisture from the ground.

He'd had visual of one body, but sensed more people

down here very much alive. Whether hostages or rebels, he didn't know. They were to the left, farther ahead where he wouldn't be able to see them until he reached the bottom of the stairs, stepped out and would be without cover. He moved inch by inch, registering and evaluating each and every sound, letting the cool of the basement surround him and revive him a little. The elevator shaft had been hellishly hot.

He stole down another step. Another body came into view. Black pants, white coat, same as the first. Another one of the kitchen staff. His stomach tightened.

When Kate and he had been down here, there'd been crates of salt to his left. But he couldn't count on them still being there. If they weren't, then with the next move he would be out in the open.

He didn't hesitate at the last step, just went around the corner.

The crates were there.

The surviving hostages, only eight, sat twenty or so feet from him on the floor, tied together and gagged this time. His gaze went to the two little girls first, who were pressed up against a young woman. He put a finger to his mouth lest somebody made some noise and betrayed him. The woman signaled something with her eyes to the kids. They stayed quiet. She fixed him with an urgent look and glanced toward the back of the basement, then at the people next to her.

He got it. He'd figured there were some rebels down here.

He quickly skimmed the rest of the hostages, taking in the red-rimmed eyes and exhausted faces, registering that Ivan was among them. He had expected him to hold up better and protect the rest.

He stepped farther out, not exactly into the open, but away from the cover of the salt crates, keeping his focus on the dark places in the shadows, looking for the enemy. A man or two, no more. Just enough to keep an eye on the hostages. The rebels couldn't spare more when a desperate battle was raging above.

He saw movement in a maze of boxes, shot at the shadow of a man and was shot back at. On instinct, he rushed forward, keeping low to the ground, putting himself between the rebel soldier and the hostages. Then a blunt force hit his left shoulder from behind, as if he'd been smacked by a football at top speed.

But this wasn't a varsity game, and he knew what being shot felt like.

This was it.

Chapter Ten

Kate stood back, higher up the stairs, waiting for Parker's go-ahead signal. But instead, when he got to the bottom, he stepped around the wall and she couldn't see him. She couldn't see anyone. She had no idea what was going on when the first shot exploded.

Her brain was screaming to get out of there. Her heart pushed her forward, toward Parker.

More shots came. She held her gun at the ready as she carefully crept down the stairs, pressed against the wall, going sideways so she would present as small a target as possible if someone came running up. Parker had told her to do that. He'd given her a dozen small tips for staying alive while they'd been stuck in various places in the last three days.

Not that he followed his own advice. Whenever they were together and heading into trouble, he always went first to block as much of her as possible.

She listened, jittery enough to jump out of her skin

at the next shot. And another, and another. Still nobody
had said a word down there. She could smell her own
fear in the air, her mouth as dry as the dusty vent ducts
had been. She was no soldier. Her index finger twitched
on the gun's trigger. *Not good.* What in hell did she think
she was doing here?

Saving Parker.

She steadied her hands and eased down another step.
She saw the dead bodies first. Hostages. Her heart
clutched. She moved lower, and then she saw him in the
crossfire, ducking bullets as best he could with no cover.
Her heart tripped when she spotted the blood on his
shoulder. A man sitting among the hostages was shooting at him from one side. Ivan? What— Another took
potshots from behind the solid cover of a stone wall in
the far corner.

She aimed at Ivan. His Russian dress uniform—obviously it had been a cover—stood out. He was sitting
among the hostages, making it hard for Parker to fire
back as men and women scrambled around, some
shouting, trying to get out of harm's way unsuccessfully,
frustrated by the ropes that bound them. She spotted the
children—*alive,* thank God, still unharmed. They were
crying, but their voices were lost in the cacophony of
the attack.

Parker ducked behind some boxes finally, not that
they offered any protection. The bullets Ivan shot at
him sliced straight through the cardboard. And he was
still open to the attacker on his other side. He was
focusing on holding that man back, reluctant to shoot
toward the hostages.

The pop and bang of bullets echoed in the basement. At any moment the rebels could reach them, following the sounds of a gunfight. But before that happened, there was a chance that the Russians could gas the building, or one of the human-bomb rebels could blow it or if Piotr had another capsule, he could set that off.

Moving, trying anything seemed futile against such overwhelming odds. Part of her wanted to fall to the floor and curl up where she was, and hope that when the end came, it would be quick. Her mind was numb with the possibilities of death.

She couldn't afford numb. The problem manager in her mind took over.

Parker needed her help. The girls needed her, and so did the other hostages. She drew a deep breath and cleared her thoughts as best she could, resolving to work on the disasters that threatened them one at a time. First, the one right in front of her.

She gripped her gun. Nobody had noticed her yet in the mad fight. She had a different view of Ivan than Parker, a better angle. She adjusted the gun's sight until she had the man's head in the crosshairs. When she got him, she wanted him to drop instantly, without being able to cause any more damage to Parker or the kids or the other hostages.

It was different from target practice. There she normally visualized the hit and focused on the hole the bullet would leave in the paper. But she blanched at the thought of a bullet busting through Ivan's skull, even if he *was* the enemy. A real person was nothing like the shadow outline at the range.

And what if she missed? There were hostages around him. Bet Parker never thought about missing. He saw what had to be done and did it.

She had to try. He had seconds left at best. Nobody could last longer in his current untenable position.

As the hostages scrambled away from between Parker and Ivan, scared that a stray bullet would find them, Ivan filled the gap by grabbing Katja and holding her in front of him.

Parker couldn't do anything now. But she could. Ivan still hadn't noticed that she'd come down the stairs, and in her direction, his side and head were still unprotected. Katja, however, did look at her, tears streaking her cheeks.

Cold fury steadied Kate as she watched the hard grip Ivan kept on the child's arm, yanking on her when she struggled against him. She took a deep breath, held it so her body wouldn't move, then squeezed the trigger.

She didn't hit her intended target, little wonder. But the bullet did go through Ivan's neck. He dropped his gun and Katja at the same time to clasp both hands to the wound, turning to give Kate a surprised look. A couple of men from among the hostages threw themselves on top of him the next second. Anna, the young woman who'd sat next to her in the gym at the beginning, threw herself on the children to protect them from the bullets that kept coming from the corner. Another hostage finally got hold of Ivan's gun and shot back.

She could only pray that he was a good shot and wouldn't hit Parker.

The sound of boots came from somewhere above her head.

No, no, no. She lunged back up the stairs, taking them two at a time, and locked the door, knowing the simple lock could only hold them for a few seconds.

She clicked the safety on her weapon and shoved it into the waistband of her pants. A handful of wooden boards lay on the shelving that lined the staircase. She grabbed those and wedged them against the door.

She searched desperately for anything else that she could use to strengthen the barricade, knocking tools and a length of rope to the ground, finding an axe that she could think of no use for. Then she accepted that this was the best she could do, and ran back to Parker.

Whoever was in the corner of the basement was still shooting at him. She stuck her head out from the cover of the staircase, then ducked back quickly when the next shot came her way.

"Stay where you are," Parker called out.

She didn't have to be told twice.

At least he was still alive. The same couldn't be said for Ivan. The hostages were using his body for cover. They seemed to have finished the job she had started. His neck looked broken.

Another one of the hostages had the gun now, the tall, young guy whose cooperation she had tried to get unsuccessfully in the gym. He wasn't shooting, however. She supposed he couldn't clearly see the rebel soldier in the corner from where he was and he didn't want to risk hitting Parker. She appreciated the restraint.

Anna was still protecting the children. Everyone was

trying to get their ropes off. She wished she could get to them and help, but Parker had asked her to stay, and if she lunged forward she might distract him.

To hell with that. She had to help. She could just warn him that she was going over. She opened her mouth to call out just as he dropped and rolled, found better cover, the giant steel toolbox. He'd left streaks of blood on the cement floor where he touched down. *Shot.* He'd been shot again. Judging from the blood on the ground, this time it was more serious than just a graze. He looked strong and alert, as capable as ever, but at this rate, she was worried how long that could possibly last.

They'd made it this far together. There was no way she would hang back in the stairway and watch him get killed.

The hostages seemed to be able to manage on their own for now. She had to get to Parker and help him, see how bad his latest injury was.

"Coming." Kate bent low and dashed toward him, yelling, "Cover me!" to the hostage who had the gun, hoping like hell that the man spoke English.

He did, and she reached Parker with only a few bullets whizzing by her. Blood pumped through her ears so loudly she could barely hear what he said, but she had no problem interpreting the black thunder on his face.

"I said stay, dammit," he yelled, popped up to fire a few shots over the large steel box then ducked back down again. "Kate, listen to me." He cupped her face with his free hand, forcing her to look at him. His whole body was wound tight, his features hard, his stance promising violence. But not to her. His hand remained gentle. "I'm trying to keep you alive."

"I'm fine."

"You were in a safer position on the stairs. Do you want to die?" His tone reflected his frustration. He let her go and popped up to fire another round.

"Do you?" She grabbed his arm then put her gun on the floor and ripped his shirtsleeve off, used it to wrap the arm and slow the flow of blood. The bullet had gone clear through the thick cords of muscle.

He kept taking shots the whole time, not at all interested in making her job easier. She did it anyway. He could be stubborn, but so could she.

"Are you okay?" he asked when he dropped down again and looked her over.

She was not okay. Frankly, she thought it was a major miracle that they were still alive. She was hungry and tired and ached just about everywhere. She was pretty close to losing it, more scared than she had ever been in her life. But Parker needed backup. And the hostages were depending on them.

"Good as new," she said.

He gave her a look that said she hadn't fooled him. "It's almost over."

She hoped he was right.

"I can't see him. I'm never going to hit him from here. I have to get closer," he said.

She didn't want him to go. "I'll cover you."

He moved fast, in a zigzag pattern. She shot round after round, aiming well over his head to make sure she didn't hit him by accident. She didn't stop firing until he was safely behind a half wall.

And then he disappeared.

She blinked, trying to bring his outline into focus in the deep shadows. But as hard as she stared, he didn't seem to be there. She hadn't heard any noise, either.

Silence enveloped the basement. The rebel soldier was probably listening for Parker, trying to figure out where he was. The hostages waited for their fate to be decided. They knew their best bet for getting out of here was Parker. Because even if the Tarkmez soldier in the corner got put out of commission, they still had a full rebel team in the building. Kate glanced toward the staircase, surprised that nobody had broken through her makeshift barricade yet. Could be that whoever was coming this way had been waylaid by the Russians. She hoped so. Their plate was kind of full for the time being down here.

A second ticked by, then another. Silence stretched, and as more and more time passed, the tension became nerve-racking.

Maybe Parker had passed out from blood loss. She couldn't accurately judge how much time had passed since he'd gone. It felt like an eternity. Could be he'd reached the rebel and they'd silently knifed each other to death.

Another minute or so passed before the rebel called out, words she didn't understand. Didn't sound like he was giving up, more like taunting.

Okay, that one was still alive. What about Parker?

She wished he, too, would say something, but understood that it would give away his location.

The muted sounds of gunfire came from a couple of floors above them. Sounded like the Russians were well into the building.

The rebel in the corner made a surprised sound, drawing her attention back to him. There was a single gunshot, then some scraping noise. Then complete silence again.

"Parker?" She didn't worry about giving away her location. Everyone already knew where she was.

For a second, no response came, and her heart stopped in midbeat.

The battle seemed to be intensifying upstairs. But her full attention was on Parker as he came out of the shadows. He looked tired and bloody, but he walked tall, his eyes finding her immediately. And what she saw in those eyes took her breath away as effectively as the danger had just moments ago.

She had been crazy to think she could ever walk away from him.

He stopped a foot from her and picked up the TNT belts from the floor, even managed a grin, although she could tell it took some effort. "Let's leave with a bang."

"You know what to do with that?" she asked as a vivid picture of the whole building collapsing on their heads flashed into her mind.

"Does Bugatti make the best cars?" His grin grew wider.

Not only did he know his way around plastic explosives, he looked as though he actually enjoyed playing with them.

He handed her his knife. "Why don't you go check on the hostages? I'll take care of the escape route."

"Okay," she said, and did as he asked.

Half the hostages were already free of their ropes, having helped each other. She helped the rest.

"Almost over," she told the ambassador's daughters, who were tightly hanging on to each other. "We are leaving here in a minute."

"I want my mommy," the younger one said as new tears welled in her beautiful brown eyes.

"Soon," she lied and ran a soothing hand over her mussed-up hair. "Would you like something to eat?" She emptied her pockets and shirt and every bite of food was snatched up in a second.

Only one of the hostages stayed motionless on the ground. Anna.

Kate moved to her side. "Are you okay?" Then she gasped as she turned her and saw the blood on the woman's chest. A stray bullet had found her as she had shielded the children with her body.

"Parker?" She pressed her hand to the wound, and Anna's eyes fluttered. "We're going to get you out of here," she whispered to the woman.

The girls pressed up against her, one on each side, hanging on to her, watching Anna wide-eyed.

"Keep her still," Parker said, looking over from where he was rigging up the charges.

"Is she going to die?" Katja asked.

"No, honey. She's hurt but she is going to be fine."

The sounds of fighting from above were growing louder. The Alpha troopers were getting closer.

Parker said something in Russian to the hostages. Everyone put on their gas masks, shoving in the last pieces of food first. Kate helped Anna and the girls.

"It feels funny," Elena said, trying to take hers off after a few seconds.

Kate stayed her hands. "Let's pretend it's a game," she said. "Do you know what Halloween is?"

The girls shook their heads.

"Do you ever put on a costume to look like a princess or a pirate or anything like that?"

"A masquerade?" Elena's voice sounded strange through the mask and they giggled.

"Let's pretend it's a masquerade."

"What are we?" Katja asked with caution, not completely buying the story yet.

"Monsters," Kate said, offering the first thing that came to mind. "Undersea monsters."

"Where are your fins?" Elena asked.

She improvised. "We are finless monsters."

"Everything in the sea has fins," said Elena doubtfully.

Kate's mind worked in slow motion, unable to ignore the dying woman in her arms. She couldn't fall apart. She couldn't let the kids see how desperate the situation was. "Not everything." She scrambled for an example, relieved when she found one. "The octopus doesn't."

"You don't look like an ocpopus." Katja touched her hand. "You don't have enough arms. You look like Shrek. Except for the ears."

She glanced around at the others and could see no re-
semblance to the animated figure, except that the gas
masks had a greenish tint. "Do you like Shrek?"

"She loves *Shrek*," Elena said. "We watched it in
Russian and in English, too. Mrs. Miller lets us watch
movies in English. She said it helps our pronceation."

Pronunciation, most likely. Kate smiled without cor-
recting her. "Sounds like a smart woman. Your English
is very good."

"Where is Mrs. Miller?" the younger one asked.

"She got hurt," Kate said after a moment of hesitation.

"Is she dead?" Elena asked.

"I'm not sure," she told them. She hated lying but the
situation was still dangerous. They had to keep their
cool. They had to get out of here. It would be better for
the children to stay as calm as possible. She couldn't tell
them in the middle of utter chaos that their parents *and*
their nanny were dead.

"You should be Princess Fiona. You know, when she
is an ogre," the younger one said. "Your voice sounds a
little like Fiona."

Her gaze sought out Parker, who was now working
with a couple of men by the wall. He had a makeshift
scale made from a stick, two small boxes and some
rope. He was measuring TNT against bags of salt.

Measurements that would be crucial.

She hoped his scale was up to the job.

Next he inspected the walls of the two-hundred-year-
old palace. God knew what TNT was going to do to
them. Parker knew, she corrected herself. He looked as

though he knew exactly what he was doing. He was drilling a hole straight through the wall. Probably to measure the thickness.

"I have to go to the bathroom," Elena said.

"Me, too," her sister chimed in immediately.

"Can you ask that lady?" Kate motioned with her hand toward one of the hostages.

But Katja wouldn't let her go. "I want you to come with me," she begged.

The woman must have understood English, because she came over to put her hand on Anna's wound. But Kate was reluctant to let go, and when she did, she couldn't look away from the blood that covered her hands. And the girls were reaching for her.

She wiped her palm on her black slacks as best she could before Katja and Elena grabbed on to her. Not that she had any idea where to take them. She headed toward an out-of-sight corner of the basement, hoping they would come across an old mop bucket.

But Parker was speaking in Russian again. Then to her. "Get behind cover."

"Can you wait another minute?" she asked the girls, relieved when they nodded.

She followed the rest of the hostages to the half wall Parker had hidden behind earlier. They squatted snugly against each other. Everyone except Parker.

Then he came flying around the wall. "Keep your heads down. She's gonna blow."

Kate tightened her arms around the girls. "Plug your ears."

The explosion that shook the basement the next second knocked them off their feet.

August 12, 03:10

"STAY DOWN," Parker said in Russian then repeated in English for Kate's sake. He straightened to look at his handiwork in the settling dust, and smiled. "Okay. Let's get going."

He strode to the hole first, kicked a few bricks out of the way, checked a couple more overhead to make sure they wouldn't fall on anyone. He looked through the hole. The basement floor in the neighboring building was at least eight feet below them, the space narrow. He looked closer as the dust settled. Maybe it wasn't a basement at all, but some sort of secret passageway that had been walled off. The important thing was that it led out of here.

"Hurry." He helped the first guy over, held him by the arms and lowered his bulk, the man's feet dangling. Then he let go and the man landed with a thud on the floor below. Parker tossed a flashlight after him. "Everything okay?"

"Da," the man responded in his own language.

The next man had an easier time as he had assistance both from above and below. Then came the next and the next, Parker getting a number of handshakes and thank you's.

The children went next, clinging to Kate.

"I'll be coming in a second," she soothed them.

And he after her. He would see her to safety then

come back for Piotr. That would have to be dealt with. Soon. Once he had made sure Kate was safe.

He helped a woman down, looking at Anna. Now that the girls had gone ahead, Kate was back at the young woman's side again. Getting Anna down would be difficult. She was unconscious and wouldn't be able to hang on to anything.

Kate caught his gaze. "I think I saw a good chunk of canvas on the shelf by the stairs. We can lower her in that." She ran off for it.

Parker helped another guy in the meantime, then the next woman. It was slow going. She was shaky from nerves and exhaustion. All the hostages were dehydrated and weak from hunger. Whatever little food Kate and he had been able to share hadn't meant much after three days.

The woman slipped several times, and he was about to recommend that she wait and be lowered in the canvas, too, but then she finally made it, teary-eyed from the effort.

Only Anna was left. She was coming to, but was still too weak to move. While he made a rudimentary bandage for her chest to slow the blood loss, he explained to her how they would lower her through the hole.

"You need help up there?" he called up the stairs. The force of the explosion could have knocked over the shelves. Kate was taking too long.

No response came. The short hairs prickled at his nape.

He pulled his gun. "You go. Quick," he told the

hostages who were already on the other side. "Stay here," he instructed Anna. "I'm going to come back for you." Then he was off, running for the stairs.

Empty.

His heart about stopped, his lungs too tight to draw in air. He couldn't let anything happen to Kate now. They had a way out. They'd made it this far, against all odds. In minutes they would be free and clear.

But Kate had disappeared, and the basement door was open. He saw the boards on the stairs, figured she had put those up earlier. She'd been under a lot of stress. She hadn't thought to check that the door opened outward. The boards had meant nothing. And the explosion probably had blown the door open. Then Kate went up. And someone who had come to investigate the noise grabbed her.

Parker moved up the stairs with care, watching for any sign of a possible ambush waiting for him at the top. He should have gotten her out of here immediately, no matter the cost. He should have thrown her across his shoulder, should have knocked her out if he'd had to.

If anything happened to her—

He never had any trouble with his focus; his survival depended on it in his line of work. But he was having trouble now, thinking beyond the fact that the bastards had her. It would take them minutes to figure out that she wasn't one of the embassy staff. She didn't speak Russian.

He got to the top, gun ready, moving inch by slow inch when he wanted to fly to her. But he couldn't get killed. To save her, he couldn't afford as much as a single wrong move.

He stepped forward, low. Quick look to the left. Clear. Kicked the door shut so he could look behind it. Nobody there. The hallway was empty in both directions.

For a moment he thought of Anna, waiting for him down below. He wasn't going to forget about her, but for now she had to wait. He hoped her weakness came more from lack of food and water than from her wound. She wasn't bleeding that badly. Then again, she could be bleeding internally. He had promised that he'd be back for her. And he would. But he had to get Kate before it was too late.

The sounds of combat filled his ears. He listened for Kate's voice. Any words of arguing, crying or screaming. He heard nothing.

Out-and-out war was being fought on the floors above him. Machine-gun fire, small explosions. Smoke lingered in the air. Judging from the sounds, the battle was at a fever pitch, neither side holding anything back.

Anger and desperation gave him new strength, until he could barely recall his own injuries. He pushed forward with grim determination.

The building was a death trap.

And he had lost Kate.

Chapter Eleven

August 12, 03:30

"Don't. Please." She fought against the beefy man who was dragging her along, keeping his gun firmly pressed against her temple. Piotr. She recognized him from earlier when he'd fought with Parker in the kitchen.

The man with the chemical-agent capsules. The man who had nothing to lose. That put her at a serious disadvantage when it came to negotiating with him. He probably figured that since he had succeeded in avenging his father's death, he could die happily now, whatever happened. Great.

"Can we just stop and talk?" She tried anyway. She'd come too far to give up now.

He didn't bother to respond. He held his gun in his left hand. His right wrist, which Parker had shot, was bandaged with a piece of blood-soaked cloth. Didn't seem to slow him down much.

He had come out of nowhere, from behind her as she had tried to free the canvas for Anna from all the junk on one of the shelves. The explosion had rattled the door enough to shake off the boards. He must have had the lock already opened by the time she got up there. He'd been lurking outside, waiting.

She could have screamed for Parker, but she didn't want to draw Piotr's attention to the people who were escaping through the basement. She wanted to keep him away from the rest of the hostages, from Anna and the kids. So she went with him, struggling only to slow him down as much as possible.

Parker would come for her. She knew it in her heart. In the past she'd been angry at him for never being there for her, for always being away when she needed him. But in the last couple of days she'd gotten to know him better than she ever had before. And she realized that when she'd truly needed him, he'd always been there.

Maybe he hadn't come along to pick out china patterns, but he had been there in the Florida night when those thugs accosted her. There were times a woman *thought* she needed her man. Then there were times when she *truly* needed him. So he'd never gone shopping with her. But the truth was, while she'd been out shopping, he'd been out saving lives, lives of people like Anna and the kids below. She wished she'd known that.

"Move it." Piotr shoved her roughly.

Parker will come. She fixed the thought firmly in her mind. She believed in him and trusted him one hundred percent. She'd thought him undependable before, too focused on his reporting career to care about others. She'd been wrong. She wanted to live long enough to tell him that.

But living even a few more minutes seemed less than likely.

She no longer had her gun, was grateful that at least her mask hadn't been ripped away from her face. Her captor wore his own. Smoke rolled through the hallway he dragged her along. Smoke and maybe something else. Bodies lined the floor, most of them rebels, only two Russian elite-force soldiers so far that she could see.

She looked for signs of what had killed the men. Plenty of bullet holes in the bodies. Which didn't mean that there wasn't gas in the air.

He dragged her into the back staircase that was deserted at the moment. They went up.

"Please let me go. I have nothing to do with this. I'm an American." She figured at this stage she had nothing to lose by revealing that. Things were already as bad as they could get.

"I know all about Americans." The man then picked up speed as fresh gunfire sounded from above.

"Listen to me. I'm the American Consul. I can be your ticket out of here." She gasped for air. He was going way too fast, not letting her catch her breath. "We can walk right out of here, the two of us. Nobody will hurt you as long as you have me."

They exited the staircase and rushed down the long corridor ahead, took several turns. The man shoved her into some nicely furnished parlor that looked as though it had seen its share of fighting tonight. Chairs and antique tables lay broken on the expensive carpet, bullet holes pocked in the walls. The lights were off, but she could see clearly since floodlights lit the front of the building from the outside and the large French doors that lined one wall let plenty of light into the room.

They'd come up two flights of stairs and she had no idea of her location otherwise.

"We have to go back down. We have to get out of the building. We can go out the front. The media is there. Nobody will shoot you with me in front of you."

Movement caught her eye on the other side of the French doors. Her breath caught. Parker? The Russians?

It meant the difference between life and death. She didn't dare look that way, afraid that if it was Parker, she'd give him away. But whoever it was didn't come in. She waited, her captor talking into his cell phone, barking questions and instructions she didn't understand.

Come on, Parker. Come on.

She moved so he would have a clear shot if that was what he was waiting for, pulling away from Piotr as much as he allowed her. She waited for the shot. Nothing happened.

Her captor put away his phone and focused on her. She had to keep him occupied.

"I know the freedom of your people is important to you. If you die here today, you won't be able to fight for it again. It's useless to die now. This battle is lost. But if you stay alive, you can help your people win the war. I can help you get out of here safely."

She was handling the situation. Managing the problem. She managed everything. That was who she was, what she did. Except she'd never been able to manage Parker, and she realized only now, too late, that a man like Parker could never be managed. Should never be managed.

Piotr grabbed for her with his left hand as quick as a snake and ripped her gas mask off, tossing it aside.

"I'm fighting for no people. I'm fighting for me," he said. "I already got what I came here for."

And she remembered now Parker telling her that he wasn't even Tarkmezi. He was Russian, with his own agenda—an agenda that had already been accomplished. Which didn't leave her with much leverage.

She gasped the smoky air. Her lungs contracted as if they were ready to collapse. Oh God, there *was* gas in the air.

She clawed at her throat, scared out of her mind now, her eyes filling with tears. But a few minutes passed and she was still alive, and she realized her reaction was caused by the smoke and her own panic. She fought to slow her breathing and get a lungful of air.

"Who are you?" Piotr watched her dispassionately with eyes that looked small and watery blue through the glass of his mask.

"I'm a Consul of the United States of America. We have to help each other." She coughed.

"What are you doing here?" he asked, then, "Doesn't matter." He had relaxed his gun for a few moments, but now he pressed it hard against her head again.

She gasped for breath, expecting it to be her last, casting a desperate glance to the French door. And caught sight of movement again, and this time, she could see what it was. She could have cried with despair.

Out there, in the night breeze, fluttered the white,

blue and red cloth of the Russian flag. That was the movement she had mistaken for Parker.

They were at the front balcony of the building, the place the rebels had used to throw out bodies of hostages to make a point in front of the press who camped outside.

And she was the last hostage they had. Parker was even now saving the others through the basement.

Her limbs froze. She understood with terrifying clarity what Piotr's plan was.

Parker was coming for her. She had no doubt of that. But he had no way of knowing where she was. And there was fighting all over the building. He might be held back for a while yet.

Time was something she no longer had.

What they said about your life flashing through your mind before you die was true. Scenes of her and Parker flickered across the TV screen of her brain—the good times and the bad. She wanted to tell him that she was sorry that she had walked away without giving him a second chance. God, she wanted to tell him so much, wanted to feel his arms around her one last time.

But the cold metal of the barrel pressed against her temple as Piotr shoved her toward the French doors that led to the balcony.

"This is for that interfering bastard friend of yours," he said.

HE KNEW exactly where they would take her. And if he was right, she didn't have much time.

Parker burst into the staircase.

Unfortunately, two rebels crashed through the door on the level above him at the same time. He shot without hesitation, got one of them, but the other flattened himself in the doorway. Parker crept upward, glad that whatever negligible noise he made was swallowed by the sounds of battle above.

When he came to the turn in the stairs where he presented a clear target, he blanketed the enemy position with fire. No answering shots came. He found out why when he reached the top of the stairs. The second guy was dead, too.

He stepped over the bodies, ran up one more flight and pushed the door open slowly. Thin smoke settled like fog in the hallway. He heard plenty of fighting, but saw none of it at the moment and was keen to take advantage of that.

Something heavy crashed to the floor above him. Much heavier than a body. Furniture? He ran toward the front of the building.

He found fighting as soon as he turned the corner. A black-clad Alpha trooper was holding off two rebels. He had nothing against the Alphas; they were a fine special-forces team. But right now, the guy was standing between him and Kate, holding him back, and that he could not allow. The rebels had noticed Parker and were shooting at him already. He shot back, clearing the way before him.

The guy in black didn't give himself easily. His skill level was several notches higher than the rebels' and his bulletproof vest was a good one, with a ceramic insert that stood up to rifle fire as well as handguns. But there were places it didn't cover. And Parker was an excellent shot. The man went down.

He picked up the guy's semiautomatic rifle and checked it for ammunition. Half a magazine. He shoved his handgun, which was close to empty, into the back of his waistband then broke into a run.

He found the right hallway, but didn't know which was the right room.

An explosion came from somewhere above, toward the back of the building. The rear balcony? Gunfire intensified. A full-on attack. Did that mean the hostages had made it out so the Alpha troops knew they no longer had to worry about them?

He opened one door after the other. Some rooms stood untouched, while others showed signs of combat: smashed furniture and bullet holes in the walls and flooring. Then he got to the right one, could hear Kate's voice through the closed door. He couldn't make out the words, but the fear and desperation came through. He backed up a step and kicked the door in.

"Parker!"

Two things claimed his immediate attention: Piotr, who held a gun to Kate's head and was just about to take her out to the balcony, and the Vymple team guy, who entered the room through another entrance at the same time as Parker had.

Vymple was the Russian special forces. The Colonel had told him they were here along with the Alpha troops, but this was the first guy he'd seen.

Parker's gun was trained on Piotr. Piotr kept his on Kate. The newcomer put Parker in the crosshairs. A three-way standoff. And two out of the three men in the room probably didn't care much who lived and who died.

Kate coughed.

The smoke was getting thicker. She was the only one who didn't have a mask.

Piotr surprised them all by tossing Kate aside in a sudden movement, practically slamming her into the floor, and shooting at the Russian with a fierce cry, hitting his target with the first shot, right through the left eye glass.

The next second his gun was on Parker. Kate was now between him and Piotr so he had to be careful. She was coughing again, trying to come to her feet, but went down again.

Was she hurt? He could see no blood. Dammit. What was in the air? He needed to know how much danger she was in.

"I don't know how my friends missed you, but I'm not going to make the same mistake, McCall."

"Since when do you have Tarkmez friends?"

"Since they promised to give me what I want."

"Victor?"

"My only regret is that it was over so fast. I would have preferred to savor it."

"So he's dead. You have what you wanted."

"What I want is another forty years, but I'm not likely to get it. The doctors give me six months at the most. But you, you have nine lives. I sent four of my best men after you when I realized you followed me to Paris.

You're supposed to be three days dead and six feet under. And yet here you are."

Parker watched the man, wondered what his illness might be—he didn't look weakened yet, whatever it was—realized that his plan was probably to go out in a blaze of glory instead of a hospital bed. Piotr was here on a suicide mission.

He wasn't surprised that Piotr had sent the men after him. He had suspected as much. Piotr seemed to be at the center of a lot of things.

"You're all right, you know," the man was saying now. "Almost as good as I am. Just have bad judgment. Picked the wrong side."

"How about we let her go?" Parker nodded toward Kate without taking his eyes off Piotr. "Then we'll see who is better. Just you and me. A man deserves a little fun before dying."

Piotr seemed to consider the offer for a moment, but then shook his head.

Parker tossed his rifle as if giving up, then pulled his handgun from the back of his waistband. The bullet hit Piotr in the throat.

He was beside Kate before the man even hit the ground, ripping Piotr's mask off and securing it on her face. "Are you okay?" He kept his weapon on Piotr to be on the safe side.

"I think so."

But she wouldn't have been that way for long, a fact that became obvious when Piotr began to twitch on the floor, his eyes going wide, drool running out of his mouth. He wouldn't have done that from the shot. Somebody had just released nerve gas in the air.

"Let's go." He pulled Kate up and grabbed her by the arm, glanced back when she hobbled.

"What's wrong with your leg?"

"I don't know. It doesn't seem to hold me up," she said just as another explosion shook the building. "I can limp along."

"Not fast enough."

He picked her up in his arms, looking for blood again and still not finding any. So she hadn't been hit by a stray bullet. She must have torn a tendon or dislocated her ankle. No time to stop and look at it.

The smoke in the hallway was blacker and thicker than just minutes ago. He saw open flames to his right so he turned left.

"Hang on tight." He could only support her with one arm; the other he needed to hold his weapon.

The conditions in the building were deteriorating fast. They needed to take the shortest way out. One floor down and through the main lobby.

His left arm was still bleeding, not terribly so, but he had lost enough blood by now to make him feel weaker. Add to that the lack of food and sleep and he knew he wasn't in top shape. It would come down to seconds and to his last ounce of strength. He pushed forward with everything he had.

One rebel was running up the main staircase. His first shot at Parker went wide. The second didn't go anywhere. He was out of bullets. He was a young guy, without a mask, the fear on his face distorting his features.

Parker lowered his weapon and ran by him on his way down the wide stairs.

Then they were in the main lobby where four rebel soldiers held the main entrance, barricaded with desks and chairs and whatever furniture they had been able to find. One of them was wearing a TNT belt.

Their attention was focused outward so Parker had a split-second chance to step behind the row of metal detectors to the side. The Russian embassy had a pretty decent system to scan entering visitors.

Kate must have been thinking the same because she asked, "How do you think the rebels got in here in the first place?"

"Could be they had inside help." Ivan came to mind. Could be he was Piotr's connection. "I figure Piotr gave the rebels Ivan and a way in, and in exchange the rebels brought him along, giving him a chance to take out Victor, who was pretty much guaranteed to be here."

Piotr was the only Russian among the attackers, a man with connections everywhere. Ivan was also Russian. Could be he hadn't even fully known what he was doing when he'd compromised embassy security for Piotr. They'd had a deal. That was why he was the only embassy guard the rebels had left alive.

"I am sorry about before. When I left—" Kate said out of the blue as he slipped her to the ground.

He'd been focused on the rebels so her words caught him by surprise. His heart thumped. He wished they didn't have to have the masks on so he could see her eyes.

"I'm sorry, too." The words broke free from deep in his chest.

He'd been a fool. And why in hell was he holding back still?

"I was crazy to let you go," he said the words out loud. Well, more like in a whisper, although there was enough fighting going on in the building to cover the sound of his voice. But if ever there was a time to lay all his cards on the table, this was it.

Possibly their last chance, although he preferred not to dwell on that.

She nodded slowly. "If we don't make it—"

He pulled her into his arms to silence her, although the same thought lay heavily on his mind. To hell with that. They *were* going to make it. They had to. He was not going to lose her again. He'd be damned if he died just when he finally got her back. So the deal was, both of them were going to make it. He would accept no other outcome.

"I want to have dinner with you tomorrow night," he said, and wished he could kiss her, but they couldn't afford to take their masks off even for a second. So instead, he caressed what little of her face was uncovered.

Then he turned to fight. But she held him back.

"Give me one of the guns."

He hesitated only a split second before handing her the Russian-made Makarov he'd taken off Piotr.

They opened fire simultaneously. His first shot hit its

target, hers missed by inches. The remaining three rebels scattered as they shot back, running for cover.

He aimed for the one with the explosives and brought him down. The man fell behind a makeshift barricade, so Parker couldn't tell whether he was injured or dead. He focused on the other two. Kate did, too, and finished one of them off. The remaining guy, however, managed to give them a fair amount of trouble.

He was a good shot, the best of the bunch, and the quickest. Parker swore as a bullet grazed his knee. He couldn't let his legs get injured. He had to carry Kate out of here.

He waited and took his time, held back until he saw a flash of movement through the cracks in the piled-up furniture. He took the shot. There was no responding hail of bullets.

"We'd better—" Kate was moving forward already, limping heavily, but he held out a hand to stop her.

He went first, slow and cautious, rifle aimed at the spot where he had fired his last shot. No movement. He walked toward the side instead of in a straight line. In another two steps, he could see the motionless body on the floor.

"Okay." He went back to Kate and picked her up, but still kept his weapon handy. He held her tight. "You cover me from the back."

She looked over his shoulder and brought up the Makarov. "You bet."

He made his way through the barricade, kicking chairs aside, stepping over a lifeless body. Then he was at the outer door.

Wow. He was seeing two. Double vision. Not a good sign. The blood he was losing through his latest injury was pushing his already damaged body over the edge.

Just a little more.

"We can't go out armed." He dropped his rifle, hating being unarmed.

Kate's Makarov clattered to the marble behind him. He opened the door that, thank God, was unlocked. The rebels probably hadn't been able to figure out the electronic lock mechanism or override the program's password.

He was blinded by the floodlights that immediately hit him. Pain pulsed in his arm and leg, his vision growing hazier, even though there was no smoke out here. But he could make out a police cordon and more barricades—triangular cement boulders with dozens of armed men behind them. He staggered that way, holding on tightly to Kate.

Then an explosion shook the ground and a wave of fire shot out from the door behind him to claim them.

THAT WAS the picture that made the front page of *Le Figaro* the next day, as well as the front page of most major newspapers around the world. Parker lurching forward in the moment of explosion, Kate in his arms, the flames obscuring most of the building behind them.

"A rescue-team member saves one of the hostages," the caption said in dozens of languages. Neither their names nor nationality were mentioned. The gas masks had kept their faces covered.

Epilogue

As it turned out, they didn't have dinner the next night, or the night after that. Parker was immediately recalled to the U.S. for treatment and debriefing. Although the Colonel had been able to pull enough strings to keep his identity secret, the Russians were more than interested in the hero the surviving hostages were talking about. Not to the press, though. The survivors said little to the army of reporters. A gag order had been issued regarding the incident.

The official story was that the rescue had been carried out by internal embassy security.

Good enough for him, Parker thought as he drove down the Avenue de la Bourdonnais two weeks later, too nervous to enjoy the early-twentieth-century architecture of the upscale seventh arrondissement. It had taken him this long to get back into Paris. The Colonel had refused to let him go until his wounds healed.

The first gunshot, that little scrape, had given him the most trouble. The wound itself hadn't been bad, but since it had gone untreated for a while, he'd managed to develop a nasty infection. All better now, save for the slight limp he still had from the third shot, which he did his best to hide.

He found the building he was looking for, a gorgeous villa in the nicest section of the avenue. He parked right in front of the house, allowed to do so by the security guard. He was expected.

His heart beat an expectant rhythm as he stepped out of his rental Renault Mégane convertible, or cabriolet, as they called it around here. Not a bad car. Might have to consider one for his collection. He grabbed the ridiculously large bouquet of pink roses from the passenger seat.

He ran up the walkway, nodded back to the security guard who opened the door for him. The hallway reflected Kate's taste, classy but with a swirl of heat. The antique furniture was French to match the historical building, the art modern and full of fire. He recognized a few pieces from the condo they had shared together: the four-foot-tall, red Murano glass vase, prints of the bold paintings of Raoul Dufy that Kate collected.

Then everything else disappeared as he looked up and spotted her at the top of the wide curving staircase.

"Hi." She gave a shy smile, stealing his breath.

She wore shimmering black silk that hugged her body, her hair swept up to leave her graceful neck free. She wore the earrings he had long ago given her.

He desperately wanted that to mean something.

She had said she regretted the past. Said it when she'd thought they'd both be dead the next second. He wasn't sure how much stock he could put in that, although he wanted it to be true.

"Come on up," she said with a smile. "We'll be having dinner on the balcony."

He took the steps two at a time, feeling embarrass-ingly eager. Then they were on the same level, her jewel eyes shining. At him. He handed her the roses, still unable to say a word.

"Thank you."

"Sorry I couldn't come earlier." He leaned forward, not sure what to do. In the end, he brushed his lips over hers.

She didn't pull back. "How is your arm? How is your leg?"

Did she notice his limp? "Better. Great." He swept in for another kiss. "You taste like strawberries," he said.

She smiled. "I just tested our dessert."

"You ate my dessert?" He tried to sound outraged, but couldn't pull it off.

"A tiny taste. Quality control."

"A taste for a taste." He lowered his head again and this time kissed her as though he meant it.

She opened to him, letting him take what he wanted, taking what she needed in return. She gave him back all that he had thought he'd lost.

"How is your ankle?" he asked a while later.

"I tore a ligament when I fell. It'll heal. Anna has been released from the hospital."

He knew. The Colonel had told him when he inquired about the hostages. Turned out Anna was the inside man, well, woman in this case, for the French. Every embassy in every country has inside men-slash-women, sometimes several: admin staff hired in the host country to observe and report to their own government on the comings and goings at the embassy.

"She called me to see if I could tell her how to reach you. She wanted to thank you for going back in for her."

"No thanks are necessary." He didn't remember much of that part of the night. He'd been half unconscious from pain. He'd left Kate with the French police at the ambulance, then had charged back in through the fire with a commando team to show them where he'd left the injured young woman.

To his surprise, they'd found Ivan, too, still alive, and brought out both of them. The hostages had broken his neck, but he would survive—a paraplegic. He had given a full confession already, confirming Parker's suspicions about his connection to Piotr.

A Tarkmezi warlord had apparently put out word that he needed someone with a connection at the Russian embassy in Paris. Piotr, who needed the warlord's favor on some gun deal, made a point of finding a "friend" via blackmail. Then, when he realized what the warlord needed the connection for, he got himself on the team, knowing that it would allow him to meet the leader of Russia's antiterrorist unit—the man who'd killed his father. Meet him and take him out. A tangled mess of private agendas.

"I heard the girls are back in Russia," he said.

Kate smiled. "With their aunt. They have a brand-new baby in the family. Katja is very excited not to be the smallest. I called them."

He smiled. She was the type of person who would. She'd make sure the kids were happy and if not, she'd do something about it.

He lifted her into his arms, not because she seemed to still favor the bad ankle, but because he wanted to hold her as close as possible. "Which way?"

"Second door on the right."

He was there in seconds, making his way in. "This doesn't look like the balcony." He grinned toward the sprawling bed in the middle of the room.

"Oh dear, did I get turned around again?" she asked, all innocence.

He felt his blood run a little faster. He walked with her to the bed to lay her on the silk sheets. He wanted her now, fast and hard, but he wanted even more to do everything right this time. There were still things he wanted to clear up between them.

"Before we— I want to come clean about one more thing. I've said before that my uncle and aunt had raised me because my parents were gone. That's not completely true. My mother is still alive somewhere."

He drew a deep breath. He had never told this to anyone. He expected the Colonel knew, that it was in some background check in his file, but the Colonel wasn't the type of man to bring something like this up.

"My mother was a showgirl in Atlantic City, ran by the name of Ruby Russel back then. My father was a cabby, stupid in love with her. She'd leave us from time to time for another guy, always came back in a week or two." He blocked the emotions that came with the memories. "Then, when I was about eight, she left for good. Left for Vegas. About six months later, my father was late coming home. He was always late, no big deal. Sometimes he went to sit at the end of the pier near our apartment and drink a beer, staring at the water.

"I went looking for him. He was there." He could still clearly see him outlined against the moonlight over the ocean. "I yelled to him, but he couldn't hear me over the waves. I was at the end of the pier when he pulled a gun." One he had kept for protection. "By the time I got there, I couldn't see anything but his blood frothing on top of the water."

"Parker." She reached for him, held him. She was crying.

He didn't want her to cry for him. "I told you because— Back when we were— It scared me how much I needed you. I couldn't forget what needing my mother did to my old man."

"Needing other people doesn't have to be bad."

"I know that now. There were other things, too. My life is— You're all light. I thought that the darkness I worked in would somehow suck you in, like what happened with Jake's wife, Elaine. But I'm not going to let that happen, you know?"

He needed her. He needed her the way a dark room needed a candle. He was at a loss as to how to explain what he felt. He held her tightly and looked up, out the oversized, curved window that opened to the sky. "Even the night sky has its moon and stars."

"Is that your way of saying that dark and light could work together?" She gave him a tremulous smile.

"Yeah. The whole yin-yang thing and all."

"I missed you," she said, her clear, luminous gaze holding his.

"I missed you, too." He lay beside her and kissed her again. "But this goes beyond missing. It's not a quick trip to the past, Kate. This is what I want and I want it forever."

"I guess this means you won't be satisfied with a one-night stand?" A mischievous grin played on her full lips, sending his blood racing through his veins.

"Be my wife."

That had the power to make her go all serious.

"It didn't work before...."

"I'm going to make it work this time. I promise."

She didn't say anything.

And he felt nervous all of a sudden. "I'm going to ask for domestic assignments. I'll take on some training at the home base so I can be with you more."

Still no word from her, the look on her face unreadable.

"I want us to get a house like you wanted before. Big yard, dog, cats, canaries, whatever you want," he said. "I want kids. I—"

She put a finger over his lips to stop him, and finally smiled, wide and bright. "I'm okay with what you do. Really. And— Okay, okay. Yes! To everything. It was yes from the beginning. I just didn't want you to know how pitifully in love with you I am." Her face softened with emotion.

"You are?" His heart expanded. "I love you, too." Never stopped, never will.

"Is there a reason why we're still dressed?" she asked.

He was the type of guy who always rose to the challenge. He had them both naked in record time. Her soft skin felt incredible against his. He turned her on her back and came up on his elbow next to her, drew a hand downward, starting at the hollow of her neck.

"I could look at you for a week straight and it wouldn't be enough." He wanted to soak up this moment, the two of them together, safe, in love.

"We just made up. Are you telling me that you're going to disappoint me already? Parker McCall, you'd better do more than look."

He grinned and dipped his head to kiss the nearest nipple, drinking in her sigh of pleasure.

Her body was perfection, but that was the least of the attraction. She was his heart, his soul. He was never going to lose her again.

He caressed her flat abdomen, drawing his fingers to her hip bones and lower. He wanted to get lost inside her, but was holding back, equally needing to savor this moment. He kissed his way down her body and up her inner thigh, relishing the soft trembling of her muscles.

He tasted her, devoured her, needing to make her his, wanting to delete the memory of the time they had spent apart.

And when she arched her back and cried out his name, he finally pushed deep inside her. And her body welcomed him home.

Much later, when he had made love to her every way possible, they lay replete in each other's arms, steeped in pleasure.

"So when does your next mission start?" she asked, even her voice sounding satiated.

"Immediately."

"Oh." She snuggled closer, as if reluctant to let him go.

He liked that.

He gathered her tight into his arms. "My main mission from now on will be to love you senseless and never let you go. We are going to make this work. How fast do you think we could be married?"

She lifted her head to look at him and smiled. "I'd bet pretty fast. We are in the city of love," she said and pressed her lips to his.

He loved Paris.

* * * * *

MILLS & BOON®

Need more New Year reading?

We've got just the thing for you!
We're giving you 10% off your next eBook or
paperback book purchase on the Mills & Boon
website. So hurry, visit the website today and type
SAVE10 in at the checkout for your exclusive

10% DISCOUNT

www.millsandboon.co.uk/save10

Ts and Cs: Offer expires 31st March 2015.
This discount cannot be used on bundles or sale items.

MILLS & BOON®

Why not subscribe?

Never miss a title and save money too!

Here's what's available to you if you join the
exclusive **Mills & Boon Book Club** today:

+ *Titles up to a month ahead of the shops*
+ *Amazing discounts*
+ *Free P&P*
+ *Earn Bonus Book points that can be redeemed
  against other titles and gifts*
+ *Choose from monthly or pre-paid plans*

Still want more?

Well, if you join today we'll even give you
50% OFF your first parcel!

So visit **www.millsandboon.co.uk/subs**
or call **Customer Relations on 020 8288 2888**
to be a part of this exclusive Book Club!